Silvermo

HAVE A
OF 50 GREAT NOVELS

OF

EROTIC DOMINATION

If you like one you will probably like the rest

**A NEW TITLE EVERY MONTH
NOW INCLUDING EXTRA BONUS PAGES**

Silver Moon Books Ltd
PO Box CR25 Leeds LS7 3TN

Silver Moon Books Inc
PO Box 1614 New York NY 10156

*Distributed to the trade throughout North America by
LPC Group, 1436 West Randolph Street, Chicago, IL 60607
(800) 826-4330*

If you like one of our books you will probably
like them all!

**Write for our free 20 page booklet of extracts from
early books - surely the most erotic feebie yet - and,
if you wish to be on our confidential mailing list,
from forthcoming monthly titles as they are published:-**

Silver Moon Reader Services
PO BOX CR 25 LEEDS LS7 3TN
or
PO Box 1614 NEW YORK NY 1016

or leave details on our 24hr UK answerphone
0113 287 6255

<u>**New authors welcome**</u>

www.silvermoon.co.uk
www.silvermoonbooks.com

NAKED TRUTH first published 1998
Copyright Nicole Dere
*The right of Lia Anderssen to be identified as the author of this book has been as-
serted in accordance with Section 77 and 78 of the Copyrights and Patents Act 1988*

CONTENTS

NAKED TRUTH
your full length new novel
by Nicole Dere
(author of *Voyage of Shame, Sisters in Servitude* and *Virgin for Sale*)

All this is is fiction: in real life practice safe sex

NAKED TRUTH by Nicole Dere

1.

Keith had always been fiercely jealous, Vee knew that. Had known it right from the start, when they had first begun going out together, when she was still a fresher at college. She had found it thrilling then, powerfully so. He was quiet, ruthlessly ambitious and determined to succeed. So different from the other loud-mouthed, crude, beer swillers in the set she moved around in. He didn't even seem particularly interested in her, only in his goal of a First Class Honours and a foot on the ladder to high flying success. So he became something of a challenge.

He seemed to stand on the by-lines, as far as the sexual manoeuvres which figured so largely with most of her contemporaries were concerned. He was good looking, in a lean, aesthetic way. His angular face, crowned by a neatly clustered mop of blond curls, had an intensely serious expression most of the time. His smile was guarded, contained, giving little or nothing of himself away. The blue eyes were deep, unknowable, they stared with a cold dispassion that sparked a shivery thrill secretly inside her.

It was her own diffidence that roused his interest. She knew he fancied her, at least physically, in spite of that distant front. He found her gawky schoolgirl charm attractive, he told her later.

After a few close encounters, she had surrendered her virginity a couple of years earlier to a groping friend of her brother's, who had been hasty, messy, and appallingly clumsy. David, her brother, only eighteen months older than she was, had practically played pimp, bringing the 'chum' round when their parents were away for the night, laying on alcohol to oil the wheels of her seduction.

What was really bad, so bad that Vee had almost succeeded in pushing it away from her conscious memory, was that she had secretly wanted her brother to make love to her. She had flung herself against David in torrid open mouthed passion, feigning drunkenness, and he had fled, from his own as well as her incestuous desires, she suspected, and left her to the less than tender mercies of 'chum'.

When it was done, she was glad in a way that she had got it over with, she was like all her school mates now. But it wasn't repeated. In fact, it was what had finally driven her into the arms, and, on one never to be forgotten rainy November afternoon, into the bed of her bosom pal, Ruth, acknowledging at long last the lesbian inclinations she had been fighting against since earliest adolescence.

She was glad the fight was lost. Or won. She and Ruth remained lovers throughout the two years of their sixth form schooling, revelled at how easy it was.

Keith wanted her, she could tell, despite her nervous, schoolgirlish, giggling shyness - maybe because of it. "Vera's a dreadful name, isn't it? Most folks call me Vee." Then they were kissing, seriously clinched against a tree in the breath-steamy dark. His mouth was demanding, hard, his teeth clashed against hers, until the soft inner surface of her lips was cut and tender.

The next time was on her bed. Sunday afternoon was the traditional passion time. She pictured girls groaning, crying, thrummed with buzzing sexuality, abandoning themselves to hot sex. All about her, sexual odours wafted compellingly on the breeze through the deserted corridors of the building. She was both terrified and damp with weak-kneed excitement at her racing thoughts.

They quickly graduated to the bed, but on top of the coverlet, both minus shoes but minus nothing else. Their mouths clamped together, bodies and limbs heaved and twisted as the bed springs danced to their writhing. She could feel him,

6

he thrust his trapped hardness unmistakably against her, while his sweaty palm inexorably claimed the cold smooth contours of her nylon covered leg, to the swell of her rigid thigh muscle. Eventually the hand extended its claim, under her blouse, to the ticklish bare midriff, and the fragrant sheen of her skin.

His clumsy but determined fingers flipped out her breasts after something of a struggle, and those fingers touched and brushed over the tiny hardness of a nipple, and she flushed.

"You've got an erection too," he teased tightly, and she couldn't force a smile.

Under her skirt, his hand finally slid between her legs, to caress her already wet vulva, tracing the cushiony outline under the protection of her tights and her tiny knickers. Finger pads rubbed up and down the length of her labia, bringing up their grooved outline like a brass etching under the sticky gauziness of her underclothing. She was twisting and shivering, her hips moving in rhythm to his stimulation. The wet patch spread, and she breathed raggedly, moaning through her open mouth. On and on his hand rubbed, until she was sobbing, ready to burst with excitement. He grabbed her wrist with a free hand, pulled her down to the domed bulge of his own excitement still trapped his pants.

"Are you on the pill?" The brutal question smacked her to crimson faced reality, at the same instant as the hand between her thighs ceased its movement. With a wounded howl, she swung her legs away from him, and clutched the creased blouse across her chest, hobbled, doubled over ludicrously, to the tiny basin, hung there, great tears splashing down her shiny cheeks.

"I've got a contraceptive," he said. But it was too late. His own clumsiness made him retreat further. He would not accept blame. He was tight lipped, still cruel in the awful embarrassment. "I'm sorry. I thought it was understood."

Later he returned, courting her with flowers and with a

7

slightly awkward charm. "I had no idea. You've never - you're a virgin, aren't you?" He mistook her blushing, hangdog silence for consent. And was in turn even more intrigued. Genuinely startled even, filled with the idea that she would be his, belong to him in actuality, him only. No one else before him. He began to love her, in his possessive way.

Ironically, now she wanted to give herself to him. Burned to do so. Wept for it. And now he refused. "We'll wait. It'll be good for us. We'll be really sure. Besides, it's sort of cute. You know, the way it used to be. The way it should be."

They did indulge in sex. All the titillating, torturous foreplay, spread out over many hot, sweetly frustrating sessions in each other's beds, or rather on them. Never under the covers. That helped to fight temptation. But he grew bolder. Bared her breasts, while she tearfully apologised, and pouted at his fond taunts, his mouth suckling as he drove her wild. And, finally, he got round, or through, her knickers, and fingered her, patiently, tormentingly, as she drew nearer to, but not quite over, the crest of her bucking wave. Except that, at last, she did - clenching and unclenching, gasping in the shuddering climax that trapped his aching wrist between her squeezing, convulsive thighs.

She, too, with fearful pleasure, saw and touched his penis, thrusting pole-hard from his fly, learned to stroke and caress, learned the quickening rhythm which brought its culminating, thrilling, scaring reward, of pumping hot, odorous semen scalding her quivering hand and fingers.

"We can't do this!" she wept one afternoon, when the heavy smell of their sex, and the stains on the cover, lay accusingly about them. Abjectly she begged him to take her 'properly', and he was adamant in his refusal. "You don't really want me," she cried. "What's the point of our relationship?" A quarrel grew, got worse. "I think we should stop seeing each other," she muttered tormentedly. She was desolated by his stiff-necked agreement,

At the end of term party, Keith was there again, coolly observant as usual. She was with a boy called Bill, and she got defiantly drunk. Couples were slinking off, and Bill was almost desperately lecherous. Why the hell not? she thought. Let's get it over with. She had almost come to believe in her virginity herself.

She let Bill take her to a coat-strewn bedroom, and amid the piled up garments she lay, giddy and sick, trying unsuccessfully to feign passion in response to his slobbered kisses. Then, suddenly, he was gone, plucked magically from her. She struggled up in smeary-eyed amazement, to see a possessed Keith delivering a series of sickening kicks to Bill's squealing figure on the floor.

Keith turned, and dealt her a ringing, open handed slap on the side of her bared thigh, and she yelped in agony. The red imprint stood out like a brand for days. He dragged her roughly upright, thrust her balled up pants and tights into her hand and pulled her from the room. Like an irate parent, he led her through the crowd, barging people out of the way. He let her get her coat, but captured her wrist immediately again, and tugged her to the taxi rank.

In the cab, he held her hand in a painful grip, and they exchanged no words. Her tights and knickers, still meshed in a ball, were in her coat pocket now. She was very conscious of her nudity under the silk dress. It had ridden up at the back. She could feel the upholstery of the seat on the backs of her thighs, even on her buttocks. Her vulva was throbbing urgently. She stood, feeling the cold night air on her, while he paid off the taxi, then, grabbing hold of her again, he marched her along the passage of the flat he shared to the austere bathroom.

"Get your clothes off!"

Hypnotically, she obeyed, snivelling softly, like a chastised infant, perversely excited by the knowledge of his unmoving stare. She stripped off, dropping her clothes on the

9

ugly little cream wooden chair, while he ran a steaming bath.

"Get in!"

She winced at the heat, but said nothing. Her skin pinked and glowed. She washed thoroughly under his admonishing gaze, blushing as she did so, but making no attempt to hide even her most intimate ablutions. When she had finished, he held out a large towel to her. It was his, she could tell. It was still damp. He bundled up her clothes under one arm and again drew her after him, naked, to his room.

Inside, he faced her sternly. "Did that bastard do it to you?"

She shook her head, "No one has," she whispered faintly. "I only want you."

He pulled her to him. "OK. You're my girl. I mean permanently. Right? Mine completely, understand?"

His blue eyes held her, blazing at her. She was shivering with fear as he bent her over his knee, spanking her like a naughty child. It excited her almost unbearably at first. She thought she would climax, feeling the rub of his clothing on her fragrant belly, the ferment of her thighs as she squirmed, but then the beating went on, hard resounding slaps, until the pain took over and she was squirming in earnest, her feet sawing the air, burning in real agony, her bottom clenching and unclenching with fire.

She sobbed desperately for him to stop.

When he did, he flung her brutally off him, so that she fell sprawling on the faded rug, weeping blindly, clutching at her stinging bottom. He plucked her up and thrust her on her back, on the bed, parting her legs roughly. She stayed like that, her jutting knees splayed, still sobbing as he tore off his clothing. His prick looked huge, lance like. He entered her at once, thrusting into her, tearing her despite her wet readiness, so that she cried out in pain. He plunged fiercely, and she joined him, flinging up her belly against his, spearing herself sacrificially, overjoyed, embracing the hard, driving burn, lost at the final flooding burst of his manhood inside her.

2

By the time they were ready to be married, her friends were warning her off. "You're besotted with him!" Ruth told her disgustedly. "He's taken you over completely, you poor little goose! He even tells you what to wear, for Christ's sake! He's walking all over you. And you're letting him, you sick little sod! And that's not just sour grapes because you won't let me in your knickers any more. He's ruining you, sweetheart!"

Vee didn't even complete her university course, for Keith was a year ahead of her. As soon as he had got the first class degree he had pursued so single mindedly, he announced that they would marry, and that Vee would leave college. She had hoped he would stay on, take up the post graduate work his department had offered, but he had already been approached by an international firm.

"We'll move to London. What's the point of you staying on here? You're not going to work anyway."

"What'll I do with myself?"

"You'll be my wife."

"That's my career?" she murmured, half seriously.

"Yes." She shivered at the uncompromising glint in those blue eyes. Then shivered again as he reached behind her neck to begin undressing her.

When he came home one evening and announced out of the blue that they were leaving for East Africa within the month, her parents were bravely enthusiastic, and brushed aside Vee's doubts almost as vigorously as he did. "A marvellous chance for you," her father said. "Congratulations,

11

Keith, my boy!"

Fired by their ready acceptance, and by Keith's fervent eagerness, she urged herself not to be so wimpish, and began to look forward to the new experience.

Ruth was working up in Scotland. They had met only once since Vee's marriage, Now she wrote insisting that she must come south and spend a last weekend at their London flat to say goodbye properly, 'before he whisks you away to the Dark Continent, the bastard!' she wrote. 'I can't wait to get my hands on you and maybe chastise you a little, you gorgeous little slut, for deserting me.' Vee made sure she destroyed the letter before Keith came home, and, with her usual diffidence, mentioned Ruth's intention to spend a weekend with them.

She watched him anxiously across the plastic topped table of the gloomy kitchen. It was one thing she would not be sorry to leave. However, he was very affable, sounded only mildly interested. He was far too preoccupied with his new duties and his preparations for departure to think about anything else. She had little idea what those duties would be. She was proud of him, of course, but she was intimidated, and felt very cut off from all that side of him. But then, that was how he wanted it, how it was meant to be. Man's stuff. Not for her to question, not the little woman's territory.

As the day of Ruth's visit drew nearer, Vee's mood fluctuated rapidly. She grew physically excited at the memory of their schoolgirl passion, then hot with embarrassment. How could she face seeing Ruth and Keith together? She recalled the dark girl's boldness. Keith would see in the first blushing glance what had passed between them. How would he feel if he knew about it? Disgusted? Disbelieving? By the time Saturday arrived, Vee was sick with anxiety. Yet she took more care over her appearance than she had for weeks. Even Keith noticed. "Jesus! She'll think you haven't changed at all, You still look like a schoolgirl."

12

She was thrilled at his remark. He rarely complemented her, even though she did try to look her best for him. Although they had been together for just over two years, and married for one, their sex life had settled into its own strange pattern. They didn't often have sexual intercourse these days. Not more than two or three times a month. Keith began to be less and less concerned about her satisfaction.

Ruth's visit was a revelation to her that some deep part of her nature had not changed since Keith had come into her life. When those lips brushed hers on greeting, and the arms came around her so comfortingly, she felt the pangs of an old hunger stir with a power that frightened her.

Ruth was at her at the first opportunity, her hands reaching with rough eagerness. Vee's reluctance was feigned. Soon she was responding to the yielding of her body's most intimate parts, the helpless sweeping over the floods of pure sensation that being a victim of lover's lust entailed. She had rarely known it with Keith, she was forced to admit. When it was over, and the tears of release were beginning to dry on her cheeks, she nestled with real longing into the warmth enveloping her.

"Poor Vee," Ruth crooned, her lips against the fine fair hair. She rubbed her fingers softly along the smooth belly to the damp tendrils of the light brown pubis, whose curls she plucked gently. "You're having a rough time of it, aren't you?" The warmth and strength of her voice released a shocking outburst of sobbing in the very midst of Vee's strenuous denial, and she buried her face into the comfort of Ruth's breast. Even in her grief, she enjoyed the feel of the satiny firm flesh, the brush of her tear soaked eyelids across the fragrant skin.

Keith was at a conference in the midlands. They still had the long hours of the night to make love. The ghost of their giggling schoolgirl selves rose to bind them with all the force of those youthful shared nights. The moans, the smothering kisses, the thirsty tongues which sought out every salty, dewy crevice, every smooth surface and curve, the rapturously exploring fingers, the twisting limb-locked bodies turning and clinging, striving to make contact along every throbbing inch, left them finally exhausted, replete with love. The room was grey with dawn before they sank into deep sleep, still wrapped about each other in the tangled ruins of the sheets.

That was how Keith found them. They woke, bleary eyed, to the terrifying sight of his silhouette, rearing darkly over them in the blaze of sunlight pouring through the thin curtains. "What are you doing here?" Vee blinked stupidly, too dazed to cry.

"I'm finding my wife in the arms of her dike lover!" he hissed. "I didn't believe it! Look at you!"

Vee gave a little cry of shame and tried to gather the sheet over her nakedness, starting to sob hopelessly, but Ruth's lithe brown figure uncoiled, rose boldly from the bed, unashamed.

"Look here -"

Keith's fist moved with blurring speed to drive deep in a vicious jab to her midriff, and she folded, with a grunting exhalation. She fell off the bed, rolled in agony on the floor, her lungs wheezing as she sought to suck in air. He picked her up like a sack, tossed her back on the bed. By the time she had managed to drag some air into her tortured lungs he had bound her wrists tightly with a tie and secured them to the bedhead. With another necktie, he captured her waving feet and trussed them together, too, fastening them to the rail at the foot of the bed.

Vee was crouched there, eyes wide in horror, holding the edges of the sheet over her breasts. He grabbed her now, dragged her out of bed and flung her crashing down into the easy chair with the wooden arms. One knee was drawn up,

14

touching her breast. She gripped the wooden arms, making no sound.

Ruth was still choking and spluttering wretchedly, her stretched out body jerking convulsively against the bonds. Her face was covered in tears as he dug his fingers into the short black hair and pulled her head up, stretching the elegant neck painfully. Her brown eyes rolled wildly as she stared at him.

"You can scream your head off, you filthy little perv," he said in a frightening rage. "I'll be glad to explain what I found you doing with my wife if the neighbours or the police come round."

Ruth fought furiously against her bonds as he picked up Vee's hair brush from the dressing table. The bed juddered, her slim body lifted and arched in vain. Her tight buttocks hollowed, clenched deeply, before he struck the first blow. There was a crack like a gun shot and she bucked. She drove her face down into the pillow, muffling the scream of torment that rose automatically at the fiery burn of her quivering flesh. He struck again, and a second flaming red outline lay beside the first. The narrow hips squirmed, the burning rounds seemed to rise to meet the punishment. Cruelly, he struck deliberately, waiting between each blow until she had savoured to the full the flaring bite of the pain scorching through her. Deep, shuddering sobs were escaping now. Her face was still buried in the pillow, which was absorbing the noise of her suffering.

Vee was sick. It was a nightmare, but she could not tear her eyes away from the scene. She watched transfixed each fall of the brush, each sickening splat, saw the quivering, dimpling cheeks grow red, until their whole surface glowed. Saw the outline of Ruth's shoulder blades moving under the smooth skin, each rippling spasm of her muscles as the agony grew worse. And still Vee sat, silent, breathless, her mouth open as the tears fell down her cheeks, dropped onto her skin. With a deep sense of shock she became aware that she was caressing herself, the fingers of one hand brushing very lightly back and forth across the lips of her vulva, still sore from the passionate love making. They blossomed anew at her strokes, and she snatched her hand away as though from a flame.

She had no idea how many blows had fallen on Ruth's bottom before Keith at last ceased the punishment and stood there, chest heaving, staring down at his handiwork. He let the brush fall, slowly undid his belt, unzipped his flies, and pushed down his trousers. He stepped out of them, shuffling off his shoes to do so, then thrust down his underbriefs, awkwardly pulled off his socks. He drew his shirt over his head, never taking his gaze from that helpless, quivering body stretched out on the bed. Vee stared, still motionless, still absolutely silent.

Now Keith was naked, and his prick stood out, pole hard in arousal. He released Ruth's ankles, and she groaned at the touch of the sheet on her behind as he turned her onto her back. Her arms were still bound above her, and her breasts were pulled into prominence by her position. She gazed up through tear-filled eyes at the sight of his naked body, merciless as he bent and seized her ankles, plucked her feet apart, knelt between them, between her gaping thighs.

Her struggles were feeble, more an instinctive reaction than anything else. She stared seemingly mesmerised at the prick, its red helm agleam with emission, fully exposed from the collar of foreskin. The column stretched massively, back to the tight bag of his balls. He wrapped his arms around her thighs, lifted her behind clear of the bed. The dome of his prick nuzzled gently at her divide, jabbed and jabbed, slid along the groove of her labia, then his hard fingers were scrabbling, pulling at her, opening her, and the thick helm drove in, forced its entrance into her damp yielding narrowness, penetrated further, burning, stretching her, possessing.

16

He plunged furiously, stabbed into her until their pelvic bones clashed, and her body arched, her slender throat turned up. This time she did scream, in sharp torment, and the pale figure slumped in the chair stiffened, and shuddered in sympathy. Then Vee stared again, in helpless fascination, watched the beauty of her husband's thrusting body, the deep hollows of his clenching buttocks, the brown thighs clamped to his side, the feet waving in response to every driving lunge.

It was soon over, though to the watching Vee it seemed as if time had stopped altogether in that weirdly sunny room. He pulled himself clear of Ruth and collapsed in heaving relaxation for a while.

Then he knelt, and slowly untied the thin wrists, moving aside and flinging her roughly to the floor. "Get out!" he snarled. Ruth was weeping softly. Vee couldn't see her face, the dark head was lowered as, whimpering quietly, she clutched at her bits of clothing and left the room.

"Now for you!"

He was standing. Her eyes were drawn to his penis, hanging now, but still elongated, still gleaming with the juices of his emission.

"Get over the bed. Here!" He did not tie her down. Instead, he made her crouch, almost kneeling, at the side of the bed, her feet on the rug, her bottom lifted high for his chastisement. "Keep still!" She did her best, though she convulsed at the first scorching explosion of pain across her behind, Her fingers were claws driven deep into the bed cover, she bit savagely at the counterpane to muffle her screams, and forced herself down for the second blow. The fire blazed again, she felt the rise of vomit in her throat, but, somehow, she stayed down, crucified, her arms outspread, her body trembling violently.

She tried to welcome the agony, to meet it, knowing how well it was deserved, but she was blubbering, pleading dementedly for mercy before the fifth strike descended. Her

17

bottom was on fire, it felt hugely swollen, she was sure the skin must split under the intensity of the punishment. Her mind fogged, drifted on the red mists of infinite pain, until she became aware that the burn was steady, the throbbing no longer punctuated by those crackling bursts of new spasms.

When at last she could move enough to lift her pounding head from the mattress, to climb stiffly to her feet, she saw that she was alone, the only sound her muted whimpers in the sun filled silence.

3

The colour everywhere was over the top, from the first huge blood orange disc of the dawn sun lifting out of Lake Victoria, blazoning the water into the brilliance of stained glass as the plane roared a few feet above its surface. Startling redness of the earth, roads like livid scars scratched over the brilliant tropical greenery. From the fairy tale Mercedes complete with dazzle-toothed, handsome driver, they saw the unreal backdrop of ragged banana fronds, looking like paper models made by school children. The huge, fringed leaves thrust to the very doors of the chocolate mud huts with their painfully glaring tin roofs.

The people caught her breath with their smiling, brown-skinned beauty. She was not prepared for it. She had expected fearful ugliness, thick lipped, sore crusted dirt. Not this serene, dignified beauty. The women especially. The bandanas and the puff-sleeved Mother Hubbard dresses, voluminous, in a riot of floral print, should have been ridiculous. Instead, they were magnificently graceful. The liquid dark eyes, the smooth facial characteristics, the finely formed features, gave the young women loveliness, the older ones majesty. The close cropped kinked hair took nothing from the swelling round of the skull, which swept up perfectly from the long slender neck, with the pure curve of a question mark.

And their figures, the round ripeness of their breasts plainly on show under the low, simple, square cut bosom. The schoolgirls were stunning, for their short, pastel coloured dresses clung to their figures, hugging the proud, high jut of their buttocks. Magnificent bottoms, Vee thought, with unenvious admiration. Rippling so exquisitely, so different from the tight, nipped in whites, her own almost flat haunches.

Still liberally stained with the fading autumnal colours of the bruising covering her behind, which squirmed uncomfortably, sweatily, under the nylon tights, and the briefs which seemed to have disappeared up the cleft, they sped that first morning the thirty kilometres from the airport to the capital. They had dressed for a chilly English evening. She could see Keith's red neck, his fingers plucking at the dark tie, the limp white collar. In his dark suit he looked as alien to the vivid scene outside as she felt.

The whole atmosphere made her head spin with its unreal quality. She had been feeling like this for days, almost spectral as she moved through the mechanics of the departure. Strongest of all was the emotion that she was so lucky to be here at all. She had thought that he would want nothing more to do with her, would discard her, and the thought filled her with terror, for she could not see any life for her without him. She had been astonished, and sobbingly grateful, therefore, when she found that she was to be given another chance.

Of course, things were different. Vastly so. The disgust she had expected was there. He made no attempt to hide it. Quite the opposite. He flayed her with his tongue, just as he had flayed her backside with the brush. The love which he had shown for her two years before seemed to have vanished. But she was his, his possession, and he would not let her go. That was the main thing, the thing for which she rejoiced tearfully, enduring his disgust, his contempt for her.

For a while she had been unable to bear even the lightest contact on her blistered skin, unable to sit, or lie on her back, or wear clothing of any kind next to her bottom. She wore a tank top and trainers only, or the rubber thonged flip flops, perversely roused by her lower nudity once she realised he was not going to send her away. She hungered for him, hoped he would use her, fuck her as savagely as he had Ruth. Her fevered mind kept on rerunning the scene of the coupling, like a blue movie.

He wouldn't touch her. She didn't expect tenderness, or forgiveness, but she hoped that he would take her for his own savage pleasure. The days - and nights - passed. Their last evening in the flat came. Tomorrow, they would travel down to her parents' for the last couple of days before their flight. Before he came in, she bathed, and rubbed herself with perfumed oil, did her hair carefully, used the light touches of make up to her best advantage. She wore the outrageous, transparent red teddy, edged with black lace, he had bought her last Christmas, and over it her diaphanous blue negligee.

Her body was taut with desire, her fingers itched to caress herself, to bring some relief, but she fought against her urge. She would beg him to fuck her, plead for him to use her as his slave, for that was what she deserved. The curl of his lip, the icy contempt she read in his gaze when he saw her, brought the tears which were never far from the surface.

"Don't you want me for anything?" she asked humbly, after she had waited on him while he ate.

Her heart began to beat wildly when she saw the smile tugging at the corners of his mouth. She followed him through to the living room. "Yes," he said. "You can service me. Perhaps it'll cure you of your obvious hatred for what men have got." He sprawled on the sofa, pointed to the bulge she could see at his crotch, and she knew at once what he meant.

She knelt eagerly, her unsteady fingers plucking at the zip fastener, drawing it down, ferreting delicately at the tight fold of his underpants, until, with some difficulty, she slid his hot penis out through the narrow slit. It was mightily swollen already, the veined column thickening, throbbing, the red helm emerging from the rim of foreskin. Its tiny mouth was agleam with juice. She slipped her thumb and fingers round the base of the glans, stroked gently, and shivered as she felt it leap at her touch, harden. Her wrist moved rhythmically until it was jutting from his clothing rigidly.

She moved, brushing aside her soft hair from her face as she bent forward and reverently kissed the glistening tip of his prick with her lips. Her tongue flickered out uncertainly, lapped at the tangy emission coating the helm. Again, she shivered, felt a deep, corresponding throbbing in her own loins. She opened her lips, her mouth formed a wide 0 and she took the head inside, sucking deeply, letting her mouth slide as far down the rearing column as she could, until she was choking at its girth stretching her jaws.

She withdrew with a loud plop, gasping for air. His prick was shining along the shaft now, where she had wetted him. She tugged at his pants, made a small mew of pleading, and he raised himself off the cushion a little, so that she could fight the trousers, and briefs, down off his hips and upper thighs. He moaned softly, shuddered, as her head pressed into his lap, her fingers and tongue stroked the yeasty softness of his testicles, before returning to work at the splendid rearing column of his penis which was straining up now.

She was near to coming herself, painfully excited as she bent low, kissing at the soaring prick, the smooth thighs and belly, the nest of dark curls. She half hoped he would seize her, brutally drag her onto her back and plunge his weapon into her running, gaping orifice.

She could feel his thighs trembling against the softness of her mashed breasts as she leaned heavily into him. She

21

licked the spongy tissue of the dome as it reared up, moved over her thrusting face. She rimmed the edge of the helm, lapped at the flange where it met the hard veined column straining under her palm. Jaws agape, she took him in her mouth once more. It filled her, surging, pressing chokingly until she gagged. The breath whistled through her flared nostrils.

All at once, she felt his fingers dig mercilessly into her head, driving her down, while his belly lifted, thrusting him even deeper into her. Drops of sweat rolled down her forehead, beaded wetly on her nose and cheeks. His fingers, twisted in her damp hair, imprisoned her. Her nose was buried in his pubic curls. She fought up, then plunged down again, his flesh driven against the back of her throat. She was vaguely conscious of her own wetness rubbing and sliding on her inner thighs. She was shivering on the brink of orgasm.

A last second fear gripped her at the sudden spasm which shook him, passed through her at the mighty eruption which burst from him. She jerked her mouth free instinctively at the first potent spurt thickly filling her, then, in an agony of frustration at her own withdrawal, licked greedily at the pumping semen, from the mid section of his column, held by her knuckles, up to the purple, shining dome, where his fluid spilt milkily over its surface onto her searching face.

Somehow, swallowing convulsively, she pulled away, ran through to the kitchen to hang over the sink, spitting and hawking, then swilling out her mouth, rinsing her face under the tap. When she returned he was dressed again.

"Quite a sword swallower, aren't you?" he mocked. "You've got so many talents you've kept hidden from me. You're a first class slag!"

Head bowed, she took his scorn submissively, as always. Strangely, she felt cleansed, relaxed. Almost serene.

After that, he had no more contact with her, but she waited

22

patiently. During the first hectic days after their arrival in Africa, she had plenty to occupy her. She had a new and, she soon realised, vital role to play - the company wife, youthful, keen, the perfect partner for the bright young rising star they all clearly thought Keith would be. She threw herself into the part gratefully, in spite of all her inner trepidation. She found that her youthful good looks, her air of naivety almost, was an asset which she manipulated to the full. Even the other women were keen to take her under their wing, and saw no threat in her vulnerable, winsome beauty.

It didn't take Vee long to sense the under currents of gossipy intrigue, the hints of scandal. There was a powerful sexual presence in the air, very different from back home. The sun was a decisive factor. It stirred their European coldness, through their clothing to the startled bareness beneath, making one aware of the body, of tactile sensations, as never before. One soon grew to love it, to be seduced by it. Vee understood after only a very brief exposure how expatriates were won over. The sense of release it brought, of freedom from shackling values they had left behind in their escape from home.

Keith was away all day, and, once they had settled in, for long nights as well, for his work, particularly in the first weeks, involved long safaris upcountry to familiarise himself with the work and the territory. She lay out in the garden of their luxurious bungalow. The sun burned through to her very centre. She felt it touch the base of her belly, envisaged her sex flowering, opening like the fluted pistil of some exotic, solitary plant. She felt herself to be expectantly waiting, damply ready to receive.

Her admiration of the rich milk chocolate shade of the local Baganda people war extended, widened, to take in the more exotic darkness of the northern tribes, who, in the office blocked, car laden context of the city, in European suits,

23

white collared and necktied, seemed even stranger, but whose burnished skin, hairless and sheened in sweat, moving to the ripple of spare muscle and corded sinew as displayed by the shamba boys, rhythmically swinging the sickle in their graceful cutting of the short grass, hidden only at the loins by a ragged pair of patched and holed khaki shorts, made her breathlessly weak with desire, hollow bellied with yearning at their savage beauty.

The pungent alien odour of their bodies gripped her until she felt she could faint, and she dreamt of placing her parted lips reverently on that shining surface, tasting that beaded sweat, and losing herself in the animal power of that black flesh, that shone with a mystical, almost bluish tinge to its velvetness.

Like her compatriots, the other 'memsa'abs', she became freer in her manner around them, beginning to treat them as true servants, displaying the familiarities which emphasised their inferiority. Menya, their houseboy, brought her morning tea in bed, long after Keith had left for his office. He unfailingly entered at the instant he tapped on the door, with his cheerful cry of, "Jambo, memsa'ab!", his eyes taking in her breasts before she pulled the sheet up to cover them.

He brought the drinks out to the terrace at the back of the bungalow, where, when alone, she sunbathed naked. Following the convention of what was acceptable between mistress and houseboy, she could roll over onto her stomach to lie with her legs pressed together, for to present one's naked back view to a known and trusted house servant was well within the bounds of decency. "Are you showing him your bare arse yet?" She heard that question put at a club dance as an estimate of the worthiness of a cook-houseboy.

She was sure Menya watched her surreptitiously from the living room, and she also had the feeling that Charles, the shamba boy, spied on her, too, despite her orders that while she sunbathed he should confine his work to the front of the huge garden that surrounded the long, red tiled bungalow.

4

Sex was palpably in the air at the club dances, when everyone drank too much, and, on the dimness of the floor, or the recesses of the wide veranda, bodies pressed and writhed together, hands cupped and caressed and probed in the acceptable eroticism of the music.

The men were decorous at first with Vee. They behaved with a cute gallantry long gone from the social scene at home and tried to impress her with easy going schoolboyish charm, or laconic white hunter ruggedness. It was the fourth week before one put a palm on her bottom, another nibbled her ear, another pressed her thigh with an impressive erection. Then it seemed de rigeur, these moments of intense, repressed passion among the swaying anonymity of the other clutching figures.

She watched discreetly. Keith was soon a groper with the best of them. She was surprised to discover she did not feel jealous. What if he were more than just a groper? What if he were one of the army of adulterers who letched their way over the continent, according to prurient women's lore? Even more surprisingly, she found herself secretly titillated by the thought. She even justified it in her convoluted reasoning. After all, their own sex life, if you could call it that, was far from the norm. And whose fault is that? she accused herself. If it hadn't been for her touch of lesbianism, things would have been vastly different.

Gerard and Mary Waters were a couple very like themselves, so Vee thought in her innocence. They became particularly friendly. It was Mary she was the more attracted to, to begin with. She was a dark haired beauty, with a foreign, Mediterranean look about her, and a flashing eyed, tomboyish vibrancy that Vee found strongly appealing and strongly reminiscent of Ruth. Zealously, she pushed this last disturbing thought away whenever it occurred. All right! So she liked the woman! There was nothing wrong with that, was there? It was natural for women to feel close to one another, to strike up a rapport. And any more deviant feelings she harboured, she would suppress, bury so deep they would never surface again.

At first, heart beating rapidly, Vee wondered if Mary was hiding lesbian inclinations herself. After one of their tennis knock-ups at the club - Mary was far too skilful for Vee to take her on in any real contest, and the pretty, dark haired figure would move around at tolerant half speed on court, while Vee ended up a limp, crimson faced wreck, agleam with sweat - Mary would strip off quite unselfconsciously in the shower and casually invite her to 'do my back for me', or offer to do the same for Vee.

Mary would sit on the narrow wooden bench, still naked, one dainty foot drawn up to the back of her thigh, the heel resting on the wooden top, and chat for long minutes before reaching for her clothing.

She would talk in the most intimate terms. The time came when she suddenly leaned back and, lifting her belly to Vee, chuckled. "Do you know, I have to trim it every few days. I swear, if I didn't it'd be down to my knees in no time!"

"You're gorgeous!" Vee burst out, then blushed for shame. But Mary didn't seem to notice anything untoward. Then, moved by an impulse suddenly too powerful to control, and by Mary's naked, gleaming proximity, Vee grabbed her in an embrace, plastering her own taller frame against Mary's and covering her lips with a gentle but clearly passionate kiss.

What came next happened with equal swiftness. Vee

squealed as she felt thin, long nailed fingers seize her by the streaming tendrils of her pubic hair, and tug until the skin beneath lifted like elastic. At the same instant, the thumb and forefinger of the other hand pincered Vee's tiny, pale pink nipple on her left breast and squeezed until the yelp was drawn out to a wail of agony, The fingers of both hands began to twist until Vee found herself kneeling, doubled over on the spattering tiles, gasping for breath against the pain which filled her eyes with tears.

She sobbed and rubbed at herself when Mary finally released her, remained huddled on the wet floor of the cubicle. Mary was standing over her.

"Come on! Out you get!"

Snivelling quietly, unable to meet her gaze, Vee obeyed. Her toes curled with embarrassment, she felt ready to die with shame. And sudden fear. "Please - I'm sorry! I don't know what came over me! I didn't mean -"

"Yes, you did, you little dike! I had no idea you were that way!"

In the midst of her panic, Vee was surprised at the equanimity with which Mary spoke. "I'm not! I mean - I've never -"

"I don't believe you, you little liar!" Mary gave a low, bubbling laugh. "And with a dishy guy like Keith, too! Well well!"

The panic caught at Vee's throat. "Oh please!" she babbled, "Please don't say anything! Don't tell a soul! I couldn't bear it! Not even - don't tell Gerard, please! He might mention - I don't want Keith to find out. He'd - I couldn't bear it if he knew!"

The tears came, faster than ever.

"Hey, all right! I'd say don't get your knickers in a twist if you were wearing any! I won't tell anybody," she continued, her light tone contrasting with the content of her speech, "but if you ever try anything like that with me again, sugar,

27

I won't just nip you. I'll tear your snatch and your tits clean off, OK?"

Later, when she had recovered from her fright, Vee began to simmer with resentment at Mary's rejection of her. Especially as it was the first time she had given way to the yearning she had kept successfully bottled inside her for so long. Right! she thought grimly, I'll show you if I'm gay or not! Somehow, she found herself including Keith in her vindictive challenge.

And that was really the point when her affair with Gerard started. Perhaps it was because he was Mary's husband. He had put his hand on her bottom, and his tongue half way down her throat, on the dance floor, as, no doubt, Keith had with Mary. After all, the four of them were an item. It was par for the course. But she knew he was willing, and eager, to go further. And quickly picked up her signals that she was ready, too.

The fear was there, it was very real. But it was a sick part of the thrill. One night, as they were getting ready for bed after a long session down at the club, her heart thumping, she asked Keith: "Do you fancy Mary?"

He had had quite a lot to drink - they both had - and he grinned lasciviously. "Course I do! She's very shagworthy!"

Vee strove to keep her voice light, to hide the tremor. "I reckon she fancies you!"

"Oh yeah? She tell you, did she?"

"Not in so many words, but I can tell. You must know it, too."

"You reckon I should try it on then?" he grinned. He pushed off his pants, flipped his underpants down and kicked them clear of his feet half way across the room. He fell back naked on top of the coverlet. She gazed at his penis, thick, brown, stirring slightly as it lay in the crease of belly and thigh. His skin was very white across his loins where his trunks had protected it from the sun's rays, in marked contrast to the honey tan of the rest of his lean body, and the dark brown bush of his pubis.

He lifted himself up on his elbow, his face transforming into the sneer she was so familiar with in private. "Hey! Is this one of your kinky ideas? You want me to fuck her, do you?"

"How do I know you haven't?" she snapped before she could prevent herself.

He gave a harsh barking laugh. "How do I know you haven't?"

She felt the crimson tide sweep up from her neck, and her eyes stung with tears. She turned hastily away lest he should see the effect his cruel remark had made, and sense the guilt his accusation had engendered.

"We could go in for a spot of wife swapping, eh?" The ugly grin had returned. "But that's a bit unfair on poor old Gerard, isn't it? He'd be rather left out in the cold, wouldn't he? And I can't imagine the delicious Mary would be able to keep both of us going, do you?"

He grunted, lay back, folding his hands behind his head. He drew his knees up and let them fall slackly open. His prick, roused by the direction of their talk and his thoughts, stirred, lifted and lobbed onto his belly, growing to a semi erection.

"Anyway, come and do your duty. Put your mouth to a better use than talking the load of shit it usually does!"

"I'm tired!" she pouted, and a thrill shot through her at her defiance. She was startled at the speed with which he leapt up, despite his drunkenness, and grabbed at her. She was still wearing bra and briefs. He seized her by the waist and flung her face down across the wide bed.

"You're getting far too big for your britches these days, memsa'ab! Time I took you in hand again!"

He clawed her knickers down off her behind, left them tangled round the backs of her knees as she started to struggle.

Her feet flailed, drummed the coverlet and she yelped at the first stinging blow with his open palm on her clenching bottom.

"Don't!" She screamed at each fierce burn. He slapped rapidly, with all his strength, until his hand was ringing and her buttocks were a livid red over most of their surface. She was sobbing abandonedly, imploring his mercy.

Eventually he did stop. She scrambled up, clawing and rubbing at the hot cheeks. The tiny white knickers slipped down to her ankles as she stood there, tears pouring, massaging her throbbing behind. He lay back, assuming his earlier pose again.

"Now then, slag! Do as you're told."

She kicked off her pants, reached behind and snapped open her bra, shrugging it clear of her breasts. She knelt, bent low over him until her hair brushed his belly and thighs. She rolled his prick between her palms, pushed it up onto his belly, held it there while she lapped delicately at the red helm with the tip of her tongue. She felt it beat and leap to restirring Life. Her fingers seized the hot shaft, moved up and down and it leapt again, stiffening to attention. The tears still on her cheeks, she lifted her head, knelt up, between his splayed thighs, pushing her fleece covered mound against his rearing penis, which she still held tightly. She rubbed its glistening tip over her bush, then touched it to the very divide of her own pulsing sex lips.

"Don't you want to fuck me?" she whispered hoarsely, thrusting out her belly in blatant invitation.

He reared up, his fingers wound savagely in her tangled hair, and dragged her head down mercilessly to his lifting flesh. She felt the wet tip of his rigid prick stab brutally into her face. "Why would I want to fuck a perv like you?" Sobbing, she stretched her mouth wide and took in the massive helm to her warm wetness.

"Thank you, Menya. You can go now."

"Ndio, memsa'ab." She blushed hotly. Was it merely her hypersensitive guilt which read that leering complicity in his gap toothed grin? After he had put down the tray of drinks, the houseboy left. They heard the kitchen door clash noisily, his singing as he made his way up the garden to the servants' quarters. Now that the moment had finally come, Vee felt empty and sick inside. She stared with wide eyed misery at Gerard.

"What if he tells Keith you called?"

"Of course he won't!" Gerard answered, a shade too emphatically. "Why should he? They don't give a damn what we get up to. The servants haven't a clue, and couldn't care less." He stood, reached down and seized her hand impatiently. "Come on. You're supposed to enjoy this."

She let him pull her to her feet. Her sandals had slipped off, she stared down at her painted toes, felt the cool of the polished cement floor on her bare soles. "You sound as if you want to get it over as quick as possible," she said. Her voice trembled, betraying the tightness of her tone.

"Nonsense!" he growled. "I just want to get it started as quickly as possible!"

It was even worse at first, when they got along to the bedroom. Her bedroom. Hers and Keith's. "We've never - made love in here!" she said shakily. "Not properly." She gazed white faced at Gerard. Tears ran silently down her cheeks. He was staring disbelievingly at her.

"To hell with it!" She reached for the buttons on her blouse, undid them with clumsy fingers. Then she unhitched the waistband of the wide, flowered skirt, let it drift to her feet and stepped out of it. She was wearing one of her finest sets of underclothes. A flimsy scrap of a bra, of fine net edged with lace. The tiny nipples and their surrounds showed mistily through the material, as did the dark triangle of her pubis through the filmy cover of the mini briefs.

31

He was quickly naked, and she moved into his arms.

"Finish undressing me," she whispered, and folded limply into his arms. He stripped away the last scraps of clothing and they came together, rolling, clinging, limbs enfolding, on top of the covers, their mouths locked endlessly together.

As a lover, he was no disappointment. She had wondered, with genuine fear, how she would feel about giving herself to another man. About being unfaithful to her husband, for, somehow, she could not count her loving with Ruth as an infidelity towards Keith. But this, letting another man possess her, enter her, fuck her! That was a true betrayal, of the man she thought she still loved, in spite of his brutal treatment of her.

It was a love he no longer merited, she told herself. He was tormenting her, treating her as his slave, the lowest of the low, refusing even to carry out his marital duties. But, argued that insidious inner voice, didn't you vow that was all you wanted, to be his slave? To be used and abused by him?

And what about that other betrayal? she cried pathetically to herself. She had revealed herself, that hidden, secret, innermost part of her that no one even guessed at, to Mary, trustingly offered the unique sweetness, the treasure of her love. And had been brutally rejected, too, as painfully as her husband's blistering thrashing of her tender flesh. They deserved what she was doing to them, both of them.

In the event, all such cloudy speculations fell away. Excitement, pure physical sensation, the thrill of loving and being loved, of exploring and discovering the raptures of possessing a new body, of being possessed, drove thought itself from her. When at last she returned from the timeless pinnacles of bliss their loving brought, she wondered dimly if it was mere convention or an acknowledgement of truth that made her cling to him with tender passion and murmur, "Oh God, Gerard! It's never been like this for me! I swear to

God! I love you, my darling!"

Above the red roofed house, Menya and Charles, the shamba boy, were sitting outside the quarters sharing an afternoon mug of tea. The houseboy gazed down at Gerard's unimposing blue Toyota parked discreetly round the side of the house, where it had rested for the past two and a half hours. He nodded towards it. "Memsa'ab na Bwana Gerardi - fanya jig-a-jig!" He held up his forearm, fist clenched, in parody of another part of the male anatomy, and shook his head in worldly wise amusement.

5

"You devious scheming little slut! Take my husband, would you!"

Mary, crackling and flashing sparks of fury, came bounding through the door into the living room and launched herself at Vee in one flowing movement. Vee started to rise, with that stomach churning hollowness, but was sent flying back in a bundle onto the lumpy bright cushions of the cane sofa. She had little chance to defend herself, and, in any case, put up only a feeble resistance.

She was no fighter, had accepted her physical cowardice from childhood. Her efforts now, weak as they were, stemmed from a purely instinctive desire to protect herself from serious bodily harm.

She held her arms up, trying to ward off the vicious blows of her attacker, then those raking nails. She felt her newly washed hair seized and yanked agonisingly as Mary dragged her off the low couch to the thin Belgian carpet. There was a loud ripping, and her dress was torn open all the way down its front. It hung in two streaming tatters from her shoulders,

33

until Mary wrenched it clear from her sprawling frame. The open sandals flew from the kicking feet and Vee, clad now only in the flimsy underwear she had donned in the excited expectation of a rendezvous with her lover, endeavoured to curl up into a ball to make herself as small a target as possible in the devastating whirl of fury which had descended on her.

Nails clawed a furrowing path down the side of her neck and shoulder, and she felt the bra strap go, then the lacy cup slip from her left breast. The merciless fingers seized the dangling strip of cloth, wrenched at it. Vee felt the remnants of the garment biting into her skin until they too yielded and flew apart, and she was huddling bare breasted, her only cover the tiny scrap of gauzy lace covering her pubic triangle.

At this point, Menya, alerted by Vee's shrieks and Mary's sobbing vituperation, managed to seize the frenzied figure doing her best to tear his memsa'ab to pieces with her bare hands and, flinging his arms about the slender waist, finally succeeded in plucking her clear of the prone and practically naked form.

He bore Mary's threshing body backwards, held her in a vice like grip, clear of the ground, while her brown legs kicked helplessly at the air. Eventually, her struggles subsided, and she hung limply, heaving with her sobs.

"Let me go! I won't touch her!" Suspiciously, watching her every move in case she relaunched her attack, Menya released Mary, placing himself between the two women.

Vee was still stretched out on the carpet, her face hidden in her arms, racked by loud sobs. "I'll leave your husband to beat the living shit out of you!" Mary gasped, and turned on her heel.

These words, penetrating as they did through Vee's dazed shock and fright, galvanised her into life. She sprang up, with an even louder wail of distress, and raced after the slim figure. Oblivious of Charles's pop eyed stare, Vee hobbled over the rough Tarmac of the drive, to grab frantically at Mary's arm as she made to get into her car.

"Please!" Vee wept hysterically. "I beg you, don't tell Keith! I'll do anything! Anything, I swear. I'm so sorry - please."

Mary's hand shot out once more, the fingers hooking into Vee's disarrayed hair, and twisted it cruelly about her palm. She forced Vee down onto her knees, where she stayed, whimpering in pain and terror, for what seemed an age, while Mary glared down at her. Mary's brown eyes, luminous with tears, shone with a murderous power.

"You'll be hearing from me!" she hissed with intense venom.

Then she flung Vee back with all her might, sending her sprawling on the gritty, hot surface. The car door banged, the engine roared, and Vee lay there, watching the car's disappearance through the dancing tears.

She was scarcely aware of Charles and Menya's solicitous and far too lingeringly familiar hands on her flesh as they helped her to her feet and assisted her back inside. It wasn't until she felt the material of the carpet under her feet as she stood in the middle of the living room that she realised her virtually nude state and their eager gaze, as well as their clutching hands on her bare skin and stumbled blindly away, towards the privacy of the locked bathroom.

All at once, she was aware of all the aches, the stinging scratches, and the red marks where Mary's furious blows had landed. She ran a bath, filled it with fragrant essence, slipped off the tiny briefs and slid with weary thankfulness under the foam. She was almost numb with the suddenness of the calamity which had befallen her.

And yet, now that it had happened, she believed she had been waiting all along for it to happen, waiting all through the three months of her affair with Gerard. There was an inevitability about it. Even the danger of discovery had seemed like a powerful aphrodisiac, spurring them on, in spite of all the obvious risks. You couldn't keep a secret. Not for that long. Not in the enclosed incestuous atmosphere of the expatriate community.

Yet, now that it had happened, she was totally unprepared for the frightening gulf she saw in front of her. She knew how awful Keith's rage would be. Yet, oddly enough, it was not the thought of his physical punishment which terrified her most. No, indeed. Rather, it gave rise to an altogether more shameful, secret sensation, which made her touch herself, caressingly, between her legs, her knees lifting to break through the whirling peaks of the foam. The physical pain he would doubtless mete out to her was at least a sign of passion, proof that she could still raise some storm of emotion within him.

But, afterwards, would surely come banishment this time. He would send her away, for good. That was the terror which stared at her, with such dread blankness. And it was a sentence which she had brought about entirely at her own volition, like some involuntary, masochistic hunger to afflict pain upon herself.

Keith was away on safari, and Vee spent a wretched, almost sleepless night, sick with foreboding. She lay listlessly in bed all the next morning. He was not due to return until that evening. Menya hovered about, bringing her frequent cups of coffee, enquiring if she was all right. "Me no say nothing. Tell nothing," he offered solicitously, standing by her bedside. Under the single sheet, which she clutched about her breast, she was more than usually conscious of her nudity, for she was wearing her usual night garb, which consisted only of one of Keith's pyjama jackets, open as always.

She smiled wanly, made no reply. Was he genuinely attempting to comfort her, or was this the opening round in a negotiated blackmail whose demands would grow more and more outrageous as time passed? It scarcely mattered, she

36

thought wearily. There was no way Keith was not going to hear about it as soon as Mary could get in touch with him. That's if he did not suspect something from the finger marks and bruises on her forearms, as well as those on her hips and other parts of her body where she had been dashed to the floor. And there were the triple red furrows running diagonally from the base of her neck across her shoulder. Would she be able to disguise them sufficiently for him not to notice? And was it worth it, trying to conceal what must all too soon be revealed? Better to make a clean breast of it as soon as he arrived home.

However, her courage failed her at the thought. She would rather endure an extra hour or two of sickening anxiety than bring his wrath down upon her guilty head by her own admission.

So she said nothing when he returned, hot and dusty, irritable with weariness and evincing little interest in her or her doings. Decently covered in a thin polo necked jumper and jeans, she pleaded menstrual pains and headache when he suggested they pop down to the club for a few drinks after dinner. He seemed content enough to go alone, leaving her to stew in her sickening juice for more long hours, imagining a stormy scene of confrontation with Mary in the bar.

She dug out a cotton nightie and was hunched at her side of the bed in assumed slumber when he returned shortly after midnight. She could smell the beery breath. He grunted and muttered as he quickly undressed, but made no effort to come near her. He was soon snoring while she lay and wept yet again for her sins in the heavy dark.

He was up and off to work at the usual time next morning. She lay tensely, listening to him moving around in the bathroom, feigned sleep once more when he came to dress before his solitary breakfast. She sighed with relief at the sound of his car driving away. She was sitting up in bed when Menya knocked and entered, could not meet his gaze as he stared at the modest nightie.

Bitterly, she decided that Mary was exacting a cruel vengeance by making her wait, sweat it out like this. She wanted to pluck up the courage to jump in her car and drive round there. Anything rather than this terrible tension of waiting for the bomb to go off. But, again, her nerve failed her.

As it was, she did not have to wait much longer. The phone rang at about eleven o' clock, when she was still lying in bed, apathetic now, dozing, failing to concentrate her mind on anything. Mary's voice, low, cold with perfect control, was at her ear.

"You said you'd do anything to keep Keith from finding out, that right?"

"Oh, yes, God, Mary, I will!" Vee gabbled tearfully, her heart turning with relief. "Whatever you want!"

"Good! You're going to be put to the test, my dear. You fail to do exactly as you're told from now on and I'll get straight to that poor sap of a husband of yours, understood?"

"Yes, oh yes!" Vee gasped fervently. Then, as Mary's crisp tones continued, Vee's mouth dropped open. She blinked in total disbelief.

"What?" she stammered, her head reeling. "I can't do that!"

Mary gave a harsh laugh. "See? You're wasting my time, cow! Now!" She repeated her orders, while Vee gaped numbly at the receiver. She began to cry, sniffling into the mouth piece, and Mary swore with brief pungency. At last Vee laid the receiver on the pillow and, moving as though in a dream, climbed out of bed. Slowly, she drew the nightie off over her head, knelt on the rug, feeling the cool hardness pressing through the thin rush matting. She kept her thighs primly together, stared at their brown shapelessness, the light thatch of her pubes between them . She cleared her throat, tried to shout, coughed, and tried again.

"Menya! Menya! Come here, kuja hapa!"

She heard his sandalled feet slop-slopping down the corridor, smelt his pleasant odour of toilet soap and tobacco. Heard him gasp, felt the stillness as he gazed at her kneeling nakedness. A sob shook her shoulders, she could not look at him. "Memsa'ab Mary," she whispered faintly. "She wants to speak with you. On the phone." She nodded at the black receiver lying on the crumpled white pillow.

His yellow, smoky eyes were popping out all the while as he listened to the incisive voice in his ear, and nodded rapidly at the stream of clear instructions. "Ndio, memsa'ab. Ndio." He handed the phone back to Vee, who was kneeling in the same position, her buttocks resting on her heels, her arms folded modestly over her breasts.

"Lie down on your back on the bed. Do exactly as Menya tells you!" Mary ordered.

Vee began to sob once more. "Please - he'll ruh - rape me!"

Mary laughed harshly. "That'll be the day. Other way round, more like. No he won't," she continued impatiently. "I've told him exactly what will happen to him if he tries anything on. Just do as you're told. If you don't want Keith to find out!"

Her body heaving with her weeping, Vee did as she was bidden, spreading herself out on top of the covers. Menya was rummaging in her drawers, pulling out her bundled tights and stockings. He used these to bind her wrists to the top corners of the bed, then her spread-eagled ankles to the bottom corners. Vee was agonisingly conscious of the gaping display of her sexual parts, the rough scratch of his fingers on her limbs, the masculine powerfulness of his proximity as he bent over her. Yet he was almost as much a victim as she was, bound by Mary's implacable commands. He stood, picked up the discarded receiver, spoke rumblingly into it, nodded once more. He cradled the phone on Vee's bare shoulder, so that she could both hear and reply.

"Comfy?" Mary chuckled lasciviously, listening to Vee's wretched weeping. "Now, just lie there and think of what a decadent little slut you are. And to think you had me fooled by that little lesbian ploy in the showers! My God! I owe you for that one, my sweet!"

"Please, Mary!" Vee blubbered, panic stricken. "What's going to happen? What if Keith comes back? What -" There was another deep laugh and the receiver was replaced. Menya was still standing over her. He heard the click, and the ensuing silence. He picked the plastic receiver delicately from Vee's neck and put it in its cradle. After one last encompassing stare at her proffered nakedness, he turned and left.

Vee lay there. At first, she was unable to prevent herself from tugging against the restraints, and quickly realised how efficiently they had been tied. Her ankles chafed as she struggled to close her legs, and her helplessness was both a cruel punishment and a wicked temptation. In spite of her fear and distress, she could feel the growing beat of insidious excitement in her loins, sending its wicked impulses through to every nerve end. She stared up unseeingly through her tears at the white plaster of the ceiling, while the room filled and grew hot with the strong morning sunlight.

Her mind drifted, fantasising, until she was brought sharply back to awareness by a sudden choked off snort, and she raised her head, to see both Menya and Charles crowding in the doorway, staring avidly at her. "Go away!" she wailed. Again the bonds burned at her tender skin as she instinctively tried to hide herself.

"No speak!" Menya answered gruffly. "Memsa'ab very bad. Jig-a-jig. Very bad!' He shook his finger admonishingly, and he and Charles burst into laughter. It was a long while before they moved away, but at least they did not offer to touch her. Only later did she realise what a tribute this was to Mary's authority and to that of the wealthy expatriates in this society.

She began to wonder if it was Mary's intention that she should be left for Keith to find when he returned from work that evening. Her reflections were disturbed by the sound of a car engine approaching down the drive, and her heart thudded in terror. Keith never came home for lunch! What was he doing here? She heard Menya call out, heard the brief rumble of a male voice answering. Footsteps coming along the corridor. She froze, staring mutely at the doorway.

In which Gerard appeared!

"Oh, thank God!" Vee burst out, sobbing abandonedly with relief as she writhed against the bonds.

To her amazement, Gerard did not greet her, but, his face looking almost as distraught as she felt, he went straight to the phone at the bedside, and dialled a number. "I'm here now." Vee heard a female voice buzzing. She recognised Mary's crisp incisiveness as Gerard laid the receiver down on the locker's top, then hastily began to strip off his clothing.

His penis, swollen thickly, was lobbing in the early stages of arousal. His fingers grasped it, gave a series of quick, savage tugs as he knelt between her thighs and brought himself to full hardness.

"Jesus! No, Gerard! You can't -"

He picked up the phone again. "I'm ready!"

His expression changed to one of deep disappointment as he listened, and she saw how his penis immediately deflated.

"No!" he said. "Oh no!"

More words hissed down the wire, and in obedience to them he untied Vee's ankles and pulled her right leg up over her head and outwards, retied the ankle to the bed post in its new and more obscene position. Then the left. Next he eased her hips forward so that her bottom was raised, leaving her to stare up at him in dread through her legs.

Her dread increased as he drew the broad leather belt

from his discarded shorts.

He picked up the phone again.

"How many, dear?" he asked, as he placed the phone where her screams would best be heard.

6

Ensnared in her new illicit relationship, this time a unique triangular affair, Vee was once more filled with a sense of impending disaster, waiting for the storm clouds to break at what she saw as the inevitability of Keith's discovery.

Surely he could not go on for much longer being blind to Menya's insolently familiar air towards her, to say nothing of his and Charles's lascivious mental stripping of her every time their lingering gaze fell upon her? And, worse, her agonising embarrassment when she and Keith were in the company of Mary and Gerard.

To her shame, she recognised the fierce excitement she derived from her involvement, and the total subservience towards Mary which the dark haired girl enforced.

She didn't know which was worse, the beatings she had to endure from Gerard, from the titillating open palmed spankings over his knee to the more serious belabourings of her bottom with hairbrush or some similar instrument, all under the avid gaze of the entranced Mary, who had never laid a finger on her after that first furious attack, or her own enforced passivity as she sat obediently in a chair at the foot of the bed and watched Gerard and Mary make long and passionate love. She hated Gerard for the willing bondsman's role he assumed. Most of all, though, she hated him for that pole hard cock, so ready to plough into the delectable figure of the wife he was all too eager to deceive in former days.

She was always terrified when he eagerly complied with

Mary's order to chastise Vee that he would leave her back-side so bruised Keith would notice. It was true she and Keith never made love any more, and her mouth was all he used to obtain sexual satisfaction. But they still shared the same bed, he would catch casual glimpses of her as she dressed or un-dressed, walk in on her in the bath or shower.

One morning, when Keith had just departed on a three day safari to the mountainous western region, Mary and Gerard arrived while Vee was still in the shower. She had not been expecting them, and was preparing to spend an hour or two lying on the sunbed on the veranda.

"Open up!" Mary shouted, rattling the door handle of the shower room, and Vee hastened to comply, grabbing a towel and wrapping it round her still gleaming torso. Mary seized her by the arm and hauled her out into the corridor. "What on earth do you think you're doing, wearing that thing? You're not a nun, you know!" As she spoke, she yanked the towel swiftly away.

Vee let out a muted scream as she saw Menya's grinning face gazing in appreciation over Gerard's looming shoulder. "You! Kwenda!" Mary ordered, and, chastened, Menya turned back towards the kitchen. She pushed Vee towards the bed-room. "Come on! Quick! We're taking you for an outing. No underwear. Just your blue flowered dress. The silky mini. We want you to look fetching."

They drove out along the principal route to the south west, the one Keith had travelled scarcely more than an hour or two earlier. The roadside native shambas straggled for miles on both sides of the narrow strip of potholed Tarmac.

Mary turned companionably to Vee, who was sitting star-ing nervously through the window from the rear seat. "We're taking you to meet George. George Kyriakos. A fascinating old stick. Lives out in Mengo, in little better than a hut. Looked after by a Baganda bibi he's lived with for years.

He's very sick. Won't last much longer. But what a character! What a life! He'll certainly appreciate you!"

George Kyriakos was a massive ruin of a man - Greek tragedy or Hollywood horror. His potbellying bulk was enormous. Pink flesh gaped between straining buttons and rumpled folds of his stained ash-dusted safari suit. The eyes in the ruined face were incredible. Ringed about with bags and purple shadows of theatrical proportions, they were femininely soft, stirring Vee to secret discomfort with their knowledge of life, the awareness of inner weakness, the pathos of the human condition reflected in their brown depths.

The face was mottled with drink and debauch. Cheeks pouched to hanging jowls, and the large billowing folds of flesh that hung and shook and flowed like a muffler onto the slope of his wheezing breast. Lips shone wetly, with a thin deadly 'Kali' cigarette hanging and bobbing, scattering its ash flakes over the bulk that spread below. Delicate little hands were heavily ringed, the fingers curled, joints swollen and matching the colour of his complexion. The nails curved into horny talons. The first two fingers of his right hand were deeply brown at the nails, fading to a jaundice yellow at the second knuckles. The small feet and ankles protruding from the filthy slacks were so swollen that the toes were grotesquely buried in the flesh. He never wore socks or shoes. The feet were bare, or a pair of blue, rubber thonged flipflops clung precariously to them.

Vee was fascinated by the monumental portrayal of illness and decay. "He's a terrible old letch, aren't you, George?" Mary said, as she introduced Vee. "This is the one I was telling you about. The little slut that Gerard was shafting. I told you she was gorgeous, didn't I?"

He held Vee's hand in his claw, kissed it slowly, leaving the wet imprint of those liver lips. He stared into her eyes until she blushed hotly to her very roots, and he chuckled softly with success when she was forced to glance away. His voice was rich and deep, almost as dramatic as his appearance. "She has that special English quality, that air of innocence" - he ignored Mary's yelp of sarcastic laughter - "that naivety one should say, that's so attractive. Such girls are almost like boys. Sweet young boys. And I have always loved young boys. All men do, I am sure, though you English will not admit it, eh, Gerard? It must be kept in the closet. It's not good to be a pouf, eh?"

They had brought him a bottle of the local banana gin, which he downed in alarming quantity, though liberally watered. His mistress, a strong, silent woman, surprisingly young, though her matronly figure was generously fattened in Baganda fashion, tended to them and faded into the background until he called harshly for her to bring water, or fetch a book.

The sparsely furnished room was littered with piles of books, old magazines, yellowing newspapers. Around the walls were dozens of paintings and sketches, some cheaply framed. They seemed to Vee to be of an excellent standard, and she was startled to learn that most of them had been done by George himself. Then she noticed an exquisite head and shoulders portrait of Mary, done in pencil.

He talked of his old days in the territory and in the Congo, tales of fantastic events and more fantastic characters, widening to a captivating philosophy of life, and glimpses of an impressive knowledge of classics and literature way beyond his admiring audience.

It was Mary who steered the talk back to sexual matters, in spite of her husband's clear embarrassment. "They'd been at it for nigh on three months," she declared, nodding towards both him and the blushing Vee.

George shrugged almost dismissively. "It doesn't mean he loves you any the less, my dear," he said urbanely. "There's nothing wrong with honest to God sexuality. You know the saying. 'A rising prick knows no conscience.' What normal healthy young man doesn't want to fuck every pretty girl he sees? Or pretty boy, for that matter." He gave his wheezing chuckle. "Where we have gone wrong in Europe," he continued, turning his gaze directly on Vee, "is in not crediting women with the same bodily desires as men. We even shrouded their physiognomy - or should I say physiography? - in mystery and lies. For so long, even young studs went to the marriage bed not understanding the workings of their wives' cunts, in spite of all their premarital experience. And girls themselves were deceived into thinking sex was something beastly. That only man should have the beastliness.

"They tormented themselves trying to ignore that secret, shrouded little tip of flesh, living in dread of what they saw as their depravity, cut off from talking of it with their own kind. Mothers even perpetuated the lie to their own daughters, ignoring their own clamorous instincts. Can you imagine what agonies our great grandmothers must have gone through if they chanced by any mishap to experience orgasm? Not that there was much fear of it happening. At least not through the sweaty efforts of their spouses, who rogered furiously, all wham bangs and thank yous. But there must have been the odd times when, driven mad by that insistent flesh, the young women found themselves unable to keep their fingers from homing in on that hot wet little patch, where they ferreted about with a tearful sense of doom. All those jokes - 'all the nice girls love a candle' - they've been with us a long time."

All three were sitting paying rapt attention to his diatribe. Again, it was Mary who rallied, gave an edgy little laugh. "Speaking of hot wet little patches, I'm sure you've got young Vee here squelching in her knickers. Or would have if I'd allowed her any! So, George, don't you think she'll make an excellent model for some of your special studies? Or are you too pissed to do anything about it now?"

His jowls wobbled as his florid face shook in vehement

denial. "No, no, not at all! Pass me that folder. Come. Get ready, my dear," he said, his brilliantly gleaming eyes fixed once more on Vee. She stared blankly.

"Come on!" snapped Mary impatiently. "Get your kit off. George is going to immortalise you."

Vee gasped in outrage as she realised what they were planning. "You want us to do it for you?" pursued Mary, with implacable intent. Crying softly, Vee reached behind her, fumbled for the zipper on her dress. She drew it over her head, held it for a second over her bare breasts before she passed it to Mary..

George's claw like hands scratched lightly at her nakedness as he arranged her in the easy chair so that the burning light of the midday sun fell full upon her.

"Put your leg out to the side. Let it hang, like that. Come on, don't be shy. We want to see your proudest treasure, my little beauty."

He made her drape her right leg over the wooden arm, hook her right arm over the back of the chair. Her left leg he stretched out in front of her, turning it slightly outward, so that she was exposing the whole of her genital area, blatantly proffering the pale curve of belly, the light brown curls, glinting in the sunlight, the long gash of her labial divide. She saw the bruise dark inner surfaces about her vulva, felt the secretly beating response to the bathing sunlight's heat on her sensitive flesh. Her breasts too, because of the arrangement of her torso, were exhibited. The small pale nipples flowered to hardness.

Despite her distress, which caused her to weep quietly all the while he was working, she could feel the throbbing depth of her arousal. She was tactilely aware of everything, the kiss of the sunlight, the touch of the lumpy cushions on her buttocks and the backs of her thighs, the film of sweat which made the back of her right leg cling stickily to the wooden arm of the chair. He worked quickly, though to Vee

47

it seemed an endless ordeal of shame. Mary and Gerard chatted desultorily, and he answered absently, concentrating on his task. Mostly, all three stared at her sprawling frame.

At last it was over. She was allowed to move, climbed stiffly out of the chair. She went towards her dress, which lay where Mary had tossed it, but the dark haired girl shook her head. "Uh-huh! Not yet. Don't you think George deserves some reward for all his labours? Just Look at what he's done." Taking Vee by the arm, she led her over to the sketch, which lay now on the table.

Vee was shocked out of her embarrassment. It was beautiful, she saw at once. She was astounded that those crippled claw hands could have created such delicate beauty. There she was, abandoned, wildly erotic, yet somehow oddly innocent too. The neat breasts, with their tiny budded crowns, the slight curve of belly, the scrub of her pubic curls, the outwardly jutting leg, the calf and down pointing foot hanging limply, the proffered genitals between those shaded muscles showing her surrender. The long curve of the vulva, the cleft of the lips, their peaks meeting in that secret fold of vulnerable tissue. Its raw beauty smote Vee. With mirroring power, she felt those sex muscles tighten, the lips seeming to push and pout and swell. Then she felt the artist's knowing gaze on her, and the rising blush flooded from her neck, quickening the beat of her blood.

"It's beautiful!" she murmured tearfully.

"Like I said, he deserves some reward, fair?" Vee's colour now drained at Mary's words. "Why don't we warm her up a little for you first, maestro? Put a little colour back into her cheeks? Ah! That should do, eh? Go ahead, Gerard. Do your stuff." She picked up the worn blue flip-flop which had slipped from George's swollen foot, and handed it to her husband. "You, slut. Bend over the back of the chair. No, that way." Urgently, she pulled Vee round, thrust her by the shoulders, folding her over the chair back, burying the blonde

48

head in the musty cushions. "We want to see that gorgeous arse getting it, don't we, George?" The pink tongue tip flickered out to lick the shining lips as George nodded greedily.

"Ohl Oh! OH!" The cracking splat of the flat rubber sole striking at Vee's behind was followed by the fierce, stinging burn, and she shrieked, surprised as always at the force with which Gerard struck. Her body jerked involuntarily, her buttocks flinching, dimpling cutely as her muscles clenched.

Sobbing, she forced herself back down over the high chair back. The muscles bunched on her thighs as she flexed for the next blow, which quickly followed. Soon both quivering cheeks were covered with the red outlines of the sandal's shape, one superimposed over another, until the whole area glowed an angry red, and Vee was pleading for him to stop, her body heaving with her sobs. The nod from Mary brought this stage of her torment to an end, and she stood there, tears streaming, while she rubbed at her throbbing bottom.

"How's that, George?" Mary asked, her dark eyes alive and shining. George's mottled face was even darker, his breath coming more noisily. His gaze was fixed on the base of Vee's belly, where the triangle of her sandy fleece showed.

"Could I have a few moments alone with her?" he croaked. His voice shook with desperate pleading.

"Why, George! You randy old goat! Be careful now!" Mary nodded at Gerard, and they went out onto the rickety veranda and down the three wooden steps to the grassy track in front of the bungalow.

"Come here, my dear!" George's throaty whisper sent shivers through Vee's naked form. It was like the command of a hypnotist, and, as though in a trance, she found herself moving the few paces across the dusty floor to his side. Once again, she felt the horny scrape of his long nails scratching over her flesh. She shivered, half in revulsion, half in a shameful eruption of excitement. His arm lifted, the talons moved lightly, almost timidly, over the slope of a breast, grazed the

49

erect nipple, then down, over her midriff, the shallow little dish of her navel, to the light curls of her pubis, and down, down to her inner thigh.

It nuzzled with gentle insistence, pushing her thighs open, so that she was standing, her legs slightly apart, permitting his exploring hand access to her vulva. He was still sitting at the table where he had been working, and she stood so close she could feel the material of his trousers rub against her leg. She was standing in a block of sunlight which streamed through the open door. Each curl of pubic hair stood out against the paleness of the skin beneath in the brilliant light, which bathed the damp, pungent folds of her flesh, burned its fierce caress on her belly and the whole of her genital area.

The throbbing burn of her scorched behind became one with the surging flow of excitement overpowering her, as he explored the groove of her sex lips, prised open their tightness, until she could feel the imperious beat of her sex, the oily wetness of her inner passage, waiting hungrily. Tears trickled down her cheeks. She stood, weeping silently.

All at once, he fell forward on his knees, with a hoarse kind of sob, and buried his sweating face into the fold of her belly and thighs, his arms flung about her hips, sucking and slobbering, drinking in her beauty, while she shivered, forcing herself to remain still, staring down through her tears and stroking the stubble on the back of his neck.

She felt the stirring pulse of orgasm approaching. Suddenly, he almost dragged her down onto the floor with him as his weight pulled heavily on her hips, and he levered himself back into his chair. He was making an alarming noise, fighting for his breath, eyes bugging, his face a dark, uniform purple. She screamed for help, and the door to the interior of the house burst open. The Baganda woman hurtled in, and shoved Vee aside before she turned to George, grabbed some appliance from the pocket of his safari jacket and

50

squirted it into his working mouth. Gradually, his breathing resumed some sort of evenness. The woman held a glass to his lips, helped him to take a few sips.

The dark shadows of Gerard and Mary appeared against the blinding light in the doorway. The woman glanced up, then turned and surveyed Vee, her gaze conveying her contempt as it travelled slowly from head to toe. With a gasp, Vee recollected her nude state and crossed her arms over her breasts.

"Go!" the woman said.

7

Masturbation was the only physical relief Vee enjoyed these days. Mary made sure Gerard never touched her except to beat her. He got his thrills from making love to his wife, with Vee as captive audience.

At home, Keith continued to shun any notion of sexual intercourse. and she was far too moulded in her subservience now to try to initiate or even suggest it. Fellatio was the only sexual act he required, and then only irregularly. She learned to recognise the signs; they had no need of words.

It was usually when he returned, drunk, from an evening at the golf club. There was even a strong sexual thrill in her servility, its total one-sidedness. He would sprawl in the living room, fully clothed, and she would rise and go to him, kneeling between his slackly open legs.

She would struggle to release his penis from the constrictions of his clothing. It was rarely a quick event. In his alcoholic state, although his desire was unmistakable, fulfilment took a great deal of time, though he seemed to derive plenty of groaning, twisting, weakening pleasure from the delicious torment.

51

Eventually, though, his fingers would grip convulsively in her hair, while he thrust savagely into her gagging, gaping mouth. She was exhausted, running with sweat, soaked with his sperm and her saliva, lips, tongue, mouth, raw and swollen. Every bone ached. Her knees were throbbing abominably, an angry red from the pressure of the polished cement floor, and it was agony when she finally moved, with the slowness of a cripple. By the time she came out of the bathroom after cleaning herself, he was snoring loudly, a hunched shape across the gulf of the double bed.

When disaster broke, Vee was totally unprepared for it, in spite of all the hours of fearful imaginings she had suffered. Its beginnings lay in a vindictive remark flung out by a petulant loser in the golf club bar after a marathon boozing session at the end of a monthly mug competition. Keith's suspicions were aroused, and it was not too hard to get them confirmed.

Vee was in bed. She heard the car come down the drive, wondered, ashamed at the tremor of excitement, whether he would want her to service him tonight. Whether, indeed, he had already found sexual satisfaction, for she was convinced he must find relief with someone. Again, she was shocked at the perverse thrill such a painful speculation caused her.

He beat her cruelly, almost with a cold precision, as though icily manipulating his fury. He held her by the hair, lifting her off her feet, swinging her round, slapping her around the face with great, open handed blows that left her burning, her head dizzy and singing. He flung her to the floor, and kicked her several times, under the ribs, and on the backs of her thighs, until she was coughing and choking.

She was only dimly aware of events now. The pyjama jacket had gone, ripped from her. She huddled up, her forehead pressed to the floor, her rump and back proffered to take his punishment. There was a pause, then a swish in the

52

air and a crack, as a line of breath snatching fire ran across her back. A sting bit into her side, like a scorpion's bite, as the end of the narrow belt curled around and struck. The fire flashed over her behind and her hips and the backs of her thighs, and she couldn't restrain herself. She writhed and bucked, squirmed and screamed. One merciless hand dug into her hair, holding her down. The crack of the belt rang out like pistol shots. Her buttocks were seared, again and again, and the agony spread over the backs of her thighs, her back itself, until there was only red pain, everywhere, and she stretched out, yielding to its power, surrendered to it, felt it cutting through her flesh to her very centre, a seductive agony that made her wrenching cries those of a gut release.

The pain, and her own cries, distorted everything, but she could hear the low rumble of voices behind her, and, somehow, could see clearly, a vision in her mind's eye which would stay with her always, the dark, staring faces of Menya and Charles, crowded in the doorway, her own bloodily streaked and welted nakedness stretched out on the thin rug, with Keith towering astride her like a giant lion tamer, the belt snaking down by his side.

The burning pain swept through her, from shoulders to the backs of her thighs, in great, throbbing tides to which she surrendered utterly. Even the great, gulping breaths she was forced to inhale because of her wild sobbing sent further fine ripples of agony through the blistered skin. She felt timid brown hands on her arms and legs, struggling to lift her, and the pain flared again at the slightest move.

The next day Keith called upon Gerard. He punched him as he answered the door, then kicked viciously, until the hunched, semi-conscious figure was twitching helplessly, covered in blood and vomit and tears.

He was amazed at the resistance Mary put up. She sobbed,

and swore foully when he picked her up and carried her, her feet threshing, into one of the spare bedrooms. Her struggles revealed an appetising exhibition of shapely limbs and white underwear as he tossed her on her back on the counterpane. "Go on then, scream," he urged, with grim satisfaction. "Maybe your gallant husband will drag himself out of bed to come and fight for your honour. I hope so!"

"Bastard!" she sobbed. But she quietened immediately, though she fought him furiously while he ripped her skirt and blouse, then the bra and briefs from her writhing frame. "You filthy bloody rapist!" But then he lay across her, crushing her down into the yielding springiness of the mattress, his mouth closed over hers, hard, demanding, thrusting. His hand fanned out over the wiry tendrils of her pubis, and she lifted her mound against his pressure, feeling his fingers like steel against the cushioning. They bent, followed the tight curving divide of her vulva, pushed into the damp crevice of her labia, seeking out the quickening beat of her, and all at once, her muscles relaxed, she sank beneath him, her belly undulated in a different rhythm which had its own urgency, and her thighs opened accommodatingly. Pelvises clashed in the mutual hunger, and they soared to their grunting, whimpering climax. Mary cried out sharply as she came, sobbing and plunging wildly, spearing herself on his potent maleness.

On the fourth day, Vee was able to bear the touch of her silk dressing gown, so that she was decently clad, and reclining, without too much discomfort, on the cushions of the settee in the living room, when Keith at last returned. She had heard from no one, no one had come near in all that time. Slowly she levered herself up into a sitting position as he strode into the room. The cold blue eyes held her in their stare.

"I've had it out with Mary and that scum," he said. "And I want you out of here by Monday. You can move into one of

54

those Salvation Army cottages out at Mbira until I can get you a flight back to UK. I want you out of my life as soon as possible!"

He had disappeared down the corridor to the bedroom before she started to cry.

8

Mbira was several miles outside the city, on the road to the north. The Salvation Army ran an orphanage there, on a beautifully kept ten acre site. The lawns were smoothly cropped, the hedges trimly regimented, with bougainvillea and Canna lilies making bold explosions of symmetric colour from the red earth flower beds.

A number of small guest cottages were tucked away among the trees on the far side of the compound from the orphanage buildings. These cottages could be rented out for a modest fee. Advertising was by word of mouth only, so that the clientele should remain reasonably select, and, apart from certain peak periods, demand was not high. Vee found that the one next to hers was empty, which was a great relief. She shunned people, had a habit of breaking into tears without warning. She was still bemused. She had difficulty in holding on to any train of thought, and her mind felt like fluffed out cotton wool.

Helpless, apathetic almost, she had put up no fight, pleaded no defence. She had scarcely spoken to Keith, or to anyone else, murmuring monosyllabic acknowledgements when he did deign to speak to her. She moved in a daze of misery, packing her cases, sitting for long intervals when she was able to sit again with her hands folded on her lap, staring unseeingly ahead of her. She made no attempt to contact anyone, and, significantly, no one attempted to get in touch with her. She thought fleetingly of going down to the Club, but she knew she hadn't the courage for it. She was obviously the villainess, the outcast who had got her just deserts.

The night before she was due to move out to the cottage, she managed to stir herself into making one last desperate effort. Keith had spent all his evenings and nights away from her. Clearly, he could not stand even seeing her, and came home in the early hours, when she was safely bedded down in the guest room. He was gone long before she ventured forth in the morning. You must at least have one last try, she urged herself, otherwise you'll be simply tossed out of his life forever.

The prospect was stunningly bleak. What had she got to lose by one final attempt? Even another thrashing would be better than this cold ignoring of her. So, although her heart was racing, and her stomach churned emptily, she spent a long time in the bath, perfumed and groomed herself, put on her prettiest underwear, even pulling on a pair of dark, sheer nylons to clip to the narrow ribbons of the suspender belt. She remembered how, in the distant days before their marriage, he had delighted in seeing her thus, had even enjoyed making love while she wore only such stockings and suspenders.

In elegant high heels, and her blue silk mini dress, she sat nervously in the living room. Menya came in after washing the dishes of her solitary evening meal. "You no go to bed?" he asked pointedly. He had become almost impossible since the disaster.

She cleared her throat, spoke shrilly, trying to hide her anxiety. "No. I'm going to sit up and wait for Bwana. You can go now. Thank you." He looked as if he were about to say more, but after staring at her until she could feel her colour mounting, he turned abruptly on his heel and went out, clashing the outer door shut behind him.

For all her perturbed state, she was actually lolling asleep in the armchair when the noise of the car engine awoke her. Her heart was thumping, she rose rapidly, one hand to her hair, trying to rouse herself. She would simply throw herself at his feet, beg him not to discard her, offer to serve him in any capacity he wished. She heard his footsteps, the door started to open, she stared in pathetic fear and pleading...

And then she was gazing, her jaw sagging, her eyes wide in amazement, at the vision of the tall, giggling figure of the African girl clinging possessively to Keith's arm. Her dress was even shorter than Vee's, so that her gleaming, magnificent legs, innocent of any covering, were on show almost from the tops of her thighs. And what legs they were! They appeared to Vee to go on forever. The girl was wearing a huge Afro wig, which added to the impression of height. In her heeled, strappy sandals, she towered over the gawping Vee.

Her skin was of a deep velvet blackness, the shade of the northern tribes. Similarly, her features were of the more traditionally Bantu type, in contrast with the lighter skinned, finer features of the Baganda people in whose region the capital lay. Her thick lips glistened with a lipstick which was exotically dark, almost black. A look of surprise spread over her pretty face, nowhere near as extreme as the ludicrous astonishment of Vee's expression. Keith did not look shocked at all. In fact, Vee recognised with dread the evil gleam of anticipation in his face.

"Ah-ha! The little woman! Waiting up for us, how sweet! Mira - this is Vee. My little blonde bibi! The slut I told you about! The one I'm slinging out on her arse tomorrow, right, Vee?" The tears rose, misting her vision as Vee swallowed, nodded desolately. "Get us a drink, will you? Might as well make yourself useful on your last night. Whisky and soda for me. What about you, Mira?"

"Beer for me," the girl answered coolly, entering into the

spirit of the situation at once. "And not cold, either!" she snapped. "I'm not a bloody mzungu, not one of your ice cold Europeans! Make it a warm one, hey?" Blindly, startled at her own servile acceptance, Vee found herself turning away, moving out to the kitchen to get a bottle of beer, then returning to serve them both their drinks.

She quickly realised that they were both already drunk. "Why don't you join us?" Keith grinned wickedly at Vee. "Have a nightcap before you go to bed." He pulled the squealing figure of Mira down onto the settee with him, and she fell, kicking feebly, into his arms. He planted a noisy kiss on her lips. "We won't be long before we'll be hitting the hay ourselves."

His hand stood out palely against her shining skin, the long, rippling muscles of her thighs, as it travelled slowly upward, displacing the short dress until Vee could see the white of the lace fringed knickers.

"I think I'll go to bed now!" Vee choked, striving to hold back the threatening tears.

"Get a bloody drink!" Keith snarled, so fiercely that Vee flinched. White as paper, she went over to the cupboard. Her hands shook as she poured herself a small measure of brandy. She did not add anything. She came and sat down again in the deep arm chair opposite the entwined couple on the sofa. She was all at once terribly conscious of the shortness of her own dress, and her sheer stockings, as she felt her eyes drawn to the white triangle of the girl's crotch, plainly on view now as she sprawled back in Keith's arms, and which stood out so excitingly against the darkness of Her thighs.

"So, Mira," Keith said. "What do you think of my lovely wife? Do you think she's beautiful?"

Mira's dark eyes held her with obvious contempt. She made a thick sound of disapproval.

"She is skinny - like a boy!"

"Oh, don't tell her that, for Christ's sake," Keith chortled.

58

"You'll make her day!" He fought out from under Mira's encompassing arms. "Come on, wench! Let this black bibi see just how sexy you are. Strip off and give her a real show!"

Vee gasped. A huge sob rose, shook her with its force. A bitter desperation rose in her gorge until she could scarcely breathe. Suddenly, with another sob of masochistic hopelessness, she thrust herself back to her feet. Very well! He wanted to inflict this final humiliation upon her. So be it! She reached behind her, found the zip fastener, drew it down, and slid the front of the dress off her shoulders. She gave a little shake of her hips, helped it down over her flanks until it fell about her ankles and she stepped out of it.

The girl gave a loud hoot of derision. "You beat her pretty damn good!" she exclaimed, gazing with new respect at Keith.

"Not as good as she deserves," he had responded coldly. And his words cut Vee as badly as ever the belt had. The tears were starting to flow, but she no longer cared for anything. Somewhere in the recesses of her mind she was shocked at the degree of sexual excitement she could feel tightening those secret muscles deep within her belly. She stood for a few seconds, in the lacy bra and the transparent white briefs, with the narrow little suspender belt showing through.

Keith roared his encouragement. "Atta girl! Gerrem off!" She was crying audibly now, and the tear drops shone on her cheeks, but she reached behind her once more, groped for the catch of the bra. It parted, she shrugged the flimsy cups off her breasts, flung the garment aside.

"She has titi like little girl!" Mira giggled.

Keith swung on her at once, and started clawing her dress from her shoulders. "Come on then, sugar! Show her what a real pair of tits looks like!" Angrily, she pushed him off, then undid her dress herself. Her long legs flashed as she struggled to get out of the low settee, then she was standing close to Vee, looming over her. The floral dress had fallen to cling about her waist. She was wearing a cheap white cotton bra, which she now undid, and, like Vee, let it fall from her.

Vee stared in involuntary appreciation. The full breasts rose as she breathed in deeply. Their proud beauty was proclaimed as they jiggled and shook. The large surrounds of the areolae were dark, and the nipples themselves, many times larger than Vee's pale little teats, were long, swollen with promise, creviced, a dark, ripe purplish colour. She gave a long, harsh peel of triumphant laughter. Vee blushed. Unconsciously, she had folded her arms over her own modest breasts. Now, Mira's hard black fingers fastened on her wrists, tugged her arms away from her bosom, exposing them once more. "Skinny little bitch!"

"Have a look at the rest of her!" Keith mocked, leering up at them both. "Go on! Finish her off!" Again, Mira gave a hoot of scornful pleasure. Her splendid hips shimmied and her folded dress dropped around her feet. She reached forward, hooked her fingers in the fragile little knickers Vee was wearing, and with one vicious yank, dragged them half way down her legs. The lace trimming tore, streamed pathetically, then Mira bent and hauled them all the way down. Vee stumbled, almost losing her balance as the African girl stripped them clear of her.

Vee was weeping at the ridiculous picture she presented in only the stockings and the suspender belt. She crossed her hands over the light fleece of her pubis, but, once again, Mira seized her wrists and pulled them away from her loins. Vee gave a little scream of alarm as the dark fingers grabbed at the hairs over her mound and gave a sharp tug, lifting the white skin beneath them.

Vee stood, made no effort to prevent her aggressor, while those same cruel fingers tore at the fasteners of the suspender ribbons, unclipping them from the dark stocking tops before they whipped the belt off. Finally, they clawed and scrabbled their way down the length of Vee's trembling limbs as Mira brought the clinging nylons down to the ankles.

Vee toppled, fell back into the depths of the arm chair once more as Mira completed the act of undressing her by hauling the gauzy material clear of her feet. Vee's scream was altogether louder, and filled with genuine terror as the fingers finally settled in the silky blonde hair and dragged the cowering form upright, with a victorious cry.

Mira hauled her weeping victim round, holding her in front of the grinning Keith. "There she is! Like I told you! See? She has hips like a boy! And buttocks, too!" Vee shrieked at the loud slap Mira delivered to the part of her anatomy in question.

The dark girl was wearing only the white briefs. "Show her what a real arse looks like, then!" Keith challenged, and, at once, Mira bent and thrust down her knickers. She kicked them away to the corner of the room. She turned around, slowly, showing off her magnificent body, and Keith gazed up, his prick straining at the contrasting, deeply rousing spectacle of the two naked girls. He chuckled evilly. "Be careful. My wife'll get turned on by you, my lovely! She likes girls. Don't you, perv? You know what a dike is, eh, Mira? You know - a lesbian?"

The girl's eyes widened, she stared back at him with a disbelieving grin. "What? She likes to play sex with girls?"

"Right on! Why don't we all go along to the bedroom and have some real fun? This could turn out to be the best night you and me have ever had, slag," he said to Vee. "And on your last night, too!"

Vee felt sickened. She almost welcomed the imprisoning hold of his arm around her waist, the other arm capturing the giggling Mira in like fashion as he steered them both along the corridor to the master bedroom.

He had to overcome Mira's indignant reluctance to allow Vee anywhere near her, but presently the black girl lay back, propped up by pillows, Keith holding her as he lay beside her. "Let her get us both going." He pushed the dusky thighs open, and Mira gasped, caught in both a strange excitement and disgust, as the blonde head dipped between the raised knees, which fell apart at Vee's gentle pressure on the insides of her thighs.

Vee's own heart was pounding with a mixture of fear and throbbing desire. The strange exotic aroma of the proffered mound filled her. She thought of the activity which had surely taken place earlier this evening between Keith and this lovely girl, now spread so nakedly under her very nose. The tight little scrub of tiny curls, so different from her own, beckoned. The upper folds of the vulva lifted, the pout of the labia presented itself temptingly. The outer surface of the divide was a dark mushroom colour.

With softly probing tongue and timid fingers, Vee prised at the tight divide. The startling pink of the inner surface was exposed, blossoming open, like a shell or a delicate tropical bloom. Vee's head dipped further, lapped at the musky treasures, imbibing the pungent moisture while a shudder of ecstasy passed through her crouching frame, from head to toe.

Talon hard hands dug into her scalp, hauled her lapping tongue away from her goal.

"Don't forget me!" a voice growled, over the thunder of her blood, and she turned to Keith's loins, her breasts rubbing lightly against Mira's thigh as she moved herself across to where he lay, equally blatantly on display. His penis was mightily elongated, and thickly swollen. It lifted at Vee's first caress, she saw the veins swell, the long column stiffen, the mighty glans bathe her with its fluid as it pushed against her, as though returning her reverent kiss. She licked at its soaring shaft, from the yeasty base of the scrotum, up, to the red shining dome of the glans, then her fingers clutched at its surging power, its deep throb transferring through to her own clamorous dampness.

Suddenly, her transformed world exploded in a stab of pain as Mira's hard heel, the curiously pale yellow sole of her foot, drove with full force into Vee's shoulder and neck. The long leg thrust out, flung the startled Vee backwards, catapulting her off the bed. She rolled, scrabbled, fell onto the rug.

"You fuck off, you crazy bitch! Leave us! We make love proper!"

With a grunt, the dark girl heaved Keith on top of her. The magnificent legs parted, the thighs wrapped themselves around his waist, pulling him into her. Vee had staggered to her feet, now she fell back onto the hard wooden chair which stood at one side of the bed. Forgotten, she stared breathlessly at the stirring sight of their bodies joining, witnessed the brief lifting flurry, the guiding hands as Keith's rigid penis plunged slowly into that pink embracing depth, and he sank down, and into her, ramming fully home. She gave a rapturous cry of need, and welcome, his white buttocks tautened, dimpled wonderfully, they bucked as one in the fury of their coupling.

Entranced, utterly forgotten, forgetting even herself, lost in the splendour of the vision in front of her, Vee watched, unconscious of the tears trickling steadily down her cheeks, unconscious, too, of the two fingers which stroked, then inserted themselves inside her own flowing, beating sheath, and moved rhythmically back and forth, while she sat there, her muscles tightening, her body rocking, in hungry, mindless response.

9

The days drifted by. Sister Teresa, the thin, upright matron of the orphanage, called in occasionally, always around four. The precise Scottish accent matched her short, iron grey hair, her neat, well tailored uniform, and her rather formal manner. She showed no curiosity, and Vee was thankful for her lack of interest in her circumstances. Apart from the African gardeners, and the young boy who came in for an hour to do some hasty, careless cleaning, she saw no one. She fixed her own simple meals, and needed no more than a weekly visit to the Indian grocer's nearby.

Keith's solicitor phoned, and arranged a meeting for the following week. He was overly cheerful and brisk. "Actually, the sooner you're out of this place the better, Mrs Green, believe me. Have you been following the news recently? There's trouble brewing, mark my words. Something's going on up north. You know they've restricted travel now? No one's getting up there without a special permit. The army's on alert. Haven't you noticed all the troop movements around town?"

She realised then how isolated and self centred her world had become. She never bought a newspaper or listened to the local radio, preferring to play her own music on her Japanese cassette recorder.

Keith rang that evening. She was angry with herself at her emotion on hearing his voice, glad he could not see the tears that splashed onto the back of her hand.

"Listen. I'm trying to get you on a flight as soon as possible. Things are hotting up with this bother up north. Apparently, all hell's broken out up near the border. All travel's been stopped. Everybody's staying put for the moment. But flights out are all fully booked. People are starting to get families out. There's talk of laying on some extra flights. I'll see what I can find out from the High Commission. But be ready to leave in a hurry if necessary. You might only get a day or two's notice. I gather you're seeing Jack again next week. We may have to finalise the divorce after you've gone... I shan't be seeing you off."

She was leaden gutted with misery when he rang off.

Vee woke to a brilliant dazzle of moving lights sweeping over the ceiling and walls. At the same time, she heard a motor roaring outside the window, voices shouting. She did not realise where she was. She reached over for Keith in panic, and came to full awareness. Terrified, she identified some sort of heavy vehicle revving up, seemingly a few feet away from the walls of the cottage. Figures passed the window.

She crammed the edge of the sheet in her mouth and hid her face under it, whimpering and shivering in abject fear. She became aware of muffled bangs, rapid stutters of sound, which her racing brain told her was gunfire. She had heard it countless times on television and in the cinema. It was unreal.

Then there was a deafening crack. She felt the bed move, the tremor pass through the room. There was a rippling descent of glass shattering, and a pungent whiff of cordite. An overpowering smell enveloped her, sweet, penetrating, and, with a shock, she discovered it was her own urine, and that her legs and the mattress beneath her were soaking.

Crying shrilly, like a frightened child, she clambered out of the sodden mess, felt the liquid drying icily on her bare skin. There was another crash, the floor jolted, and she fell down on the polished cement, screaming, her hands over her head. Running feet, voices yelling desperately, more rapid fire, shouts. She grovelled on the floor, hands over her head still, among the broken glass and the heavy, acrid fumes of the shells.

Suddenly, the clattering din accelerated, was all round her. In a paralysis of fear, she found herself staring at a heavy, muddy combat boot, rolled her terrified head round to stare up at a giant, clad in camouflage jacket and trousers, festooned with webbing and belts and holding a stubby automatic weapon in his hands. A huge black face. Broad and shining. His teeth showed in a dazzling grin, his expression portraying his astonishment at the spectacle of the pale naked figure curled at his feet.

"Don't hurt me!" Vee whimpered, Somewhere in this ultimate madness came the awareness of her bladder relaxing once again, the last dribbles of urine being passed over her quivering thighs.

She was lifted. Only gradually did she awake to the sensation of being hauled roughly up from the ground and being flung over this giant's shoulder, her upside down head bouncing madly as her captor raced with her out to the open. There were other dark shadows. They were lit by flashes, then the growing flicker of the flames which were swiftly engulfing the end of the row of cottages. The man ran with her to a Land Rover, into the back of which she was tossed unceremoniously. She fell in a heap on the hard metal floor. Bodies piled in, boots trampled her, they were all about her, big, muddied. She was down in a forest of them, of dark, gaitered legs.

All at once the floor went wild beneath her, flinging her up, banging the breath out of her body. She cannoned off the hard limbs that hemmed her in as the vehicle buffeted over the rough ground.

After some time, the buffeting eased, and was replaced by a steady thrumming that passed through every bone and nerve. The tyres sang and the engine whined protestingly. The Land Rover was being driven at top speed on Tarmac, Vee was not aware of when the gun fight had ceased or when the wild bucking had steadied. She was no longer capable of registering time, or even sensation, for she did not notice the physical abuse her body had been subjected to. It was a rude awakening when she felt rough hands touching her, lifting her body, naked except for the buttonless pyjama jacket which clung to her shoulders and hid nothing, passing her like a roll of carpet from one to the other, until she stood giddily in the dust of a track, in bright morning sunshine.

Her legs buckled and she sank down on her behind, with the unsteadiness of a newborn foal, Deep laughter rumbled round. Grinning black faces leered at her. At first, despite the bright sun, she was aware only of the chill of the air. The last white snakes of morning mist were wreathing the tops of the tall eucalyptus trees, and the stark thorn bushes. She saw that they were on a narrow, dirt track, the bush thick all around them.

Then the tide of pain washed over her, from every throbbing muscle, and, in the same instant, a deep, choking shame at the awareness of her nudity, for the jacket, ripped and filthy, streamed open. She saw her breasts, the bush of her pubis, the stains of dust and sweat marring her skin, felt the burning gaze of the men's eyes covering her every intimate exposure. With a sob, she tried to clutch the buttonless jacket over her breasts.

Some soldiers were urinating noisily. They had turned their backs. She saw the crinkled, sweat darkened olive slacks, heard the potent splashing of their liquid, saw the steam rising, smelt its heavy aroma. New panic overwhelmed her. The girls at the Club had talked in hushed outrage of various cases of rape, of animal brutality. A British girl - an air hostess - had been murdered in her bungalow, just a year before Keith and Vee arrived. A gang had broken in during the night, raped her repeatedly, done other unspeakable things to her, finally strangling her. They were bestial, everyone knew. And here she was, alone and naked, with a dozen savage killers, hundreds of miles from anywhere. No one would even find her bones.

She must run! Simply get up and run. They would perhaps shoot her. Instantaneous death. She would not feel the pain of the bullet that killed her. But her legs refused to move. Apart from this incessant trembling, her muscles had yielded all their strength. She was lost, incapable of the slightest resistance. She could not even die with dignity. She had a powerful urge to fling herself on her belly in the dust, to grovel at their feet.

She heard a sudden cry of alarm, and she was grabbed, plucked up easily by the waist, by the same giant who had lifted her from the cottage floor. He held her to him like a baby, crushing her, one plate-like hand comfortably enveloping her behind, the other pressing the back of her head, clamping her face to his sweat drenched shirt. He ploughed through thorn and razor-like man-high grass. She felt it lacerating her thighs and calves, then she hit the ground with a thud. The giant covered her, so that all was blackness. She lay very still under him, pressed intimately to him in a parody of love.

She heard the whisper of a jet, rising in seconds to a mind rending roar of suffocating proportions as the fighter hurtled over at treetop height. Dust swirled madly, the thorns and grass in which they had buried themselves threshed, and the air itself seemed to be sucked away from them. The roar vanished, all was still.

No one moved. An urgent whisper ordered them to remain still. Vee felt that paralysing weakness again. She was glad of the umbrella bulk covering her. She realised he must be holding his weight off her. She felt a strange sensation. What was happening? With freezing shock, she became aware of those great thick fingers moving, scrabbling between her thighs. They ferreted through her pubis, pressed the pad of her mons, brushed the tips of her labia, prised the outermost folds open.

She shivered. Her buttock cheeks clenched responsively, her inner thighs gripped the spade like, invasive hand. She wanted to scream, to laugh hysterically. God! She could actually feel a faint response, that flowering open, the yielding quiver. It couldn't be real!

A voice called out. The men moved, slowly, cautiously. The giant moved too, with one last fondled caress of her bare rump. She felt the deep rumble of his laughter, and she blushed hotly.

They journeyed on, hour after hour. The terrain changed, to the open, more rugged hills of the far north. In a well hidden valley, they stopped for the night. A fire was made, a large sufuria of rice and beans was placed on it. Vee sat where they had placed her, leaning her back against the wheel of the Land Rover. No one took any further notice of her as the short tropic twilight ended and a numbing coldness crept over her.

She tried to comfort herself. The giant's good humoured fondling of her genitals had been reassuring somehow. The sneaking brevity of it. Surely he would have raped her before now, they all would, if that had been their intention? Perhaps they did not find her sexually attractive. She recalled Mira's cutting contempt of her physical appearance. It was always said that Africans liked their own big breasted, big buttocked, rounded women, that they found the slight bosomed, slim hipped Europeans repulsive.

The giant loomed over her. She had gathered that he was a sergeant, held authority over the other men. She smiled timidly, humbly, took the plate heaped with food he gave her, and the chipped tin mug. She could manage no more than a few mouthfuls of the thick mixture, scooping it in with her fingers, as the others were doing, but she gulped at the hot, sweet tea greedily. Once more, in spite of the unsavoury state of her filth encrusted body, she was deeply aware of her nakedness, and his eyes upon her.

When they resumed their journey in the damp grey of dawn, after a breakfast of thick porridge and the inevitable sweet milky tea, Vee was allowed to ride in the cab, squashed beside the sergeant, her bare thigh nudged by the driver's hand every time he changed gear on the rough track. The early chill gave way to steamy heat until she could feel the slippery pool of her sweat on the backs of her thighs on the thinly upholstered seat.

Her buttocks ached, then her back, and legs, then every muscle, and still they hammered on along the deserted and rutted track. The scenery changed dramatically, the open grassland giving way to more mountainous slopes whose steep sides were thickly forested. The air became lighter, fresher, and Vee knew they were deep into the wild beauty of the northern region, the homeland of these bulky, very black men who had taken her prisoner.

Jokes were made about these Northerners, who were despised by the lighter skinned, more graceful southerners. Far more advanced, the Baganda had been favoured by the British when they had taken over the last century, with the result that the educational system had concentrated upon them. They held the top administrative and commercial posts, and when independence came, they made sure they retained their privileged position. But unrest among the other tribes in the neglected north had been simmering for years.

They reached the rebel HQ late in the afternoon. They were bouncing along the boulder strewn, twisting track, the forest slopes seemingly as empty as ever, then suddenly there were other soldiers in front of the vehicle, appearing from the bush on either side, waving their weapons, their teeth flashing as they whooped and yelled. Vee sat terrified, afraid to meet the crowding stares as the newcomers jostled to get a look at her, yelling their delight. The Land Rover bounced on slowly, accompanied by a growing horde of the guerillas, then they were in what appeared to be a large village of mud and grass huts, blending with the trees to make detection difficult from the air.

Now the shouts rang out in a fearful roar. Hundreds of the ebony black faces thronged about them. Women and children appeared, some of the women bare breasted, several naked except for a small brown sporran of bark cloth over their genitals. Vee was pulled roughly from the truck, the blanket snatched from her. She stood, staring at her dirty feet, her fingers nervously tugging the hem of the jacket as far down over her thighs as she could make it reach. She tried unsuccessfully to stem her tears, all too aware of the sorry spectacle she presented.

The crowd had formed a tight circle about her. Pot-bellied naked children edged up to her, giggling, and shot out timid hands to poke her bare legs, or to pluck at the pyjama top, then fall back, shrieking with awesome delight. All at once the crowd receded magically she heard hissed cries of 'Simba'.

Simba! Lion! Lion! - and she stood before a huge man, bulkier even than her giant sergeant, though with the same wide features, the same imposing girth and jut of belly. She knew it must be General Mavumbi himself.

She did not know what to do. She had a wild urge to throw herself down at his feet and beg for mercy. Some last shred of self control held her back, and, in the end, she remained with her blonde head bowed, standing trembling before him, snivelling like a naughty child.

His deep voice was as impressive as his size. "I am Mavumbi. You are a prisoner of the Liberation Army. You will not be harmed, unless you try to escape. In any case, it would be foolish to do so. If you were not shot by my men, you would die within two days in the bush. You must simply do as you are told, obey orders, and you will be kept alive."

She dared to glance up into his broad gleaming face. He was wearing a red banded peaked cap, khaki drill shirt and trousers. They were spotless, and pressed to knife edge creases, but they bore no insignia. On his chest, a pair of gold framed mirror sunglasses dangled from a narrow leather strap. Thoughts of their blank pitiless stare sent little quivers of alarm through her.

His thick lips parted and the dazzling teeth showed in a grin. "We have another guest since this morning. Come. I will show you to your quarters." He turned to go, then spun back to her. He spoke as though in afterthought, but his grin was broader than ever, and the crowd hooted with shrill delight at his words. "Ah! One other thing. In order to discourage you from wandering too far, and so that everyone here can see that you are one of our guests, it is necessary for you to discard your clothing." She gazed in dismay as he paused. "Though in your case, I see that this advice is scarcely needed."

She gasped, stood there helplessly, when suddenly she felt her legs kicked from under her and she toppled hard to the dusty bare earth. Cruel hands plucked the strip of the open pyjama jacket from her shoulders and flung her headlong in the dirt again.

The whole episode had taken no more than a second. Mavumbi was still half turned, smiling. "Ah," he raised his eyebrows in polite enquiry, "I regret I do not know your name, Madam."

She scrambled up, feeling horribly exposed and ridiculous. A huge sob escaped, taking her by surprise. "Mrs Green. Vera Green."

The general chuckled. He stared obviously, his gaze encompassing her naked body. "Well, I can see you are every colour but that one. Perhaps black would be a better name." He roared at his witticism, and the crowd about him whooped.

Soon she was trudging head down in his wake, aware of

72

all the eyes fixed on her nude figure. The crowd tagged along, stirring the dust of the beaten roadway, until they came to a large hut, in front of which was a small roughly fenced compound. Vee stared, her own misery in abeyance as she saw a pale form in the doorway, framed against the dimness of the over-hanging grass roof.

A white girl, entirely naked like herself, gazed back at her! She was tall, willowy, with a wonderfully youthful figure. Her long hair streamed down on both sides of her face, hiding most of her firm breasts. It was of a dazzling white gold, many shades lighter than Vee's own fairness. A very small patch of hair over her mound, over which her slender hands fluttered instinctively, was almost as light. There was a lingering hint of coltish adolescence about the long legs, in spite of the womanliness of the figure.

The two Europeans stood staring at each other shyly, despite the incongruous circumstances of their meeting, as though waiting to be introduced. "You will stay here," Mavumbi rumbled. He nodded at an extremely young soldier, who, sloppily dressed in a uniform that looked too big for him, was holding a long, old fashioned service rifle, of the kind that Vee recalled seeing in old films of the war. "If you attempt to leave your quarters, the guard will shoot you."

He turned on his heel and left, but most of the crowd stayed where they were, staring mercilessly, chattering and hooting with laughter. The guards made sure they did not encroach beyond the makeshift fence.

At last the blonde girl spoke. She was foreign, her English carried an attractive trace of accent.

"Come, let us go inside. I hate the way they look all the time!"

She gestured, and Vee thankfully followed her into the cool, dim interior. Some woven rush matting was spread on the floor. A stout wooden pole rose from the centre to the conical roof. There was no furniture at all.

"My name is Katya Burnsen," the girl said. "I am Danish. How do you do?" She held out her hand. Vee told her her name, made to grasp the filthy hand, then she gave a small cry and suddenly flung herself at the startled girl and clasped her tightly in her arms. Their naked bodies brushed enticingly as they hugged, their faces pressed together and their frame shook in a catharsis of weeping.

The dimness of twilight did not last long. The hut took on a ghostly gloom in which their pale skins shimmered insubstantially. Then it was opaquely dark. The curious spectators vanished, and smells of wood smoke and cooking drifted in. The two girls huddled closer, without actually touching. Vee drew her knees up under her chin, wrapped her arms around her legs. She couldn't stop shivering, She felt guilty at the huge relief, and pleasure, she found in having this lovely companion to share her misfortune. They had talked non-stop, telling each other of their backgrounds, though, of course, there was a great deal which Vee did not reveal.

Katya was out on a holiday visit to her parents. Her father worked for one of the United Nations' agencies, had been out in East Africa for five years.

"I go to school back home," Katya said. Just two days ago, she had celebrated her eighteenth birthday with a barbecue in the garden of their bungalow. "I am going to training for a nurse after the summer when I go back home."

Her voice caught on a sob as the implication of her words struck both of them. Who knew what would happen to them now?

"Oh, my dear!" Vee cried, her voice rich with sympathy. She reached out her hand, touched the smooth skin of Katya's shoulder, then they were half lying, clinging, seeking every inch of contact to comfort them in their fear. Vee was shamefully conscious of her excitement at the sight of Katya's pink-budded high little breast only inches from her suddenly yearning lips.

All at once, she felt the young girl stiffen in her embrace, draw back a little, as though only just realising the intimate nature of their actions. Awkwardly, she eased herself out of Vee's arms, and stood. She moved over to the door way, called out so harshly that Vee's heart started racing with alarm. "Hey! You! We're freezing here! Bring us some blankets!"

The young guard said something, gave a sneering laugh. "You can't treat us like this!" Katya's voice rose shrilly. "Who do you think we -" There was an abrupt cry as he grabbed her by her arms and pushed her down in the dust until she was kneeling in front of him. His hand moved quickly as he cuffed her head.

Vee flung herself forward, crouching beside Katya. She put her arms around the thin shoulders, half shielding her, at the same time gazing up at the young soldier with a pleading expression. "Please! We're sorry! We didn't mean - it's just we're so cold. And scared. Couldn't you find us something?" She shivered violently, pulled Katya closer to her. The guard muttered in disgust, but he had calmed down, responding to Vee's humble approach.

"Wait!" he snapped, and moved out of the compound.

Katya wiped at the tears on her cheek with the back of her hand. "Pig!" she spat, in the direction of his retreating back. "You mustn't cringe to them!" She turned accusingly on Vee. "Don't let them see you're afraid of them. We must stand up to them!"

"No!" Vee cried in fresh alarm. She glanced around anxiously. "We mustn't make them angry! Don't you see? Just do as they tell us - then they'll leave us alone."

"Don't you believe it!" Katya answered. "I don't believe that!" Vee's insides hollowed with new fear, both for the lovely youngster and for herself.

"Come!" The young guard had returned. Now he beckoned them imperiously, pushing at them with his rifle butt, and they moved out onto the roadway. Kerosine lamps were burning, hung on the outside walls of the huts, and several open fires glowed redly. Groups of people sat around them, taking their ease, children dodged about at their games, It was a peaceful enough scene, yet both the girls moved self consciously, their arms hugging their shoulders, trying to hide as much of their nude bodies as they could from the prying eyes.

Raucous insults and laughter sped them on their way to the largest of the buildings. It was much more impressive than the surrounding huts. its walls were made of cement blocks, it had a tin roof supported by metal pillars.

On a wide, roofed over veranda, a long trestle table was set up. Men were sitting over the remnants of a meal. The food had been placed on dishes, there were plates before each of them. Clearly, these were the leaders, and Vee guessed that this was what stood for the Officers' Mess. As confirmation of her speculation, she saw the general's huge frame seated at the head of the table.

The bottle of beer in his fist looked tiny. He levered himself upright, came towards them, led them through into the inner building, to a small office.

Vee's eyebrows rose in surprise at the sight of the pretty figure sitting at a desk. The military uniform of shirt and slacks somehow served to emphasize the shapely femininity. The girl was young, and Vee was painfully reminded of the attractive whore, Mira, that Keith had brought home on her last night at the house.

"This is Lt Awina," Mavumbi said. "One of my aides." His thick lips spread in a smile, his teeth flashed. For a fleeting instant, the girl looked distinctly uncomfortable, and she threw a malevolent glance at the two unkempt naked figures before she replaced her expression with a look of cool disinterest.

"Now. You will answer all our questions as fully as you can. We must have all necessary information about you, and your families." He nodded at Vee. 'You first. Full name. Address. Next of kin. Age."

Vee answered everything, and the Lieutenant wrote her replies down. Surreptitiously, Vee studied the bent head. Her close cropped woolly hair was bound in the traditional tight circular plaits clinging to the rounded skull. She had the flat nose and broad lips of the Northerner, and the brilliant black skin. She was slim, her neck was long and graceful, her shoulders square. High full breasts strained the material of her drill shirt enchantingly.

When it came to the young Dane's turn to be questioned, Katya spoke out before the general had completed his first sentence. Her voice shook, but she spoke forcefully. "This is an outrage!" She gestured at her stained body. "You must give us clothing! You cannot keep us like this! We are not animals! We demand that you - a-r-r-rgh!"

For a man of his bulk, Mavumbi moved with lightning speed. His hand shot out, grabbed Katya by her long golden hair, twisting it like rope in his massive grip and forcing her down onto her knees, holding her thus.

"Demand?" he roared, while Vee stared petrified. "Shut your mouth, you white slut!" His left hand moved quickly, struck the sobbing girl a heavy blow across one cheek, then back again across the other. Still holding her by the hair, he hauled her up and bent her over the desk in one fluid movement. The lieutenant moved with admirable swiftness, grabbing at her papers and leaping back just in time as Katya's helpless frame crashed down on the wooden surface, The General held her easily while she threshed and kicked out hopelessly.

"You must learn a little respect, white meat! You say you are not animals. But this is what we do to animals who dis-

77

obey, eh?" He rattled off a command in the local language, and Lt Awina smiled with malicious satisfaction. Quickly she undid the broad army canvas belt about her slender middle and handed it over. The general's ham fist closed over it, knotting it around him. Katya's shriek rose piercingly at the first appalling crack on her squirming bottom. Her hips twisted, her body writhed, making the desk judder, her long legs kicked out helplessly behind her, but he held her down. A red fiery imprint came up over both clenching cheeks. He struck again, and again she bucked, screaming wildly, sobbing hysterically. By the fourth or fifth blow, her bottom was criss crossed with the angry red lines, and her struggles had subsided to the involuntary flinchings at each cracking report, She wept dementedly and blubbered for mercy between her agonised screams at each scorching stroke.

He flung her aside and she collapsed in a heap, moaning and clawing at her throbbing backside. He smiled at Vee, gestured at the desk.

"We had better deal with you too. You British are notoriously stiff necked. Our former masters!" he chortled.

"Oh no, please! I beg - I won't- I'll do whatever you say, I swear!" In spite of her frantic tears, Vee laid herself down at once, feeling the smooth hardness of the wood mashing her breasts, its sharp edge digging into her lower belly and the tops of her thighs. Her hands were folded under her, she laid her cheek on them, turning her head to the side. Her buttocks dimpled, clenched rock hard as she waited for the first painful blow to fall.

There was a pause, she heard his deep rumbling laugh. "Look, lieutenant. I see someone has been here before us. What is this?" She felt his huge hand passing over her quivering behind, feeling the taut rounds, on which, through the dust and dirt, could be seen the fading pink stripes of Keith's beating.

"I think we have what you English call a dark horse here."

Her shame was forgotten at the blaze of torment which rippled over her tender skin at the impact of the broad belt. Her throat ached with the power of the abandoned scream which rose. Its deafening note rang on in her reeling brain, even as the next scorching fire flared over her writhing flesh, and the burning red swell of the fresh blows rose to mar the pale smoothness. The breath caught in her, she hung there, afire, sobbing, as successive strokes thudded into her resilient globes and brought up further blossoms of redness. She was limp, save for each arching response to the falling scourge, its agony spread its fine lines until she was one generalised mass of pain. Only the steady throbbing of her abused body told her when the ordeal had ceased.

He picked her up, held her up on her feet by her hair, continuing to hold her while, with his free hand, he plucked up the sobbing Katya, who had lain curled up all the while, lost in her private world of misery. He held the pair of them at arm's length.

"Do you think you can learn to be obedient now, my little white cows?" He shook them with playful force. Their breasts heaved, shaken by convulsive sobs.

11

The return of the two girls past the fire and lamp lit huts, with their cheerful, noisy throngs gathered in the compounds, was even more ignominious. They trudged heads down, their shoulders shaking with the force of the sobs which still erupted periodically, their hands inadvertently stroking the blistered flesh of their behinds.

At least when they reached the hut which served as their quarters, some provision had been made for them, for there was a large dish mounded high with the white 'posho', the maize meal which was such a staple diet of the northern tribes, and another filled with a mess of dark beans and some thick gravy. As well as a gourd of water, even more welcome was the sight of two coarse grey blankets, which the girls immediately drew around them, both for warmth and concealment.

There were no eating utensils of any kind, and the laughing young guard squatted down with them in the middle of the flattened earth floor, showing them how to roll the posho into round balls with the fingers before dunking it in the bean stew. He chuckled, and with a further shake of the head, he left them to it.

Katya gave up after only a few mouthfuls. "It's disgusting!" The tears spilled yet again down her cheeks.

"We'll have to get used to it," Vee advised. "We must keep our strength up. We mustn't get sick. Not here."

Although the water was tepid, it seemed clear, and tasted reasonably pure, and they shared most of the contents of the bellied gourd. Their guard had hung a lantern in the open doorway of the hut. The girls surveyed each other in its dimly flickering light.

The slightest movement sent spasms of pain through their weary frames from the scorched and throbbing rounds of their buttocks. "I need the toilet," Katya muttered forlornly. She stared with revulsion at her battered and encrusted body under the draping blanket. "And I wish there was somewhere we could wash."

Afraid that she might give way to another foolish outburst, Vee rose, clasping the rough blanket about her shoulders, and went over to the doorway, "Excuse me," she called out nervously. The soldier was lounging outside the fence, chatting to a companion, also in uniform. "We need to go to toilet. The choo," she added, using the Swahili word. One of the men muttered something, and both burst out laughing.

"Of course, madam," the guard answered mockingly. "If

you would come this way!" Self consciously, the girls followed him, clutching their makeshift covers around them. They did not go far. The communal latrine advertised its presence before they arrived by the powerful stench borne on the night air. A rough fence of woven branches and grasses had been erected, behind which a long, deep trench had been dug. Planks of wood had been laid to act as duckboards on either margin of the trench. There was no roof or any other screening of any kind.

The sentry pointed with his rifle, stood there, grinning. He made no move to depart. "Go away!" shouted Katya, in outrage, and once more Vee felt her heart race with alarm.

"It doesn't matter!" she said hastily, but the soldier guffawed quite good naturedly and turned his back, moving out beyond the fencing to the trackway. Embarrassed at the crudity of the facility, the girls squatted, folding their blankets to hang like scarves about their shoulders, a little distance apart and keeping their backs to one another. Vee dug her toes into the roughness of the wood, and tried to breathe as shallowly as she could to avoid the full effect of the noxious fumes drifting up from the pit beneath her jutting knees.

Back at the hut, the sentry unhooked the lantern. His shadow loomed in the doorless opening. "You stay inside now," he warned. "Sleep." He moved off, bearing the lantern with him. The girls' breath caught in convulsive, echoing sighs of despair. The earth floor was cold, and hard as iron. There was not even any grass or straw to ease their discomfort.

After a few miserable, shifting minutes, Vee sat up. "It's freezing cold," she murmured. "Why don't we try to get comfortable? With each other, I mean." She felt herself blushing in the dark. "If we put one blanket down and lie together, cover ourselves with the other, we can keep each other warm."

"I stink!" Katya answered pathetically, and choked on a fresh sob.

"No more than me!" Vee said. "Come on! I need you - I really do!"

She knew at once that Katya was glad, as glad as she was herself, to feel the human contact. Soon, they were wrapped tightly together arms and legs around each other, they were pressing their bodies together, their mingled breath adding to warmth they were able to create under the musty wool, which they drew over their heads and shoulders as if it would protect them somehow from all the terrifying miseries which surrounded them.

Vee's lips brushed against the tangled locks, nuzzled the delicate ear of the Danish girl, placed light kisses on the tear dewed cheek.

"We've got to help each other," she whispered. "Stick together. There's only the two of us." She squeezed the pliant body even tighter, felt their soft breasts rub together, and quivered with a shameful yet strong inner excitement. She was thrilled to feel the instinctive response from her new companion.

She hugged Katya closer, squeezed her thigh between hers, pulled her close in a clearly passionate embrace. "We have to obey them. Whatever happens, you understand, Katya, don't you?"

She felt the shivering body against hers heave in another racking sob. The young face pressed against hers. Vee felt her nod. "Do you think -" There was a heavy, painful pause. "I am a virgin!" Katya's sobbing voice went on. "I have never - had sex. Not fully, properly, never!"

"Oh, my darling! Come here, my love! Let me hold you!" Vee hugged her, her mouth moved over the wet face, bestowing light kisses all over it, until her lips met those of the sobbing girl, and remained there, gentle, loving, but with increasing passion. Vee's blood was thrumming, she felt the thick rise of desire, thrust her body against that of the girl in her arms. Katya stiffened involuntarily, in shock, then Vee

82

felt the muscles relax, that lovely flesh surrender, moving against her in tender reciprocation.

Vee was half lying on her now, hanging over her. Their mouths locked again, this time open, searching. Vee's tongue moved, slid into that delectable wetness. They were both gasping when they broke the kiss, their heads spinning. Vee's lips brushed against the delicate ear once more. "I can help you," she breathed softly. "Make you ready. So that -"

"Oh no! I am not intact!" Katya's reply was louder, almost shrill with surprise. "At school, we have - all the girls, they have, er, vibrators, yes? My girlfriend she shows me, she used it on me. I - just haven't done it yet - with any boy -".

"How about with girls?" Vee whispered faintly. Her hands were moving, one caressing a warm breast. She could feel the small nipple brushing in rubbery hardness against her palm, her teasing fingers. The other hand crept between their bellies, the fingers strayed through the wiry little tuft of pubis adorning the swell of the mound.

This time, the stiffening of the body was far more noticeable, the movement to restrain her clear. The tone was even more shocked.

"Oh no! I'm not - lesbian!"

"I know," Vee crooned. "Neither am I. But now, like this with everything happening to us I just want to feel close, really close. I want us to be as close - as we can be." Katya's hand had clamped tightly over Vee's wrist, preventing her from exploring more intimately the quivering belly on which it was resting. "Just lie still, my darling," Vee whispered, her lips again brushing against the earlobe, which her teeth now nibbled, drawing an automatic shiver of response which she felt against her. "You don't have to do a thing. Just relax. Go to sleep. I've got you. My love."

Katya was crying softly again. "No, no!" she muttered, like a child tossing in a bad dream. But the iron grip of her hand on Vee's wrist relaxed, and fell away. With a huge sigh, she let herself go limp once more. Vee wriggled, moving on top of her, pushed with her knees against the long thighs, which parted after a mere token resistance. Vee's sensitive fingers moved and trailed over the curve of Katya's mons, traced the groove of the labia, which she stroked lightly until she felt the slipperiness of those outer folds yielding their moist, virginal secrets.

Vee came slowly awake, reluctantly surfacing from the warm, sensual world of her dreams which, for a few seconds, merged confusingly with reality. She felt the warm length of her companion's body fitted limpet like to the shape of her curving back. Katya's arms were slipped through Vee's, the hands cradling Vee's breasts. Full awareness returned, together with the agony of her sore behind, and the pressure of the unyielding ground on her left hip. There was a dull grey light filtering into the hut, and a chilling damp which set her teeth chattering despite Katya's clinging contact.

A figure was standing over them. Vee gave a muted scream as she realised the soldier had pulled the blanket off the entwined couple. His grin flashed in the dawn gloom. "Come. UP. You must wash. Then work."

The white mist was hanging thickly about the camp. Katya was still whimpering, only half awake, as the girls, huddling under the blankets, trooped after the sentry, who led them past the latrine, on along a narrow grassy pathway beyond the last of the huts. There was a small round pond, steeply banked at one end as though it had been man made. Several figures were already crouched at the muddy edges, either washing or drawing up water in the silvery metal 'debis', containers made from old petrol cans.

At the guard's insistent gestures, the girls dropped their blankets. The water looked black, and was freezing, striking up through their shivering frames with numbing force when they stepped into the muddy shallows, but they were so relieved at being able to cleanse themselves that they forced themselves to wade out a little way and crouch until the icy liquid covered their hips and lower bellies. They washed as best they could, rubbing vigorously, with blowing breath and little moans, even at their faces and necks, before hastily clambering out again.

They used the blankets as makeshift towels. Their bodies were shaking as though suffering from ague as they shuffled back along the track. But they did not stay at the hut longer than to shed the blankets, again at the guard's command. Hugging their own shoulders now, once more they hurried in his wake through the slowly waking camp, where bleary, heavily swathed figures paused to stare with frank interest at the pale nude forms.

He led them back to the HQ building where they had been questioned the previous evening. An elderly man in ragged khaki shirt and flapping shorts, grinned toothlessly at their approach. Two young boys, no more than ten or eleven years of age, stood staring wide eyed at the newcomers. They wore only shorts, as holed and venerable as the old man's clothing.

"This is Achoke. Boy for Officers' Mess," the sentry told them, indicating the skinny old fellow. "You work for him. Do as he say. OK?" He turned on his heel and left them.

The old man smirked lecherously. "Kuja! Fanya kasi msouri. Mimi bwana mkubwa!"

Katya gazed wonderingly at Vee, whose kitchen Swahili was scarcely adequate. "He says that we must work well. That he's the the big man - the boss!" Vee translated. Katya snorted in disbelief, but he began to pull them about by their arms, issuing a spate of orders, much to the delight of the two youngsters, whose grubby faces split in identical grins of dawning pleasure at this unexpected diversion. It was the boys who showed the dismayed girls what to do. One of the first jobs was to set out the places at the long table on the veranda, where the officers, about a dozen or so, would take their breakfast later.

Achoke supervised them, carrying on an endless tirade, mercifully incomprehensible. But then he produced a metal spatula, with a long wooden handle whose paint was chipped and worn, and with this delivered a series of stinging swipes across the girls' bruised backsides at every opportunity, so that they were soon skipping about, yelping in pain struggling to carry out the unfamiliar tasks as quickly as possible, while the two kitchen totos hooted with laughter.

A large enamel teapot was filled with strong tea, already sweetened with sugar and pale with milk, from the crude looking iron stove whose wood burning interior was already fiercely alight. It was placed on a round tray, together with two large enamel mugs. A dish was filled with hot water. Achoke said something, bringing the spatula down with a loud splat across Vee's bottom for emphasis.

One of the sniggering boys told her, in quite good English, "You and other one must take this tea and water to the general." He pointed across the wide roadway at a building set apart from the others, and of clearly superior design, with two wooden steps leading up to its own narrow wooden veranda. There were slatted wooden shutters drawn closed across the window openings Vee picked up the tea tray, and Katya the dish of water, and nervously they made their way over in the rapidly increasing light of the new day.

There was a wooden door, also closed like the shutters, and Vee put the tray down on a small table on the veranda, while she knocked timidly. "General!" she called out, her voice unsteady with nerves. "Your tea is here."

She gasped at the suddenness with which the door opened, and with surprise at what she saw. The exotically dark, and very lovely, figure of the young Lt Awina, stood framed there. Vee had time only to take in a fleeting glimpse of the high, conical breasts and the dark circles of the nipples, the splendid curve of belly and long thighs, with their tiny little scrub of tight curls over the mound, before the girl came to them, knotting a brightly flowered sarong about her hips carelessly as she did so.

"Hah! So! You are making yourselves useful. That is good!" She was frowning, her thick lips were set in an exaggerated pout, and her lovely face had the look of one just awakened from sleep and not too pleased about it - "Ah! The hot water. Put it down, girl! Over there!" Bad temperedly, she indicated the table, and Katya, still goggling at the lovely breasts, whose nipples had hardened in the cold air, hastened to obey her.

Awina turned back to Vee. "You! Pour me a cup and pour another for the general." She smiled unpleasantly. "Take it in to him and wake him! Do it gently - he's not in a good mood when he first wakes." She reached out, pulled Vee round by the hips. "How is your backside?" She nodded when she saw the darkening stripes. "You don't want more, do you?" Vee shook her head, but the African had already turned impatiently towards Katya. "You! White hair! Bring me my towel and toilet bag. They are inside."

One side of a mosquito net had been tossed aside, and the sheets displaced, so that the upper half of the bulky figure stood out in dark contrast with the white bed linen. General Mavumbi grunted, turned with a deep growling sigh. He was like a beached whale. His massive shoulders were a dusky chocolate shade, as were his great thick arms, and the smooth mound of jutting belly. His face looked even blacker, then a huge, pink cavern appeared as he gave an almighty yawn, and swung his legs out from under the covers.

Vee stood there, trembling, holding onto the mug of steaming tea, and tried not to let her eyes stray towards the conflux of that great belly and those vast, meaty thighs. Without success. She saw the tiny patch of his pubis, and a startlingly small, wrinkled penis, of a delicate, lighter mushroom shade, curling in the crease of his flesh and shrouded in the folds of foreskin.

Unselfconsciously, he patted and held his round belly, cradling it proudly, "Give me the tea! You don't find me staring at you like that!" She jumped, started forward, handed it to him. Katya meanwhile had found Awina's toilet things and beat a swift retreat to the veranda.

Mavumbi stood, his great body quivering as he raised his arms high and gave another great bellowing yawn. Vee shivered as she saw his prick stir, seemingly stretching itself also, as though only just coming awake. Suddenly it was at least twice its former size, thick and long, the head poking out, lifting slightly in a potent curve, over the tight pouch of the testicles.

Deep laughter rumbled in his throat. "What's wrong, Green? You've never seen a real man before? it's true then that the white bwanas' pricks are all so small they can never satisfy their women in bed. Come here."

Somehow, though her face burned with shame, Vee could not take her eyes away from his penis, bobbing now, and growing even bigger while she gazed. The great helm, an even paler shade than the mighty column, rose hypnotically. She felt her feet move, take a hesitant step, then he seized her wrist in an iron grip, pulled her forward, and at the same time, down, so that she was kneeling, that huge dome literally in front of her riveted stare.

"Why don't you get acquainted?" he murmured thickly, the chuckle of laughter rich in his deep tone. "As you haven't met such as this before!"

Her hands reached out, timidly, her fingers grazed the satin surface of the pulsing shaft. It reared, swelled at her feathery touch, stiffened magnificently. She could see the gleaming slit of the small mouth, shining with the dew of his emission. It was only centimetres away from her. Her nostrils were full of his male odour. The yeasty excitement of it made her blood thunder. Her fingers curled, a little more firmly, held the throbbing shaft, and felt it respond powerfully. She began to stroke, starting off the rhythm of stimulation, and pursed her lips in a delicate little bow which fitted to the gleaming pungent tip.

She tasted the salty fluid in a quivering ecstasy of fear and hunger. Her pink tongue flickered out, brushed the spongy tissue of the helm, her fingers tightened, drew him towards her searching tongue, her nibbling mouth.

She heard the door crash open behind her, and she fell forward onto hands and knees as the general pulled away from her embrace with appalling abruptness, The deep rumble of his laughter echoed above her as she stayed crouched there, her eyes stinging with tears.

"Get this white witch away from me!" he guffawed, "Before she eats me altogether!" His prick was thrusting out like a bowsprit, but he showed no embarrassment. His laughter redoubled as Vee was suddenly sent sprawling ignominiously onto her stomach by a well placed and vigorous shove on her behind from Awina's bare foot.

12

General Mavumbi sat at the head of the table, enjoying to the full the assertion of power which the two pale, nude figures stationed on either hand emphasised.

Their bodies were fragrant, their hair hung and gleamed silkily in the lantern light, for they had been groomed for the occasion. In the early evening, after a long and wearying day doing the menial chores, making beds and sweeping out the officers' quarters, including the general's hut, as well as washing dishes and preparing food under Achoke's critical eye and flicking hand, they had been sent off, led by Jackson, one of the pair of kitchen boys, to the unbelievable luxury of a covered bath house with hot water.

The spurt from the crude iron pipes of the shower stall which they shared was somewhat irregular, but they did not mind that in the least. They were even given rough towels, a sliver of sweet toilet soap, and a bottle of cheap shampoo. Their spirits could not help lifting a little, in spite of their anxiety at Achoke's admonition, translated by Jackson as, "Tonight you must be looking sexy for Simba!" The boy rolled his dark eyes and clicked his teeth, before bursting into fits of laughter at the girls' blushing expression.

Vee had an added private worry, which she did not share with Katya, for, as she had picked herself up and scrambled out of the general's bedroom that morning, she had not failed to observe the malevolent glare which had followed her from the young lieutenant, who was clearly the general's sleeping partner.

In vain, Vee tried to reassure herself that there was nothing else she could have done, that General Mavumbi had forced her to caress him like that, dragging her down to kneel before him and thrusting that great prick into her face. She had the feeling somehow that Awina would not see it that way, or, even if she did, it would make no difference to her antagonism.

Though the two prisoners had already endured the ogling of the officers in the morning, it had not been so prolonged or so public, for they had appeared in ones or twos. They had not lingered for breakfast was a snatched, hasty meal, and quite basic. Dinner was much more of a social occasion, which was why the general had wanted to present his captives at their best.

Vee was all too conscious of Awina's burning gaze fixed on her from lower down the table. She wondered if the officers sat according to rank. Surely, she would have thought, given the intimate nature of the lieutenant's relationship with the general, she should have been sitting much closer to him? Vee had also quickly noticed that Awina was the only other female present at the table. In any other circumstances, she would have admired and felt for the lovely girl, having to uphold her position in front of all these men. Particularly in view of the African male's attitude towards women and the controversial feminism which was only just making itself felt on the continent.

But now the girl's dark eyes fell on her with such ill concealed malice that Vee was afraid all over again. "They look just like those high class whores they use as strippers in the Nairobi night clubs!" Awina said now, as conversation turned yet again upon the hostages. Her remark, passed in English, brought an immediate blush to both the European faces.

One of the men said something which caused a burst of laughter. "Talk in English, you uncultured ape!" Awina snapped. She nodded at the embarrassed pair standing beside the general. "Out of courtesy to our honoured guests!"

The man she had unflatteringly addressed did not appear to take any offence. The general nodded. "Quite right, lieutenant!" He turned, chuckling, towards Katya and Vee. "My men are very flattering, my dears. Some of those girls in Nairobi are very beautiful eh? Very sexy!" He laughed deeply. "But I think it's true. I think you would make excellent strippers. Don't you think so?" he asked the table in general, and there was a chorus of assent.

"I think all white girls are good at that," Awina announced. "They are all whores at heart." She looked at her fellow officers, shook her head in mock sadness. "And they have bewitched our own people. Everywhere you look, in the papers, at the cinema. We are always encouraged to copy them, to try and make ourselves skinny like them. To make our skins lighter. A black girl now is shenzi - uncivilised. Our men all want us to look like these bean poles -" she nodded at the two embarrassed figures, while her colleagues erupted in good natured cheers. "Tiny little titties like young girls and flat bottoms like little boys!"

Vee and Katya became alarmed when the men lingered on at the table, and they were kept busy serving the large bottles of beer, from which the officers swigged, dispensing with glasses. But though the talk grew more raucous, it was clear that discipline was strong. No one stepped out of line, or offered anything more frightening or violent than a fairly brief grope as the girls brought the beer.

Awina left not long after the meal was over, but not before she had flung one last hostile glance in Vee's direction.

At last, the general rose, and his officers stood, too, dispersing with loud good nights. "You two, wait here," he said, and strode off across the roadway to his sleeping quarters.

Katya's blue eyes looked huge with fear, Vee tried to smile reassuringly, and moved close. She slipped an arm around the slim waist, hugged her. "Don't worry," she whispered. "It'll be all right."

They both quivered with dread at the sudden roar which erupted from across the road. The deep voice continued to thunder for a few brief minutes, then there was a shrill cry of pain. The door opened, light spilled out onto the veranda, and they saw the slender form of Awina coming out, still buttoning up her shirt. She was weeping. She turned away, but was still within earshot as the massive bulk of Mavumbi appeared in the doorway, naked to the waist. "Come!" he called simply, beckoning with his hand, and they moved over to him, clasping each other tightly as they went.

He was sitting on the edge of the bed and gestured impatiently for them to close the door. "Both of you, make yourselves useful!" he growled, holding up his still booted feet, and they knelt, one at each leg and unlaced the heavy combat boots. They tugged them off, then the thick socks. He stood, unbuckled the pants and slipped them down. He stepped out of them, and Vee gathered them up, folding them neatly to lay them with the discarded shirt on a chair. Clad only in a pair of white Y-fronts, over which his huge belly thrust, he fell back onto the bed and held up his arms.

"Come on, the pair of you. Let's see if it's true what Awina says, that you're all whores at heart."

Katya began to sob pitifully. Vee put her arms around her, led her to the bed. "What's wrong with her?" the general asked. His voice feigned surprise. "Don't tell me she doesn't want it!"

Vee cleared her throat. "She's a virgin!" she murmured, and cast a pleading look at his grinning face. She saw at once from the expression of eager lust which spread over his broad features that she had blundered.

"You!" he growled roughly at Vee. "Get on with what you started this morning." He nodded crudely at his bulging loins. "And you, little one, come here!"

Paralysed with fright, Katya stood there, shivering and weeping, until he leaned forward, caught her roughly by an arm and pulled her down with him. She gave a little scream and began to fight, panic stricken, her long legs threshing as he captured her wrists, held her clawing hands away from him. He loomed over her, swiftly pinning her down, reducing her to sobbing submission. Only when he felt her go limp did he release his restraining hold on her.

"That's all right. I like a bit of fight. Shows you value what you've got. But learn from your friend here. She knows what it's for, don't you, eh?" He jabbed Vee painfully with his foot. "Meanwhile, I gave you an order, bitch!" He lay holding the sobbing Katya easily in his arms, and Vee bent over him. Carefully, she eased the tight underbriefs down, drew them off. His already massive prick flopped out, heavy with its fecund promise, and that rich odour sent her nerves tingling as she dipped her head in homage. Its yeasty flavour filled her lapping mouth as she bestowed feather light kisses along its throbbing length, while her fingers stroked at the column, which reared and hardened almost at once in response.

Still clutching Katya in his arms. clasping her to his side, he rolled onto his back, his great legs lifting, the knees bending, slackening, and Vee knelt between them. She took hold of his penis near its base, and her movements were more vigorous now, massaging it until it stood up from his belly like a pole. Her blonde hair fell either side of her working face, brushed his thighs as she stretched her gaping mouth as wide as she could, and encircled the soft dome, taking it into her suckling wetness until it filled her entirely and she was gagging for breath, her nostrils flared like some wild creature.

Vee sucked noisily, until she was forced to withdraw in order to breathe, and the glans re-emerged with an audible plop. Her head bobbed again, her jaws stretched, and once more she took in as much of the straining column as she could, until she felt it press chokingly at the back of her throat. It pulsed mightily, and her own vaginal muscles spasmed in acute response.

All at once, the great hams buffeted her aside, and rolled over, dragging the petrified Katya underneath him, sobbing loudly. Her white blonde hair spread out over the crumpled pillow, her eyes were closed, her head tossing from left to right. The great expanse of his dark buttocks rose, nudging Vee as she crouched in forgotten proximity, watching the vast bulk engulf Katya's slim form. He scrabbled furiously, forcing the thighs apart, the great column stabbing at the pale flesh.

Instinctively, the pale knees lifted, the narrow feet waved in the air as the Danish girl's limbs encompassed the mass of dark flesh descending on her. The thick fingers, with their contrastingly pallid nails, pulled ruthlessly at the tight divide of Katya's labia, brutally forcing an entrance for that nuzzling dome, which sought blindly to penetrate, and all at once succeeded. The pinioned frame twisted, the feet scissored as the slim body shuddered at the shock, and the pain, of such a huge invasion, then once more seemed to relax, the strength ebbing from the struggling victim as the potent shaft sank remorselessly into her and she screamed and screamed.

The broad backside quivered, dimpled as he thrust against the virginal resistance. Again, there was a corresponding shudder from Katya, again a limp yielding, then their coupled bodies were moving in a new rhythm, and Katya's initial cries of pain changed to short grunts which drew echoing responses from the smothering bulk driving down on her until the bed shook. Vee could feel the springing of the creaking mattress, was buffeted still by the writhing limbs of the joined pair.

Katya's knees lifted higher, almost level now with the great slope of the general's shoulders, her feet crossed over the broad, undulating plane of the back. Vee stared at the narrow, faintly dusty soles, watched the pink little heels begin to drum against the dark flesh. Katya's wild screaming began again. The frenzied plunging grew more violent, and now Vee could see that the transfixed form beneath the huge shape was lifted, impaling to meet each spearing thrust, until there was a final, cataclysmic juddering, a micro-second when Katya's slim body was raised clear of the bed, clinging to him, soldered to his flesh as the spasm fired through him.

Then they collapsed, leaving Katya crying desolately. Covered by the general's inert mass, she wept for her lost innocence, and for the terror which had swept her away, and from which she was now returning with the dim awareness that she would never be the same again.

The general dismissed them with a single word, the curtness of his command flaying their sensitivity as badly as any physical abuse they had suffered. The encampment had settled for the night, and at first they could hardly see to move in the blanketing darkness, but gradually their eyes grew accustomed to the gloom, and they could make out the edges of the track, the shape of the trees, the silhouette of the round huts. Dogs barked. They both gasped with fright at the sudden looming appearance of a figure, then shook with relief as they recognised the quiet voice of their young guard, whose name they had learned was Edward.

Vee realised that Katya was stumbling, walking stiffly, and weeping with shock and pain. "She is hurt," she said strongly, concern making her bold. "I must bathe her."

"Wait." Edward led them back to their hut, lit the lantern, which he suspended on the central pole. He left without another word. Katya stood dumbly, spreading her legs at Vee's gentle insistence, letting Vee inspect her in the poor lamplight. The gash of the vulva gleamed rawly, the outer labia swollen, distended, and there were darker streaks of blood on the inner thighs, along with the thick residue of Mavumbi's semen, but the bleeding was nowhere near as copious as Vee had feared.

She turned away, huddling forward, shielding herself at Edward's return. He was bearing a dish of water, some clean rags, a bar of soap and a towel. His face looked extremely boyish in the flicker of the lantern. He frowned with awkward concern, and embarrassment. "I leave light," he said. "You put out when you finish."

Vee reached out impulsively, lightly touched his sleeve. "Thank you."

Katya's weeping had almost ceased. Vee made her lie down on the blanket and spread her legs wide. She bathed the area of the genitals carefully, leaving the cloth draped over the swollen cleft of the sex lips. "Lie on your side," Vee instructed. "Hold the cloth between your legs. Draw your knees up. That's it." She positioned the girl, then knelt and leaned over her. She kissed the soft lips tenderly, and though

96

Katya did not draw away from her embrace, there was a wooden acceptance, with no response. The blue eyes, washed with the tears, did not meet her own. Vee stood and turned out the lamp, then fitted herself around the curving back, snuggling in tightly as she pulled the blanket over them. She felt her own body's treacherous beating of desire at the contact of the cushioning buttocks on the front of her thighs, and her lower belly; unable to prevent herself, she slipped a hand under Katya's arm, and fitted her palm around a warm breast.

"You'll soon be better now, my darling." She kissed lightly at the nape of the neck, kept her lips there. "I love you," she whispered. There was no answer.

13

The next morning, though the vaginal lips were a little puffy, and a little more pronounced, there was nothing more to show the frenetic activity of the previous night, except for Katya's stiff, hunched gait, the strained lines of her tragic young face, and the shame in those blue eyes which could not meet Vee's tender gaze. At her deeply felt compassion, those blue eyes misted once more with tears, and the sweet mouth curved. "I hate him!" the Danish girl whispered, a shudder passing through her.

Over at the mess hut, Vee was astonished to see a slim female sitting alone at the table, eating. She recognised the scowling features of the lieutenant, whose superb figure showed to full advantage in the simple clinging sheath dress of a bright but cheap floral pattern, with a matching bandanna fastened at her woolly skull. Beneath the dress's hem, which ended at mid thigh, her bare legs shone with freshly applied perfumed lotion. Her feet were encased in flimsy plastic sandals. She pushed aside the bowl, rose as she saw them approaching. Her venomous look took in both of them.

"I am leaving to go south. To see what those bastards are prepared to offer to secure your freedom - if anything! Personally, I think you're useless sluts! I hope you stay with us a long time!" She stepped very close to the cringing Vee. Her finger and thumb shot out, caught hold of a nipple, already erect with the early morning chill, and Vee gave a muted scream at the flash of agony which speared through the sensitive flesh. The dark fingers twisted cruelly, pulling the soft round out of shape, forcing Vee to double over as though bowing obsequiously.

"I'll be back in a few days!" she hissed, in a tone rich with threat, before she released her and stormed out, leaving the trembling Vee striving to hold back the tears, while she massaged her throbbing breast.

The second long day passed in a daze of menial tasks, with Achoke's grumbles and painful swats from his instrument, and the laughing mockery of the two kitchen totos, to speed it on its way until once more the girls stood, freshly bathed, one on either side of the general's imposing figure, during the evening meal. "Report to my quarters when you've finished your chores," Mavumbi said, nodding at the remains of the meal which covered the long table. He called out something to the elderly cook, who cackled and nodded enthusiastically.

"I told him not to keep you too long," the general grinned. "And not to work you too hard. As I said, your hardest work is yet to come."

He was lounging naked on his bed when they timidly knocked and entered. Vee had been afraid that the trembling Katya would not obey the summons, and had held onto her tightly all the way across the wide earthen track to the veranda. And, indeed, once inside, Katya burst into a paroxysm of sobbing She leaned against the plasterboard wall, her hands clasped tightly between her legs. "I can't!" she wept, the white gold mane tossing as she shook her head. "I won't!!" Vee looked on in dumb misery, her own eyes brimming with tears, her heart fluttering as she waited for the storm to break.

To her amazement, she heard instead the general's rumbling laugh. "Would you rather be beaten?" he asked.

"Yes!" Katya sobbed wildly, and he nodded.

"Very well. Come here!" The tears streaming down her face, on which the fine strands of her dishevelled hair clung as they hung over her shoulders, Katya advanced slowly, her hands still covering her vulva. He rose, towering over her as she stood there, her head down. "Turn round! Bend down. Touch your toes!" There was a fractional pause, the willowy form gave a little start as though she could not take in his command, then she did as she was bidden, though a huge sob, appallingly loud in the quiet of the room, shook her as she moved.

Vee stared breathlessly. In spite of her alarm, she felt a warm flow of appreciation at the pathetic beauty, and utter vulnerability, of the lovely creature. The golden hair brushed the floor. The pale haunches rose, elongated slightly by her stance, the deep cleft of the buttocks showed entrancingly in the lamplight which fell full upon her. The rounds stood out whitely, the central divide's shading contrast highlighted, and the peeping display of the puckered sex lips, fringed by the light coloured curls, at its very base. Though she kept her feet together, there was a touching little space between the tops of her thighs which allowed such an intimate view, and which brought a lump to Vee's throat.

Mavumbi had moved, and, as he turned towards Vee, she saw the thick hawser of his prick curving out, already roused. He caught her gaze, grinned savagely. "You! Go round the front. Pull her legs apart and hold her down!" Vee moved quickly, put her hands on Katya's shoulders, felt them quivering as she stared down at the flaxen head on a level with her own sandy pubis, almost touching her thighs.

The general had picked up a short cane, an officer's swagger stick. Vee could see the muscles bunching on the curving back below her, and on the thighs, saw the tight buttock cheeks hollow in anticipation of the pain which was to come. Instead, with an evil grin, the general pointed the stick directly at the cleft of the backside. One end of the stick was tipped with metal, and he pushed this gently against the peeping fold of the vulva, penetrating just a fraction. Katya gasped, and jerked convulsively, her head flying up as she propelled herself forward cannoning into Vee and pushing her back a few steps.

Mavumbi roared with laughter. "What are you squealing for? You've had far more than that up you now, you stupid girl!"

Sobbing desolately, lost in her shame, Katya made to bend over again, but he nodded at the bed, his gaze still on Vee. "Put her over there. You'd better sit on her head. Keep her down."

Although she continued to weep noisily, Katya made no move to resist, letting herself be pulled over to the bed and bent over, with her toes trailing on the floor and her bottom thrusting like an offering. Vee tried to keep her weight off her, yet at the same time straddle her head, kneeling with thighs splayed, their inner surface tantalisingly grazed by the profusion of Katya's tangled locks.

"Hold her!" Mavumbi ordered again, and Vee spread her hands on the heaving shoulders.

The cane whistled briefly as the black arm rose, then fell with a loud crack. The prostrate body jerked, Vee felt the head thresh, bump against her mound, and encircling thighs. Vee pressed down to hold the arching back onto the springy mattress. Katya's scream was muffled by Vee's smothering body. The long legs scissored, and Mavumbi waited sadisti-

100

cally until the first violent spasm had died before he struck again, equally hard, and the bucking figure writhed in fresh agony.

Six strokes were delivered, cruelly spaced, so that the full torment of the burning pain could be savoured at each pause. All six cuts could be seen, the thin red lines of fire criss crossing one another over the pale resilient flesh. By the sixth, Vee could feel the captive frame beneath her had ceased to struggle, except for those involuntary twitches at each falling blow, and the screams had faded to a deep gut wrenching sobbing which Vee could feel transmitted to her own body. She was also acutely aware, much to her private shame, of the throbbing arousal between her legs at the jerking of the helpless head beneath her.

Katya was limp again now, the only movement those great engulfing sobs. Vee stared over the pale back to the massive bulk of the general. She could see his penis, fully erect, rearing over the curves of Katya's behind. The dome, exposed, pointed directly at her, its eye gleaming with the juice of his excitement. She thought he was about to plunge it into the weeping girl's exposed crevice as she lay still pinned there, but he dragged Katya upright by the hips, toppling Vee backwards in the process. He flung the limp girl back onto the hard wooden chair.

"You need experience, girl!" he spat, "and you shall have it. For now, watch and see how fucking should be done!"

Vee had little time to reflect on the implied insult in his words, for he leapt on her, grabbed her legs and hauled them wide apart. Desperately, she encircled him with her limbs, lifting them high about his waist as he crashed down, and she felt that gigantic prick stabbing and sliding over her belly. She scrabbled, caught hold of the rearing column, steered it to her own vulva, flicking and lifting her hips, stretching herself to take in his solid girth. She felt it thrusting for a second at her tightness, then her vaginal lips parted and the length of the shaft drilled into her. The fiery torment took her breath, she could not even scream. Her narrow orifice, wetly ready as it was, was stretched to capacity. She felt his hardness hammering against the neck of her cervix.

Impaled, burning through to her very centre, she rode the fury of his assault, buffeted by the colossal bulk of him.

Hazily, she tried to recall how long it was since she had been fucked, then lost the ability to think as pure sensation took over, and she grunted fiercely, spearing herself, pain and pleasure fused and mounting, battering the softness of her flesh against his consuming hardness. The world thundered to the force of their coupling, their mutual hunger and need. She was not aware of the scream which ripped from her throat, the convulsive clutch of her fingers digging into the great shoulders, the final frantic rutting at the burst of the orgasm shattering through her every fibre, dipping, soaring, then exploding once more, at the very point of surrender, when she felt the mighty surge of him pumping deep within her.

There was so much Vee wanted to say, to explain to her beautiful companion. Yet, she reflected sadly, how could she, when she could not explain it properly to herself? How could she account for the primitive, animal excitement, the magnetism of that powerful black body possessing them so completely. so purely - as pure as their own lost excitement at their submission, the submission which brought its own sweet, paradoxical sense of power at the very moment of ultimate surrender?

So they said nothing to each other of those things, pretended that they were helpless victims to his will.

Vee concentrated all her energies, and her passion, into convincing Katya of the sweetness and the strength of the love they could share for each other. And the rightness of the physical expression of that love, the passion it could rouse.

It became increasingly difficult to share such treasured moments. They were called upon nightly to service the general - "Like prostitutes!" Katya wept bitterly. And she was learning the art of pleasuring a man, and learning fast, in spite of her horror. She was shocked to the core when Mavumbi first demanded that she should use her mouth to arouse him, in the way that she had seen Vee do, yet, with Vee's guidance, she managed to overcome her repugnance, and the two of them crouched like acolytes between those meaty thighs and lapped reverentially at the soaring column of the phallus between their nuzzling faces.

But there was no force about the passionate embraces the girls shared in the privacy of their own hut, usually all too briefly, at least in Vee's eyes, in the cold greyness of dawn before they were compelled to drag themselves forth for another day of servitude. There were times when Vee wept, too, though she hid her tears from her companion, at the sweet frustration of their loving, for, apart from the eagerly reciprocated kisses and the closely pressing embraces of their warm bodies, it was a one-sided consummation of their love.

Whether from ignorance, or innocence, or maybe even, painful as it was to contemplate such a thing, a natural revulsion against such an act, Katya lay passively whenever Vee's mouth, and exploring fingers strayed to that region below the divinely heaving breasts where the core of their bodily desire lay.

Indeed, the first time Vee's lips had moved from the sweet pink tipped mounds to trail over the fragrant, palpitating belly, pausing only to lap worshipfully at the shallow little dish of the navel before they centred on the quivering thighs, and the moist folds of secret flesh that lay between, the pliant young body had stiffened, a hand had clutched convulsively at Vee's hair, which spread over the heaving flanks, as though to prevent any further violation of her clamorous flesh. But Vee, trembling with urgent hunger, would not be denied. She persisted, gently, and the hand fell away, the young body surrendered, with another deep sigh, while Vee, delirious with pleasure, sank to slake her thirst at the musky fount of passion which yielded its last citadel to her irresistible caresses.

Time ceased to have any normal meaning for them in the days that followed. The divisions of daylight and darkness, the routine of their servitude in the officers' mess, those strange, isolated hours which they shared with the charismatic leader in his bed, Vee's own snatched moments of bliss under the coarse blanket in the twilight of their hut - all of these rolled by with strangely little relevance to the normal passage of time.

They were shocked one afternoon by a commotion, an excited running and shouting which made their hearts race. They were kneeling over the big dishes of greasy water, cleaning the pots and pans, when Jackson came racing back, teeth and eyes flashing. "Lt Awina!" he cried in English. "She has returned! And she brings a mzungu with her - a white man!"

The commotion came nearer, they heard a jeep draw up, the engine cut. Mavumbi's deep tones bellowed their names, and they hurried out into the blinding sunlight, their hands still wet from their task. A large crowd had gathered. They cheered loudly at the sight of the two naked figures, but it was not this roar which made the girls suddenly colour up in a rush of shame, while their hands moved helplessly from breasts to fleece covered mounds. Nor was it the impressive bulk of the grinning Mavumbi, or the travel stained but still lovely form of the coolly mocking Awina.

An elegantly handsome European, dressed in immaculately tailored and well fitting drill shirt and khaki denim slacks was climbing from the jeep. His hair was a dark bronze, with hints of redness catching in the sunlight, which caught also at the luxuriant growth of moustache tapered to two fine points a fraction below the corners of his smiling mouth.

If he had been shocked at the vision of the nude girls, he recovered his poise with admirable speed, and advanced with hand outstretched. Aware of their foolishness, toes gripping and flexing with their embarrassment, the girls found themselves returning his handshake, murmuring the polite formula of greeting.

"Hi!" His teeth sparkled, his tanned face, and tawny eyes, gazed at them with frank directness. "How do you do, Mrs Green, Miss Burnsen. I'm Frank Tully. International News. I'm here to get some pictures!"

14

"Go and put some clothes on, you shameless whores!"

The girls blinked, gaping open mouthed at Awina's verbal attack. As they stood there in dumb astonishment, she hurried forward. Her fingers were like steel around their upper arms as she dragged them away from the stranger and hustled them into the dim interior of the mess hut.

"Come with me!" she hissed, and continued to tow them along at a furious pace out of the back entrance of the kitchen, and across the compound to the long low structure where the officers had their individual bedrooms. She thrust them into the end room, They could tell from its neatness, the cheaply framed pictures on the rough walls, the small embroidered cloth draped over the crate which served as dressing table, and the faint fragrance which hung in the air, that it was hers.

She delved into a giant suitcase which stood against one wall, on which its raised lid rested, and which served as a drawer for the clothing neatly folded within. She pulled out two pieces of brightly patterned, thin cotton cloth, the 'kitengis' which local girls, and white women too, wore as wraparounds. Awina flung one at each of them. "Cover yourselves, sluts! And keep yourselves covered! Titties as well! Our visitor will think you are completely shenzi!"

Stung by the injustice of her words, the girls nevertheless had the good sense to say nothing. They draped the thin cloth around them, knotting the upper corners over their breasts, the upper half of which showed enticingly above the cloth.

"Wait here! Don't move!"

Awina went out, pulling the door to but not bothering to lock it.

The girls stared at each other, then moved together, held hands as they sat down on the edge of the creaking metal bed. "International News, he said. To take our pictures? Does that mean -?" Katya's voice faded, as though afraid to voice the hope which had made their hearts race.

Vee nodded, squeezed her hand tightly. "It means they know about us - outside. Back home. I'm sure it won't be long now." Oh God, I hope so, she prayed vehemently.

Awina returned shortly. The sun was low, the light mellowing towards sunset. "Come with me!" she muttered, and the girls scurried after her. Strangely enough, they were suddenly newly conscious of their bodies, of their nudity under the clinging fineness of the cloth. Awina led them through the late afternoon ease of the crowded encampment to the general's own quarters. He was standing on the veranda, talking to a small group of men, but he ushered all three females through into the crowded privacy of his bedroom at once.

Vee could feel herself blushing at the thought of their other visits to this sanctum. It was the first time they had seen the spartan little room in daylight. Her discomfort was aggravated by the general's deep, knowing chuckle at observing them covered by the kitengi cloths. "I didn't recognise you!" he beamed.

106

"I'm not surprised!" Awina said, with bitter sarcasm. "Really! Did you have to let that news reporter see them like that? Naked!" She gave an exclamation of disgust, "What on earth will he think of us!"

"He can think what he likes!" Mavumbi countered strongly. "They are our prisoners. We do what we like. That's what he's here to see!"

"He'll think we're nothing but a bunch of uneducated savages!" Awina fired back. Her dark eyes were blazing, her face alive with her anger. She made a great effort to control her fury. "In the last ten days the eyes of the entire world have turned on us. On our cause." Her arm shot out, she gestured towards the closed door. "That mzungu, he's a big man in the press. His story, his pictures - they will go everywhere. We are hot news! The capital is packed with foreign journalists. They are flying in from Nairobi every day. Television crews." She shook her head. "I don't think you realise -"

"I don't think you realise who's in command here!" the general thundered. "If I want them to go around with their arses showing, naked as baboons, then that's how it will be. These whites have to learn they no longer run things here. And soon their brown faced lackeys in the south won't, either."

Though the young African girl had quailed a little at the force of his riposte, she spoke out spiritedly. "If we want international sympathy and support for our cause, then we have to appear humane. Civilised, on their terms."

"I didn't notice you showing much sympathy when I leathered their backsides with your belt their first night here. Or since," he sneered cruelly, "when I've been fucking the hot little bitches every night!"

The blow struck home. Vee saw the hurt and humiliation on the lovely features, though the girl tried hard not to let her emotion show. She did not answer, and the great hulk of

107

a man swept on, his disgust rising. "You are as bad as they are, with your western ways, your perfumes and your powders, your frilly knickers and what not! That is what education does to a woman. No wonder no man wants to marry you clever bitches! Too many foreign books! They take away the life, drain it from those parts that really matter, and stuff your heads with nonsense instead!"

"I haven't noticed you complaining!" she cried.

"Nor you!" he replied, with final brutal insult. It was like a slap in the face. Vee heard Awina's soft gasp. "You can play it your way to a point with that reporter," he went on, "but I want him to know that we are not treating these two whores like VIP guests in the Hilton. Is that clear? And I want him off the camp and on his way by tomorrow afternoon. Now get out!"

The sun was almost down below the tall trees edging the village. The long shadows of the three figures stretched before them. Awina seized their arms once more, her fingers like painful claws on the softness of their bare arms. Her lovely face smouldered with rage. "You go to your hut and stay there. Don't report to the mess tonight. The mzungu will come to you after dinner, Answer his questions, let him take his pictures. But don't tell him about the beating, or how roughly we've treated you." Her head tossed savagely back towards the building they had just left. "Or how you've been spreading your legs for Simba every night. Unless you want the whole world to know what whores you really are!" She thrust them away, and the girls hurried off, whimpering quietly with fright.

"Is it really only ten - eleven - days since we were taken?" Vee said wonderingly. Their incongruous initial shyness was only just beginning to wear off in the presence of this handsome man, who appeared to them to be as exotic as an alien from another galaxy. They found it impossible to believe their sudden fame in that outside world from which he came.

"Believe me, you're headline news," he told them. "Everyone knows your faces. You've been on television practically every night." He tapped the bag at his side. "And these pics will travel round the globe. If they'll let me, I'd like to get some shots around the camp. The ablutions and so on. Where you wash, toilet facilities."

Katya gave a derisory little cry, and Vee shot her a warning glance.

Frank Tully said delicately, "When we first met outside the officers' mess. You being starkers. That lieutenant, Awina. She sort of suggested that it's quite common for people, some of the young girls, to go round naked. When they're working. How did it grab you? Did you mind?" He smiled, trying to sound as casual as possible. He had already sensed the caution in the girls' answers to his questions about their treatment by the rebels, and guessed they were keeping some things back, through fear or embarrassment.

"Mind?" Katya's voice shrilled with h er outraged sensibility. "You think we have a choice?" she asked, her voice breaking with emotion.

"Katya!" Vee said, the urgency in her tone plain, But all at once, the Danish girl's reserve of strength broke. She brushed aside Vee's hand, which had reached out gently towards her, and stood. Dramatically, she flung aside the thin covering, exposing her beautiful body, whose curves and planes were highlighted and shadowed in the light of the lantern hanging above them. Frank stared up at her. Vee had risen, too, and tried to take hold of her, to screen her, but once again Katya shook her off. She faced the reporter, the tears streaming down her face.

"This is how we have been the whole time!" she wept. Her fists were clenched at her sides, she forgot to conceal herself. "We have been beaten! Look!" She turned, ignoring Vee's cry of shocked protest, and, bending slightly, thrust her bottom almost literally in the journalist's face. Though the belting Mavumbi had given both girls had faded to pale insignificance the marks of the caning he had inflicted upon Katya were still quite clear. "That was some nights ago, I don't know how many. Because I wouldn't -" her voice caught on a sob.

"Don't, darling!" Vee pleaded, but the mane of gold hair tossed defiantly

"I don't c-care what they do!" Katya sobbed. "They should know the truth about these animals back home!" Her breasts shook as she gulped, fighting against her grief. "I was a virgin! He - the general - he raped me. Both of us! Every night he makes us go to him. Together! Makes us do things - have sex with him. Each night!"

She broke down, and Vee clasped her to her, mothering her. A shadow loomed in the door way, and they saw Edward, the young guard. He advanced warily, holding his ancient rifle. "What is happening?"

"It's all right, Edward," Vee answered soothingly. "It's just Katya is upset. All this talk of home. Of her family. You know?" She smiled at him over the quaking shoulders. His eyes were wide as he stared at Katya's unclothed rear view, and Frank Tully hastily picked up the discarded cloth, draped it over the weeping girl to conceal her. He nodded in support of Vee's explanation, and the boy nodded in turn, somewhat sheepishly, and went out again.

Vee released the sobbing Katya, and put her hands on Frank's arm. "You mustn't print any of that!" she said, her low tone rife with alarm. "They'll punish us! God knows what they'll do! Promise!"

"OK," he answered placatingly. "But I'm going to let the authorities know what's really going on, don't you worry!"

All at once, Vee gave a soft moan and flung her arms around him. He felt the softness of her body, its sinuous shape pressing to him, smelt the damp freshness of her blonde hair as it nuzzled under his chin, Her tears wet his shirt front, and he hugged her to him. Now she shook, too, with muffled weeping.

"We just want to get out of here. To be safe!"

He thought of the vision of the Danish girl's lovely body, lit by the lantern, savoured the feel of this other slim form pressing so close. Ashamed at himself, he felt his prick stiffen, throb against the tight restriction of his clothing, and he eased his hips backward slightly, afraid that the girl would feel his erection.

Escorted back to his rough quarters by the young guard, he sat on the edge of the narrow camp bed, waited for his excitement to die before he undressed. He wondered how intimate would be the photographs he would be allowed to take tomorrow. If only he could capture the girls naked, as he had first seen them, out in the open, preferably with their captors surrounding them. These thoughts were not helping to quieten his blood, he thought wryly.

He had just slipped off his socks and shoes, then his shirt, when there was a gentle tapping at his door, and he heard the husky voice of Awina. "Mr Tully, are you awake?" He stood, opened the door. She had a short white towelling robe pulled tightly about her. His eyes were drawn to the deep V of her breasts, contrastingly dark, showing between the folds of the robe. Her closely kinked hair had drops of water in it, shining like miniature jewels. She smelt of perfumed soap and gave off the damp fragrance of the shower.

He had been deeply attracted to this outstanding young woman from their first clandestine meeting in the crowded anonymity of the Suzy Bar. At first, he had thought she was another of the educated girls who were turning their talents towards prostitution in order to supplement their income. Many of them were stunningly good looking, and had good jobs as secretaries or waitresses in the city's hotels during the daytime. He thought this one had come up with an ingenious scam concerning the kidnapped Europeans in order to make herself a considerable bonus. But she had quickly convinced him that she was indeed what she purported to be, a member of the Liberation Army, and a trusted member at that. And one who would bring him an exclusive scoop that would make his own fortune on the international press scene, as he had always hoped.

He liked African girls, had enjoyed a good many during his time in the region. Unfortunately, he never got the chance to pursue his private inclinations towards the lovely rebel, never even found the opportunity to be alone with her, not even during the rough two day journey to the rebel stronghold, the final hours of it blindfold. Now here she was in his bedroom! And wearing only a bathrobe. As for him, all he had on was a pair of slacks and a mighty hard-on which threatened to split them in two!

"I just came to see how the interview went. If our prisoners cooperated with you. Gave you the full picture, as it were." She moved, sat down on the protesting bed, and crossed her legs. The robe fell open almost to the top of her chocolate coloured thigh. Her feet were bare, one swung with a hypnotic rhythm in the air. He gazed at the narrow little line of pinkness just above the sole, which contrasted so exquisitely with the darker skin above.

"I don't know about that!" he grinned. His heartbeat quickened, with both excitement and an edge of fear. "But I'm sure you haven't!"

In the fractional pause that followed, the tension was screamingly apparent. She stared coolly at him. "Really? What do you mean?"

"Come off it!" he replied strongly, standing close in front of her. He could see the swell of her breasts rising, moving the fold of the cloth. "I'm not that thick! I saw how they were when we arrived. Naked. Terrified out of their wits. Like they are now. And I saw the marks on the Danish girl's backside. Someone's given her a damned good thrashing. And more than once, I'll be bound. They've had more than that done to them, too, haven't they?" He dropped on one knee, dug his fingers into the gleaming thigh, pressing hard. "Haven't they?"

She made no effort to push him away, or wriggle free. She laughed scornfully. "Rape? Is that what they told you?" She shook her head in amusement. "The only one who's touched them is the general. And they couldn't wait to open their skinny legs for him, believe me. Maybe they thought it would help, keep them safe. Or maybe that's just the excuse they gave themselves, but don't let them fool you into thinking they've been forced into it. The only noise you'll hear are the howls of delight when they come, the lying little whores!"

"You sound like you're a mite jealous!" he smiled, and for a fleeting instant he saw the hate and pain flicker in the dark eyes which told him he had stumbled on a hurtful truth.

"Of those skinny, shrivelled no-tits?" she exclaimed, her woolly head shaking in vigorous denial.

"You don't have to be!" he murmured thickly. He reached out, caught hold of the lapels of her robe, and ripped them apart. It fell open, exposing her gleaming body. She remained sitting upright as he leaned forward, pressing himself blatantly against her knee, rubbing his straining groin against her, while his mouth fastened on those ripe thick lips, and his tongue flickered between the even teeth to the passionate wetness beyond.

Her sharp breasts were heaving when the kiss ended. He saw the deep burnished hue of the rounds, the exotic shading of the generous areolae and the dark violet tint of the swollen nipples, towards which his mouth now dipped eagerly. He nuzzled, lapped, then took one teat inside his mouth, relishing the rubbery roughness of its texture on his tongue. His hands still gripped the edges of her robe, and he pulled

113

them down off her shoulders and arms.

Her need was as great as his. She stood, leaving the robe, a ripple of white, discarded on the blanket beneath her. And now his breath was warm on her belly, made her shiver as he clamped his arms about her hips, pulled the smoothness of her flesh into him, cradling his head between her thighs, where he felt the rough rasp of her small pubic patch on his cheek. He kissed the apex of those thighs, drank in the musky fragrance of her, felt the play of muscle as the curves of her buttocks flexed at his caress.

He stood, too, now, and her fingers stroked at the huge bulge of his penis beneath his clothing. "You will be sympathetic to our cause?" she whispered, her mouth against his, the rest of her body also moving against him.

His fingers dug into the full rounds of her bottom, grinding her loins against his as a foretaste of the passion they were to share.

"Of course!"

He bit at her long neck and smiled in male triumph. "But still, I think, as a white man, I ought to give you a taste of your own medicine."

He swung her round as he spoke, pulling her down with him and bending her over his knee. She gave a gasp of shock, then a muffled squeal of mock alarm. "There are people next door!" she hissed. "If I scream, they'll come and beat the shit out of you!"

"You'd better keep quiet then, hadn't you?" The pale heels of her legs kicked out as she lay across him. She made no other movement, and he slapped with an open palm at the clenching globes of her behind, so delightfully spread below him. She made small mewing noises, squirming her hips, thrilling at the rub of her belly on his trousered thighs and the feel of her own thighs fanning her excitement by their rapid friction. But then he struck harder, until his palm was stinging, and her flesh throbbed hotly, and she reached for a

114

corner of her robe and stuffed it into her mouth, biting down on it.

Her bottom was burning when he stopped, and she turned on his knee, his image indistinct through her shimmering tears as she lay there. His hand was gentle now, It nestled between her thighs, brushed the moist palpitating folds of her vulva, parted her beating flesh to the wetly flowing centre of her desire, its slippery slopes yielding gladly to his invasion, while her trembling body hungered madly for more.

15

When Awina appeared, Vee was brooding, deep in misery. She had lost count of how long it had been since the journalist had appeared and disappeared again, within a day. Was it one week? Two? She blushed at the subterfuge he had employed, with their connivance, to obtain at least one photo which reflected something of the true circumstances of their imprisonment. Vee had been extremely reluctant. It was only when Katya had added her pleas to those of Tully that Vee, ashamed of her cowardice, had agreed.

He had managed to snatch a brief moment in the dimness of the hut when they were unobserved, He had called in Edward, persuaded the compliant youngster to adopt a martial pose, holding out the 303 Service Rifle, with his two captives looking suitably cowed in front of him. At the crucial second just before the flash bulb popped, the two girls had cast off their kitengi cloths, letting them fall at their feet to reveal their nakedness, and Edward's bug eyed expression of outraged decorum. The boy had protested volubly, but young Katya had seized his arm, led him to one side and argued earnestly, with such success that, though he muttered sulkily, he said nothing further.

"You will be my maid!" Awina's words jerked Vee back to the present. "You'll sleep on a pallet outside my door. Then I can get you whenever I want you. And I'll want you a great deal, I should think!" She chuckled. "Anyway, it' s time you and the Danish cow were separated for a while. From what I hear you and she will be wearing each other out if we don't prise you apart!" Vee's crimson blush told that the bolt had struck home, and Awina gurgled with delight. "She'll be kept busy enough with our gallant leader, I suspect!" she went on, a scowl replacing her expression of pleasure.

Vee strove to keep back the stinging tears. As if their suffering wasn't enough! Though they should have expected something like this, Vee reprimanded herself. Two nights ago, Mavumbi, no longer diverted by having his two captives servicing him together, had immediately and brutally coupled with Vee, leaving Katya to stand ignored in the shadows watching the writhing bodies. To the horror of both, he had then dismissed Vee, ordering Katya to stay behind.

Vee had lain in the unaccustomed solitude of the hut, shivering under the blanket, frantic with worry for her friend and reluctant lover. Eventually, she had dropped into a troubled sleep, to be woken in the grey dawn - the time they were normally required to report over at the mess hut to assume their daily duties.

Katya was crouching stiffly, her face drawn, etched in lines of agony. She turned wordlessly, and Vee was sickened at the sight of the angry red lines imprinted on the pale bottom. She supported her along the damp track to the pond where they took their hasty morning bathe. Vee even found the courage to protest to Achoke when the cook began an abusive tirade, accompanied by swats from his trusty spatula, aimed at the exhausted Danish girl.

Vee was afraid to ask Katya what had taken place in the general's room after she had left. Apart from the obvious fact of the beating. And why had he thrashed only Katya? Why not her, too? Vee was sure that Katya would no longer attempt to deny or defy him, no matter how repugnant she found his forced possession of her to be.

Then, last night, when the evening meal was over, and the general had risen from the table after a lengthy drinking session, he had said casually, "Green. You can have the night off. You're wearing me out with your insatiable appetite, I'll make do with our little Danish friend tonight."

They had said nothing, but the tragic looks the girls had exchanged had been eloquent enough. Katya had not put in an appearance even at dawn, and Vee had had to bear the full brunt of Achoke's bad temper, and double the amount of work, to prepare the simple breakfast for the officers. And now this bombshell, delivered with such malicious pleasure, by the lovely African girl.

A sudden cut across the outside of her left thigh brought Vee back to the present. Awina was holding a short swagger stick, identical to the one Mavumbi had used to chastise Katya. Vee felt the thin hot line coming up on her brown skin. "I'll tell you your duties. And you'd better get them right, skinny cow! The rest of the time you'll continue to help Achoke here in the mess. Clear?"

"Yes."

"Yes what?" The cane swished, struck again, and Vee gave another skip of agony, rubbed at the sting on her flank. "That's no way to address an officer."

"Yes, sir - er - I mean, madam!"

"That's better." Awina suddenly giggled, an incongruously girlish sound. "I think you'll make a good maid. Don't you?"

"Yes, madam," Vee murmured.

Her duties were not too onerous, and, contrary to her expectations, Awina did not resort much to physical violence. An occasional slap, or a light cut with the bamboo switch sufficed. Although Vee felt keenly the humiliation heaped

117

upon her by her new role, she was careful not to offend, and her abject servility gave the lieutenant all the pleasure she needed.

One of her first tasks in the morning was to bring a basin of hot water from the great cauldron in the mess kitchen. Then she hurried out to return with a mug of the steaming, sweet, milky tea. Awina was usually awake by this time, her black head peeping snugly from the blankets up to her chin. Vee laid out the scented soap in its plastic holder, the face cloth and the folded towel, beside the basin which she placed on the cloth covered crate.

The first time she performed this duty, she hovered indecisively, then made to go, but Awina called her back grumpily. "Stay! I haven't dismissed you!" She swung herself out of bed. She wore a simple kitengi cloth of bright, deck chair stripes, which she allowed to fall carelessly to the matting as she moved to the crate. Vee stared in shy admiration at the tall slim figure displayed with such unselfconsciousness, though she sensed that Awina was well aware of her covert stare and derived much pleasure from it. Certainly, she turned and stretched provocatively, her darkly tipped conical breasts proudly high as she reached her arms up sensuously towards the roof, then brought them down, allowing her hands to slide lingeringly over the curve of hip and the tops of her thighs.

Vee learned to lay out clean clothing - the tiny white cotton mini briefs which were all Awina wore in the way of underwear, the drill shirt and trousers, the thick woollen socks. Another job which she learned to perform meticulously was the polishing of the heavy black boots. Jackson, the grinning kitchen toto, showed her how to rub in the greasy polish, making small circles on the smooth leather, then spitting and rubbing, spitting and rubbing, until the boots reflected the light like mirrors. She also had to shine up the buckles of the canvas belt, the one the general had used to thrash them so painfully - and the gaiters.

After breakfast, Vee tidied the small room and made the bed. She used a broom of bundled twigs to sweep the cement floor, carrying the strip of rush matting outside to shake it free of dust. She then had to do the laundry, with hot water from the kitchen, hanging the clothes on the lines strung across the grassy area immediately behind the mess building. She invariably coloured with embarrassment at the inevitable comments and sniggers from the boys and Achoke when they saw her pegging out the tiny underpants. She knew they drew unfailing pleasure from the spectacle of a naked mzungu performing such menial tasks.

The most painful aspect of this new regime was the separation of the two captives. Vee suspected it was by design that they were allowed scarcely any time together. And none in private. Katya seemed to be spending less and less time in the officers' mess, and more and more at the general's side. The Danish girl's face coloured deeply, and took on an expression of acute shame, as she muttered reluctantly, "He makes me go with him - around the camp. In his office, when he's working, or seeing people he makes me stand there. Bring the tea, or drinks. I am his slave!" Her voice shook, the blue eyes swam with tears, and Vee's heart ached. Another, much lower part of her anatomy ached, too, with a hunger to feel the sweet young flesh wrapped around her, to taste the nectar of those kisses she had forced, and which had now been snatched so cruelly from her.

There were other worries. "What do you call this, eh?" Awina, back from her after-work shower, the towelling robe cast aside on the narrow bed, stood splendidly naked holding out one of her drill shirts. "You call this ironed, you lazy little cow? Do it again, right now, before I take the skin off that skinny behind of yours!" The charcoal iron was an instrument whose intricacies Vee had found difficult to master, even though the smiling Jackson had tried to teach her its use.

But Vee persevered, concentrating on the moment, learning the myriad duties her life was now taken up with, until it seemed even her mistress was impressed with her effort, if not her skill. "You'll make a good housemaid yet," Awina teased. "I think I will offer you the job. You can stay here forever."

Vee could not help speculating whether the gradual thawing of the lieutenant's attitude towards her had anything to do with the fact that the general never sent for Vee now, leaving her to slumber comparatively undisturbed on her draughty pallet outside her mistress's door. He also never sent for Awina, Vee noted, which no doubt accounted for the lieutenant's glowering hostility towards the Danish girl. Luckily for Katya, at least as far as her relations with Awina were concerned, she was seen less and less frequently in the communal officers' mess.

The quietest part of the day was in the heavy heat of the afternoon, after the midday meal had been cleared away, for which there were often very few takers anyway. The boys and Achoke would disappear to snatch a siesta, in common with the majority of the inhabitants of the camp, and Vee would sit in the shade against the kitchen wall, where the washing flapped or hung limply in the indolent atmosphere. This was the time when she could allow her mind to drift, to think of other times, other places, though such thoughts did not always bring her comfort.

What was happening in that unreal outside world? Frank Tully had said that they were famous. She tried to imagine it. Not only out here, but back home in England, too. What about her parents? Were they celebrities now, making appeals on television, being interviewed on News at Ten? Inevitably, her thoughts would turn to Keith and their troubled relationship. How was he handling it? Would everyone know that their marriage had been about to fall apart, that he was in the process of sending her away in disgrace? She thought of the adverse publicity, and how much he would hate it, the damage it might do to his career. Surely, after this, after all that had happened to her, he no longer felt that implacable hate towards her? She nourished a tiny hope, beating in a corner of her heart like a fragile new born bird, that they might after all be able to resurrect something of their life together, make a new start. She prayed to be given the opportunity to try.

Her head had nodded onto her chest when she started awake. Except that at first she wasn't sure that she had woken, for a figure in military uniform was towering over her, had just kicked her painfully on her bare thigh, and was yelling at her furiously. She scrambled blearily to her feet, her heart thundering with alarm, and staggered in his wake back through the kitchen, then out again into the blinding sunlight. She was almost running after him.

He led her across the compound to the general's quarters. She saw him sitting at his desk on the veranda. A small group, amongst whom was Awina, clustered about him. Then Vee's stomach hollowed when she saw the pale form of Katya, her shoulders heaving as she sobbed. She was kneeling in front of the desk.

Vee's insides had jellied. Someone thrust her down by her shoulders, and she sank beside Katya, her eyes huge with her fear. "You bitches!" Mavumbi roared. "You treacherous mzungu bitches!" His desk was covered with newspapers, and magazines. He leapt up, came round the desk, holding a magazine, which he flourished in front of them. Vee saw that the print was in German. But it was the rather poorly reproduced black and white picture which caught her gaze, for she saw her own naked body, and that of Katya, and between them the white teeth and eyes of a startled Edward.

"So! We are animals, are we? Murderers and rapists, are

we? By God, I'll show you what harsh treatment is, you whores!"

Mavumbi issued a rapid stream of orders, while the two girls knelt there, sobbing pitifully.

They watched in horror and disbelief as two heavy logs were carried into the compound and dropped onto the red earth directly in front of the general's hut. There were rusty iron rings, set in pairs, along the length of each. The girls were hustled down the steps by many rough and eager helpers, and stretched out on their stomachs in the dust. They kicked helplessly, but their struggles served only to add to the jeering merriment of the thick and growing crowd gathering about them.

Their aggressors did not try to force the girls' feet. through the iron hoops, merely using them to tether the helplessly kicking limbs with strips of leather. The other log was trundled into position so that their arms, stretched out above their heads, could be tied to the corresponding rings on its rough surface. Thus the pair of them were staked out, their struggles instinctive and useless, their sobs dying to whimpers of terror.

Mavumbi used a whip with several long slender strands of soft black leather, in which knots had been fastened at intervals. He was accurate in his aim, and the jerking bodies could do nothing to avoid the blows which whistled down upon them in rapid succession, so the majority of the burning strokes fell on their clenching buttocks, which were soon scored and crisscrossed with red weals. Inevitably, though, some of the blows landed on the hollowed backs, or the backs of the threshing thighs, so that soon it seemed to the howling victims as though the whole of their bodies were afire.

A fine sheen of sweat broke out on their scorched flesh, to which the dust clung stickily as they squirmed, their fair hair flowing and mingling at the anguished tossing of their heads.

122

Lost in the private mists of their torment, only gradually did they realise that the whipping had ceased, and the roars of the crowd had diminished to an excited chatter. Mavumbi, his black face shining with sweat, its stains evident between his massive shoulders and under the arms of the straining material of his shirt, boomed, "Well ladies! How's that for savage punishment, eh? And that is merely the overture, my little harlots. The best is yet to come, as they say!"

16

Eventually, the crowd thinned out, people drifted away. The naked pot-bellied little totos grew tired of swiping at the pale, dusty figures with their branches, and moved off, leaving the snapped off fronds lying in the trampled earth. The girls' sobs died, too, and they groaned fitfully. Their heads shook, their limbs and muscles twitched now and then, tormented by the fat flies which settled on their sweat drenched bodies.

Even these movements sent darts of agony through them from their wealed and throbbing skin. The rough bark of the logs scraped against the fronts of their shins and the bridges of their feet because of the way they were secured.

They made no attempt to communicate. Each was wrapped in a private world of shock at the brutal punishment, and present physical misery. The Danish girl did figure in Vee's random thoughts, but only as an object of mean resentment when she thought of Katya's responsibility for that infamous photograph which had brought this dire punishment down upon them.

Mavumbi's ominous words kept echoing in her head. 'Merely the overture.' What other horrors could he have planned for them? As the air cooled, the evening shadows lengthened. People went about their business, ignoring the racked out bodies. Vee began to wonder if they were to be left pinioned like this all night. Perhaps for days! Though one entire day exposed to the sun would be sufficient to burn and dehydrate them catastrophically. The chill of the approaching night would be torture enough, Vee thought. She moved, the muscles in her shoulders and back ached abominably, her breasts were crushed painfully against her rib cage by the hardness of the ground under her.

She was half dozing, in a stupor of apathy, when she suddenly felt a booted toe prodding between the cheeks of her flayed bottom, pressing into the cleft itself.

"How's my naughty little housegirl? You've neglected your duties, haven't you? Come, you little hussy!" Awina was standing over her. Tearful with relief, Vee felt the girl's fingers fumbling with the tight bonds, releasing the ankles, then the wrists. Vee whimpered in fresh agony as she moved stiffly, crouched to kneel with her forehead on the ground, unable to stand, while the blood flowed back into the cramped, chafed limbs.

Awina stooped and pulled her roughly to her feet. The lieutenant held onto her, otherwise she would have fallen. She began to lead her away, one arm round her waist.

"What about Katya?" Vee croaked, turning her head back towards the still staked out figure, whose curtain of blonde hair lifted now to stare mutely at them.

"Don't worry about her! She'll be taken care of, believe me! The General knows it was her fault, or I couldn't take you away like this."

The pressure at Vee's waist drew her on, and, ashamedly, she turned away again, and hobbled over towards the officers' quarters and the sanctuary of Awina's small room.

She was amazed to find a bowl of soapy water standing on a large towel which had been spread over the centre of the floor. Over the fragrance of the suds, the sharp aroma of

124

disinfectant advertised its presence. "Get in. Stand in the dish." Even more astonished, Vee obeyed, felt the blessed warm water close about her feet and ankles. She stood with an air of unreality while Awina carefully washed her weary body with a face cloth, from neck down to the immersed feet. Vee shivered as she felt the cloth rub at the fleece of her mound, then gently insist, until she parted her thighs a little, to allow access to the folds of her vulva.

Despite her exhaustion, and her throbbing pain, a spasm of excitement made her catch her breath at this stirring contact. On, down the thighs, and knees, the black skull below her as Awina knelt to perform this menial chore.

Vee could not suppress the hiss of pain at the first touches of the warm cloth on her bottom. Awina dabbed gingerly at the welts which spread over the slight curves, both upward and downward. Eventually the bathing was completed, though Vee, weary as she was, felt that she would have liked to stand there forever, passively submitting to the dark girl's ministrations.

After wrapping her in a clean towel, and patting her dry, Awina ordered her to lie face down on the narrow bed, where she proceeded to smooth in a wonderfully soothing cold cream, whose perfumed fragrance hung heavily about them, as the dark hands moved with slow caresses over the tender flesh.

By the time this leisurely task was ended, Vee's pulse was racing, her vaginal muscles tingling with a powerful arousal. Her reeling brain told her that, from the slow caressing of Awina's hands, she, too, was finding the experience deeply sensual.

"Is that better, my little housemaid?"

Vee could feel the breath warm on the back of her neck, Awina was so close, her voice a breathy whisper. The bed creaked and moved as Awina abruptly stood up, and Vee closed her eyes, which felt suddenly moist with sadness at the passing of these precious moments of closeness.

There was a rustle of cloth, a sharp intake of breath, then a nervous little giggle which sounded as tentative and fragile as Vee's own sigh.

"You're very pretty, white one. So fine, delicate. I don't want to hurt you."

Fingers ran through the tangled spread of locks over the pillow, then Vee shivered at the feather soft touch of those dark lips on the wounds which marred the paleness of her buttocks. She turned, wincing with pain, to see Awina kneeling by her side, a strange, vulnerable expression of yearning on the lovely face. She was naked, except for the white briefs. The pointed breasts, their nipples swollen with desire, quivered inches from Vee's gaze.

"Edward said you and the Danish cow make love," she whispered raggedly. The dark eyes were wide, naked as her body in their appeal. "Could you love me?"

Vee wondered fleetingly if she were dreaming, then, the throbbing pain forgotten, she moved, they came together, breasts, bellies, thighs, brushing, thrusting, locking, while their mouths clamped together in a blaze of passion that was as powerful as it was sudden.

The bed shook, they twisted like wrestlers seeking for a hold, though the delirious Vee felt from the first the flowing weakness, the willingness to be conquered, in the dark, lovely flesh against hers. She was on top, parting the jutting knees, which fell away helplessly, and then her mouth was everywhere, devouring greedily, from the thick, parted lips, to the throbbing cones of the erect nipples, down over the undulating belly, and its tiny scrub of pubis, to the ripe, unfolding treasures of the sexual cleft lifted and offered in such helpless need.

"Oh, my God! You have killed me, you delicious whore! I have died and gone to heaven!"

126

Vee lifted her head from the warm breast, smiled blear-ily. She wondered if she had been dreaming, or if she had really heard Jackson's piping voice calling her mistress to the dinner which was almost over, and the replete, sleepy voice rumbling from the warm flesh against which she was pressed telling him to go away. Somewhere in her drifting mind, Vee acknowledged that she should be horrified, scalded with shame that everyone must know by now of her loving with the beautiful African girl, but she pushed it away. Later, all that would come.

But not much later.

"Go and get us beer!" Awina patted her lightly on the shoulder, and Vee's heart began to race as they slowly disen-tangled themselves from their embrace. All at once, the tor-ment of her sore body flowed back, and she was bent like a crone as she made her way fearfully out into the narrow pas-sageway, then along to the mess building. The kitchen boys were dealing with the piles of dishes. They snorted and snick-ered as she delved in the huge cooler, grabbed two of the large bottles from the vast number clinking in the melting ice, and scurried back to the haven of the tiny room.

Awina was standing over by the basin of water. She was holding the white knickers she had just picked up from the floor where they had fallen earlier when Vee had dragged them from the kicking feet. "White witch!" she smiled. She took the bottle, neatly flicked off the metal caps with the opener. She held it up. "Essential equipment for the NCO." She swigged eagerly from the long neck of the bottle, giggled when the frothy foam spilled down between her breasts.

"Drink up, mzungu. Here's to your victory." She touched the ice cold bottle to the soft fold of tissue between her thighs, and gave an exaggerated shudder. "My God! I thought I'd got over all that lesbian shit. Left it all behind at that expen-sive boarding school where we learned all your decadent western ways! Then you come along and start me off making those disgusting creamy little messes in my pants again. You must have noticed! I've been mortified with shame at the thought of you washing my smalls, seeing what a filthy creature I am!"

Vee's head was spinning. She felt still as though this was not real, this stolen intimacy. "I thought you - you hated me," she offered humbly.

Awina gave a hard laugh. "Hated you giving me the hots! Setting me off again. It was a white bitch that seduced me in the first place." She laughed again, in more gentle reminiscence this time. "Mary Ayres. Let's get back to bed and I'll tell you about it."

Vee felt her heart melt with gratitude as she hastened to comply with Awina's order, and they settled themselves, bodies snakily entwined, blonde and black heads nudging on the pillow.

"The general's right when he talks about how unfit us educated women are for this society. You bloody whites have ruined us, you hear? I should have been married now with at least four totos. I'm already an old maid by our standards. And all because my daddy thought he was being oh so modern and enlightened, sending a girl to the whites' school. That's all he did it for. To show everyone how rich he was, and how he was as good as the whites who used to rule us. After independence, when they opened up the schools like St Margaret's to everyone, everyone who could afford it, that is, there were lots like daddy who wanted to show how progressive and powerful they were. Even us black shenzis from the north!" she laughed in satirical self mockery.

"And of course, there were still plenty of you whites around, trying to cling on to your privileged status. As you still are, only you have to be a bit more subtle about it now, eh?" She gave another mocking laugh, the underlying bitterness showing through. "There's a great chumminess now, of course. A wonderful liberalism - no more 'Whites Only' at the sports clubs. All pals together, eh? Mary Ayres was pally all right. And her chums. It was all a bit of a giggle." She mimicked a shrill European voice, the drawling refinement of upper class accent, with cutting accuracy. "Awina what a lovely name! I had an ayah called Awina once! This is a knife and fork, my deah! This is loo paper, we don't wipe our bums on banana leaves at St Margaret's!

"But she was keen enough to get into my school knickers, however much she liked to make fun of us. I didn't even have hair on my belly, and she was in my bed every night. She couldn't get enough of my little black cunt!" Suddenly, all the emotive bitterness was gone with the next infectious giggle. "And to tell the truth, I couldn't get enough of her superior little poking white fingers and her wicked pink tongue!" She seized Vee's hand tightly and pulled it down to the scrub covered mound nestling against her thigh. "There! Enough true confessions for tonight. Now, do what you do best, white bitch, and make me squeal for mercy!"

Waking in the grey light, trapped by the warm black body and the clinging wreckage of the bedding, Vee hardly knew where she was at first. The dark hip slamming against hers roused her. "Go and get my water. And my tea." Awina grunted, heaved herself over, dragging the blankets with her, and Vee, shivering, put her foot out onto the cold floor. A wave of deep contrition and shame swept over her.

She hurried through to the kitchen, where the grinning boys and the rumbling Achoke were waiting. Ignoring their sniggers, she hurried through to the front of the building and gazed across towards the general's quarters. The two logs were still there. She sighed with relief as she saw the emptiness of the space between them. She stared at the closed door and shutters of Mavumbi's room. Was Katya reinstated there, after all? Whatever the Danish girl might think about it, Vee found herself hoping fervently that she was.

Katya did not appear, even to collect the general's morning tea, and his hot water, which Jackson took over to him. Vee was afraid to ask, but vowed that, at the first opportunity, she would endeavour to find out Katya's whereabouts.

People stared at her striped behind, and made laughing comments, most of which she couldn't understand. She wondered if she dared ask Awina if she might wear the kitengi they had been given during Frank Tully's brief visit, She knew, however, that she would have to tread extremely carefully, that she could not make any assumptions, despite the new level of intimacy she shared with her mistress.

That was made very plain by the role Awina adopted towards her in public that first day, for she was even more cuttingly harsh and casually dismissive towards her, abusing and making mock of her in front of others until Vee's eyes stung with wounded tears she had trouble in hiding. Perhaps, she wondered dismally, the lovely African was already regretting the weakness which had made her yield to her own sexual appetite and surrender herself up to Vee's ecstatic passion.

It was not until mid afternoon, when the lethargy settled on the drowsy encampment, that Vee found an opportunity to slip away from the kitchen area. She searched where she could, going to the pond, the latrines, the bath house, even the bare hut they had shared, but there was no sign of Katya. She began to feel more and more uneasy and when the kitchen boys came back, yawning hugely and scratching themselves after their siesta, she asked Jackson if he had seen anything of her. He shrugged, shook his head.

By evening, she was seriously alarmed. As she knelt, cradling Awina's boot between her thighs while she untied the laces, she plucked up courage to enquire. "Where is Katya? I haven't seen her since - since yesterday."

"Forget her!" came the bald reply. Awina stood, shrugged off her shirt, unbuckled the heavy canvas belt, then unhooked

130

the fastener of her slacks. Vee tugged them down, and Awina lifted her legs while Vee dragged them clear. She stood there, grinning down at the crouching figure, then pulled the blonde head tightly into her loins. Vee felt the moistness of the thin cotton, the rasp of the pubic curls, and her nostrils filled with the pungent flavour of the damp sex lips beneath. "There! See how hot I am for you, you wicked witch! Early to bed tonight!"

That evening, her legs shook when she served Mavumbi at the head of the table, then stood slightly behind his chair. She tried to summon up the nerve to ask him about her missing companion, whom she had not seen since Awina had led her from the scene of the whipping. But those stripes were still throbbing painfully, and her fear closed her throat. Mavumbi made no reference to her, at least, not in English, and Vee suffered dumbly, not least for her own cowardice. She would tackle Awina again, she vowed, Surely, after they had made love, she would at least give her some reassurance as to Katya's condition?

But the black girl was already sprawling, magnificently nude, the long legs wide apart, on the bed, when Vee came in after finishing her duties in the kitchen. "Don't wait! Come and do your worst! Or your best!" the throaty voice commanded, and Vee moved, her head dipping subserviently, to obey.

17

"Simba wants you! You are to take this to him." Vee gazed dumbly at the grinning features of Jackson as he held out the tray with the mug of tea on it. The dank mist tendrils clung about the camp, the sun had not penetrated the greyness of the dawn.

131

"What about Awina?" Vee croaked, nodding back towards the long row of rooms. where she had just left the arms of her sleeping mistress.

"You better go now, damn quick!" Jackson warned. and Vee took the tray. Her heart thumped painfully, her knees shook as she crossed the damp ground, skirting the twin logs which lay in her path. She mounted the veranda of the general's hut, feeling the cold grittiness beneath her bare soles, and tapped nervously on the door. She did not know whether to be relieved or alarmed to see that the general was alone in his bed.

He pushed aside the sheet and blanket. She stared at his naked hulk, found herself automatically covering her loins with her hands.

"Come!" he growled. "Don't hide yourself. You're no virgin." He chuckled, shook his head, letting his gaze travel critically over her cowering frame. "Wazungu! No breasts, no backside! Why are you whites so thin? Like boys!"

You still shag us! she cried fiercely, in her mind, but she was tremblingly silent. "The other one just the same," he went on grumblingly. "Scarcely any more meat on her! You like sex?" he asked suddenly. "I think so, eh? You like with men, with boys. With girls, with blacks, with whites."

He laughed cruelly, shook his head once more in amusement. Vee floundered, her face crimson, her throat choked with impending tears. His body looked incongruously young, innocent. His belly was smooth and round, a rich chocolate colour. It reminded Vee of a heavily pregnant woman. It thrust out from under his breast, ballooned up from his loins, so that the insignificant scrub of tight little pubic curls was almost hidden.

The penis was soft still, vulnerable looking as it curled against the crease of his thigh. It looked shorter because of its stubby width. The glans was paler. It peeped delicately from its thick collar of foreskin. The bag of his testicles

132

looked small, nestled beneath the curving column.

"I think you are a whore, a natural whore. Is that why your husband beat you?" Her eyes gazed at him, luminous with the tears that welled up. She could not speak, shook her head. "Rouse me!" he growled, and, when she gaped at him blankly, gestured brutally towards his loins. "Now!"

Her frightened eyes stared directly into his, and, along with the cruel animal conquest, she saw, too, an inner mocking knowledge. It felt as though he had glanced for one microsecond at all the darkest sensations lurking under the stone of her character. How could he know? How could he tell that, in the very core of her terror, beat the quivering pulse of her excitement, the shameful heat that brought her on her knees, her hands lifting, cupping in prayer, her lips opening, fearful tongue peeping forth to pay its homage, to make its shocking submission to that looming, exotic phallus towards which every part of her flowed?

Even as her stomach clenched, the muscles of her throat spasmed with the hot bile of threatened vomit, she moved, opening, stretching her jaw, taking in his girth, suckling, her senses lost to its power.

All at once, she felt her scalp lift as he hauled her face away from his loins, dragging her onto the creaking bed. Blindly, she lifted and spread her legs, braced herself to take his entry, even scrabbled with frantic fingers to guide and facilitate his bludgeoning manhood, to open herself wider to ease him.

Still the brutal thrusting shocked her, and she cried out at the clash of pelvis, the tearing of her soft flesh and the white hot stab through to her cervix. The great, blubbery, crushing, sweat-slippery weight engulfed her. She whimpered, raised her knees and thighs about his bulk, raised her hips to take his pinning thrusts. He pounded her. Smothered in the burden, the feel and smell of him, her mind spun away and she registered only sensation - the bursting pain, and, under it, the counterpoint to its pistoning rhythm, the dark, fluttering beat of her own excitement.

It was soon over. She felt the mighty surge, the electric jolt of his final, releasing spasm, the potent explosion overflowing to her, and then, in the very instant of the dying afterthrust, her own shocking, breath shattering climax, catching her almost unawares at the violence of eruption, the consuming force, as, jaw clenched, grunting in wild ecstasy, she battered herself under his bulk.

Then she lay skewered in martyrdom, her mind empty, her body utterly sated, until awareness opened the floodgates of despair, racking her from head to toe. All the while, he lay dead on her, still deadly in her. When he moved, slid coldly out, she felt her shame and desolation could not be surpassed.

"Where's Katya? What's happened to her?"

She was astounded herself to hear her catchy voice, quavering with fear, ask the question. She stood there, aching, sore, feeling the cold seep of him from her distended labia, her fear, just for that moment, overcome by her desperation.

To her surprise, there was no backlash of anger, no violent reaction. He sat up slowly, wiping at himself with a corner of the sheet, turned his great head towards her with that spreading grin. "She's not like you. She has a lot to learn. Besides, she's scarcely more than a child, in spite of her age. If she was one of us, she would have been a wife, a mother, long before now."

His words made her think fleetingly of the lovely girl with whom she had spent the night. "I've sent her to join the initiation class. Some of our young girls they are of an age to become women." He chuckled evilly. "White head will become one of them. She too will become a true woman!"

Vee felt the cold fear spread from inside, devouring her with its panic. Initiation. A true woman. The general's phrases rang in her head like a sickening bell. The horror of what they meant stifled her. She thought of all the mysterious, horrifying ritual connected with such things. Circumcision! Surely that was what he meant by this talk of becoming a true woman? She tried to smother the choking terror which rose like a scream into her throat.

"What will they do to her?" she whispered.

He laughed, as though he was fully aware of her terror. "Of course, it's not like it used to be in the villages back home. But we have a few youngsters here girls who are ready to be taught the basics. To be prepared for making proper wives and mothers, for our young bloods."

"But she's - she's -" Vee's voice died away, she shook her head hopelessly. "Where is she? Where have they taken her?"

"They have a place, on the edge of the village. They should really be far away, in the forest, where no one can find them, but it's too dangerous. So we've given them a small compound on the edge of the camp. Just past the dam, and the vegetable shambas," he added helpfully. "I don't advise you to go anywhere near, though." He chuckled again. "The mamas and their assistants don't like being disturbed, I can tell you. They don't even like me showing my face there!"

Vee caught at Jackson's arm. "You know about Katya?"

He grinned, glanced around. "She go with initiation class." He giggled salaciously. "The girls who are ready to become women." Again, panic fired through her as she thought of the barbaric rites associated with such practices. Did they practise female circumcision in the north? She thought of the beautiful body of Awina. There was certainly no sign of any mutilation there, as Vee well knew by now. But then Awina was not exactly a typical village maiden, as she herself had told Vee. She had gone to secondary school, her father was rich and powerful.

"Where is Awina - Lt Awina?" she amended quickly.

Again, he grinned. "She go work. She very damn angry

135

with you. You jig-a-jig with Simba, yes? I think she beat you when she come."

Without waiting to hear more, Vee hurried away from the mess huts, heading towards the pond, and the rows of vegetable gardens. Her anxiety about Katya overcame her own stomach churning fear. There must be something she could do to save her. From what the general had said, this class or whatever it was was run by women. Elders of some sort. Surely they could see that Katya was not like one of them, that she could not be subjected to... to what? Vee shivered with dread at her imaginings, even as she hurried forward.

She picked her way through the large expanse beyond the pond, which had been turned into a neat patchwork of tiny plots, intersected by narrow raised paths just wide enough for one person to pass. The women and children were weeding the shambas. The pendulous breasts and the high, firm little cones glistened freely as the workers bent forward in their distinctive straight legged pose, the lower halves of their bodies draped in the bright, simple cotton kikois or sarongs. They glanced with curiosity at the hurrying figure, pausing in their labour to watch her progress through their midst.

Widely spaced, silvery columns of eucalyptus trees stood at the far edge of the shambas. The sun dappled space between the trunks was thickly covered with the pale yellow fallen leaves, and the breeze set the high branches above dancing with the continuous sighing sound of waves breaking. The whole atmosphere was of light, cool airiness, with the vast wash of sky overhead.

But then Vee saw through the trees the split bamboo fencing, and the tall grass roofs sloping steeply in the traditional hive shape. She faltered for an instant, felt the tremble in her knees, and forced herself on before her courage should fail her.

There was an unlocked gate in the fencing. As she passed

through, she heard girls' voices singing in unison. They sounded loud, aggressive, challenging. About a dozen girls were sitting on the grass in front of the larger of the two huts, their backs to Vee. An imposing woman of statuesque proportions stood facing the girls. She was wearing the traditional sarong of the matron. The heavy metal necklaces hung across the tops of her full breasts, the bracelets covered the right forearm almost to the elbow.

There was a shrill cry, an outraged yell of protest. Vee saw two younger women, dressed in similar fashion to their leader, who had been sitting at the front of the class, but who now rose, pointing at her.

An instant later two men appeared, one on either side of her. They too were not in uniform or modern civilian clothing, but had only a simple loincloth wrapped about their bodies. Their burnished dark skin shone smoothly in the sunlight. All this, Vee noticed in the fraction before they had seized her, twisting her arms painfully behind her, and frogmarching her forward, through the small group of astonished, chattering girls.

Dimly, she heard Katya's voice cry out her name, then the heavy hands forced her down upon her knees in front of the imposing figure of the woman, who seemed to tower over her as Vee squinted up into the sunlight.

"I'm sorry!" she whimpered abjectly. "I didn't - I wanted to see my friend -"

The thick lips curled in disgust. The large hand swung up and then across towards her in a swift blur, and she flung her head sideways instinctively. The open palm struck her a ringing slap, and her vision was cut off in dancing tears as the fiery pain stung the side of her face. The soft inside of her mouth was cut against her teeth. She tasted blood. Now the cheek was burning, branded a livid red.

She sobbed breathlessly, gulping in fear and shock. The woman in charge rattled off a spate of orders. The two young

137

men, grinning now, moved. One reached out, grabbed her by the ankles, the other held her by the wrists, and they lifted her clear of the ground. They began to swing her back and forth, as though they were playing a game, then released her, so that she sailed through the air in a flurry of limbs for a couple of yards before landing on the hard ground with a force that knocked the breath from her body.

The bone wrenching thud left her stunned, choking to fill her tortured lungs. She was lying against the base of the mud wall of the smaller hut. It was many minutes before she could regain her shattered senses. The singing and haranguing went on. Everyone ignored her.

When she was sufficiently recovered, she was able to pick out the bent form of Katya sitting in the midst of the others. Another shock awaited her, for she realised why the girl had looked so startlingly different. Her fine long white-gold hair had been removed. Her head had been shaved, so that now only the lightest pale stubble remained, and the large round of the skull was revealed in all its prominence, emphasising the long slenderness of the neck, which now seemed as delicate as a flower stalk.

Vee's head and face throbbed from the blow, while her joints ached. Her hip burned where she had fallen so heavily. There was an angry red graze, and it felt as though she could scarcely move, though she had the sense not to try. She did not want to incur any further displays of wrath.

The songs went on and on. The big woman spoke a verse, the girls chanted it, then they would fit it to the loud, monotonous rhythm of the tune. Three girls kept beat on tall, slender cow hide drums, which they gripped between their ankles. At least Vee was lying in the shade. The young girls were in the full ferocity of the sunlight, and their shaven heads and bodies shone with sweat. The sharp body odour hung pungently in the air.

Vee saw with a pang of acute anxiety that Katya's head

drooped forward almost on her chest. Her lips looked cracked and pale. Her mouth was hanging open, and her eyes were deeply ringed with hollow shadows. The flies hovered and buzzed and swarmed about the sweating mass. They tormented Vee even more, constantly alighting on her face, even on her lips, greedily feeding on the perspiration that streamed from her.

Her mind wandered, drifted, her awareness gone, so that when the girls suddenly rose, she jerked back to consciousness. She saw that, like the others, Katya now wore the tiny brown flap which covered her genitals. Its beaded string snaked darkly across those narrow hips.

Once more, Vee found herself the centre of attention. The two male guards pulled her roughly to her feet. She groaned at the pain the movement brought, but they dragged her before the leader once more. Vee stood there, head down, sobbing quietly, while the big woman's voice rang out scornfully. Clearly, she was pronouncing in very uncomplimentary terms on this vile foreigner who had violated their code.

Her hands were forced behind her and someone swiftly and expertly bound her thumbs tightly together. The big woman's hand landed derisively on her right breast, hefted its slight contour, tweaked the small pale pink nipple, rolling it between thumb and finger until it hardened. The harsh voice poured out a scornful commentary, and the girls hooted with laughter, and gave their strange, shrill, undulating cries. Vee's head stayed down. The hand swept contemptuously over her belly and the bony hips, pinched the tops of her thighs, in clear condemnation of their scrawniness, then those cruel fingers plucked painfully at the soft brown curls of her pubis, Again, the explosion of laughter, the screams, and the loud slap of hand claps.

At the termination of the leader's speech, there was a deafening shout of applause, so that Vee looked up in renewed alarm. She screamed as the glistening black bodies

139

closed in smotheringly. The world tilted dizzily, then she was spread out, the sun beating down on her as countless pairs of hands lifted her high aloft, at the ends of their uplifted arms. She screamed again, kicked out feebly, but the sounds of her protests were drowned in the high pitched cries of glee.

The long fronds of grass thatch hanging down from the roof brushed down the length of her body when they carried her through the doorway of one of the huts, where she was dumped on her feet again. She swayed, disoriented by the move, and by the dimness after the blinding glare full on her face. She tottered. Her vision swam back slowly, and she gasped, for there, in the dusty half light, illuminated by the window opening high in the wall to their left, was a row of objects that looked at first glance like the posts of a miniature fence.

There were seven of them, each about eighteen inches apart, rising from a long beam of wood. Rounded and tapering, they resembled stalagmites. They were all roughly the same height, about twelve to fifteen inches from tip to base, but the diameters of the upper portions varied considerably. The thinnest, an extremely slender object, was no thicker than a stick, a finger width, then they increased in girth until the thickest was several inches across.

Vee's eyes widened in alarm as their purpose became clear to her. The base of these phalluses was a light brown, the colour of the baked mud which formed the outer surface. The upper tips were worn smooth and shone blackly, as though polished, the darkness fading unevenly a little way down the stems. She had no time for further reflection. With hands still bound behind her, Vee was thrust forward, placed at one end of the column, in front of the slimmest upright. The girls formed an eager circle. The big woman called out a question, grinning hugely, and the girls screamed their answer, their heads shaking.

Vee was nudged along the row, the pantomime re-enacted before each post, until she arrived at the thickest. "No!" she wept, but her tormentors manipulated her easily, until she was straddled over the final column.

She could feel the faint indentations where previous victims had dug in their heels. They positioned her carefully, with slow enjoyment, while she wept and pleaded with them. She offered no resistance. One of the senior women stepped forward and coated the upper surface of the phallus with some strong smelling grease, smearing it until it glistened. Vee screamed as the woman turned to her and applied the same substance to her genital area, even spreading her labia and probing the inner surface with her fingers.

They spread her splayed out knees, fingers pressed on her shoulders, and all her muscles clenched as she felt the cold hardness of the tip nuzzle her. On and down. She felt her tissue yield, the inner lining began to burn, then the tight ring of muscle burned against the unyielding intrusion. The invasion continued. She felt the grudging surrender, and she gasped at the shock of swift, awful penetration, the awful, stretching, splitting sense of the lifeless object boring into her. The interior muscles clenched and tore in agonising protest. A warm wetness came suddenly, and faintness welled up. At the same instant, there was a surrendering relaxation. She felt it in her belly. Dimly, she heard the yelling, was aware of the stench of closely packed bodies, of her own acrid fear sweat.

The burning was steadier now. She felt utterly exposed, pinned on a rack of degradation. Then an unspeakable, white, tearing flash of pure agony at which she shrieked. Her throat ached with the sheer abandon of her scream as they lifted her off the instrument, which shone with her blood.

She became aware of a delicious coolness. Someone had placed a dark glossy leaf, thickly coated with some soothing ointment, between her sprawled legs. She was lying on a grass pile, they were wiping her face and body with wet cloths. A steadying hand lifted her head supportingly, another held a cup to her lips. She drank and choked, the fiery spirit bit at her, burned its way down. The warmth began to glow and spread, in her stomach and belly, coursed through her limbs, absorbing the agony, lifting away the pain.

"Thank you," she murmured weakly, crying, her head sinking back to the grass. Her eyelids were heavy, she couldn't hold them open, and she drifted out of her helpless, abused body, away from the shame and the humiliation and the fear. Gladly, she allowed herself to go.

18

Vee's brain felt as though it were spinning crazily. Her body was warm and languorous, her limbs moved slowly as she drifted up through the deep layers of unconsciousness. Am I still dreaming? she wondered, sensing the unreality of her returning world. Then she didn't care, surrendered to the unbelievable joy of the moment. Tears spilled over. "How did you get here?" she asked tremulously, as Keith bent over her, tenderly brushing back the hair from her eyes. His wonderful fingers moved on down her responsive flesh, brushing off the pieces of grass.

She wanted to move, but somehow couldn't find the energy. Still that lazy, cosy warmth spread through her. Had she been ill? Was she drugged? But what did it matter? Keith was there, miraculously, and gazing at her with a tender love such as she had not seen from him in an age. He bent so close to her that their lips were almost touching, would touch, any ecstatic second, his breath mingled warmly with hers.

"Don't worry, darling. You're safe now. Everything's going to be all right."

142

His hand moved intimately, possessively, across her belly, the heel of his palm pressed tightly at the apex of her thighs, the cushiony flesh of her mons, and she shuddered, her muscles locking rigidly, her belly jerking at the rippling orgasm his touch produced. She sighed, and released a sob of abandoned joy, her frame quivering again.

The strong, sensitive male fingers played with the slippery folds of her melting cleft, explored with sure tenderness her pulsing inner core, found the quick of her desire, and she closed about the hand, capturing and squeezing, lifting her deeply clenching buttocks, shaken by another powerful orgasm. It flowed on until she cried, rolling her tearwet face in a torment of ultimate delight against the cushioning flesh that held her, the lips that clamped fiercely about her own trembling mouth.

Lips that moved as his strong arms settled her down on her back and the magical hands opened her, lifting and parting her thighs until they rested on his smooth warm shoulders as his mouth blazed over her flesh, from throbbing breasts, over the quivering belly, down to her wildly surrendered loins.

Her spinning brain thought that this could not be, she must surely die at this lapping. sucking heaven, she could not stand such feeling, as the spasms built and built to the crescendo of their explosion.

She came, on and on, seized and buffeted, torn apart by the potency of the climax. It soared, wave after wave, until she felt consciousness slipping away from her. She howled for mercy, sank almost gratefully into the darkness.

She was on her back, legs spread immodestly. She shivered, felt the after tremors of the potent sexual release, at the same time felt the soaking wetness between her thighs. The big woman and her two acolytes were kneeling beside her, gazing at her. Someone was wiping at the sticky mess. There was the blessedly cool, cleansing touch of water, a cloth gently wiping her clean. Too weary and lost to be embarrassed, she lay there, the fog persisting in the cloudiness of her mind, letting them do what they would. She rolled her eyes about her, seeking in vain, as she knew she would, for her husband.

"Good dream, yah?" The big woman smiled. Vee could hardly believe her words. it had been so real. She could still feel his caresses, her body tingled with them. Bitterness welled up, the tears spilt, ran down the sides of her face. She gave a choking sob as the misery engulfed her at the realisation of the truth. That drink. Her head still swam with it. The magic brew, which had induced such mind bending illusions that her body, too, had been deceived. She was stunned at its terrifying power. The big woman was stroking her, the huge palm amazingly gentle.

"Come."

The three of them lifted her easily, carried her outside. It was evening, almost sunset. They took her into the other, smaller hut. The girls filed in after them. They did not shout or jeer this time. They spoke in hushed whispers, as though waiting for some momentous event. Vee was placed on a high, narrow table, like an operating table, she thought, and then her heart pounded with fear at the aptness of the comparison. There were leather straps hanging from a horizontal pole above.

They tied her ankles, lifting and spreading her legs exactly as at a gynaecological examination. Vee was shivering with renewed terror. The horrors of the rape with the phallus came flooding back, though she realised bemusedly that, for a while, it had been obliterated from her memory, and, indeed, the physical pain, which had been so acute, had vanished after their ministrations. Now, however, she was sure something equally horrible was to be perpetrated on her.

Weeping hopelessly, she felt them prise open her outer labia. Something was inserted - later, she was to witness this operation being performed upon Katya. It was a contraption

144

made from two short twigs, fastened to form a kind of frame. This served the purpose of a dilator. The women were holding her by the thighs, though, apart from the instinctive, flinching jerk at each touch, she gave no resistance.

The leader spoke, her fingers lightly probed the gleaming raw tissue of the exposed surfaces, and the girls crowded closer, staring wide eyed. Among them, Vee saw, through her shimmering tears, the outline of Katya's head. The girl was trying to shrink back, and being held by her colleagues.

Vee waited, tensed, for some new, excruciating agony, while the leader's strong voice continued. She seemed to be explaining some point of anatomy to the riveted audience, using Vee's helpless body as a model. Then, instead of the torment she was anticipating, Vee felt a shameful stirring at the tight caress of her inner flesh, just above her vaginal entrance, and centering on the normally hidden core of sensation, the clitoris.

The tiny peak of flesh was roused, then captured in a pair of extremely fine tweezers. Utter panic seized Vee at the thought of its removal under the knife, but, almost before her brain had time to record such a terrifying notion, she felt the tiny fold of flesh being drawn out, raised and elongated from its glistening surround, while skilful fingers swiftly bound a collar of fine cotton around it, tightly enough for Vee to whimper a little with the sharpness of the pain.

The whole procedure took little more than a minute, but to Vee, spread-eagled, peeled back, exposed to her very centre, it was a timeless ordeal. Then her ankles were released, she was set on her feet, and there was this burning, quite heavily felt appendage, once more hidden in the secret folds of her flesh. Yet she was acutely aware of its beating, engorged state - a permanently, shamefully rousing state, despite the soreness and the stinging tightness.

It was a weird sensation, both painful and titillating in its bizarre way. It focused attention, demanded it, on that part

145

of her anatomy, for she could not help but be conscious of it, the binding constriction against which it seemed constantly to beat and strain, whether she was moving or still.

She had hoped that when they released her from the table they would allow her to go. The darkness was coming down. Her head was still muzzy from the concoction they had given her, though she guessed it had helped a great deal to deaden the pain of the cruel abuse she had suffered.

It occurred to her that she might have slept through a whole day and night, or perhaps even longer. Now, she suffered the added fear of what punishment Awina would inflict on her for such dereliction of duty. Though the relationship between them had changed, because of the physical intimacy they shared, it was still very much that of mistress and servant. The black girl was still largely an unknown quantity, and Vee feared her.

When the youngsters had filed out of the hut, Vee tried, haltingly, to ask for permission to return to the main compound, but Oduori, the bulky chief of the initiation class, brusquely silenced her, "You will stay. You will join the class. Though you are old enough to be the mother of many sons, you are ignorant like a little girl. You will be initiated."

"But -"

Vee quailed before the roar of displeasure. "Silence, heathen!" Oduori called out, and, magically, the two young men appeared. They seized the weeping Vee and tied her wrists together with a thin leather strip. Her hands were bound in front of her, and they made her raise her arms above her head before they thrust her down, bending her over the table on which she had been spread before. This time her feet trailed on the floor, her behind raised in readiness for the punishment she knew was to follow.

One of the young men held her carelessly by her hair. The other stood behind her and proceeded to thrash her with a thin cane, which cut painfully, bouncing off the taut cheeks

146

of her bottom. Vee began to wail and wriggle madly, much to the amusement of the watching women, whom she heard chuckling deeply.

Shockingly, the sting of the cane, and the vigorous squirming of her belly and thighs against the hard surface of the table, set off a tingling excitement which was intensified by her bound clitoris to such a degree that she gnawed at her lower lip in an excess of sensation. It was soon over. They untied her, and she straightened up, blubbering and rubbing at her throbbing buttocks, despite her knowledge of the shameful spectacle she presented.

"Go and join your little white friend. She has no courage at all. She is like water." Gratefully, Vee fled. The girls were sitting about, near the open air kitchen where the cooking fire was burning, and the air was rich with the preparations for the evening meal. Katya was curled up on the ground, quite alone. They hugged, fell into one another's arms, weeping, oblivious to the sniggers of those around them.

Presently, Katya had recovered sufficiently to tell Vee of her ordeal so far. She grimaced at the fat with which her body gleamed. All the girls oiled each other with the strong smelling stuff, to enhance their beauty, and to protect their skin from the burn of the sun and the cold at night. The Danish girl stared at her solemnly. "They have not - done what they did to you yet. The tying of the clitoris. That will come later, they tell us. But they have done something. Look."

Glancing around to make sure the others were no longer watching them, Katya opened her thighs even more as they sat facing one another, and lifted the flap of her apron. With some difficulty, she pulled at the narrow band of bark cloth beneath that hugged her genitals tightly. She managed to pull it slightly to one side with her fingers, then she pulled back the outer lips of the narrow divide of her sex. Vee saw something pale, a smooth rounded surface filling the small aperture.

147

"It is a stone," Katya muttered. "It must not be removed. It feels - funny."

Later, Vee learned that they were known as 'love eggs' and were made from the distinctive soap stone quarried to the west of the country. Their texture was as smooth as marble. The pebbles, of varying sizes, were inserted in the vaginal passage, where their constant chafing kept the girls in a state of teasing irritation. The girls were made to wear them for days before the tying of the clitoris. The others in the class had already gone through these stages in the elaborate rituals.

Vee was embarrassed at first at having to be with these adolescents, for the African girls were far younger than either Vee or Katya, the oldest being no more than fifteen. But the white girls had the considerable consolation of being at each other's side. They could even sleep together in the communal hut. All the girls paired off, lying huddled in tangled union beneath the blankets provided for them, even though one of the female keepers slept on a mattress of grass near the entrance.

Overt lovemaking was forbidden, and the initiates were prohibited from removing their sole garment, except for their ablutions, which were strictly supervised, but from the sighs and rustles and wrigglings, and thrusting of hot bellies together all about them in the dark, it was clear that the girls made amorous contact aplenty.

Next morning, after their breakfast of the thick, cloying porridge and the sweet, milky tea, they were assembled in the larger hut. The narrow table was still there, centre stage, and Vee's heart sank when she was once more called forward by Oduori.

The two younger women stretched her out on it, and then began to anoint her body with a heavy aromatic oil from her shoulders down to her feet, until its musky perfume filled

148

the entire hut, hung heavily in the charged air. She gasped, and bit at her lips as their fingers probed into every crevice, delving into the cleft of her buttocks and the fleshy divide of her labia.

Then her embarrassment was temporarily forgotten. She gaped, and gasped, along with all the others, at the dramatic entrance of one of the young men. This time, his body was entirely nude, and gleamed with its own coating of the oil. From the black scrub of pubis, his slightly paler penis curved, long and thick, in semi erection. He stood, feet apart, the muscles on his lean thighs bunched, his belly projected forward, proffering his prick for their admiration.

You could almost smell the girls' tense excitement, feel their pounding blood as they watched, their eyes fixed on the unfolding drama.

Oduori spoke, moved easily to Vee, pushed her knees open, drew them up, lifting her thighs, placing her in the classic pose to receive the man's penetration. Dazedly, Vee realised that this was to be a practical lesson in the mechanics of sexual intercourse. She closed her eyes against the tears of shame that stung them and lay back helplessly. Oduori's voice droned on hypnotically, Vee felt fingers prising her open, felt the nuzzling of his member against her narrow divide, then the slow entrance of him into her gripping tightness.

Her feet were raised, her thighs embraced the warm feel of his body lowering slowly on top of her. Then, all at once, she gave a strangled squeal, wriggled madly at the inexorable slide of his rigid column into her vagina, for the sensation of her bound clitoris at the friction his flesh caused was unbearable. She squirmed madly, her hips hammering against his crushing body, her feet kicking wildly in the air. Mercifully, she was not aware of Oduori's pungent comments or the shrieks of the delighted audience.

The copulation was not allowed to continue for more than

thirty seconds or so before, to Vee's sobbing relief, he slid smoothly out of her. However, her relief was short lived. Again, Oduori closed in, to turn her over onto her front, and force her to kneel, her bottom raised, her head resting hidden in her folded arms. Again, she felt that remorseless penis driving into her receptive sheath, this time from behind. He knelt, holding her by her hips, and, for a short while, the intense wave of pleasure flowed over her so strongly she felt her responsive wetness further lubricating the passage in which his impressive weapon plunged. But, again, the pressure of the clitoris drove her mad, so that she was turned once more into a wildly struggling, howling creature, while the staring girls hooted and clapped.

Other positions were demonstrated. She lay on her side, her leg hooked over his thrusting hips, facing the gleaming black body of the stranger buried to the hilt in her. She sat, straddling his lap, while he knelt, and she clung weeping, her head on his gleaming chest, her hands interlocked behind his neck. It was at this point that the first of the building orgasms erupted, transforming her into a demented thing, head flung back, her whole frame jarring and shaking with the force of the climax, so that he had the greatest difficulty in holding onto her.

Finally, she was made to stand, her head once more thankfully hidden in her arms on the table top, as she stuck out her behind, her legs, knees straight and tightly locked, her thighs wide apart, while he, standing behind her, entered her, plunging home with one magnificent thrust. She felt the power of his driving belly and thighs buffeting her bottom. Within seconds came another tidal wave of sensation, and she threshed, lost the consuming power of the climax, so that she was not even aware until later, at the messy aftermath, that he too came, flooding her with his potent discharge.

Drifting in a restless half sleep, Vee felt a tugging at her

150

ankle. A shadowy figure crouched beside her, indicating that she should go outside. Katya stirred, muttering something as Vee eased herself from her embrace of the girl, but she did not wake up.

Vee shivered in the night air, hugging herself, blinking owlishly to remove the trailing clouds of sleep. Someone was waiting for her - a girl, dressed only in the maiden apron, though Vee could see that she was older than the other initiates. In fact, she slowly realised, staring in admiration, this was a beautiful young woman. Her breasts were high and proud, the dark nipples long and roused, hardened by the cold. The neck rose, long and graceful, from the slender shoulders. The waist was narrow, the hips slim, the buttocks and thighs far leaner than was customary, and, therefore, to Vee's eyes, far more attractive.

The tiny brown apron, the beaded necklets above her breasts, the metal bracelets on her left wrist, all enhanced the naked beauty.

"So! This is what you do to hide from me, eh, little stick insect?"

Vee gaped in amazement, then gave a small cry. "Awina!" The next second she was pressed tightly against the splendid body, and their mouths were fastened in a passionate kiss.

19

"I came to find you earlier," Awina said, long seconds later when they finally relinquished their hold on one another. "But they would not let me into the compound. I was not dressed properly, they said." She glanced around, though no one was within earshot. Vee was surprised; it was hard to imagine anyone pitting strength against this formidably determined young lieutenant. Vee had seen how much power she commanded in the rebel stronghold. It served to emphasise the extraordinary influence this unknown and isolated corner of the community must exert.

"Anyway," Vee said, "I'm out!"

"Oh no, not really. I have to take you back. They will not let you out until you have been initiated."

"Oh God, no! Please get me out!" Vee almost screamed.

"If they think I want you out they will keep you even longer. Oduori is very powerful. She has the ear of the general. She is the keeper of tribal culture." Awina frowned again. "It is a damned nuisance. I am used to you, little insect. I will have to make do with Jackson, or Joseph again. Those boys are fools."

Vee gasped as a hand shot out and grabbed a handful of her hair. Awina tugged it with playful force, shaking Vee's head from side to side. "You are a naughty girl! I should punish you!" She gave a final pull. "At least they haven't shaved your head. I think perhaps they will spare you. Married women can grow their hair." She seized Vee's hand. "Come. Let's go into the schoolroom." She pulled her towards the smaller hut, the scene of Vee's public humiliations. "We can sit and talk. It is too cold out here."

The floor was covered with the traditional rush matting. Awina left her briefly, then returned with two blankets. She spread one over the matting. "Let us lie together," she said casually. "We can keep each other warm." She sat gracefully, patted the space beside her.

Shyly. Vee joined her, She felt a faint stir of excitement, which made her wince, for she felt the distinctive sharp twinge of secret flesh stirring in its tiny bonds. Awina chuckled. She reached out to a low round stool and upended it, holding it by one of its three short, thick legs. The base of each leg swelled out in a clear representation of the male erection. "You can see what is the driving force behind our culture. What our forefathers were obsessed with. Every-

152

thing they carved - even our furniture - looks like a penis!"

She lay back on the coarse blanket and held out her arms. "Come here. I won't bite you," she grinned sarcastically. Disturbed. yet deeply affected, too, Vee moved hesitantly. and the girls lay side by side. Vee revelled in the silk smooth, cool sensation of Awina's firm flesh so intimately connected to hers. Hotter, more urgent feelings came to the surface. feelings which were clearly reciprocated. Awina's body pressed closer, her arms tightened about her, and their lips came together.

Then Awina's strong arms were loving her, pushing her over, while the fingers plucked at the beaded strings of Vee's apron. But the knot that held the inner flap to the back of the waistband remained obdurate. "Those bastards make it impossible!" Awina tried to force her fingers in through the side of the flap, but it was extremely tight.

"We're not supposed to take them off," said Vee. "I guess they make sure." She felt Awina's impatient thrusting movement against her, and she saw the lips so close to hers part in a grin.

"Well, they didn't tie mine." Her hands left Vee's hips and moved to her own. She wriggled swiftly. She grabbed Vee's wrist, and fiercely guided her hand to the bared loins. The dark girl gasped. "You must do it to me then, angel. I'll work out how to get to you later. Please! Oh God!" She scrabbled, guiding Vee's fingers more specifically to the already wetly welcoming, slippery cleft. Vee needed no second bidding. She was afire with desire. Excitement burned so strongly that the pain of her constricted clitoris became screamingly apparent. She twisted back and forth vigorously, groaning aloud. There was only one way to lose this discomfort, and she embraced it eagerly, obsessively bending to lose herself in the gloriously proffered, delicious, dark flesh that meltingly rose to engulf her.

Becoming Awina's lover somehow fitted with fatalistic inevitability into the crazy pattern of total physical obsession that the next two weeks brought. Scarcely a conscious minute of that time passed without acute awareness of her very alert sexual force, and a great many unconscious ones, too, for the initiates were given regular and liberal doses of the potent brew which could induce shatteringly vivid erotic dreams. The sleeping hut echoed and re-echoed to the sighs and groans, the tossing of fevered limbs, and, frequently. the climactic yelps and screams of the girls, about which they were delightedly and mercilessly teased the following morning by the mamas.

Both Vee and Katya lived on the edge of fear, and of shameful excitement too. The verbal haranguing, the lectures, the songs, they were entirely ignorant of, although occasionally someone might make a brief attempt at translation. However, there was visual stimulus enough - and participation too. Vee was present at the tying of Katya's clitoris, and she herself had to endure the insertion of a 'love egg' which, together with the effect of her bound and distended clitoris, drove her wild with clamorous arousal, so that when, that night, they all took part in the seemingly endless 'jumping dance', which consisted of the participants standing in a long row and performing a series of increasingly vigorous leaps in the air, accompanied by the singing of an infinite number of doubtlessly obscene songs, she was hotly, finally screamingly eager. She was covered in dust, awash with sweat, when at last the fevered pitch of sexuality within reached its explosive climax, and she collapsed with a threshing, jerking abandon on the earth where many had already fallen, and subsided into weeping exhaustion.

There were demonstrations - tableaux of living, explicit sex techniques - performed either in the 'school' hut, on the narrow table, or in the open air, before the breathless, wide eyed gaze of the young captive audience. Although more often than not either of the two younger mamas provided the willing partner for the young men in these exhibitions, Vee was sometimes called upon to take an active role, to her intense shame and her captors' amusement. Any perceived reluctance an her part was swiftly rewarded by a caning, again in front of the highly diverted onlookers, so that she strove hard to hide her emotions at these painful times.

As a backcloth to all this, Awina visited her almost every night, apparently with Oduori's gracious consent, and Vee found herself as eager for her role of lover as the beautiful young lieutenant. No matter that it was the white prisoner who indubitably took the active part in their lovemaking. Vee was besotted. thrilled to be the harbinger of such wild passions as she was able to release in the turning, whimpering figure spread helplessly beneath her. After all, she was living practically every waking minute with this sweet yet torturous sense of unfulfilled excitement within her.

Katya was pierced with jealousy, literally red eyed with it, from her bitter tears. "Duh - don't see her any more!" she sobbed, clinging to Vee desperately.

"I have to, sweetheart," Vee murmured, suffering too. "I daren't refuse. You know how it is. I have no choice." Katya wept inconsolably, and Vee's private pain was increased, for she knew only too well what a willing victim of circumstance she was.

The end of the initiation came with great drama. There was an air of anticipation. The girls were in a new fever pitch of excitement, though it was some time before Vee and Katya discovered the reason. It was Awina who told Vee during their nightly rendezvous. "Each girl is given to the man she has chosen. Oh yes - it is mostly the girl's choice, though she is often guided by her family. There will be a big ngoma - a dance. Then the girls go off with their partners. For the honeymoon."

She laughed cruelly. "I wonder who you and your little

friend will get." Vee gaped at her in dawning panic. Awina's broad grin softened a little. "I think perhaps you will not be given a partner. You have a husband. But your skinny little friend with the chicken head. It could be the night of her life!"

Vee was horrified. Later, she appealed to Awina. "Please - you can't let them just give Katya to a man!"

Awina smiled wickedly. "Probably it will be good for her. I thought Simba would have kept her to himself, but he thinks that would cause too many problems with some of the other officers."

She caught hold of Vee, pulled her head down to her bare breast.

"Anyway, how will they take notice of me? I have had to plead with them to let me keep coming in here to see you. Humble myself before them." She gestured at her nudity, the discarded scrap of cloth, the beaded necklets. "I can do nothing."

Not that you want to, Vee thought bitterly. Any attempt to approach Oduori or any of the other guardians would merely bring some extra brutal and degrading punishment. The two 'ghosts', as the white girls were called in the vernacular, had already sampled enough harsh abuse to know that they could expect no favours.

Despairingly, Vee acknowledged that to warn the younger girl of her impending fate would simply push her over the edge of hysteria. Besides, there was always the hope, forlorn though it seemed, that Awina was enjoying a sadistic joke at their expense.

One of the final rituals of the Initiation was the removal of the clitoral bindings - a delicate operation which they all had to witness. Many lewd comparisons were made of the sizes of the angrily scarlet little triggers. At first, the release made the soreness worse. Then came a maddening itch. The aprons had been removed, and the smooth stones, and the

156

naked girls spent the day indelicately hawking and scratching, unable to leave themselves alone, to the cackling delight of Oduori and her team.

The last night came. All the girls had looked forward to the final hours of unbridled and unfettered love in the darkness of the sleeping hut. Even Vee was praying that Awina would not pay her clandestine visit on this last night, for she wished to spend it with Katya. There was much consternation, and heartfelt disappointment when, at each sleeping space, four stout pegs were driven into the ground, and the girls made to lie on their backs while wrists and ankles were tied to the pegs with straps of the softest padded leather, but which held firmly against even the most determined pulling.

When they were staked out, tormentingly close to one another, yet not touching, the mamas came round each one, and supported their heads while they were made to swig copious draughts of the fiery spirit. Wickedly caressing hands moved over captive flesh, until the air was filled with the sighs and gasps and groans of the frustrated occupants.

The night was endless. Vee sank rapidly into the weird scenario of dreams thrown up by her subconscious. Dreams peopled by a host of unlikely participants, others more expected, in a wild variety of sexual permutations. Ruth, Gerard, Mary, Keith even the ruinous carcass of George Kyriakos, figured in her fantasies.

One of the most powerful featured her brother, David, who came to rescue her from her present captivity and to confess his undying love for her. They made love furiously, endlessly, they even coupled on the reclining cushioned seats of the plane which carried them back to England, where they settled down to a life of bliss, boldly challenging the rooted prohibitions of their society. It was so real she woke sobbing in the cold grey dimness, wrists and ankles burning where she had chafed constantly against the supple restraints.

All the girls were exhausted in the morning, but they were given a root to chew which revived them and kept them on a nerve tingling 'high' all through the preparations - the bathing, the painting of the face and body, which Katya and Vee had to endure fully. They were given the beaded collar, the iron bracelets, and another fringed apron, this time with no protecting crutch piece underneath, so that at every movement the pudenda was provocatively displayed.

Heads were shaved once more, Katya's copious tears a source of unfeeling merriment, and Vee was thankful of her status as a married matron.

At long last, in the heat of the afternoon, they were ready. They formed a line, and with the distinctive, swaying, hopping step, hands on the hips of the figure in front, singing and chanting in unison, they set off, out of the gate, through the eucalyptus grove and up through the village, where the path was lined with cheering crowds.

The feasting and dancing went on long into the night. And the drinking - the girls drank more of the blood-stirring secret spirit, and the pairing off began. Katya seemed in a trance, semiconscious with the drink. All at once, she was being pushed forward, and suddenly Vee recognised the gangling, grinning form of Edward, the young guard who had been appointed to watch over them in the early days. He appeared before them, decorated with tribal markings, wearing the anklets and armlets of a young warrior. His genitals bulged beneath the skimpy loincloth.

Katya's piercing scream ripped out above the hubbub, then she fell forward, fainting, as he swept her up over his shoulder. Vee watched the pale little buttocks, peeping above the blackness of the arm that lay possessively across them, disappear through the jostling, drunken throng. Vee stared after them. She felt numb and sick. Her head was reeling, her heart pounding. The sense of her utter helplessness pinned her like a weight. Somehow, she found the strength to fight against her inertia. "No!" she screamed, and staggered to her feet, pushing, fighting, to follow, to save Katya from a man who had every reason to hate her...

Then suddenly Vee was pitched forward, sprawling head first in the leaves at the side of the path. There was a deep bass rumble of laughter. Some force plucked her easily up from the cool earth, held her easily in his arms. She lay there, the brief spark of her rebellion quashed, overcome once more by her weakness, her inability to move. She stared blearily. That broad, grinning, shining face. How did she know it?

All at once, she remembered the day and night of her capture, the journey, the giant of a sergeant. He of the massive, solid bulk, the sheepishly exploring fingers. She had not seen him since then. His unit served in the bush, in a dangerous commando role.

She lay back like a baby as he moved purposefully forward with her. She felt that deep, bubbling laughter transmit itself to her yielding frame, as the shouts and the singing grew fainter behind them.

20

Vee's mind was slow to clear. Sensations flooded through her first - light and warmth, the rough texture of blanket wool against her damp skin, the stale atmosphere of the confined space, overlaid with the sharp outdoor smell of canvas. The morning sun came strongly through the stretched sheet only inches above her head. Awareness came, too, of the hard unevenness of the ground pressing her soft flesh, and of the aches and pains that emanated from almost every part of her battered frame.

The aching of her belly and the soreness between her legs brought at that same instant the memory of the elemental sexual activity in all its force, the furious rutting of the huge sergeant, and her shocking complicity, her surrender to the screaming animal in her that came bursting to the surface in such violent consummation.

And when she turned her head, there he was. Her lower limbs were still sweatily entangled with his, the blanket slipping from the hulking body. The hairless expense curved smoothly like the carcass of a beached whale. The belly, for all its girth, looked solid, firm. She could see, just visible in the gap of the fallen blanket, the dark, tight, somehow inadequate scrub of his pubis. Its blackness was deeply highlighted against the soft chocolate shade of his skin.

Their stretched bodies filled almost the entire volume of the low one-man ridge tent. She could hear voices outside, reduced by distance, but still clear.

He woke!

The cracked red of his eyes stared at her blankly, simply. Then the great, sparkling teeth flashed as the pale thick lips pulled back in a grin, that smile of simple, unalloyed pleasure that made her liken him even more to some friendly great animal. "Jig-a-jig!" he announced gruffly, catching her completely by surprise.

Before the import of the word had even registered, the wall of flesh rolled over her, the ham hands captured her thighs and swept them up and about his broad waist. He bludgeoned into her, excruciatingly hard, tearing her tenderest flesh, so that she gasped, bit her lip as her face pressed into the muscled hump of his sweat moist shoulder.

She gripped him, raised her knees still further, instinctively riding his thrusts to accommodate him, and, as she did so, she felt her own stirring beat of excitement, fluttering stronger and stronger, in spite of all the discomfort.

When he came, after no more than two or three pounding minutes, her body was clamorously ready to continue the plunging ride to its own explosive conclusion, and she threshed madly, her head rocking from side to side, as she hammered herself against his pinning weight, the dying hardness buried deep within her spasming sheath. and slipped in ecstasy over the cataract of her own climax. He lay on her, a dead weight, pungently, wetly, while her blood thrummed crazily for a torturous interval, until she recovered a sense of her thinking self and wept for shame and humiliation.

The return of her towering sergeant marked a watershed in Vee's status in the rebel camp. Perhaps it was the initiation which had, in its strange way. identified her in relation to the community, but Vee felt it was rather the decisive action of the sergeant, who had, with his unthinking simplicity, swept her off her feet and carried her off to his tiny man made cave. Until that momentous event, everyone, with the exception of General Mavumbi and Awina, had treated the prisoners with a certain natural deference that inhibited them in any excess. It might have been the shocking fact of seeing their white skin so nakedly exhibited. Whatever the reason, they had hesitated to carry out any serious forms of physical abuse.

Certainly, no sexual threat had ever been offered, other than the ordeal with the leader himself. Now that the sergeant had so spectacularly changed this state of affairs, and Katya had been carried off by Edward, Vee felt a vulnerability that she had not experienced since the earliest days of her captivity. It seemed to her that the hulking figure had demonstrated so clearly her availability, which others had never dared to assume, and now, fearfully, she saw that knowledge in all men's eyes.

True, Awina protected her. The morning after the ngoma, Vee had finally escaped from the claustrophobic tent to seek refuge in her mistress's room. The 'gentle giant' had come later to claim her once more, naively assuming that 'the skinny white one' was now his for the taking. In the compound outside the officers' mess, Awina had, in a monumental display of spitting she-cat fury, disabused him of this assumption. It was tense for some moments. Vee could see that his brute masculinity was at odds with this pretty young female of such stinging tongue, in spite of the lieutenant's insignia on her shoulders. It was pathetic to see his final retreat. Pathetic, and a great relief.

The mobile patrol was gone again the next day. But now Awina warned her, "I cannot protect you always. Other men will want you. You may have to accept it."

They did. The novelty of the 'white meat' pulled them, as did the inescapable barrage of propaganda from outside media which had deluged their country and promulgated among the rising generation the pale slimness of the western woman as the essence of sexuality and desirability. Again, it was Awina's intervention which largely prevented her from becoming common property, available to all who had a lust for her.

The very next night after the ngoma, as she lay sleeping on her pallet in the corridor outside Awina's door, three very drunken men appeared, crying out for the 'malaya mzungu', the white prostitute, Vee fled shrieking into Awina's room, and eventually the drunks were dispersed. The African girl at first seemed extremely angry with her, but Vee had learned that Awina's outward manner could be deceptive, or at least could change dramatically within seconds. Next day she told Vee, "You sleep in my room from now on." Then she gave one of her dazzling, radiant smiles, and reached out to fondle Vee intimately. "It means you will be all the handier for me when I want you, eh?"

But she could not keep her from the general's regular use of her body. Nor, what was much worse, from having to service certain of the more privileged officers, a generous concession from their leader. Though her almost nightly visits to their rooms, and their beds, were carried out with discretion, it did not make them any less painful for Vee to bear. Nor did it help in the close and cherished sexual bond she had forged with Awina. The lieutenant's ill disguised jealousy caused her to take out her bad feelings on the hapless victim.

One morning, Awina used the excuse of a badly pressed uniform to give vent to her frustrations. "You stupid white cow," she raved, while Vee stood dumb and miserable, choking back the tears. She yelped in alarm as Awina's fingers suddenly wound about the blonde locks and dragged Vee face down across the end of the bed. There was a whistle of air, and Vee screamed louder at the sudden flaring agony which rippled across her bottom as the short bamboo swagger stick made resounding contact with the quivering flesh. Vee squirmed and kicked helplessly, pinned down by that merciless hand gripping her by the hair, while the cane descended five more times in swift and fiery torment.

"Therel" Awina panted, in mean triumph, as she stood over the blubbering Vee, who clawed at her throbbing backside as she crouched on the floor. "Perhaps that will teach you not to be so lazy, you idle little slut!"

In spite of her very real woes, Vee's thoughts had not been entirely preoccupied with her own misery. She had had time to dwell on the hapless Katya, and to wonder with some dread how she had survived her ordeal. She had wanted to seek her out, but had been expressly forbidden to do so.

"The warrior huts are out of bounds!" Awina had grinned, enjoying her discomfiture to the full. "The honeymoon is for seven days and nights. The lovers never leave the bed!"

But, eventually, after more than a week of the new routine, Awina, her conscience perhaps pricked by the red stripes across Vee's buttocks, told her carelessly, "The honeymoon period is over. You can visit Mrs Chicken-Head in the new wives' quarters this afternoon, if you like."

Full of trepidation, Vee made her way to the small circle

163

of beehive huts, within its own fenced off compound, which the 'newly weds' occupied after an ngoma ceremony. The sun was already quite low, the shadows lengthening, the light mellowed. The haze of cooking fires drifted on the air. Vee recognised some of the figures tending the blazing twigs underneath the blackened pots. They called out raucously, cheerfully, and Vee greeted them shyly. She noted how proudly they wore the bright cotton sarongs that covered the lower limbs completely. With much giggling, they directed her towards one of the huts, outside which no cooking fire burned.

Vee stepped into its cool dimness, bending to pass through the low doorway. Katya was lying on a mattress, her pathetically shorn white head in the crook of her arm. She gave a wounded cry, then they were clinging and kissing frantically, tongues and lips tasting their tears.

"Oh, my darling, I've missed you so!" Vee held her, feeling every tremor of pain through her own responsive body. Long minutes later, they had recovered sufficiently to smile tremulously, and to release one another, though they continued to hold hands tightly as they sat on the grass stuffed mattress.

Vee tried another smile. She nodded at the small pile of bright cloths. "At least you can cover up now. You don't have to go naked."

"Oh Vee!" Again, they clung together tightly. Vee's mouth sought to draw out all the hurt that was in the anguished sobbing, both her own and that of the lovely girl in her arms. "It hurts so! He is so big -" Katya shook her head, fought for some measure of control again. She shook her head hopelessly, gestured through the open doorway to the distant figures bending over the fires. "I can't - I'm not like them. I can't be a wife. The cooking - everything!"

Soon after they had stepped outside, Katya self consciously draping the sarong about her hips, Edward appeared, in his drab uniform of baggy trousers and shirt. He was carrying two old fashioned enamel coffee pots. "He brings food from the mess," Katya explained, blushing.

When the girls exchanged their final, tearful embrace, Edward awkwardly touched Vee's arm. "I take care of her. I take good care." Vee nodded gratefully, stumbled away, blinded by her tears.

She tried to visit whenever she could, usually in the afternoon, when she had her brief freedom. They were able to be on their own. Katya had a patch of garden, she was trying to cultivate vegetables under the mocking tutelage of the other girls. They were also teaching her how to cook. Their days were far more leisured now that they were wives. They collected firewood, tidied their huts and the communal compound, cooked, washed clothes. They enjoyed playing at housewives and gossiping, revelling in the sudden improvement in their lifestyle, their elevated status. Their chief job, as they well knew, was to be child bearers, so they made the most of their pampered existence, which would not last. The sharpness of their cruel behaviour towards Katya had eased, just a little.

Being so close to Awina, Vee was able to keep track of time's passing, though sometimes she wondered if this was an advantage or not. She was shaken when she calculated one day that they had been held prisoners for more than three months. Yet she was uncertain why she should be so surprised. It might as well be three years. The time before her capture was in the dimness of long ago, it seemed. Even the visit of the white journalist and the violent aftermath was consigned to the distant past. Their life, servile as it was, seemed to have settled into a long established pattern.

The intimate nature of her relationship with her beautiful mistress occupied a great deal of Vee's thought. She was quite sure that Awina's occasional outbursts of anger towards her were caused by her jealousy of the fact that her fellow

165

officers were making regular use of Vee's body. Usually, these displays of temper did not erupt into physical violence, as on the occasion when she had thrashed her. At worst, there might be the odd slap, or kick with a well placed boot. And, always, afterwards, there would be some clear sign of her penitence, some small or large favour granted to her in recompense.

Although, for a long time after their relationship had become a sexual one, Vee's role was to be the active partner in their lovemaking, that, too, changed, not long after the ngoma. Vee had believed she was more than content to play the part assigned to her. The powerful excitement with which she approached her task was in itself an aphrodisiac of such force that her body found spontaneous release while she went about ensuring that of her exotic new lover.

The texture and taste, the musky odour of that heavenly dark flesh so totally abandoned to her during those rapturous moments, had been enough to trigger her own climactic response. She thought she wanted nothing more.

But then, suddenly one ecstatic night, she found her lover as passionate as she was to be the bearer of those ultimate sensations. Each kiss, each search of mouth for hungry flesh, each stroke and squeeze and rubbing of hand and limb was strenuously matched. Like twin champions, they wrestled and threshed, so vigorously that they were forced to spread the bedding out on the rush mats, for the narrow cot quivered and creaked in alarming danger of collapse. Thighs locked, hips twitched, bellies thrust and slapped in soft abandon together. One would roll uppermost, upward thrusting knees would slacken, part, fingers search out the wet crevices of love, and tongues thrust in joyous conquest to the warm cave of submission.

Then the shivering thighs would harden, muscles bunched, those other weakening hands find strength, and their fingers in turn storm the stronghold of melting desire. The coupling frames would topple crazily, now reversed, one kneeling, thighs astride the trembling belly. On, until the love play grew more and more stormy, and the black girl, with a sob of half frustration, half plea, fought Vee down, threw her body furiously over hers, and, capturing the slim wrists, pinioned her arms above her head. The fine, strong teeth sank with passion into the proffered neck. Vee stiffened, felt that magnificent body spread over her, shivered throughout her frame, and tearfully, joyfully, surrendered.

It was almost dawn when they finally lay in total exhaustion among the tangled sheets. Sore and stinging, bruised and utterly sated, they still sought contact in this after-storm calm. "My God!" Awina groaned, with a small laugh that contained something of the wonder she was just now experiencing. "You are a tiger. No more stick insect. My white tiger. I feel you have eaten me up, every inch."

Vee nodded. She turned to face her lover, felt the crinkly hair touch her forehead, pressed their sweat damp brews together. "It's never - I know you won't believe me - but it's true. It's never been like that for me before. With anyone!"

"And me," Awina answered. She spoke softly, solemnly. "I am not a lesbian." Then she gave a small laugh, shrugged. "I guess that is nonsense. But it was true until tonight. I let you do it to me. In school we fooled around. We would lie in each other's arms and kiss. I let girls put their fingers in me sometimes. But it it was not making love. Nothing ever happened like this before." She shook her head vehemently. "Not with a man! No! Never like this!"

She reached out yet again, drew Vee into her. "Curse you, white tiger! Woman lover! Lesbian! What have you done to me?"

More days rolled by, turned into weeks which slipped by unnoticed. The long dry season came to an end. The white morning mists hung about the tall dripping trees, reluctant to depart, and the skies were grey and louring, until about mid afternoon, when the sun would return with its brief burst of fiery splendour, every bit as potent as before.

Smoking charcoal braziers appeared in all the huts at eventide, and were kept burning all through the night, while even the totos covered their nakedness with ragged dresses, or T-shirts and holey shorts.

Vee sneezed and streamed, and shivered miserably on a morning so that Awina took pity on her and allowed her to wear a kikoi. The flimsy covering was more of a psychological than a practical help, but she was grateful none the less. And there were still those magical moments when she clung hungrily to Awina under the blankets, with the brazier glowing cosily in the corner of the fume-filled hut. Then the cold receded, and young flesh on flesh responded with a different kind of fever, and mouths met and re-met in ever renewing ecstasy.

One night, in the early hours, Awina was strangely withdrawn after the almost desperate passion of her lovemaking which had left Vee wetly, sorely, but blissfully exhausted. The black girl, instead of settling down to the limb locked sleep towards which Vee was drifting with sweet anticipation, propped herself on one elbow and stared at the fair head so close on the pillow. Despite her sleepiness, Vee became aware of the scrutiny, and opened her eyes to gaze at the dark face contemplating her.

"What is it?" she asked shyly.

Awina grunted. "God! You white bitch! I'm going to miss you so much!"

Vee's heart began to thump. "What? What do you mean?

What's happening?"

The dark eyes regarded her sombrely. "I have to go away again tomorrow. You may not be with us much longer."

Vee pleaded to be told more, but Awina shook her head. "No questions! I shouldn't have said anything. Nothing's definite yet."

"But -"

Almost angrily, Awina covered Vee's lips with her own, lifting herself over the supine figure and pressing her down. She caught the thin wrists and pinned them by the side of the tousled head. Deliberately, she let her breasts rub insistently against Vee's slighter, paler mounds, until both girls felt the slow, stirring rekindling of passion. Thighs and bellies pressed in slow mirror image.

"I'm meeting someone from your government," Awina whispered, her face still close to Vee's. "Don't say a word to anyone, you hear? Not even to the Danish cow - otherwise, I'll be in trouble. Give me your word!"

"Of course." Vee puckered her lips, began to return the gentle kisses. "I knew there was something different in the way you loved me tonight. I -" Suddenly, her eyes filled with tears. "I'll never forget you. I love you."

Awina's smile was sadder than ever. "I bet you say that to all the girls!" But those thick, luscious lips descended fervently to claim Vee's eagerly upheld mouth.

Vee felt strangely vulnerable and isolated after Awina's departure next day. She was shocked at the confusion of her emotions. Her heart should have been beating with wild joy at the prospect of her imminent freedom. Why then did she feel this clawing fear hollowing at her insides, and the loneliness? It shocked her to acknowledge how close she had become to Awina, and, perhaps as a consequence, how far apart she seemed to have drifted from Katya.

Of course, she urged herself, it was not really her fault.

After all, she could only see Katya briefly now, in the afternoons, and in such public circumstances.

The physical intimacies she had sought were a thing of the past. Vee had the feeling that Katya was relieved. She had been, at first anyway, a reluctant lover. The precarious quality of their existence had been the vital spark which had brought her to an acceptance of a sexual relationship between them. Now, she seemed embarrassed in Vee's presence, and guarded. What was more, she seemed to have come to terms remarkably with her status as Edward's concubine, or whatever the term was for the role she occupied with the young soldier.

The first night after Awina's leaving proved that Vee's anxiety was not ill founded. She wondered if she were merely being hypersensitive, but it felt to her as though there was an air of general tension which communicated itself to all levels. It began badly, when the general came across to the mess hut in the early evening and saw Vee wearing the kikoi draped round her body from breast to mid thigh.

"Get that thing off!" he roared. "Who the devil do you think you are, white slut? You're getting ideas above your station!"

Terrified, Vee pulled the thin garment off and dropped it on the ground. Lately, now that the novelty of sex with a white captive had worn off, she had been called upon less and less to satisfy the desires of the officers, while Simba himself had not sent for her for weeks, Jackson had told her that the general was working his way through the new young wives who had formed the recent initiation class, and that Katya, too, had been sent for. Vee had found herself too embarrassed and estranged from Katya to ask her such a delicate question. It was sufficient that she herself was not having to couple with the menfolk, especially as the bond between her and her mistress was growing daily, or nightly, closer.

170

"You'll wait on us at dinner tonight!" the general roared at her now. "And you'll wear what nature gave you, scrawny as it is!"

There was a new maliciousness about Mavumbi's behaviour that frightened her from the outset. He made her stand close to him, beside his chair, and he let his great greasy hand fondle openly between her thighs while he ate and chatted. "I'm just checking," he told his laughing subordinates, deliberately speaking in English so that she should be spared no shame, "to see if her cunt hasn't closed up. I know our gallant young lieutenant's been doing more than her duty in these regions, but she hasn't really got the equipment for such things, has she, white meat? I bet you've been missing it, haven't you?"

All at once, he seized her round the waist and pulled her forward over the table, the dishes spilling and scattering as she sprawled, her feet waving in the air.

"Look at this!" he bawled, and the sobbing Vee felt his hands hefting and pinching at her bottom. "Not a mark on it! You've been missing that, too, I bet, eh, white meat?" He kept his hand spread over the clenched rounds, holding her down easily, for she made no resistance, only her feet waving as a token instinctive protest.

"She likes a good beating, this one!" he informed the ogling company. "You know, it excites these decadent white bitches. Releases some chemical that gets them all worked up. I read it in one of their clever magazines."

He let his thick fingers probe deeply into the tight divide until they pressed against the hidden slit of the anus, and Vee gasped.

"I guess it's because the wormy little pricks of their bwanas are so unsatisfactory. You'll never be the same now that you've tasted what real men's pricks are like, will you, Mrs Green? Will you?" he bellowed when she failed to answer, and gave her behind a resounding slap.

"Nuh - no, sir!" sobbed Vee.

"Well, let us make her day on both scores!" the general grinned. "Hold her, gentlemen. Take her ankles, and her wrists!"

The two nearest men needed no second bidding, and Vee felt herself mercilessly exposed, spread like a star on the table top, amid the litter of the meal. A cane had appeared, and Mavumbi made it whistle through the air, the sound striking fresh terror in Vee's thumping heart. But, as if to prove his earlier point, wickedly he struck her with nowhere near his full strength. In fact, the first strokes were almost parodies, taps which stung only a little, and raised the faintest of pink marks on her clenched buttocks.

"See how she wriggles!" the general guffawed. "She'll be begging for more soon. Am I teasing you, my little slut?"

Gradually, he increased the force, until the hot fire flared across her tender flanks, and she yelped aloud. The last few strokes were delivered with violence enough to cut more deeply, to set the rounds quivering, and to raise livid lines of angry red that throbbed abominably. When they released her, she knelt there, weeping pitifully, her head down, her blonde hair trailing in the morsels of spilt food and drink, her hands clawing at the fiery torment of her bottom.

Worse was to follow. She had expected that she would be ordered to the general's room. His voice was worse than the caning he had delivered when he said coolly, "Well, gentlemen, I'll leave her to you. She's warmed up for it now. I hope you'll be able to give her something to remember us by!" And he left her, still kneeling there, sobbing and thoroughly degraded.

An endless nightmare followed. Rough hands seized her, she was borne aloft, carried through into the nearest bedroom, flung on her back on a narrow bed. For the first minutes, the room was shamefully crowded while her first assailant swiftly peeled off the clothing from his lower limbs.

172

The dark penis thrust out like a lance as he dived unceremoniously between her spread-eagled thighs and hammered at her. She lifted her knees, her feet turned towards the ceiling, and in pure self preservation, she scrabbled frantically to capture his stabbing column and guide it into her. Her labial cleft was already moist, but the bludgeoning thrust of his prick jarred her, and the fury of his rutting made her whimper with pain. He came after no more than a minute or two, though she had little time to endure the shame of his withdrawal before his place was taken by another rampant penis, another crushing, driving weight between her sprawled limbs.

A third, a fourth - she tried not to count, tried not to feel the burning pain, the friction of sweat slippery bodies on hers, the discomfort of her tender thighs as they hugged one body after another to her. Tried, too, to forget the most haunting, darkest shame of all, to bury it far beneath her conscious memory, for, somewhere in that kaleidoscope of heaving rutting flesh, rising imperiously over all the agony, came the unstoppable thunder of her own blood, her own threshing, finally shatteringly fulfilled excitement, that made the rest of the desolate, weeping ordeal even more atrocious to bear.

The ending of their captivity came with a swiftness that left them with a numbing sense of unreality. Vee was still hobbling like a crone, her bottom bruised and scarred, her genital region swollen and tender to the lightest touch, when Awina returned four days later. The time had slid by for Vee in a daze of numb despair after the multi-rape, though no one touched her again, or scarcely acknowledged her. Then Awina was back, and she was lying weeping in her arms, hardly able to comprehend the rather terse tones of her mistress and lover.

"You're leaving at dawn tomorrow. We have achieved all we're going to get out of those bastards! Some recognition of our struggle. And some help. Not that they'll ever admit it. But we're keeping our word. So! This time tomorrow, you'll be in your husband's arms again!"

But her bitter taunts vanished when, in the privacy of her room, she examined Vee's naked body and saw what had been done in her absence. "Oh my God! The swine! The filthy swine!" She bent, tenderly traced the dark bruises on the delicate inner surface of Vee's thighs, then the softer, bruised tissue of the labial divide. Her tears mingled with the sweet saliva from her lips and gentle tongue, and Vee shivered with ecstasy.

Aching, tired flesh, sated appetite, was found to be rechargeable. This time, they knew inescapably that this was the last, and they made love with a hunger, a yearning that neither would forget, abandoning their bodies to each other with a new willingness to possess and be possessed, exploring inches and surfaces, slopes and crevices never before exposed to their love. Teeth bit, salty tongues licked, fingers picked and probed, on and on, until they felt for those magic seconds, minutes, hours, that their flesh had indeed fused.

It was greyly light, the noises of the waking day had begun, when Vee sank into the sweetest sleep she had known since parting from Keith. It seemed to last no more than a micro-second before she was being roughly shaken back to reality. Awina, dressed in a crisp uniform, was towering over her, the room was full of daylight. "Put on your kikoi. There is a sweater, too. The landrover's waiting."

She turned, was gone, without goodbye.

Shivering, feeling sick and empty, Vee wrapped the kikoi around her waist, pulled the thick sweater over her head. She went outside. The landrover was drawn up right outside the mess tent. Katya was standing there, her white gold hair a tangled mass, her face drawn and pale. She looked totally bemused. Armed uniformed figures crowded about them, Mavumbi came striding from his quarters, snapped without

174

ceremony, "Get in! You're going home."

"No! Please, sir! She must stay -" A wild figure, in shirt and trousers, burst through. It was Edward. His eyes were rolling, his black face contorted with emotion. "She is my wife!"

Katya was staring, looking more bewildered than ever. Tears began to roll down her ashen cheeks. "Get her in the truck!" Mavumbi hissed, and Vee realised he was addressing her.

"Come on, Katya," she said gently, taking her arm. The Danish girl shook her off, stared at Edward, almost as distraught as he was.

Mavumbi rattled off an order and two men grabbed the weeping Edward, dragged him away. Katya gave a cry, and made to follow them, whereupon Mavumbi flung his great arms about her and, hoisting her in the air, dumped her through the raised rear doors of the vehicle. A figure who was already inside grabbed her, held her down, as she began to scream and struggle. Vee scrambled inelegantly after her, the door slammed, and they were off, bouncing on the uneven track, passing in seconds through the morning bustle of the camp, the roar of the engine muting Katya's agonised sobbing.

She ceased to struggle, and the soldier released her. When Vee put her arms tentatively round her, she accepted the embrace, collapsed against Vee's breast in a welter of grief. Vee's lips nuzzled at the white gold hair as she whispered, "We're going home, Katya. It's all over. We're going home."

Vee's words, meant to encourage, had a startling effect. The golden head lifted once more, and the blue eyes gazed at her in a naked anguish which shook Vee. "I'm pregnant! I'm going to have his baby!"

175

22

Vee watched the small group of upturned black faces fall swiftly away beneath the clattering chopper. At the last glimpse of the rebels, she saw the bulk of her sergeant, solid, statue like, diminishing in the whirlwind. She felt her muscles stir at the memory of his hugeness inside her. She raised her hand in a little wave as the group vanished in a swirl of pale dust, and she noticed the British official opposite staring at her, then, in particular, at her brown, bare, scratched, dirty, leg, which projected in full splendour from the folds of the kikoi.

All at once she was engulfed in mortifying shame in front of these white people, so clean and elegant. She became aware, in newly dawning revelation, of her general unsavouriness, and, above all, her nakedness under this inadequate makeshift clothing.

They landed in the grounds of the large modern hospital, Britain's gift at the country's independence. The crowd looked terrifyingly large, though, in fact, access to the grounds had been strictly limited. The journalists and cameramen fought and jostled to get to them, calling out, waving microphones with forlorn hope. Surrounded by police, the two girls were hustled away into the ground floor of the glass tower, where a more official welcome waited.

"Papa!" Katya's scream cut through the opening remarks, and then Mr and Mrs Burnsen, weeping openly, were hugging and kissing their daughter, while the African government ministers strove to look on benignly.

"Hello, love." Keith was standing there, white with tension, looking unbelievably young, and clean. His image dissolved in a flood of tears and she flung herself blindly at him. Her arms clasped about his neck, but they did not kiss. She pressed the side of her face into his chest, her thin frame convulsed with great sobs. His arms came up to hold her, but, even in her abandonment, she sensed his stiffness, the almost recoil he fought to disguise.

Vee was privately stunned at the transformation which her young companion in misfortune had undergone. The physical changes were only just becoming apparent - the riper, increased size of her breasts, the general air of blooming health, the more generously rounded curves, despite the ordeal of captivity. But it was her mental attitude which confounded Vee. Far from rejoicing at their rescue, Katya was torn with doubt and confusion, and Vee was shocked to realise that the girl was feeling a deep affection for the awkward young boy soldier she had been forced to live with - and regret at being parted from him.

Most shocking of all was her fierce determination to keep the baby. Her parents, and the doctors who treated her, assumed that the pregnancy would be terminated with all speed. No difficult matter. They, too, were shocked at Katya's refusal to cooperate. "She's unwell - in her mind, I think," her distraught father told Vee, and appealed to her for help.

"There's one thing, darling," Vee murmured wretchedly, when she was alone with the Danish girl one evening, "This baby - how do you know it's Edward's?"

Vee was appalled at the tragic look which Katya gave her. "What do you mean?" she whispered, her face white.

"Well," Vee stumbled on, "you were - didn't you have to sleep with the general? After you and Edward - after you went to that compound? Couldn't it be - well, couldn't the baby be the general's?"

Katya's eyes gazed at her with a haunted, wounded expression that brought the tears to Vee's eyes too. "No!" the girl whispered, then cried out fiercely, "No! No!" The white gold head shook furiously, then she fell back onto the bed and sobbed heartbrokenly.

Meanwhile, Vee had her own griefs to contend with. She swiftly understood that, in public, Keith was keeping up the image of the faithful husband tortured with anxiety for the safety of his virtuous wife. That was the role he must have played throughout the months of their imprisonment. He therefore visited the hospital every day, smiled bravely for the staff, and for the world's media, and kept his arm firmly about her shoulder when they were seen together. In private, there was an awkwardness which hung between them.

One morning after they had been at the hospital more than a week, Vee went along to Katya's room, to find her bed empty. She met Mr Burnsen in the corridor, his face split by a smile of pure relief.

"Katya has agreed. She's having an abortion."

Vee nodded, smiled too. "I'm glad," she said. Was she? she wondered. Suddenly, she was deeply dismayed at the depth of emotion which welled up inside her, so that she had to mumble her excuses and beat a hasty retreat. She locked herself in a toilet and began to weep desolately. She realised suddenly, with genuine shock, how physically roused she was. Her hand slid between her thighs, under the lifted night-dress, to caress her tingling flesh, tracing the contours of her vulva. Her body ached to feel the passionate warmth of Awina, to savour the musky heat of her loving once more.

Keith had still not so much as kissed her on the lips. All at once she was assailed by the feeling that he would never make love to her again. She snatched her hand away, and, instead, used it to dash away the tears which were pouring down her cheeks.

In the end , the tragedy was that she would never know if the break up with Keith would have been inevitable. She actually went back to live at the bungalow with him. Menya had gone, thank God, replaced by another houseboy. "Sleep in the spare room," Keith said baldly, his face red, and she fought down her dismay. He had brought her home. He had not thrown her out. That was all that mattered. He was away all

178

day, and most of the evenings, too, but still she clung to that flicker of hope. It would take time. And now they had time.

One day, feeling guilty but unable to prevent herself, she went snooping about his drawers, his desk, scarcely knowing what she was looking for. She found a file containing all the press cuttings about her captivity.

She spent the whole day reading through them, sickly fascinated. The British press were mostly full of vague allusions to their conditions and full of salacious speculation. But the foreign press was not so delicate. There was an American magazine in particular, carrying Frank Tully's article, She recognised his picture at once. The article pulled few punches, describing their conditions and the sexual servitude they endured under the rebel leader. The centre piece was the blown up, intimate photograph he had taken in the hut that night. She stared at her image; the small points of her naked breasts, her solemn, wide eyed stare. She was amazed, and humbly grateful, that Keith could even bear to look at her again. She knew how much his pride must have been hurt at all this. She put the file carefully back, determined he should never know she had seen it.

Katya returned to Europe. Vee exchanged a tearful farewell, they kissed tenderly on the lips, Vee praying that all the intimacies they had shared could be translated into that one embrace.

"Write to me," she whispered. "I'll never forget you." She let her fingers brush softly against that fine hair, which had grown back with added lustre, but which was now shaped in a more sophisticated, shorter style, transforming Katya from girl to an elegant young woman.

"I'm coming back soon," she whispered in return, and Vee glimpsed the veiled determination in the blue eyes. "I'm going to find Edward again."

Vee was lying on her bed after a lonely dinner, wearing a

pretty satin negligee of pearl. The sheer gown beneath hugged her body with seductive softness. Her shining hair, in its simple style, had been carefully arranged, her nails filed and polished. She was subtly perfumed, looking her best she felt, wishing as ever to appear desirable in the eyes of Keith, longing with an intensity that left her weak for him to find her so.

He came crashing through the door, that awful mad glare in his eyes. He flung a thick, heavy magazine at her. It fell across her thighs.

"Look at it!" he thundered, his words choked with rage. "Look at it!" She had a sensation of falling. She thought he was going to strike her.

She turned it over with nerveless fingers, flicked at a page, and there, in glossy abandonment, was George's pencilled portrait of her, the one in which she sprawled in the chair, in all its erotic detail. The promise of the peak nippled breasts, the fluffed curls of the pubis, the proffered lines of the vulva, the exposed out turn of the thigh, the delicacy of the hanging, tapered calf, the pointing toes.

On the opposite page were the other sketches George had done of her. The captions, the article, were in English. 'Sexpatriots in the sun. The truth behind lovely kidnap victim, Vera Green. Lover tells all.' There wasn't much. There was no need for more words after that explicit pose. Gerard wasn't even mentioned by name - out of his professed wish 'not to embarrass the beautiful Mrs Green, who has already suffered enough'. A fine irony, the final touch in a devastatingly effective act of revenge - for which, she heard later, he received $200,000. It was a revenge aimed more at Keith than at her, she guessed, and hit the mark disastrously. And so perfectly timed, after all the effort Keith had put in through the long months of her capture to hide the truth from the world.

"So, here we are again then!" Keith snarled, with a bitter

kind of triumph. "You must have been missing it all so much."

She made no effort to struggle, or even to plead, as he hauled her up from the bed, and stripped the thin silk from her body. When he thrust her down once more, she pressed her face into the satin of the covers, clutched at their softness with her fingers, muffling the screams which rose in her throat at the wicked sting burning over her flanks as he chastised her for the last time. The chosen instrument, purely by chance as it was the thing which came nearest to hand, was the long handled, imitation tortoiseshell hair brush, which he had bought her when they first set up home together, and which had figured in the early days in the stinging, stirringly naughty spankings which had roused her so fiercely.

He struck now with a savage force that tore the breath from her, and her frame quivered at the fiery consummation. She could not prevent her body from jerking instinctively at the agony he inflicted upon it, but, after every blazing stroke, she pressed herself submissively against the yielding mattress, surrendering to the pain and to the punishment she felt she had richly earned.

POSTSCRIPT

Even on the plane home, days later, her bottom was still tender, so that she shuffled uncomfortably and had hardly any sleep. She was using her maiden name, and was thankful that there were no reporters waiting at the airport. They milked the story without her help. She was not even able to go to her parents' home, though it was doubtful if they would have welcomed her had she done so. Her notoriety as a fallen idol, or at least heroine, was briefly such that she had to shun any of the places where the media might latch onto her.

She was too beaten down to care. She arranged a meet

up with David, her brother, in the anonymity of London, where she found a dingy bed sit, not through lack of finance, for Keith had insisted she take a generous enough settlement, but she was determined to make herself independent of him as soon as possible.

The meeting with her brother was painful for both of them. Vee suddenly remembered the vividly erotic dream she had had during the initiation class and her forbidden adolescent fantasies. She found herself clinging to him, lifting her mouth, open, for his kiss, pressing her thigh and loins to his, so that he almost thrust her away to break the embrace.

She felt even more desolate. "I don't know what to do," she wept.

"Go back to college," David advised. "Finish your degree. You can get a teaching job meanwhile. They'll take you on unqualified in Inner London."

She took part of his advice, finding a post at an inner city comprehensive, relearning the knack of living in the present, and keeping memory at bay. And the present, bleak as it was, had plenty to occupy her thoughts. Her pupils of both sexes were rowdy, often totally unmanageable. There were times when she was stomach churningly afraid of them, sick with fear. She was a bad teacher, she knew very soon. Most of the time she dreaded facing her classes, longed for the escape of the final bell at four o'clock, woke up with a lump of apprehension in the pit of her stomach each weekday morning.

Uncomfortably, she perceived that dark, masochistic element at work in her personality, that kept dragging her back to the ceaseless battle, the obscene insults. There were other dark tendencies, too, the long, coltish legs of summer, the sharp little breasts of the girls, the tight, pert behinds and promising bulge of the boys. But fantasies, indulged in the lonely, steamy solitude of her lumpy bed, were harmless after all. To compensate, she assumed a persona of prim old fashionedness, a strait laced schoolmarminess at odds with her still youthful prettiness, a combination her students delighted in. They vied with each other to shock her, and were never disappointed.

Summer ended at half term, and a wet autumn heralded a dank, bitter winter. School finished, with the hectic pre-Christmas festivities. The biting cold made her muscles ache, and she thought longingly of the warm bath of the African sun, every time she saw her almost faded tan. She felt even more isolated at the excesses of good will all about her, She lied to her parents, sure that she would only be an embarrassment at their home during the holidays. She derived a kind of masochistic pleasure almost from her loneliness, lying in the warmth of her bed like a little animal in its lair, daydreaming, allowing the slow, sexual yearnings to filter through her body, tormenting herself by lying perfectly still, trembling still, until she could stand it no longer, and her hand would creep with lover's stealth to a breast, her other hand sliding lasciviously down her belly, across her thigh, to the clinging dampness of her sex.

She didn't dress, kept the gas fire going, and moved around the flat naked, constantly, teasingly aroused. She liked that strange sense of unfulfilment her behaviour brought. She held onto it as long as she could before she was forced to bring herself swift, consuming release.

Two days before Christmas, she decided she had to visit the nearby launderette. She dressed in front of the fire. All these clothes! She was wearing a clingy body warmer these days, instead of bra and pants, and she wriggled into the tight garment, smoothing it to her contours, fastening it awkwardly at the crotch. She eased it into place, sliding an index finger in the high, cut away ribbing of the legs. She pulled on a pair of thick black tights, then the heavy skirt and sweater. With the scarf and bobble hat, and winter coat, she felt weighted down, like a deep sea diver.

The launderette was busy, but not too crowded. She sat through the procedure, then dried the first lot, pulled them out and replaced them with the remainder. Another fifteen minutes and she would be back home, free to strip off again.

"'Ow do, miss. O'righ'?" The voice startled her. A burly coloured youth slumped into the plastic bucket seat beside her. Wayne Grainger. A sixteen year old whom she tried unsuccessfully to teach six periods a week. He was a tearaway, one of the many in 5C, a choice collection of misfits she had been saddled with. There were a lot of coloureds in the school, probably three quarters of its population. She found it oddly comforting. She could relate to them more than the pimply faced or make up plastered whites, though she was sure they didn't realise that.

He was grinning at her and staring with a rude directness that made her blush uncomfortably. "Not out wid de boyfrien' ternight then?" She shook her head, smiled distantly, freezingly. "Very nice. Oh yus. Very choice!" he drawled, with exaggerated slowness.

At first, she did not realise what his words referred to, then she saw with amazement that he had reached down deliberately into her canvas bag and picked out a pair of knickers. Her tiny white tango briefs, with the twin cotton roses on the front panel. The little crumpled triangle of lace and cotton looked minuscule and startlingly white against the brown and black of his hand. He rolled them in his palm, then brushed them very delicately over his thick lips.

Vee blushed deeply, shivered, felt a shooting, twingeing spasm of her vaginal muscles, exactly as though he had caressed her there. She fought against the breathless constriction at her chest. "Put them down," she managed faintly. "Huh how dare you!"

His grin widened He held up the knickers even more prominently, and Vee squirmed with burning shame at the amused gaze of several onlookers. "Wot's 'at?" he enquired in a parody of wide eyed innocence. "Wo'd you say? Pull 'em dahn? I'd love to, but not 'ere, darlin', know wot I mean?"

Galvanised into action, she snatched at them, and he moved his hand deftly, avoiding her clumsy grasp. Tears of helpless rage blinded her. He dropped the garment insolently back into the bag. "Let's not get 'em in a twist, eh? Only bein' friendly, like. Don' take offence, eh? Stay cool, darlin'."

"Don't call me that!" she snapped unsteadily, breathing hard. "You're going to be in serious trouble!"

"Ooh, please, miss." The mockery of his tone stung her. "You gonna spank me, are yer? Tell my mum of you, I will."

She flung herself out of the chair, tugged at the door catch of the rumbling drier. In clumsy haste, she pulled out the articles of clothing, thrusting them into the bag. More delicate underthings. She felt a violated sense of his eyes on them. As she made to go, he seized her wrist in an iron grip, pulled her back into the seat. "Come on! Don' be so toffee nosed, miss. We ain't in school now. Lighten up. Come dahn the caff. I'll treat yer to a coffee, seein' as it's Christmas."

"Let go of me!" she hissed through her teeth, struggling not to cry. Suddenly, he released her hold, flung her away in disgust.

"Go on then, fuck off!" he snarled, dark eyes blazing. "All the fuckin' same, incha? Bloody stuck up toe rags! 'Oo d'yer think you are, so bleedin' special? Don' wanna know us black barstards, do yer? Can' even speak to us ahtside school. Go on, piss off!"

His rage startled her. Without thinking, she fired back, "Listen, sonny! I lived with you black bastards for three years. I was a prisoner of you black bastards for nearly six months!"

Oh no! She groaned at her own stupidity. A new life, a new name. And, miraculously, no one had known her, no one had recognised her, despite her notoriety. It had never happened. Just as David had said. 'Nobody looks at anybody here. We don't see anything.' And she had blown it all.

He was gazing at her in astonishment now. "Hey, miss. Wo'd yer mean? Sorry fer gittin' yer mad. Let's start again, eh?" He continued to talk, polite, friendly. He picked up her bag, linked her arm with antiquated courtesy, led her to the door and the brightly lit cold night. Unbelievably, even to herself, she allowed herself to be escorted outside before she made a belated, stumbling protest.

"Aw, c'mon, miss. I don' mean no 'arm, honest. Just a coffee. Be 'uman. I won' tell nobody. I jus' wanna talk to yer. I've alwus thought you was smashin', miss. Even though you think we're scumbags!"

"No!" she murmured involuntarily. He had her bag. Confidently, he held onto her, steering her through the still crowded streets.

In the steam-weeping coffee bar, they found a quiet corner booth and sat opposite each other, knees touching. Wayne beamed a grin. His dazzling teeth flashed, and with a painful clarity, Vee remembered her sergeant. The boy nodded at her bag, on the seat beside him, his dark face alive with mischief.

"They're real pretty, your knicks. Jus' like you. All dainty, delicate like. You're a real toff, incha, miss?"

She shook her head helplessly. His deep, uneven voice poured on over her, its childish banter having a curiously hypnotic effect on her. "We gotta get acquainted proper like. I wanna know all about you. Wot you meant back there. You bein' in prison."

She stared at him like a frightened, trapped rabbit. 'No!' Her lips formed the word soundlessly. He merely grinned. He took her cold hand in his rough palm and kept it there, his fingers playing firmly over her knuckles. Her huge eyes pleaded with him. "Don't!" But he grinned again, shushing her protest.

Inside her head, she screamed out a warning against the

invidious lassitude that was stealing through her body, the tight, clenching, weakening spasms deep in her belly. She felt the swelling, dampening tightness between her legs. The vivid premonition of danger crushed the breath from her even as she throbbed to its fatal excitement.

She gasped. She felt his fingers softly, insistently, rubbing along the ribbed tights, at the inside of her knee, then on, up the quivering softness of her inner thigh. She began to weep quietly, but she did not move, except to clench her hands more tightly on the plastic surface of the table. "We'll go back to your place," he crooned thickly. She watched the movement of his gleaming throat, in the solid, muscled column of his neck.

The precipice was there. She felt the gritty stones, the sliding, sharp definition of the brink. "Don't hurt me," she begged. The tears shone on her cheeks.

He laughed deeply, a terrible, primitive, male animal laugh, and, as they left together, placed his broad hand with possessive claim over her buttock through the thick winter coat.

BONUS PAGES

Here are a couple of reviews which are quite fun - they are from a journal called Desire!

<u>Biker's Girl on the Run</u> comes with the warning, 'This is is fiction: in real life practice safe sex - with a willing partner,' which in itself should give you a little of the flavour of this, the latest in a series of sex-saturated, Mad Max-style post-apocalyptic biker romps, in which our heroine manages to stay bare-ass naked throughout the whole duration of the book!

...Sarah Fisher's <u>The Contract</u> is the latest from Silver Moon's sister imprint (note the SM abbreviation), which specialises in CP, sub/dom-orientated fiction for women. It's not all welts and stripes though, as this tale of pleasurable pain also contains much in the way of good, old-fashioned, dirty, rumpy-pumpy. What more could a woman want?

Our next book is I CONFESS! by Dr Gerald Rochelle. Here is how it starts:-

CHAPTER 1

Maria looked up at the ornate ceiling of the entrance to the church to see the carving again. The woman was naked and suspended by a rope around her waist. Her long hair hung in swirls over her face and her arms reached down at full stretch as she clung desperately to her ankles. Behind her, a naked masked man wielded a cane and was bringing it down hard onto the woman's taut buttocks.

There was also a carving of another woman, blindfolded and tied by her wrists to a post, being beaten by three naked men: one with a chain, one a rope and another with a long knotted whip. Yet another depicted a woman, spread-eagled on her back and manacled to the floor by her wrists and ankles. She was being fucked while two other men forced their cocks deep into her mouth. The last woman in the series, the most realistic and therefore her favourite, clothing in tatters, hung suspended by a rope around her neck, and was being beaten across her buttocks and breasts as dogs snarled menacingly around her feet.

Maria had gazed up at these same carvings as a young girl. She had wondered what it would be like to be whipped and chained, and how it would feel to be beaten, fucked and humiliated. Often she had leant against the wall of the entrance, gazing up as she lifted her school skirt and slid her fingers down the front of her white panties. She had dribbled from the corner of her mouth as she slowly inserted her fingers between the pink folds of her young cunt, and gasped with anxiety and joy as strange shivers of excitement coursed jerkily through her limbs.

Maria had been brought up a strict Catholic, and had been used to confessing as a young girl, but it had been years since she had come here to pour out her sins.

She stopped just inside the heavy oak doors, and for a few moments stood in the silence. She stared down towards the dimly lit altar. Candles flickered on the white cloth that draped it and the gold candlesticks stood up glistening with darkly etched veins mysteriously entwined around them.

She jumped as the door closed behind her with a low thud. She must be even more tensed up than she had expected.

The metal-capped heels of her shiny black shoes clicked on the stone floor as she walked over to the small wooden confession box that was built into the wall behind some towering grey columns. She paused at the closed door and peered through the lattice-work front; she could just make out the dark figure that crouched like retribution inside. Without hesitation, and falling into the old habit, she reached up and drew back the heavy red curtain that hung in velvety folds

189

from a brass rail fixed between the side of the box and the wall.

She paused for a few seconds, just to let her eyes get used to the dim light inside, then, bending slightly, she pushed behind the dark shroud of the smooth curtain.

There was a narrow seat fixed to the side of the booth and below that, raised only a few inches from the floor, an even narrower shelf for penitents to kneel on. She knelt down as she had always done before, but the hard wood hurt her knees so she got up again and slithered onto the little seat. It was cold and she shivered. She turned her shoulders towards the grill in the side of the confession box and, as if sensitive to her presence, it slid back.

She looked through the open grill and saw the white teeth of Father Thomas, it was as if no time at all had passed since she had last crouched trembling there.

He waited in silence. She felt sure that he recognised her even after all this time and a wave of embarrassment swept over her as she wondered where to start. She squirmed her bottom around on the narrow wooden seat, tightening the muscles of her buttocks and lifting the soft flesh inside her panties away from the cold wood. But it was no good, it only felt worse, so she eased the tension in her buttocks and felt the her panties press down against the smooth surface of the seat.

Maria's thick black hair was cut to shoulder length and lay tousled around her pale face. She had full lips, bright blue eyes with long lashes, and was slim and very attractive, although, as people sometimes told her, she looked too vulnerable and could have made more of herself.

She had a small delicate frame and was not very tall, but she had shapely hips which curved out from her narrow waist. She had firm thighs and her compact calves led down to slender ankles. Her feet were narrow and her carefully filed toenails were painted with the same bright red varnish as her fingernails.

She had to wear a black suit for work and her skirt was quite short. The cold wood of the seat was pressed against the bare flesh of her smoothly curved thighs as they peeped out between the flattering tops of her fine, sheer stockings and the plain edge of her white panties. She wriggled her bottom again and nervously pulled her skirt down as far as she could, but she could only get the hem halfway down her slender thighs. She wore a white shirt which was open at the neck and her jacket was buttoned up tightly around her slim waist. Her small, firm breasts were secured snugly in the cups of a flimsy, embroidered bra. A small sewn flower just poked from the open neck of her well-ironed shirt as it nuzzled snugly between the curves of her cleavage.

Now she was sure that he recognised her, but still she could say nothing...

She had not felt tongue-tied when she was a child; then there had been so many things she seemed to do wrong that she could hardly wait to pour them out. She would wait anxiously all week to do her confession on Friday. She would write down all her sins in a little notebook then read them out carefully, one by one, to the thoughtful, shadowy figure behind the fretwork panel.

'Oh Father, what must I do to put these things right?' she would beg as she sat forward eagerly on this same hard seat with her hands clasped tightly between her legs. 'I feel so dirty, so sinful, so horrible! What must I do? Oh Father, how can I be punished?'

Father Thomas would listen quietly, occasionally drawing his long fingers down his thin moustache and tugging at his pointed beard. Every now and again, when she looked through the grill, she would catch sight of his flashing white teeth and staring eyes and imagine that he was a wolf. Sometimes, she pretended that she was Red Riding Hood and that he was going to eat her and that she did not care if he did, as long as she could tell him how bad she was before he sank his pointed teeth into her neck. She tingled all over at the thought of that first bite and tingled more as she felt herself wanting to bleed for him and be sucked dry as he gnawed and slobbered at her throat.

Sometimes, as she leant forward to pour out her secrets, she thought she saw him staring at her budding breasts. It caused a dark terror to well up inside her and she trembled with fear. But it was not a fear that she wanted to run away from; it was a fear that seemed to delight and beguile her, it was a fear that she wanted more of and it forced her to lean even closer to the lattice-work grill.

In a way, she sincerely believed that she tried not to be sinful. But how could she confess if she did nothing wrong? The two things went hand-in-hand, she did not so much want to be sinful but she could not bear the idea of having nothing to confess. She wanted to be purified but she did not want to be pure, for if she was pure she would never be able to confess again. Her life was driven by this perverted desire to confess; driven by a need to be forgiven for being so sinful. Her badness was the means of acquiring purification, and as the act of purification was what she needed more than anything, she always needed to be bad.

Wrongdoing stalked her everywhere: by the time she was thirteen, her lists grew so long that sometimes, when she came out of the shadowy booth, she was sweating and exhausted.

Sometimes she felt a tingling deep in her stomach as she told Father Thomas every detail of her sinful behaviour. She would squeeze her hands tightly together and move them higher up her thighs, feigning to ease the delightful pain that the confession bestowed on her. He knew everything about her yet still she wanted him to know more. He knew all her sins and always forgave them, but still she wanted to be more sinful and suffer the pain of confession and forgiveness.

Then the problem got even worse.

One summer, there had been some men working on the road outside her convent school. There were three of them, all dark haired and swarthy. She saw them from a distance as she approached one warm morning. She was wearing her new white panties and a light cotton dress. Even before she got close to them she felt an excited fear prickling across her skin as she sensed their rough masculinity. Their torsos were naked in the warm sunny morning and they leant lazily on shiny steel shovels with hard-skinned hands. They flexed their glistening muscles and looked up eagerly as she approached; then they leered at her and instantly she felt a sting of shame and fear run through her ripening young body.

Their hole was right across the gates to her school. It was deep and contained a heavy iron railing against one of its sides; it looked like the entrance to a subterranean cavern. The three men stood around its rim, pushing each other and laughing as she approached nervously. There was no way around them; she hung her head, drew her brown leather school bag up onto her shoulder and scurried towards them, hoping to get past as quickly as possible. As she drew alongside them she could smell their sweat; it was sweet and sticky and hung heavily in the air like steam rising from overrun horses.

The one nearest her said something, she did not know what, or could not understand. Then, as the others chimed in, she gripped tightly to the leather strap of her satchel and ran past them shaking with fear. When she got inside the school gates she looked back at them and they laughed and jeered at her. They leant back on their shovel handles and as they stretched their bodies backwards she could see how their stomach muscles ribbed up hard and shiny with the tension of their laughter. She turned and ran inside, shaking and gasping for breath.

The next day it was the same, but this time she did not hang her head so low. As she came up alongside them the first one shouted something. Again she could not really make it out, only the word 'panties'. It frightened her as it had done the day before, but this time she also felt something that thrilled her. When she got inside the gates she turned and looked back at them and this time she noticed the way the material of their trousers mounded up at their crotches.

For the next few days, though she dreaded running the gauntlet of the workmen, she also found herself looking forward to it. One night she woke up sweating with her fingers probing high between her thighs and she lay awake for quite a while before she moved her hands outside the bedclothes. The next morning she felt so guilty she cried as she wrote down what had happened in the little notebook.

Every day they were causing her to be sinful and providing her with everything she needed. On the Thursday morning of that week, as she excitedly pulled up her satchel and ran towards the hole in the road, her heart sank when the men were not there. She stood at the rim of the gaping excavation and looked down into it.

There were two girls from the school down in the bottom of the hole with the men!

It was muddy around their feet and the girls' white ankle socks were spattered with dirt. Both of them were crying. They were being bent over in front of the three men with their bottoms up. One of them had her panties pulled down to just above her knees and Maria could plainly see the rosy darkness pressing out from between her young buttocks. One of the men was pulling down the panties of the other girl but they were tight across her bottom and were hard to get off. He had to pull at them roughly and the white, sewn edges cut into the girl's slender bottom.

The girl who was having her panties removed looked up in tearful appeal. Maria recognised her, she was in the fifth form. As the girl turned, the man swung back to her and ripped her panties down violently. She gasped as he pressed one of his hands on her back to force her to bend over even more, then spanked her hard across her rounded bottom. She let out a bleating cry. Maria saw the expression of pain on the girl's face before she was finally forced to turn away by the pressure of the man's hand on her back. There was another smack and an even louder scream and Maria turned and ran.

Her heart felt as though it was going to explode. She felt violated and frightened by what she saw, but even more frightened by what she thought. More than anything, more than fear, or wanting to run away, more than disgust or sympathy for the girls, she wanted to go back and clamber down into the muddy hole herself and have her panties ripped off by the men and be spanked and...

She flushed terribly, wild thoughts spinning uncontrollably through her head as she ran in panic for the sanctuary of the convent school, and when she arrived she dared say nothing.

At the end of the week it was all of this that she confessed. She poured out her wicked thoughts and wrongdoing as normal, but this time she admitted something she did not fully understand. This was no simple misdemeanour. This time she had enjoyed shaking with fear every time the workmen made rude gestures and offered to 'take her little white panties down and give her a good thrashing.' This time, she told him how she had kept her fingers high between her thighs as she lay awake in her bed thinking of the mounds in the men's trousers. This time, she trembled tearfully as she told him how she wanted to be one of the girls in the hole.

As she made her confession to Father Thomas she heard him sigh loudly. She knew he was angry with her and the realisation set off a tingling in her stomach and sent shivering thrills throughout her young body. She pleaded for forgiveness and punishment; she wanted to throw herself on the floor and beg for punishment. She wanted to stretch out before him and kiss his feet until he said she was saved. She felt so guilty and yet so satisfied; she felt so fulfilled with her sinfulness.

"Father," she had begged, "I'm so wicked, I walked past those horrid, smelly men and listened to the horrid things they said. I can't get to sleep at night because I think of them; their muscly stomachs and what it is beneath their trousers that makes them bulge out at the front. I can't stop thinking about what it would be like to be bent over in that muddy hole and have my panties torn down and my bottom spanked by those rough hands. What can you make me do to put things right? What has made me so bad?"

"What did they say again my child?"

"About taking my panties down?"

"Yes, what did they say exactly?"

"They said they would take my white panties down and give me a good spanking."

"Why? Why would they do that?"

"They - they said that I looked as if I would enjoy it."

"And would you?"

"I don't know Father. I don't know what is right any more. Father, perhaps they were right, perhaps I deserved a spanking. Perhaps I still do."

Father Thomas hesitated, then, stroking his beard to its thin point, spoke softly.

"You have been very wicked indeed. Your punishment should be severe this time, very severe, my child."

She shuddered with fear and clasped her school notebook tightly against the tops of her thighs. Suddenly, this was not a game and a sense of real fear spread through her.

"There is only one thing for it,' he continued.

Her hands started to shake and she pressed them down even harder against her thighs. What would it be? Would it be enough to save her?

"No prayer will make this better," he said, "you will have to be punished directly, here and now - by me."

She felt herself beginning to sweat with dread. The pages of her little notebook were sticking to the sweat that was covering the smooth skin of her young thighs. She waited, barely breathing.

"I will have to spank you my child. I must take your panties down and spank you now." He spoke slowly as he adjusted himself on his seat. "Come into my confession box and I will bend you over my knee."

Her head spun dizzily as a sweat broke out on her face and she felt herself flushing all over. This was what she wanted, she knew that, and yet she felt so fearful. She just did not know what to think. She was terrified! She took one frightened glance through the grill, caught a brief glimpse of Father Thomas's flashing teeth, then jumped up and ran out of the church crying and horrified.

When she got home she threw herself down on her bed and sobbed relentlessly. She stayed in her room for three days, weeping and saying prayers. And that had been the last time she had entered this place. That was six years ago...

Now, new feelings of guilt were spilling out and she needed someone to lap them up and guide her to repentance and salvation. It had been six years of an ever-growing need for forgiveness, six years of remorse for refusing her punishment from Father Thomas. There had not been a day that she had not felt guilty for running out of the confession booth all those years ago.

She glanced through the grill and saw the priest's thin fingers stroking his pointed beard and his eyes flashing as he raised his head. She turned away fearfully, shrunk back into the darkness and pushed herself hard against the cold stone wall of the church.

"Father, I need to confess," she said nervously, "I need to confess so much."

There was a pause. Maria anxiously looked through the grill again and saw Father Thomas' white teeth shining between his thin lips. He still reminded her of a wolf. For a second she imagined him slavering at her neck before sinking his teeth deeply into her throat. For a moment she was enthralled by the thought of him sucking her blood and drying her to a husk.

"Begin then, my child."

She turned away and stared down between her legs; her knees had fallen slightly open and she quickly drew them back together again. She pressed the palms of her hands against the tops of her smooth thighs as they stretched out from beneath the hem of her black skirt. She took a deep breath.

"Oh Father, I have been so wicked, I just don't know where to start."

"Start at the beginning," he said.

And now our serial, ERICA (expanded version), by Rex Saviour. This is Episode 9 but that need not stop its enjoyment by new readers. Rex is trying to cure Erica of her fear of being touched, beaten, snakes etc by densensitisation - that is, exposing the patient in gradually increasing doses to what she fears most. So far this is not working out too well!!
Now we open the part III, RADIO CONTROLLED...

PRELUDE

So, Great Lord, it is said that you enjoyed what I have written so far, and I am spared to continue with my story.

So be it, but I have to tell you that I find the conditions in which I am confined exceeding distasteful.

If I go onto my balcony I see a beautiful river and colourful trees, but I also see visitors to the Palace arriving in these diabolic trishaws harnessed to naked women, and I see road sweepers wearing nothing but straw hats and standard length smocks. These smocks barely pass the hips of the shorter women, and are obscene on the taller ones. No wonder these poor creatures are raped by any passer by. The surprise is that they return to their sweeping as if nothing had happened; I can only guess at what severe discipline they are under.

Very well. Your subject are Sahdists, you worship the Marquis, you believe that cruelty is a virtue, but it is all so one sided. Men are always the aggressors, it appears, and every woman I have seen is a victim. I have to live with that if I come here, which obviously I should never have done.

Especially I should not have brought my poor Erica here!

I must put up with what I see outside, I suppose, but I really must protest about the living wall. How can I sleep in a room that is decorated with living women in such suffering? True, there is little sound, for your gags are very effective, but I cannot shut my eyes to these writhing bodies that seem to be built into the wall, some facing in, some facing out, some tense with dread, some in present torment. Such beautifully supple bodies! Such quivering breasts and bottoms! How do you keep their flesh in that state of constant motion when they are so tightly bound? I can only assume that the wires I see penetrating sensitive places periodically become hot enough to cause considerable agony.

So, as I continue with Erica's story in order to save her from some similar fate, I curse you, Mighty Lord, with all my heart.

Your Kingdom of Balikpan is an abomination, and you fit well upon its throne.

3-1

At twenty-two, Erica was a pleasure to own, even when one has toothache, as I did that day. Looking back, that should have made her specially careful not to rub me up the wrong way.

It is ironic that the concept of radio control arose from a trivial act of rare defiance on a bad day, because after I devised and fitted her with my greatest triumph, the remote-control dildo which she called the stinging snake, any further question of defiance became totally unthinkable.

It all started when she came reluctantly downstairs, blushing, pretty as a picture, dressed exactly as I had ordered.

"Turn round," I said. "Let me look at you."

Shy though she is, I have taught her to show her clothes like a mannequin. She blushed again as she turned, posing as if she was on a catwalk. One thing was most incorrect - she was holding down the back of the dress. However, I decided not to complain about that as it was perhaps rather short for decency. One likes to be fair.

"Excellent," I said. "I thought we'd pop out for a lunchtime drink at the Fox."

I could see by the way she still fussed with the hem of the dress that she was uneasy about that.

"Don't worry, dear," I said. "You look fine."

"But Uncle Rex - is this really the dress you meant?"

"What's wrong with it?" I asked.

"I haven't worn it for years and years!"

That didn't prevent it looking good on her. I specially liked the way her neat little breasts threatened to peep out at any moment. As I have said, it was very brief, but she had the figure for that, trim waist and long bare olive-brown legs that invited a fondle.

"You look fine," I repeated. "I thought we'd have a pub lunch there. I really like their jumbo sausages. And isn't it the day they have a little band?"

"Yes, Uncle Rex."

She didn't sound too enthusiastic about that.

"Cheer up - I know I don't dance very well, but lots of men there are quite keen, aren't they?"

"Well - it would be nice to try somewhere else -"

"Not meet our friends? Don't be silly!"

She could see that I would get impatient soon, but still she pressed her luck, down on her knees now, clasping me round the waist, rubbing her cheek against my crotch and looking up pleadingly. Her fingers caressed me timidly and her big blue eyes seemed more full of fright than usual that morning. I am not her uncle of course, I am her step-father. But she called me uncle before I paid her mother to marry me and then get out of our lives, and I allowed her to continue to do so.

"Oh please, not there!" She was getting quite distressed. "Specially not when there's dancing!"

"But I arranged to meet Tom. You like Tom don't you?"

She shuddered.

"He seems to like you."

"Oh God! Mayn't I at least have some knickers then?"

"Aren't you wearing any?"

She stood up and raised the hem of the dress reluctantly, then, not daring to lower it without permission, stood before me and fidgeted about whilst I lit a cigar. I was pleased to see that she had shaved herself that morning. She has this beautiful red-gold hair which was never too obtrusive over the sex, but I still prefer her bare, and what I prefer is what I get.

"I shall have to punish you tonight for the blasphemy."

"Yes, Uncle Rex."

"And you ought to be ashamed of yourself, intending to go out like that! Go and put your knickers on immediately."

"But I don't have any."

"Don't you dare lie to me!"

"But - but -"

"You have a perfectly good pair."

I had burned some underwear the day before, when I had become angry at her shyness. She must think I had burned it all.

"N-no."

"Oh yes. Go and look properly."

Two minutes later she was back, a pair of black knickers in her hands, embroidered in gold.

"I c-can't wear these, Uncle, not with s-s-snakes on them!"

It was a battle we had had before. She just would not wear snake-embroidered underwear, however much I beat her: her fear and loathing of snakes is too strong.

According to systematic desensitization I should have forced her to wear them. However, somewhat against my better judgement, I decided not to press the matter at that moment.

"I suppose I'll have to take you out as you are, then," I said, "but it's pretty shameful for me. Is that the way to accompany me when I take you out for a drink?"

"No Uncle, no!" She knelt again, clasping me even tighter and looking up imploringly, tears in those pleading eyes of hers. "Couldn't we go to a shop on the way? Oh please? The men at that pub - they might put their hands up my dress."

"WHAT!"

She put a finger to her lips, a gesture of hers when she wishes she hadn't said something. "The - the men there - they might put their hands up my dress!"

"Might they indeed?"

"Well, yes."

"Why would they do that?"

"I - they're nasty -"

"Have you been shameless in there?"

"No! God no! I hate them doing it, I hate it, I hate it!"

"Are you quite sure you don't encourage them?"

"Oh God, no!"

"Kindly do not blaspheme!" She never seemed to control her tongue. Although blasphemy was something she had had innumerable beatings for, she was no better than when I first got her.

"Sorry Uncle, I forgot."

Perhaps the blasphemy was intentional this time, to divert me. "It is not a thing to forget!" I said, as I made a note in my little lack book and she watched me apprehensively. "But to come back to these men at the pub. You say you let them put their hands up your dress?"

She looked up and saw that I was getting cross about her forwardness. She licked her lips and her fingers returned to my flies: I could feel them trembling. "Well - if there's a crowd and I have to fetch your drinks - or if one of them dances with me -"

She gasped as I yanked her suddenly to her feet by the handle in her hair - it was one of those days when it was formed by two pigtails tied together.

"DO THEY?"

"Yes well one - some -"

"SOME?"

"Most of them - sometimes they do p-put their hands up my dress, yes."

"And you let them feel you? With no knickers on?"

"I - well - if you don't allow me any -"

She had a point there. I don't usually allow her any. It was a point I chose to ignore, however.

"I've told you not to lead men on like that!" I said. "Do they try to put their fingers in you?" She didn't answer but I

203

saw guilt in her eyes. "This is disgraceful! At a pub of all places, where I have friends! Disgraceful!"

She was down on her knees again, sobbing openly now.

"Well, since you don't like that dress, you may take it off."

She took off her dress and handed it to me, then rebuckled the belt at her waist and stood to attention. She looked gorgeous just in the belt and those smooth sheer black stockings and extra-high heels.

She was trembling, but she made no effort to cover herself with her hands as she had used to do. And she kept her eyes open and on me, and parted her lips. A distinct improvement. Perhaps desensitization was beginning to work, at least against shyness.

"Well?" I said, smoothing the stockings up over her curvy thighs. "What happens when you displease me?"

Speechlessly she stood up and unbuckled the broad black leather belt she is obliged to wear at all times. She kissed it from end to end in the little ceremony we have devised, then handed it to me and bent over the sofa arm as usual, spread her legs, went up on tiptoe, and covered her eyes with her hands. I let my fingers stray a little before the prayer.

"Oh Lord have mercy upon this Jezebel and strengthen the arm of your humble servant that he may chastise her to good effect, Amen."

"Amen," she replied, in that little-girl voice she uses when she is punished, "and may the punishment I am about to receive do me good."

I inserted her ear-plugs, then, when I had lighted my cigar, brought the heavy belt down with a thwack on the chair seat, close beside but not touching her. I did that a couple of times. She can sense the blows alright, she jumped a mile each time, and, as usual, her bottom started twitching and she began to whimper.

I went up to our room and looked through her wardrobe.

I found a button-up jersey and a skirt that was even briefer than the dress she was complaining about.

I went back downstairs and pinched her quivering bottom a couple of times, enjoying the way her whimpering increased, then gave her a single slap and removed the earplugs.

"Get up. I've decided not to punish you."

She jumped up and flung her arms round me, kissing with passion, tongue tip busy. "Oh thank you Uncle Rex, thank you, thank you!"

"Until I can think of something special," I added.

"Oh!"

"Perhaps this evening. You may ask me then."

"Yes, Uncle."

I tossed her the jersey, then the belt. She looked good, parading up and down for me with them on, for the jersey was both thin and tight, specially with all the buttons down the front done up.

Then I tossed her the skirt.

"Better?"

"Well -" She walked up and down to show me how brief it was, but did not say anything.

"BETTER?"

"Oh - yes, Uncle Rex!" Untrue, but she knew it was the right thing to say. She will go to great lengths just to postpone a beating for a few minutes, never mind several hours, always hoping I may forget or something will crop up to get her out of it. "It's lovely, Uncle Rex."

"But you say men at the pub touch you up?"

"Well - they might -"

"You think they'll do it in that skirt?"

She was in a quandary now, not knowing what to say. "I think they might, yes!" is what she came out with at last. She was blushing very prettily

"Can't have that, can we? It isn't nice, is it?"

BONUS PAGES

"N-no." She spoke hesitantly now, her eyes wide open as she looked at the two wrist straps I produced, something I had never used before.

"These are to help you keep your skirt down," I said. She held out her arms as I strapped the buckles on her wrists like watches, except each had a bulldog clip instead of a watch. "Now, stand at attention again." When her arms were well braced back I fastened the clips to the hem of the skirt.

"There. That should stop them!"

"Well -"

"Grateful?"

"Oh! Oh, yes, Uncle Rex!"

"Show me, then!"

She came and gave me a long kiss. She had to stand on tiptoe to reach my lips, but she kept her hands to her sides.

"Now a hug," I said.

When she put her arms round me the skirt was pulled nicely up at the back. She must have felt the draught! And when I massaged her bare bottom with the fingers of one hand, it quivered in anticipation of the pinch and her lips became more eager on mine, her tongue more frantic. I gave her a friendly nip or two and the frightened kisses they produced were more delicious than was proper. Although she was bonded legally to me as my absolute property for another few months, my conscience kicked. I had to accept that my lust would be aroused as the desensitization progressed: it was a sacrifice, but one I must make if I was to cure her, and that of course was a sacred as well as a legal trust.

Stephen, the landlord of the Fox, was the focus of a group of people interested in such matters as bondage, corporal punishment and domination. People came from a widening area as the word had spread. It was not a club as such, just that his friends naturally tended to drink in one particular bar and some of them dressed pretty outrageously, or brought peculiar partners, or behaved in a rather unrestrained fashion. The ambience of the place was an attraction to voyeurs also and ensured that his pub and this bar in particular was always crowded: those who did not appreciate the freedom of expression soon stopped coming, but on balance he was more than thriving.

He sometimes said he ought to rename the Fox. He wanted to call it the Sir Stephen, after The Story of O, but he hadn't got round to it yet, although some of the decoration was rather daring.

Stephen was always pleased to see Erica and I. I think business had improved even further since we started coming.

There was a hush and all eyes turned on her as we entered: she declined a drink, and it was amusing to see how carefully she kept her hands to her sides as she stood demurely beside my table, upright as a ramrod and lips parted as I required.

She was blushing, and did not respond to any of our friends, though several waved and called out, or even whistled.

"There's John," I said. The big man was perusing some papers at the bar. John is an unlikely solicitor, but he is a good one and quite a Godly man. He came frequently to my country estate to check on the desensitization treatment, because I was legally as well as morally obliged to treat Erica during the three year period during which she was my property: a period now coming close to its end, as Erica was almost twenty-two.

"Why don't you go ask John over?"

"He - he seems busy, Uncle Rex?"

"No harm in asking."

That was as near to a command as was necessary these days. She walked over rather stiffly, her arms carefully held straight down at her sides, and got his attention at last. He followed her over to me and put his papers on the table, then turned to her.

"What, no kiss for your Uncle John?"

The way she still kept her arms down whilst having to lean against him and stretch up on tiptoe to reach his lips was very erotic, and he obviously appreciated it.

"Give us a hug, then."

Ever so reluctantly she raised her arms, and catcalls and laughter broke out all over the pub. He took his time over that hug. He always appreciates being the centre of attention.

"Go get us another round, dear," I said.

She walked over to the tight-packed bar, hands at her sides, clutching the five-pound note. Her progress back with a drink in either hand was tumultuous. It took her several minutes to negotiate the close-set tables between the bar and us.

She was blushing a lot, too. I think she may be ashamed of being depilated, but I keep her so because I think she looks better like that. One or two people were certainly appreciating the smoothness of her sex to the touch, and I was proud of her.

I always encourage her to dance at the Fox, and when the music started it was amazing how many men queued up to partner her after John. Judging by her squeals and blushes, and if desensitization works as well as my books say it should, she will soon be totally cured of her deep shyness. And yet, when I sent her for another round of drinks, she seemed, if anything, rather more reluctant than before.

She had only just taken up her position behind my chair, more than somewhat flustered and short of a few buttons on the tight jersey, when Stephen strolled over.

"How about some photography?" he asked, absentmindedly turning up Erica's skirt and patting her on the bottom.

"A few of the punters have been asking."

"Sure," I said. "Why not? She'll be happy to oblige."

"What? What, Uncle? I didn't know -"

"You know now," I said. "Up on the bar with you and pose for pictures."

Her shyness made her an excellent model for expressions as she walked up and down on the bar, hands stiffly to her sides, and there were many flashes going off.

"Will she take the skirt off?" came a loud voice.

"Won't make much difference," came another.

"Volunteers to do it," said Stephen. "If Rex doesn't mind?"

"Not at all," I said. "Feel free."

There was a rush to climb onto the bar, and eventually a dark slim man with a moustache won by pushing everyone else back. Quite a tough customer. He was waving a bottle in his hand, and well lubricated from it all already by the looks of him as he wobbled towards her, his free hand out-stretched.

I could see Erica wondering whether to jump down amongst us, but when she looked at all the close packed and eager faces all round her she very sensibly decided she was safer up there.

"Hands up!" he said, and everyone clapped as the cords to the clips on her wrists raised the hem of the skirt to chin level before he undid the clips and threw the skirt to me in triumph.

"Dance!" called out several men, and he took her in his arms and started a clumsy waltz up and down the length of the bar. It was hilarious!

"Will she suck me off?" he called out.

"She'll do anything," I said proudly, knowing it was all part of her cure. "Anything!"

He seized her by the hair and forced her down on her knees, and she started to unzip his trousers... another man forced his way up onto the bar and held her arms behind her

209

as he forced her mouth onto the dark man's penis. Then, as soon as the first man was satisfied, he laid Erica on her back and raped her there and then, to the immense gratification of the other punters.

"Somebody whip her," came a shout.

"Yes, yes, the whip, the whip," came a chorus.

"Rex!" they shouted. "Rex! Rex! Rex! Show us who's master!"

So then I gave her the command to bend over, and when she was clasping her wide apart ankles and looking at the crowd through her legs, I gave her a good beating.

When I stopped for breath and looked at my watch, it was later than I thought.

"Sorry Stephen," I said, "I'm due at the dentist."

"Well, leave Erica with me," he said. "I'll let her clear a few tables."

3-2

When I returned for Erica it took a little time to extricate her from a noisy corner where she seemed to be spending more time than was justified. She seemed a bit upset, so I decided to take her for a walk in the park to cheer her up.

It was a beautiful afternoon, and lots of people were strolling around amongst the fine old trees and beside the lake. The swans were out in force, but they all had an eye for Erica, which didn't seem to cheer her up.

After all that horsing around in the pub there were very few buttons left on her jersey. She had worn it all the time - it might have been wiser to take it off. Anyway, when we saw the HQ of the model aeroplane club in the distance we strolled over in that direction, thinking there might be a kiosk of some sort, maybe selling T-shirts, but there wasn't.

However, we stopped to watch for a while. There was an open space where several model aeroplanes were flying noisily around and I was quite fascinated by the way they were controlled, little hydraulic valves pulling and pushing wires to change the engine speed and the various flaps that dictate height and direction, all this at the decision of a person with a small radio transmitter hundreds of yards away.

"I know a good game," I said. "Pretend to be an aeroplane." I am always thinking of new amusements for her, and it was her wrists being attached to the skirt (now that she was wearing it again!) that gave me the idea: she had only to raise her arms to simulate wings.

Although I found her a fairly deserted spot back amongst the trees, she was reluctant at first to raise her arms high enough for a really good effect, but when she saw I was running out of patience she did better. We had several fly pasts, improving every time. When she began making engine noises as well, one or two of the flying club members started to clap, though I think they were too far away to appreciate the real situation as she flashed through the trees.

One, a little ginger weasel of a fellow, evidently did see enough to be interested. He brought his plane over, for a better look I think. When he arrived he was more than surprised. He licked his lips and leered at Erica, and lust was written all over his face as he showed her his plane. A most unpleasant fellow, but such can prove useful.

"Interested in flying, are you?"

"Well - I suppose - yes," she said shyly. "I think they are very interesting."

She didn't dare lower her arms without my consent, and she was blushing prettily.

The weaselly man was obviously intrigued, also very uneasy, but he said nothing.

"How difficult is it to build a plane like yours?" I asked.

"Not too hard, not too hard at all. I made this one myself.

Maybe -"

He hesitated, looking at Erica.

"My step daughter," I said. "Put your wings down, Erica dear, let's have a little decency."

"Yes, Uncle."

"She calls me Uncle because it's simpler," I explained. "Erica, this is -"

"Tom," he said. "Hullo there. You like aeroplanes, do you?"

She nodded shyly.

"Maybe you'd like to BE one!" I said. "Remotely controlled, like Tom's?"

"Well -" I stared at her pointedly and raised my eyebrows. "Why yes, Uncle Rex," she said hastily, "oh yes, that would be lovely."

"Is it possible, Tom?" I asked.

"Well, we could send signals, certainly." He seemed embarrassed. "But would it be fun for her?"

"She'd enjoy playing aeroplanes more if she could do it better, wouldn't you, Erica dear?"

"Well - yes, Uncle Rex, yes of course I would."

"More realism, that's what we need, isn't it?"

"Well - yes -"

"We do!" I said firmly. "Why don't you show us what you can do now, try a few acrobatics if you like. Tom and I will sit here while you zoom round a bit!"

Tom's weasel eyes were gloating as they followed her slender figure running like a nymph among the trees, her hair streaming out behind her, glinting redder than usual in the patches of sunlight.

"I say, is this alright? She seems rather, well, strange?"

"Oh yes, no problem," I said. "She's got some hang-ups and we're trying to sort them out by systematic desensitization, that's increasing exposure to what the subject suffers from. Shyness, for example - that's what we're trying to cure at the moment."

"Oh, I see! Glad to help then!" He stood up, lechery written all over his face, and shouted to Erica. "Louder! Zroom, Zroom, good, good!" He held out his arms: "Return to base!"

She hesitated, then, at a gesture from me, ran into his arms and gave him a kiss.

"Wow!" he said. He licked his lips. "You enjoyed that, didn't you Erica, but there's lots more you could do to make it more realistic. You don't bank properly, you'd have crashed I'm afraid - we could radio signals to you, steer you round trees, that sort of thing."

"How will you steer me by radio, Uncle Tom?"

"There are several ways. You'll have to wear a belt with an aerial and valves we can activate. They could pull strings attached to your ears, perhaps?"

"Or nipples?" I suggested casually.

"What - well, I hadn't thought ... well, yes, I suppose ..."

I nudged Erica and she chipped in: "That sounds lovely, Uncle Tom. My nipples are pierced already so I could put the rings in them for you."

He gulped - I could see he was a bit shaken, but also extremely well pleased.

"Perhaps we could fly her at your meetings?" I said.

Pleasure turned to embarrassment. "Well, you know, I don't really think so -"

"We could do it on my estate," I said. "Why not come home with us now, a cup of tea and a chat? You'd like Tom to come back with us, wouldn't you Erica?"

He put his arm round her and she concealed her dislike as well as she could - she has been well disciplined in this, a stern look from me and she snuggled up to him.

"Yes, do come, Uncle Tom."

I let Erica go in his car to show him the way. I left the outer gates unlocked, the electricity switched off. I didn't want him to think we lived in a fortress.

213

I took a couple of chairs onto the lawn. "Sit here, Tom. We'll have a chat about this. Erica, fetch us a table, there's a good girl."

There was a large patch of damp on Tom's trousers already, and when Erica staggered out carrying a small table it didn't help his control one little bit. Her wrists were still clipped to the hem of her skirt, of course. I knew he was going to be useful to us so I made her carry the table a bit beyond us to give him another thrill, and he positively drooled over it. What a despicable little man he was.

"Tea?" I asked. "Erica will be maid, won't you my dear?"

"Yes Uncle Rex."

"Phew!" Tom said, turning to watch as she walked off. "Wow!" He was mopping his forehead with a disgusting pink handkerchief.

"Don't stay if you're bothered."

"No, no, it's just I never met a girl like her before. If this doesn't cure her of shyness, nothing will! Yes, well, now, about wings for her."

A few minutes later he broke off as Erica came back with the tray. She put it on the table and poured, as I had taught her, then stood beside us, waiting further orders, and I regret to say that Tom had himself quite a grope under the guise of friendliness, or maybe helping to cure shyness.

To cut a long story short, he agreed to make an apparatus so we could steer Erica by radio - he looked forward to bringing it in a few days, he said. I was sure he did. He was a very nasty little man indeed, but was to prove even more useful than I had suspected.

As bedtime approached that evening, Erica became more and more edgy. It was her duty to remind me of punishment that had been promised, but she could seldom bring herself to do so.

She did not eat much. She dare not unclip her wrists herself and could not very well ask me without reminding me about the punishment.

Eventually I took pity on her. "Bedtime," I said.

We have a routine about this. We sleep together now, of course, but she goes first, puts on her night clothes, then comes back down for a good-night kiss.

So, a few minutes later, she came down in her night smock - a filmy little thing, waist-length, that I find really attractive. The wrist-bands were still on her wrists, but the clips clipped nothing, perhaps because the smock was not long enough.

She came to me apprehensively and dropped to her knees, her fingers at my flies. Soon I felt her lips and tongue, trying to make me forget or forgive. An old ploy that seldom works, though she still tries it on if she is desperate. After a while she broke off long enough to look up.

"Good-night, Uncle Rex."

"Haven't you forgotten something?"

She raised her wrists with the cuffs on. "Well - I didn't like to take these off -"

"You've unclipped them, though."

"Yes, Uncle Rex, or I couldn't get ready for bed."

"You thought I'd forget why you had them on!"

"Oh!"

"Didn't you?"

"Oh - well -"

"There is the little matter we were discussing before - leading men on to put their hands up your skirt."

"Oh God!"

"A very serious matter."

"Yes." Just a whisper now.

"Too serious to deal with tonight. I have to think of a suitable punishment. Perhaps we'll leave it till tomorrow. What do you think?"

"Yes Uncle, I think you are rather tired tonight." How

215

transparent she was, that look of hope and tentative relief. A punishment tomorrow is never the same as one right now!

"Yes," I agreed, "I am rather tired ... Where is the belt?"

"By the bed, Uncle, but truly tomorrow will be alright."

"GO GET IT!"

She scurried off and was back with the belt in a trice. She did the usual bit about kissing it before handing it to me, then lying over the sofa seat.

"The punishment for leading men on will be tomorrow and it will have to be something special."

"Yes, I know."

"Yes, extra special, I have to think about it ... in the meanwhile..." I brought the belt down hard on the leather beside her. "In the meanwhile, you have blasphemed three times since you were last punished for it."

I cracked the belt down again and she started to whimper.

"Also, you left the belt upstairs when you know very well you should have been wearing it. A good old fashioned thrashing is what is needed now."

"Oh God!"

Her legs dangled over the leather arm of the sofa, her head and breasts were on the sofa itself, her hands clutched the smock, pulling it up her back, totally unnecessary as it would never have covered her quivering bottom anyway.

"Stick your bottom up."

She tried to hold it higher.

I cracked the belt down on naked flesh and she bit the cushion on the sofa. Her bottom wriggled but no sound.

I went round to the other side. Same again. Much more wriggling and her legs kicked up, but still no sound.

I repeated the dose several times, each blow harder than the one before, and I had started off pretty hard, but still she made no sound, although she was writhing about a good deal. She had far more control than the first time I belted her, far more.

I left her for a while whilst I had my bath. When I came back she had not moved, except that her bottom was still twitching a little. Wrapped in a towel, I sat down beside her and lit a cigar.

"We'll continue soon," I said.

I took no notice as her head inched towards me. Soon her teeth pulled aside the towel and her face was in my lap, her tongue licking my balls, licking with a lot of urgency...

I picked up the belt and ran it through my fingers, and saw her shudder.

Her mouth and tongue worked with even greater urgency, and now she presumed to slip off the arm of the sofa and insinuate her supple cringing body between my knees. Her fingers joined in the action...

She wouldn't get round me that way, of course, she hardly ever did, but it seemed that it was going to be an interesting night...

3-3

Next morning I woke to find Erica between my legs, using tongue and lips, as sometimes happens when she wishes to please me for some particular reason.

"After coffee this morning," I said, as she lay quietly in my arms a little while later, trembling nicely, "you may fetch me the belt and we will consider this special punishment, since you seem to want to get it over with."

She snuggled up to me. "Oh - no Uncle, I didn't want to trouble you, later would do."

I dozed off again, and after that she was very quiet, brooding no doubt on what was meant by special. By the time I was ready for my morning coffee she had put on her rather fetching little bare-bottom maid outfit. Unfortunately, though, her hands were shaking so much that coffee had spilled into the saucer: I said nothing about that, but she did catch a disapproving look that boded ill for here future.

As soon as coffee was served, she offered the belt and placed it beside me, then bent over the arm of the sofa, covering her eyes with her hands as usual if there was no skirt to raise. When I had finished my coffee I pulled her legs a little further apart and examined her bottom. Thanks to the cream it had fully recovered from the thrashing of last night.

I pushed the ear-plugs firmly into place, then positioned the little electric fan to blow on her bottom, as I sometimes do before a particularly severe beating. She couldn't help wriggling a little when I switched it on, and when I left her there to go to the pub she was whimpering as well.

As soon as I had a glass of wine in my hand and had ordered my pub lunch I spoke to Stephen, that most kinky of landlords.

"Mornin'," he said. "No Erica this mornin'?"

"She's fine," I said. "I just wanted a word with you about bringing her tonight."

"Sounds special?"

"It could be, if it's OK with you. You know all about the desensitization I'm using on her?"

"Oh sure, and so do some of the others. We understand very well, we're with you all the way, you know that."

"Yes, well, I've something special if those in the know could stay after hours tonight."

"Really worth it, is it?"

"I think it could be, yes."

"But not for the general public, eh?" He winked at me. "Good-oh! I'll phone around a bit, tip off a few of the reliables to come tonight and stay behind."

218

When I got back I took out Erica's ear-plugs.

She jumped a mile when I first touched her, then tensed. "Still thinking about your extra-special punishment?" I cracked the belt down beside her, and as usual she squealed as if I'd hit her. "Stay over the sofa like that. I expect I'll have a good idea quite soon, and you'll be ready."

Every time I came near her that afternoon to tell her I was still thinking I saw her buttocks clench, until at last I told her to get up as punishment was postponed for the moment.

Erica was very quiet as she stood in front of me. She was wearing a jersey only, her hands above her head as she waited for me to choose the rest of her outfit for the evening.

"We have to stop men from putting their hands up your skirt and having a feel. It's disgusting."

"I know, Uncle Rex."

"I haven't decided on your punishment for leading them on and letting them do that. It's difficult. The punishment has to fit the crime, doesn't it?"

"I suppose so."

"I'll think of something in the end. Until then, a long skirt, I think. If you'd like to go out tonight, that is?"

"Oh yes, in a long skirt, that would be nice!"

"And knickers of course."

"Oh but - I only have - oh God oh God -"

"You need them at the Fox, you see."

"Not the Fox again! Not so soon! Oh no!"

"Go and fetch the knickers, dear. I can't possibly take you there without knickers after what happened there yesterday. It was quite disgraceful."

"Oh but please -"

"It wouldn't be proper."

"Oh God! Is wearing the snake knickers to be my punishment?"

"Certainly not. They're just to keep you safe from prying hands. I haven't thought of the punishment yet."

"You could beat me really really really hard and I promise not to make a noise, but not the snake knickers, please not those, I can't wear them, I just can't!"

"GO GET THEM!"

She went upstairs very slowly and at long last came back with the snake knickers which had been a cause of controversy between us for so long, but still she just would not put them on. I had to take her into the punishment room and tie her hands to the frame, then drag the knickers up her legs against frantic writhing and kicking, not to mention screaming. It really was most unedifying.

As soon as I released her she started to tear the knickers off, so I had to tie her hands behind her back.

"Stop wriggling like that and nobody will notice your hands are tied."

"Oh God, I can't keep still in these."

"You'd better damn well try, my girl."

I put a long skirt on her, one that came to her ankles, and we were ready, decency personified. Even so she wriggled all the time and was reluctant to get into the Rolls and even more so to get out, and at the entrance to the pub I had to take her arm and walk her in.

The level of attention was noticeably higher than usual as we joined John and his friends, ardent drinkers all. John fetched me a beer and Erica stood beside us.

"Is she wriggling a bit?" asked John. "Or is it my imagination?"

"She has knickers on. She isn't used to that."

"She can't be. She's squirming a lot."

"Sorry," I said. "Do stop it, Erica dear. It's upsetting John."

"I - I need to go to the ladies."

"Don't be silly. You went just before we came out."

"I really would like to go."

"Well, you really can't. Try standing still."

John and I usually had her stand by us rather than sit.

A couple of hours later the doors were locked and there were less than a dozen left in the cosy little bar, men who were in the know and would cause no problems.

I banged on the table and comparative silence descended.

"Erica tells me that some men here have been putting their hands up her skirt," I said. That produced quite a few grins, but they entered into the spirit of the game and there a few muttered such things as 'disgraceful' and 'can't have that'.

"So we've come to put a stop to it. Erica will identify the culprit, for he is pretty sure to be amongst those present. Get up on the table, dear, so you can see us all."

The table was quite low. I helped her onto it, leaving her standing there in her long skirt, still wriggling a little, her hands tied behind her back.

"Now," I said. "Which one of these men has been putting his hand up your skirt?"

"I - I don't know -"

"Well then," I said, "they had better all have a feel, and you can see if you recognises anyone's touch."

"Oh God no!"

"Stand back," I said. "Let's form an orderly queue. Come down amongst us, Erica." I lifted her down and blindfolded her, and tucked the dress up. "Now," I said, "we'll soon get to the bottom of this. I want you to tell me when someone who touches you has done it before, and who it is."

I spun her round and pushed her into the nearest arms. She didn't guess right until the last, when it was John and he had the longest feel, and was easy because of his bulk. She was crying really hard by then.

I put her up on the table again, let down the skirt and took off the blindfold, then untied her hands.

221

"You must have been allowing more than one man to feel you," I said. "Otherwise you'd have been able to identify him."

For a little while she stood there crying and squirming, rubbing her wrists, then she pulled up her skirt and tore the snake knickers off, flung them from her defiantly.

"Well!" I exclaimed. "It's as I feared, it's all her fault for being deliberately provocative."

"No, no, oh no!"

"Is that provocative or is it not?" I asked, and the replies were unanimous. It was obvious that taking her knickers off in front of all of us was extremely provocative.

"Should she be punished?"

"Yes!" came shouts on all sides.

"Suppose we sit in a circle," I said. "She can lie in our laps and wriggle round whilst we smack her. Maybe that'll teach her not to be so provocative next time I bring her for a drink."

"Great idea!" said Stephen. "First, drinks on the house!"

"Suppose she wants to suck us off as she comes by?" someone asked. "So we don't smack so hard, like?"

"Suppose she wriggles backwards," another added. "Then we can put more into smacking her because it's to speed her up coming to us!"

"Right!" I said. "Good idea. What do you think, Erica dear, forwards or backwards?"

"Oh God oh God oh God!"

"Backwards then," I said. "Let yourselves go, we have to teach her not to blaspheme while we're at it."

"Is pinching allowed?" someone asked. "And tickling?"

"Sure, anything goes ... she can keep her skirt on but I think it will be best if I tie her hands behind her back, then they won't get in the way, make her use her mouth only."

She was up to her old habit of whimpering long before I put her hands behind her back and tied them there and lifted

222

her down and laid her face down on John's lap. It turned out that she straddled three people in the circle, her mouth in one man's lap whilst the next supported her body and the third did the spanking. As she was never allowed to wriggle backwards to her next customer until the first shot his load, the whole process made for good punishment and took quite a while.

When all were satisfied two of them had to hold her still whilst I put her knickers on again to take her home. In spite of all our efforts it was clear that the punishment had not really worked, as her hands had to be secured to stop her pulling the knickers off and she immediately started to wriggle and protest just as much as before.

"Looks like same again next week, then" I said, "if that's OK with you lot?"

Apparently it was.

Now A VICTORIAN SCRAPBOOK - Vignettes from a sterner age, by Stephen Rawlings, author of 'Jane and Her Master'. 6th extract, A MISCELLANY.

1 AN IMPORTANT ADVANCE IN MEDICINE, AND THE MANAGEMENT OF WOMEN'S DISORDERS From the Morning Courier.

[Readers who normally allow their female dependents to read all or part of the this newspaper may, at this point, wish to shield them from the details on the grounds of delicacy but, so important is it to their health, both mental and physical, we earnestly urge them to at least impart the gist of the contents to those who would most benefit from them.]

At a meeting of the London Gynaecological Society last night one of its founders, and most experienced practitioners, Dr Isaac Baker-Brown, delivered a lecture of the first importance.

Woman is so ruled by her body, Dr Brown tells us, that her brain, being smaller and weaker than man's, will often collapse under the strain, resulting in the manifold ailments of the mind that so afflict the fair sex. Moreover, he has discovered, nearly all such cases can be traced back to un-natural vice.

[We will spell out here, once and once only, the exact nature of the evil. The learned Doctor refers to female mas-turbation. Once again we caution our readers against allow-ing this article to fall into the hands of their womenfolk, without, at least, preparing them for the contents. So that there can be no ambiguity, we will go further, and define it as the stimulation, manual or by means of an instrument, of the pubic nerve, or clitoris, until passion over-spills in spasm or paroxysm]

Masturbation, Dr Brown makes clear, leads to lassitude, hysteria, inflammation of the spine, mania and, eventually but inevitably, death. There is only one certain cure for this condition, once the habit has been formed, and that is the surgical removal of the organ responsible, the enlarged end-ing of the pubic nerve, sometimes known as the clitoris. He recommends a radical incision with the scalpel, on either side of the clitoral ridge, followed by cauterisation with a hot iron, to stem any flow, since the area is well supplied with blood vessels. Since the procedure is comparatively quick, it is best not to risk the newly introduced methods of anaethesia. In any case, this operation has been made neces-sary by the woman's own unacceptable behaviour, and any suffering she endures may be thought of as part of her pen-ance.

Total success may be anticipated, the lecturer not being aware of any woman who did not become submissive and tractable after such treatment. The cases of several women, whose instability of mind was demonstrated by their wish to take advantage of the recent relaxation of the laws governing divorce, were advanced as proof of this assertion. After the surgery they all returned to their husbands and no longer spoke of such nonsense.

In a further reference to the connection between a female's mind and her bodily functions, it was stated that, at the menopause, many women are stricken by unnatural cravings for sexual attention. All husbands of such women were earnestly recommended to deny them such stimulation, which can otherwise be expected to result in the same grave consequences as unnatural vice in the younger female. In really severe cases, he recommended, the same surgical solution should be employed.

Other eminent medical men have also commented on this domination of the female mind by her bodily functions, including the deleterious effects of menstruation. Mothers are earnestly advised to take precautions to delay the onset of this dangerous phenomenum, with its mood changes often bordering on madness, by keeping their daughters in the nursery, restricting diet and exercise and, especially, forbidding the reading of 'novels' which so inflame the female brain.

2 THE PRINCESS AND THE GUARDSMAN

There is a strange story that one of Victoria's married daughters had an affair with her Art Tutor and that the Queen's medical adviser recommended she should have her clitoris removed to calm her blood. The story goes on to say that the Queen could not bring herself to have her daughter treated so, having already seen the suffering caused to another, who had the same treatment, and advised the lady's husband to have her whipped and made pregnant. Since the husband was homosexual, he entrusted both tasks to one of his guardsmen.

Louise has been suggested as a likely candidate as the offender of this story, but, although some of the facts support the idea, others seem to rule it out.

For instance, she undoubtedly caused her mother much anxiety, and rather urgent efforts were made to find her a suitable husband, when she was about twenty or twenty-one, because of her flightiness and tendency to have 'fun'. At that time Victoria consulted her doctor, Sir James Reid, on the subject. He was a man of poor diagnostic skills, but some strange views, and one who might very well have recommended clitoridectomy.

Moreover she was artistic and moved in a Bohemian circle and there were strong grounds for suspecting that she had advances made to her by her teacher, both as a student and later in life, though nothing was proved. Moreover, one Christmas while she was at Osborne with the Queen, another doctor who attended the Royals from time to time, was called to deliver an unknown young woman and subsequently arranged for one of his sons to adopt the baby.

So far so good, but Louise, who married Lord Lorne [later Duke of Argyll, what a family!] was riding and hunting and indulging in quite vigorous activities only weeks before Christmas. Moreover she never had children of her own from the marriage, nor does the story of the guardsman seem to fit with a Scottish home filled with 'men in kilts'. The guardsman story sounds very Germanic to me. Moreover, Louise was a sculptress, who achieved some success in later life, rather than a watercolourist, as in the story.

Altogether, my present guess is that the story is most likely to have been an amalgam of a number of rumours, and facts, such as the Osborne baby, concerning more than one of the daughters, and that they have been put together to form a single narrative. I have several leads going still, and will report as I find things. Have any readers come across this tale, or do they have information bearing on likely candidates?

3 TO A CHERISHED GODCHILD.

Dearest Sophy,

From the innocence of your seventeen years you ask me to tell you honestly what I most regret about my own seventy. We have kept no secrets from each other since you were a child upon my knee, and I will not do so now. You are a woman now, and able to understand such matters, yet young enough to need the guidance of the old to benefit from the lessons they can teach.

What do I most regret about old age, besides ageing itself? That is easy to answer. Never again to wake up to the hot scent of a woman. To wake to find my limbs twined with hers, her thighs sticky from last night's excesses, the fur at their tops matted and coarse. To run my fingers up the roundnesses of her belly to the even rounder swelling of her breasts. To find a nipple and feel it harden under my touch. Its owner is still asleep, but her body seems to recall the excitements of the night. My own excitement is arising again, hardening against her hot ribbed buttocks, where the raised purple welts press against my belly. I stroke a tendril of soft hair from the deli cate pink shell of an ear and nip it gently between my teeth, then kiss it. All the time her hot smell of scent and sex is in my nostrils.

Does the picture I paint arouse you Sophy? Do you under stand what goes on between men and women when true passion strikes? Not the insubstantial, milk and water emotions of the lady novelists, but the raw desires, and bodily fluids of real flesh and blood? I believe you do, for I have taught you well, and you have been attentive at my knee. You understand that woman is destined to find her greatest fulfilment when her pas sion is warmed by pain, when her blood is heated by the whip, and her belly is suffused with the warmth of surrender.

You, I believe, unlike your weak sisters, will understand where a woman's happiness comes from, and strong enough to grasp it, a joy to that man you honour by giving yourself to. Oh that I were but half my age! How well matched we would be.

Your loving Godfather,
Arthur

4 - LETTER FROM ONE GENTLEMAN OF THE WORLD TO ANOTHER.

Dear Percy,

A small, but consequential matter, left over from one of your recent communications. I must take you up on your remarks regarding my use of the expression 'fig', to describe the vulva, especially as seen from the rear.

You claim that 'peach' is a superior and more pleasing description. I would agree that peach is very pleasing and, if you used it to describe the bare buttocks, seen from behind, especially in the bending position, I would agree with you whole heartedly that it is a most felicitous and apt simile.

The peach is my favourite fruit, not only for its flavour, and the delicately fuzzy feminine quality of its skin, but because, every time I handle one, I may turn it so as to look down on the scar, where the stem that supported it was once attached, seeing there the perfect image of a pair of feminine buttocks, complete with tightly closed anus and vulva winking in the crack between the cheeks. One may even let one's imagination dwell on what application of searing strap, or horny hand, aroused that ruddy glow in her burning buttocks.

And the feel of the skin on one's tongue! Exactly like that of the inside of a girl's thighs, when one lays one's head between their delicious firmness and licks delightedly on the lovely surface. Even its scent if like that of a roused woman.

The vulva per se, though, is quite a different matter. The ancients christened it 'fig', and not without reason. The labia, especially when aroused, and even more so if depilated, [no razors please, my friend, only the exquisite torment of the tweezers], often take on the purple hue of the ripe fruit, together with the slightly wrinkled surface, while both, when split, display a delicate and exciting pink interior, to which one yearns to apply one's mouth. The swelling pouch of the engorged organ has a fecund look to it that matches the fruit, and gives promise of similar ripe pleasure.

No, I'll stick to peach cleft buttocks with purple figs pouting prettily between. Not to mention cherry-tipped apples or, in the case of the lusty Hortense, melons of the first water. Moreover, there is a delightful little grape to discover at the tip of that same empurpled fig. What a cornucopia of fruits a ripe woman is, and how sweet her harvesting.

Your very 'upright' friend,
Algernon

And now for a treat - a short story from Rex Saviour

SILVER

I was mildly excited when I saw a girl in my headlights, thumbing a lift.

When I saw her rather more clearly through the driving rain, her soaking little skirt clinging to very curvy thighs and her sweater outlining splendidly firm breasts that obviously didn't believe in bras, my excitement rose several notches.

I brought the Jag to a sliding halt beside her, and lowered the electric window.

"Please Mister -"

"Go and stand in the headlights," I said. "Hands above your head! I want to see if you have a gun!"

"Oh but -"

"Now, or I drive on."

She did as I said. What a great little figure! She was barefoot, with a mini skirt, a jersey, lots of long hair, and nothing else. I got out and walked behind her, ran my hands up and down her, not neglecting the breasts that were outlined by the jersey with her hands raised. She shrank away a little but but did not protest.

Definitely no gun. Not even a handbag.

I got back into my seat and beckoned her back to the window.

"What the Hell are you doing out here in the middle of the night?" I asked sternly. "You don't look a day over fourteen!"

"I'm sixteen," she said indignantly, shaking raindrops from her long red hair. "Today, actually!"

"Even so," I said, "I do not approve of young girls out alone at night miles from anywhere." I began to close the window, which, as I expected, put her into a panic.

"You aren't going to leave me? Oh no, Mister, please!"

"I only deal with nice girls," I said. "Obedient ones! What you need is a good spanking, not a lift."

"Oh but Mister -"

"Yes?"

"I am obedient. I like to be obedient, truly I do." The glance she gave me was full of meaning. "I promise to be good, ever so good, I'll do everything you tell me to. Don't leave me out here, all alone, I'm so frightened of the dark. And he took my money -"

"Who?"

"My boy friend. I thought he was nice. Then he met another girl at the dance tonight and they just threw me out of the car. I didn't even have my shoes on! And she took my handbag, it had all my money in it." She burst into tears. "And he took my rings and bracelets. People call me Silver, because of all my bracelets, they were my money box."

I opened the door.

"You'd better get in, Silver. I'm getting cold with the window down."

"Not so cold as me, Mister," she snuffled. Now that she was close to me I found her very sexy, sort of slimly plump if you follow me. Juicy. Ripe.

"Don't be cheeky!" I said, "not while you're with me. Doesn't your father ever punish you for being cheeky?"

She shivered. "He used to beat me with his belt when I was naughty, but that's alright because I deserved it."

"Surely you don't think being sixteen changes that?"

"I guess not." She burst into tears again. "My Mum died, you see, and my Dad ran off, so there's nobody to look after me now."

"Or to beat you."

"Well, about that..." She paused and considered the matter gravely. "A beating or two isn't such a big deal, it would

231

be worth it, wouldn't it, to be looked after real well?"

"Would it?"

She looked at me. I couldn't see what colour her eyes were, but they were big. "Yes, Mister," she said wistfully, "oh yes, it sure would, I don't mind, truly. As a matter of fact ... well, anyway, you plan to beat me, then, if I'm naughty, like I often am? On the bare bum I suppose? Hard, with a strap, like my Dad did?"

When I didn't answer - being speechless, as I'm sure you will appreciate - she leaned over and kissed me, pressing against me, a really erotic experience for a crusty old bachelor like me.

"I miss my Dad," she whispered.

"Where do you live?" I asked when I had got my breath back and my erection a little more comfortably stacked. I also had the car purring gently forward by now.

"I got out of the orphanage this morning, I was going to live with the boy who dumped me. So nowhere, I suppose."

"You'd better come home with me, then, just for tonight," I said.

"I guess so."

"And then we'll see."

"Right!" She started playing with the stereo, apparently quite at home. "Got any good tapes?"

"Yes, opera."

"Holy shit!" She leaned forward and turned on the radio, twiddling until she found reggae, which I detest, and turning it up full blast.

I pulled in to the grassy edge and turned the music off, and she looked at me, her eyes frightened now, no longer mocking, tears not too far away.

"I do not tolerate behaviour like that!" I said. "Over my lap for a spanking, or out! It's up to you!"

"I - I didn't think we were quite that serious," she said.

"Well, I am. Out. Start walking."

"There isn't even room for you to spank me."

"There will be when I come over there and open the door."

"I see." She seemed to be thinking it over. "A spanking or abandoned in the dark, eh? I just hate the dark! So it's a spanking for you, Silver, girl! It's grit your teeth and bear it time! Well, then, Mister, are you still going to take me to your house after you've spanked me?"

"Perhaps. This is a test to see if you are serious about being obedient."

"OK then."

I moved over into her seat, away from the steering wheel, and she came over my lap, surprisingly heavy, just fitting when I opened the door, so that her head was out in the rain and her feet in the driver's seat.

"You really ought to tie me down if you're going to spank me," she said, "because I can't always control myself."

"Maybe another time," I said. I was all a quiver, no breath to talk with, a strange sensation. She was heavy on my penis, wriggling against it a little, and I shifted to get comfortable.

Don't rush this, I said to myself. Fate has dealt you a good 'un. Make the most of it. Test her out properly and maybe... maybe she will come to live with you and you can spank her once a week.

One hand confirmed that she had no bra and the other was poised to lift that pathetic little rag of a skirt, and yet I couldn't quite do it.

"Knickers," I said.

She twisted her head round.

"You'd better take your knickers off."

"I don't have any, Dumbo."

"And don't be cheeky - I've told you before." I think she was testing me out, seeing how far she could go. Well, she'd soon find out!

"What's your name, then, Dumbo?" she asked.

233

"Stephen."

"OK Sir Stephen, let's get on with it."

"What's all this about Sir Stephen?"

"He's in my favourite book, the Story of O. Don't you know it, Sir?"

I didn't.

"Well, then," she said, "I think this is going to be fun. I shall call you Sir Stephen and think of myself as 'O'. Carry on, Sir Stephen, do your worst!"

She was trying hard to sound as if she didn't care what I did to her, but there was a very satisfactory tremble in her seductive little voice, and she was squirming against my swollen prick all the time.

Lovely!

But I couldn't hold out much longer, and then the thrill would be gone.

"Pull your skirt up."

"Well -"

"NOW!"

"Yes, Sir, I am your obedient servant. I do like your beard, it makes you ever so fierce."

Two timid little hands came and pulled the skirt slowly back, revealing the plumpest little bottom I have ever seen, an arse to shame all arses!

"Hold your skirt there."

"How many are you going to give me?"

"We'll see, won't we? As many as I think necessary, OK?"

"OK," she said, but her voice was definitely trembling now.

I put a finger on her flesh and felt her jump. I traced a circle with my thumb nail. I would have to speed up, or I would erupt and spoil it all.

But when I got her home...

"If this all the clothes you have?" I asked. "This bit of a skirt and the jersey? No knickers, no bra?"

"That's all I was wearing, that's what my pig of a boy friend liked. Will you buy me some clothes, Sir?"

"Perhaps. Shoes, anyway. When we get home you can take these wet things off. They're filthy anyway. I think I'll burn them."

"What will I wear?"

"I'll think I can spare you a shirt."

"Oh, but -"

"You aren't nearly as tall as I am, so it will be quite decent for a while. And the house is very warm."

"Yes, but -"

"I will not be argued with!" I confess to licking my lips. "So I've changed my mind. Take the skirt and jersey off now!"

"Oh but -"

"NOW! Or get out and walk!"

She looked out into the dark wet night and then I slid back into my seat whilst she struggled out of her wet things without another word.

"Throw them out, then close the door."

To my amazement, she did as she was told without further protest, and then actually put her arms round me and gave me a kiss!

I had left the engine running to keep us warm, and now I drove on in silence. When I glanced at her in the dim starlight I got an impression of firm high breasts, not too big, definitely not too small.

"Now you'll have to look after me!" she said contentedly.

"Is that what that kiss was for?"

"Yes, you're my guardian now, my benefactor. Perhaps I'll be your slave-girl, because you definitely can't abandon me like this! And at least your slave girl doesn't get to be spanked!. That's a relief! I rather think you meant to hurt!"

"I did," I said. I drew in to the verge again. "I do."

"Holy shit!"

235

"Quite. Stop talking all this rubbish and come over my lap as before."

It was even more delicious this time, specially the hand that held a breast, quite different without a jersey between. Her nipple was real hard, the little minx!

I ran my other hand up and down inside those splendid legs of hers, making her open them. She wouldn't be very tall, I suppose, I could tell better in daylight, but she was certainly beautifully rounded, warm and already squirming delightfully under my roving fingers, giving a little squeal or two and a special wriggle when my fingers reached her delicate bits, but not protesting.

She was actually soaking wet, as if she was enjoying what I was doing! I pushed a finger in, and all she did was wriggle.

A very amenable girl - or maybe she really did have a phobia about the dark.

I raised my hand and brought it down hard, with a satisfactory slap.

"Ow," she said, "that hurt!" A hand came feeling for the place to rub it better.

"Keep your hands out of the way," I said. "Or the stroke won't count."

"But I don't know how many I'm going to get!"

"Never mind, I still advise you to keep your hands away."

I didn't know how many she would be getting either. I intended to keep going until my orgasm, but it couldn't be much delayed. No doubt I'd do better with practise, improve my control and all that.

After three hard slaps she began to cry softly, then to sob openly. Very stimulating. I was on the verge of flooding.

After six she was heaving about like mad and howling without restraint. She had good lungs, but there wouldn't be anyone within miles of us.

"Holy shit!" she screamed. "I didn't bargain for this! I thought you were a soft touch!"

236

She tried to wriggle away from me, but I had her in a grip that was much too hard for her. I am pretty strong, actually, and tall - over six feet. Only my orgasm could save her now I had my dander up.

Slap! Slap! Slap! I began to lay into her really hard and fast, and she was really screaming and squirming, squirming and screaming, struggling like mad, all her bottom quivering and juddering, oh it was so lovely... She tried to bite me, but I easily stopped that and increased my pace and vigour, slap, slap, slap, slap.

Then I exploded, best ever, on and on and on, heaving up and down beneath her naked belly!

As my breathing eased and my heart slowed, she wriggled round and came and nestled into my arms, snuggling up and still crying softly.

At last she spoke.

"Well, then, you are really going to look after me, aren't you? I was ever so good, wasn't I?"

"If I can train you to my ways, make you into a real good obedient companion."

"Well, yes, OK Sir, whatever turns you on, I'm your helpless victim, aren't I, I'll have to be your loving kitten or your little dog or your pony or your absolutely obedient slave-girl, but not to beat me that hard next time, my God that really hurt!"

"We'll see!" I said.

She would squirm great under the slipper, I thought.

And as for the belt ...

I would be good with the belt, I thought.

She would have to ask me very nicely if I was to go easy on that!

We'd soon find out how submissive she could be!

237

DON'T MISS OUR INTERNET SITES!

OUT OF PRINT TITLES

All titles (including above) are available plain text on
floppy disc
£5 or $8.50 postage inclusive
(PC format unless Mac requested)
or can be downloaded from
www.thebookshops.com/silver

All our in-print titles (listed overleaf) can be ordered from
any bookshop in the UK and an increasing number in the
USA and Australia by quoting the title and ISBN, or directly
from us by post. Credit cards show as EBS (Electronic Book
Services - £ converted to $ and back!): Price of book (see
over) plus postage and packing UK £2 first book then £1.30
each; Europe £3.50 then £2; USA $6 then $4. Please make
US cheques payable to Silver Moon Books Inc.

TITLES IN PRINT

Silver Moon

Silver Mink

*UK £4.99 except *£5.99 --USA $8.95 except *$9.95*

QUANTUM LEAP: A TO Z

PULITZER
Was Al a traitor to his country? Only Sam can
find out for sure . . .

ODYSSEY
Sam and Al must save a twelve-year-old from an
uncertain future—and himself . . .

INDEPENDENCE
In 1776, Sam's ancestor could have been a patriot or a
Tory—now he has to find out firsthand!

ANGELS UNAWARE
When Sam Leaps into a priest, Al joins him as an angel
in a quest to ease a woman's pain.

OBSESSIONS
A woman claiming to be Sam's wife threatens to turn
Project Quantum Leap into a tabloid headline.

LOCH NESS LEAP
Sam makes a monster Leap into a physicist at Loch Ness—
but the reason behind this mission is the real mystery . . .

QUANTUM LEAP

OUT OF TIME. OUT OF BODY.
OUT OF CONTROL.

QUANTUM LEAP

HEAT WAVE

A NOVEL BY

Melanie Kent

**BASED ON THE UNIVERSAL TELEVISION
SERIES *QUANTUM LEAP*
CREATED BY DONALD P. BELLISARIO**

BOULEVARD BOOKS, NEW YORK

TO AMAH

Quantum Leap: Heat Wave, a novel by Melanie Kent, based on the
Universal television series QUANTUM LEAP, created by
Donald P. Bellisario.

QUANTUM LEAP: HEAT WAVE

A Boulevard Book/published by arrangement with
MCA Publishing Rights, a Division of Universal Studios, Inc.

PRINTING HISTORY
Boulevard edition/November 1997

The Putnam Berkley World Wide Web site address is
http://www.berkley.com

Make sure to check out *PB Plug,* the science fiction/fantasy newsletter,
at http://www.pbplug.com

ISBN: 1-57297-312-9

BOULEVARD
Boulevard Books are published by The Berkley Publishing Group,
a member of Penguin Putnam Inc.,
200 Madison Avenue, New York, New York 10016.
BOULEVARD and its logo are trademarks
belonging to Berkley Publishing Corporation.

PRINTED IN THE UNITED STATES OF AMERICA

10 9 8 7 6 5 4 3 2 1

CHAPTER
ONE

Carla Sue entered the hot, dirty trailer and sighed. Sweat trickled down her shoulder blades and gathered in the small of her back. She turned and kicked the trailer door shut with her foot. Summer was ending with a bang. For Carla, it was too hot for the end of the summer.

She walked over to the countertop and set down an empty soda bottle and a bloodied, torn cloth she had been holding. Carla reached up and touched her cheek, feeling the large welt forming under her fingertips. She touched her nose gingerly. Wincing, she examined her fingers and was relieved to discover her nose was no longer bleeding.

That fool had drawn all the blinds in the trailer. It was supposed to keep the heat out and the room cool, but it only made the trailer dark and unbearably stuffy. Carla shook her head and walked across the room to open the windows. She paused by the couch and kicked off her dust-covered shoes. Barefoot, she headed toward one of the sealed windows.

She heard the trailer's creaking wooden steps announce a visitor. She turned around and looked up at the clock, which hung crookedly on the far wall. "If that's you, Tom, you'd better be here to apologize and pack."

The door swung out on its hinges. Carla squinted into the bright sunshine. Her shoulders sagged and she brushed a stray hair away from her face. "What are you doing here? Shouldn't you be at work?" Her question was answered by silence. Carla shrugged. "I'm in no mood for small talk, if that's what brought you by. My mind is made up, like I told you two days ago. Nothing's changed as far as I'm concerned." She smacked the dirt off her skirt and noticed that her leg was scratched from the fall she had taken earlier. She turned her back on the caller and headed back to the window.

Carla had just laid her fingers on the sash when the sound of the trailer door closing made her spin around. "I said I don't want to talk." She took a few cautious steps toward the visitor. "I warned you . . ."

The visitor reached out and grabbed Carla's arm, twisting it. "Hey!" Carla protested, trying to scramble out of the grasp. Now both her arms were pinned to her sides and she was being pushed to the floor.

"Get off of me," she shouted. Her back hit the floor and she felt a knee dig into her chest, pinning her down. A gloved hand slapped her face, sending a new cascade of blood flowing from her nose. She tried to work her arms free as she grew more alarmed and terrified by the second. The knee dug deeper into her chest, cutting off her air supply. Carla stopped struggling and looked her attacker in the eyes. She could taste her blood on her lips. She turned her head and tried to spit.

The knee in her chest pulled away and she was able to breathe again. Carla watched as her attacker straddled her in one quick movement. *This old game*, she thought to herself. *Fine, just get this over with and let me be able to walk away*. Her attacker smiled at her and produced a long knife, which had been concealed by his shirt. The tip of the blade

2

was pointed inches from Carla's bleeding nose.

Carla froze and looked at the knife blade. It was a big knife. The knife plunged down quickly and stabbed through her shoulder. The pain was indescribable. Carla started to scream and the other gloved hand was thrust into her mouth. As one hand covered her mouth, the other pumped up and down, stabbing Carla repeatedly. The blade plunged deep into her chest on the fourth stab. She felt the blade penetrate and she cried out as the knife was withdrawn.

Blood flowed down her blouse. She could feel its wet stickiness as it pooled beneath her.

Carla was dizzy and exhausted. Finally the attacker released her arms as he worked down her torso with the knife. Carla tried to bring her arms up to fight off the blows, but she was too weak. She wanted to roll away, but she couldn't.

The dim light was fading from the room. The sounds she heard seemed to come from far away and she could no longer feel the pain from the knife. Carla tried to call out, to summon help, but all she could muster was a gurgling noise. Her attacker paused, the knife held in midair, dripping with her blood. He studied his victim without guilt or compassion.

Carla knew she was dying. Her blue eyes stared up at the ceiling as her life drained out of her on that hot summer day. The knife attack continued, long after Carla Sue was dead.

Tuesday, August 30, 1955

The hot, blue, electric light popped and swirled all around his body. As quickly as it had begun, the light began to fade. When Sam Beckett's vision cleared, he found himself perched on a narrow ledge. Sam peered cautiously over the edge, down his khaki-covered legs, past his shiny black shoes, to the concrete sidewalk below. He could feel his

3

hands and fingers now. Sam realized that he was spread-eagled against the side of a brick building. It must be brick, judging by the way it felt digging into his shoulders and back.

The warm summer sun beat down upon him. The clothing he wore felt damp and heavy. Humidity. Sam could feel the heavy, oppressive humidity weighing down on him.

Sam's left hand was splayed out against the building, his fingertips just inches from a window. *A jumper?* Sam thought wildly. *Have I Leaped into someone about to commit suicide?* Sam tried to reach the open window.

Loud voices came drifting out through the window. Someone was arguing. Sam continued reaching for the window frame. He almost had it.

All the effects of the Leap in were gone now. Sam was very aware of his surroundings and the predicament in which he found himself. A small crowd had gathered in the street. They were shading their eyes and craning their necks skyward. Sam took his eyes away from the window he so desperately wanted to reach, and looked down at the crowd.

That's when Sam's childhood fear of heights came flooding back. He had been afraid of heights ever since he was nine years old. He and his older brother had been playing in the barn loft. Sam couldn't remember what happened next, but he was sure it had to do with the height and clinging to a rope for dear life.

Sam caught his breath and closed his eyes, erasing the memory in the barn. He ground his body further into the brick wall. The dizzying effects of vertigo threatened to pitch Sam off the balcony. He broke out in a cold sweat, even though the temperature felt like it was over one hundred degrees. His fingers spread out along the brick, looking for the window's edge.

A boisterous voice jarred his concentration. The voice was off to Sam's right, further down on the ledge. Sam twisted his head away from the open window and carefully opened one eye.

Less than two feet away stood a giant. At least, that's

4

how the man looked to Sam. He was as tall as he was wide. He was over six feet tall and must have weighed more than 250 pounds. He was dressed in scruffy blue overalls and a grease-smeared T-shirt. Large, powerful arms and thick legs helped him maintain his balance on the narrow ledge. His face was unshaven and he had a large, bloodied gash over his left eyebrow. Blood from the cut had leaked down the man's unshaven face and dripped onto his clothing. The man squinted at Sam. He tipped and swayed on the balcony, but amazingly, he managed to keep his balance.

"Stop. Don't come any closer," he threatened. "I'm aiming to die today. Don't try and stop me."

Sam opened his other eye and felt his jaw sag. He watched in horror, waiting for the hulk to tumble off the balcony to his death.

The man shifted his feet and retained his balance. He curled his lips back and snarled, "You want to die today, too, Sheriff Williams?"

Sheriff! Sam carefully scanned his clothes. He was wearing some kind of a uniform. And maybe that was a gun belt buckled to his waist. *Great,* Sam thought. How was he suppose to talk this guy down when he couldn't even move? Sam swallowed and tipped his head back against the building. He closed his eyes and whispered, "Oh boy."

Sam heard a timid voice calling out from the window.

"Sheriff Williams? Will? Are you all right out there?"

Sam opened his eyes. A young man was leaning out the window, looking up eagerly at Sam. He was waving his hand in the air, trying to get Sam's attention. "Hey, Will, over here." He was a skinny kid between twenty and twenty-five years old. He was dressed in the same type of uniform as Sam. The kid shoved his dark, black hair out of his eyes. He offered his hand to Sam. "I'll help you inside."

Sam forced his arm away from the brick wall. He shuffled his feet along the balcony, inching toward the open window. Sam reached and grabbed the kid's outstretched

5

arm. He carefully worked his way into the window, where he was pulled safely inside.

Sam was standing in the building's cluttered attic. There were boxes stacked in one corner and some long tables and a few chairs collecting dust next to a wall. The room felt like an oven. Sam staggered over to one of the tables and leaned against it. His knees still hadn't stopped shaking. Behind him voices began to argue.

"You said he'd have him off the ledge in under five minutes, Gene."

The kid who had just hauled Sam inside turned and checked on Sam. He kept his back turned on the older man as he spoke to him. "I know what I said. It's another killer day out there today, Mayor Tilden. Maybe Will got sick from the heat."

Sam straightened up and found himself searching the faces of the kid and the older man. The older man was sweating profusely even though his attire indicated he was dressed for the heat. He wore a short-sleeved shirt and white cotton trousers. Mayor Tilden whipped a blue bandanna out of his back pocket and mopped off his glistening, bald head. His cheeks were flushed and he began to jab the air with his bandanna. "Sick or not, Tom Madison is still out there on that balcony. I hope you and Williams are both aware that he's standing over my brand new '55 convertible, which I've owned less than one week. If he falls, the chances are very good that's he's going to land all over my front seat. I'm warning you, there will be hell to pay if that happens . . . *boys*."

Gene whirled around. "I'm not a boy. Furthermore, I told you to move that car over thirty minutes ago when Tom first climbed out there," he shot back. "I told you this could happen. It's your own fault if Tom lands in your car."

The mayor raised his chubby arm and pointed his index finger at Gene. "Now you wait one minute, Gene Dupree!"

Sam took a cautious step forward. "Don't shout." His

admonition was either ignored or unheard as both men continued to argue.

"Hey!" Sam yelled, getting the attention of both Mayor Tilden and Gene. "Stop shouting." Sam headed back toward the window, separating Gene and Mayor Tilden in the process. "We've still got to get Tom off the ledge," Sam said over his shoulder as he leaned out the window.

Gene thumbed his nose at the mayor and walked over by Sam. He knelt down by the window and retrieved something off the floor.

"Are you going to come in now, Tom?" Sam asked. The fresh air was a welcome relief after the inside of the attic.

Gene coughed. "Hey, Will, you know he won't come in till after you throw it."

Sam pulled his head back into the attic. "What?"

Gene pulled his hand out of the shadows and offered Sam a big, red, overripe tomato. Gene held the tomato with great care in his hand. "I'm real sorry I was so late, Will," he began to explain. "But remember how Mr. Phillips said he wouldn't let us use any more of his produce? And after that last incident with the watermelon, he said he didn't care what kind of an emergency it was, he wasn't going to have his profit thrown, lofted, tossed, pitched, flung, hurled, or splattered all over Main Street. The way he chased me out of his store the last time, I didn't bother going back this time. And when I heard the call over the radio, I tried to get something as fast as I could. I went to Mrs. King's and got a tomato from her garden. Seems she had a bumper crop of tomatoes and most of them would have wound up in the trash pile. I didn't think you wanted me to go all the way into Dunsmoore for a melon, did you?" With his free hand Gene tugged on the gun belt slung around his skinny waist. He again offered the tomato to Sam, waiting patiently for Sam to take it. "Did you, Will?"

The mayor laughed at Gene and waved his bandanna at the tomato in the deputy's hand. "That's what you brought? You've got to be kidding. You think Tom's going

7

to come in for that measly little thing?'' He swabbed the damp bandanna over his brow.

Gene snarled at Mayor Tilden, ''It was the best I could come up with under the present circumstances.'' He turned to Sam and lost the snarl. ''I didn't think I had time to make the trip into Dunsmoore, Will,'' Gene apologized. ''You sounded pretty urgent on the radio.''

''Dunsmoore?'' Sam said helplessly. He looked at the tomato in Gene's hand. What lunatic place had he Leaped into now?

Gene's shoulders fell. ''I can still go. Is that what you want me to do?'' he asked with disappointment in his voice.

''He wants you to get that idiot off the balcony,'' the mayor roared behind Sam's shoulder. ''Is that so difficult for you to understand, Deputy Dupree?''

Sam held his hands up. ''Both of you, be quiet.'' He pointed down at the tomato. ''Again, just what am I supposed to do with this?''

Gene raised his eyebrows and blinked. ''Pardon me, Will?'' A thin trail of sweat trickled down the kid's cheek.

''This tomato,'' Sam said. ''What am I supposed to do with it?''

Gene cackled loudly. ''Good old Will, always trying to kid around. Trying to lighten the mood.'' He lifted the tomato up in the air. ''You're supposed to throw it. *You* know, Will,'' Gene prompted in a lower voice, ''same stupid routine as the last four times? Seems it's the only way Tom will get off the balcony.''

Sam could not believe what he was hearing. ''You want me to throw this tomato out this window so that crazy person will come inside?'' Sam clenched his hands into fists and looked desperately around the room.

''What's going on in there?'' Tom bellowed from outside. ''I'm getting hot out here, Sheriff Williams.''

Gene leaned out the window and hollered back at Tom. ''Will is just taking his time. Don't you worry none. He'll have you off the ledge in a second.'' Gene stuck his head inside. ''Come on, Will. You're the one who started tossing

8

stuff out the window for Tom. You've done this sort of thing all the other times Tom's been out there. What gives now?''

'' 'All the other times?''' Sam repeated in utter disbelief. He swiped at his forehead, which was damp with sweat. ''This isn't the first time Tom's been out there?''

''Hell no,'' Gene hotly answered back. ''This is Tom's fifth time. Are you upset 'cause I didn't get you a watermelon? Or is it 'cause I took so long to get here this afternoon? If you're upset with me, just tell me.''

''One of you better throw that damn tomato,'' Mayor Tilden advised. ''Tom's going to fall off that ledge and dent my car. I wouldn't want to be in either of your shoes if that happens.''

''All right,'' Sam snapped, his patience gone. Maybe that's all he needed to do in order to Leap out of here. Sam snatched the tomato out of Gene's hand. He squeezed the fruit and a thin trickle of red juice began to run down his fingers and hand.

Gene bit his lower lip as the juice ran down Sam's arm and began to drip off his elbow. ''It's really ripe, Will,'' he muttered. ''Did I mention that it was really ripe?''

''Is this how this town treats potential suicide victims? By throwing overripe fruit out windows?'' Sam retorted. He squeezed the tomato with his fingers and more juice trickled out.

Gene swallowed and spoke in a small voice. ''But Tom's not a suicide threat. I'm sure he'd come in of his own free will once the whiskey wears off. Throwing stuff just gets him inside quicker.'' Gene also wiped his forehead with his sleeve. ''We just never wanted to chance waiting him out. Don't you remember?''

''He's drunk!'' Sam sagged against the windowsill.

''Well, of course he's drunk, Williams.'' Mayor Tilden chided Sam. ''He'd never have the nerve to climb out there in the first place if he was sober.'' He shook his head. ''I think you're right for once, Gene Dupree. The heat's got to ol' Will today.''

9

Sam frowned at the men and leaned out the window. "Tom? Tom Madison?"

"About time you got this show on the road, Sheriff Williams," the burly man in the dirty overalls snorted. "I'm gonna jump and kill myself if you don't hurry up. I can't live without my Carla Sue."

"Go ahead, throw it. He's waiting for it," Gene urged Sam in a timid voice.

Sam, with disgust, heaved the tomato out the window, slinging pulp and juice against the windowsill. The crowd below let out a cheer, followed by applause.

Mayor Tilden charged the window, knocking Gene and Sam out of the way. He pressed his fleshy hands on the messy sill and leaned out as far as his protruding stomach would allow. He was straining to see what the crowd was cheering about. He let out a strangled sound as he pushed his body back inside the window. Once inside he began to shout in Sam's ear, "Goddamn it, William Williams! You lobbed that tomato right into my new convertible. It's splattered all over the new upholstery. Is this your idea of a joke?" Mayor Tilden's hands were balled into tight fists, as his face contorted and began to change from a deep shade of red to purple.

Gene Dupree elbowed his way around Sam. "If it's anyone's fault, it's your own, Tilden. I told you to move that car. You shout at Will again and I'll arrest you for interfering with a police investigation."

"I'd like to see you try," the mayor roared as he pushed Gene with his stomach. Tilden acted like Gene was nothing more than a troublesome fly that he could swat away. He stuck a thick finger in Sam's face. "As for you, Williams . . . I'm not through with you yet." He turned on his heel and left the room. He bounded down the staircase to the first floor.

"That was a good shot." Gene whistled and leaned out the window for a better look. "I couldn't have hit that windbag's car."

"I didn't mean to hit the car," Sam started to explain.

"I've never heard of a such a stupid, inane, moronic way to . . ."

A shadow crossed the window and Tom Madison leaned in. "I'm ready to come in now, Sheriff Williams and Deputy Dupree." It took both Sam and Gene to pull Tom inside.

Tom reeked of whiskey and sweat. He leaned into Sam's face, his stale breath wafting up into Sam's nose. "The watermelon was a lot better, Sheriff Williams. Bigger squash when it hits the pavement. You did nail the mayor's car pretty good, so the whole day wasn't wasted. Maybe next time you—"

"There better not be a next time," Sam warned.

The mayor came thundering back up the staircase and bolted through the attic's doorway, waving his chubby fists high in the air. "Judas H. Priest, Will Williams. You've ruined my brand new 1955 Ford convertible down there." He shouted and ranted as he danced around the small room, all his anger directed at Sam. "How am I going to explain that mess to my wife! She's going to be furious." He huffed and puffed as he whipped out his wrinkled bandanna and dabbed at his thick neck.

Gene had quietly handcuffed Tom in the corner. "You'd better calm down, Mayor Tilden, or you're going to give yourself a heart attack. Just tell your wife it was only a tomato."

The mayor whirled and stormed over to Gene. "A heart attack, my foot! You call my wife up and tell her yourself. She'll be picking up what's left of you and feeding it to our dog when she's through. She's a woman to be dealt with, mind my words." Tom snickered and Gene dropped his eyes and looked down at his shoes.

"It could have been Tom Madison in the front seat instead of that tomato," Sam reminded Tilden. "Tell your wife that when she sees the mess." So far twenty minutes hadn't passed in this Leap and Sam didn't like the mayor or his attitude. "Besides," Sam reminded him, "my deputy did warn you to move your car."

Gene raised his head. A small, grateful smile started to spread across his face.

"Hey! It's too hot to stand up here and listen to you all fussing about me and that car." Tom rattled his handcuffs. "Now that I'm under arrest, I'm supposed to be going to jail. I sure don't want to stay up here any longer."

Tom had a point. The air in this room was so thick and heavy you could have sliced it.

"Take him downstairs," Sam ordered Gene. Sam wiped his face with his sleeve and turned to the mayor. "As for the car . . ." Sam patted his shirt pocket and found a small wirebound notepad and pencil. He flipped open the notepad and began to write. "Just let me know how much it costs to clean up your car and I'll see that you get reimbursed for your trouble." He flipped the notebook closed and tucked it back into his pocket. "I'll be downstairs if you need me." Sam followed Gene Dupree and Tom down the stairs.

"I'm watching you, Williams. You'd better believe you're gonna be hearing from me. Yes indeed." Mayor Tilden tried to smooth out his ruffled appearance as he clambered downstairs.

As the group reached the first floor, Sam cleared his throat. "Let's take Tom to the jail and book him." Sam hoped this little town had a jail. "And I want a doctor to look at that cut over his eye."

Gene led Tom outside. "I'll give Doc Adams a call as soon as I can get Tom fingerprinted and booked—again."

Outside, the mayor had found a new audience to perform for and he began to bemoan the state of his upholstery all over again. Sam left the mayor behind as the humidity and heat began pressing down on him from all sides. Sam noticed that Gene's shirt was completely soaked through as it clung to his thin body. Upon closer inspection of his own uniform Sam noted his shirt wasn't in much better shape. Gene loaded Tom in the backseat of the police cruiser and shut the door. "You want a lift back, Will?" he asked.

"Sure," Sam responded automatically. He climbed in

the car with Gene at the wheel and Tom Madison groaning loudly in the backseat. Gene dropped the cruiser into gear and the trio pulled away from the crowd and headed down Main Street.

Sam rode quietly in the big police sedan. Gene whistled and adjusted the rearview mirror to get a better look at Tom. "What happened to your head?" he asked.

"Carla Sue." Tom snorted. "I really made her mad this time. She went and whacked me with a beer bottle."

Gene shook his head as he turned off the short street and headed down a side street. "Tom, you and Carla Sue have got to stop this fighting. Will and I can't go climbing out on the balcony each time you two get into it."

"I haven't seen you out on that balcony yet, Gene Dupree." Tom sat back and smiled. "Only Sheriff Williams climbs out after me."

Sam turned around. "And I don't want to climb out there again, Tom."

Tom nodded. "I know, I know. I broke our promise we made the last time I wanted to get Carla worried about me. It's just she's being so stubborn this time."

Gene stopped the car in front of a squat, brick, single-story building that sat at the end of the street. A crude, weathered sign hung above the front door on two rusted metal chains. It read JAIL.

Sam climbed out and followed Gene and Tom up the stairs and into the building.

The men entered an office area, large enough to contain two desks, a filing cabinet, a long table, and a Coca-Cola machine. Atop the long table sat a log book, phone, and radio dispatch. A small bathroom was tucked away in one corner of the room.

Gene began guiding Tom through the main office area and down a short corridor that led to the jail cells. The jail had two cells, complete with metal bed frames, cloth-covered mattresses, and pillows. Gene undid the handcuffs and opened the cell door for Tom. Tom rubbed his wrists and slipped inside the cell without a struggle. He walked

13

over to the bed as Gene shut the cell door. The metal bed frame emitted a groan as Tom sat down and put his head in his hands.

"The whiskey's beginning to wear off now. He'll be needing some aspirin soon," Gene said as he returned to the main office area.

"Let's give the doctor a call."

Gene nodded and headed for the phone as Sam wandered over to one of the desks and pulled out a swivel chair. He sank into the chair and listened as Gene talked to the doctor, explaining about the cut and how the afternoon's events had progressed. Gene cupped his hand over the receiver and asked, "Is there anything else, Will?"

"Just make sure the doctor brings a lot of aspirin. Tom's gonna have one heck of a hangover."

Gene smiled and relayed the message back to the doctor. He chuckled and hung up the phone.

Sam had just pulled open the top desk drawer when Gene spoke up.

"It was my fault," Gene said as he walked over to the other desk and sat down, pulling at his shirt collar. "I took too long getting that tomato. You would have had Tom off the balcony in no time flat and it wouldn't have cost the mayor ten bucks. I think Tilden's more upset about the ten dollars he lost than his car, if the truth be known. His wife hardly ever lets him drive it."

"Ten dollars?" A perplexed expression crossed over Sam's features. "You mean . . . a bet?"

"Yeah," Gene sighed, leaning back in the chair. "He bet Russell that you'd get Tom off the balcony in less than five minutes this time." Gene shook his head. "Sorry if I messed that up, Will."

Sam just grunted. He shifted the gun belt around his waist and glanced at the calendar on the desk. A calendar serving as a blotter was opened to August 1955.

"You looked spooked up on that balcony today."

"I wasn't spooked," Sam muttered as he began to plow through the contents of the desk. The office wasn't air-

14

conditioned and it was very uncomfortable in the small building. The little metal fan sitting on top of the filing cabinet whirled madly away in the corner, its stream of cool air fading long before it reached Sam. A clock ticked away on the far wall. Gene seemed to lose interest in the conversation and opened a file on his desk.

Sam's search yielded no clues as to his whereabouts or identity. In a last-ditch effort he pulled out the sheriff's wallet and checked the driver's license.

William T. Williams was thirty-nine years old. He was six feet, two inches tall, had dark brown hair and brown eyes. Sam memorized Will's home address and upon further inspection discovered he was carrying forty dollars in the wallet. "Dear God, I've Leaped into Andy Griffith," Sam muttered.

"You can say that again." Al Calavicci tucked his oversized cigar into the corner of his mouth and shook his head. He brought the blinking handlink out of his lime-green jacket and studied its small screen. Sam jumped and almost dropped Will's wallet.

"Did you say something to me, Will?" Gene looked up from the file he had been reading.

"No," Sam answered with a wave of his hand. He threw a blistering glare toward Al and hissed under his breath, "I told you not to do that to me!"

Al raised a bushy eyebrow. "Do what?" He shrugged his shoulders and feigned innocence. "Didn't you hear me come through the wall?"

Sam just shook his head. He put the wallet back in his pants pocket and stood up. "I'm going to wash up."

Gene was studying the file. "Okay," he answered absently.

Sam walked past Al and nodded toward the bathroom with his head.

"Not the bathroom again? Come on, Sam, can't we find a different place to talk?"

Sam just kept walking. The minuscule bathroom had a bare bulb with an old-fashioned pull chain. Sam tugged on

15

the chain and the room was lit with a blinding light. He blinked and shut the door.

Al joined Sam by squeezing through the door. The hologram's right shoulder kept melting back into the door and disappearing. Al looked like a smorgasbord, dressed as he was in a lime-green jacket, an orange shirt, cream-colored suspenders, chocolate-brown pants, and gold shoes. Ziggy's link blinked off and on in his hand, adding its own neon hues of blues, oranges, pinks, yellows, and greens.

"Where have you been!" Sam admonished his friend.

"And hello to you too." The link twittered away in the rear admiral's hand. Al smoothed out his jacket and pretended to ignore the anger in Sam's voice. "I don't want to hear one word," Al warned Sam as Al's elbow disappeared into the porcelain pedestal sink. He pulled his elbow out of the sink. Sam could see the link twitching slightly in his hand.

"What's wrong, Al?" Sam asked, forgetting how badly Al had startled him a few moments before.

Al removed his cigar from his mouth and licked his lips. "I'll tell you what's wrong." Al spoke quietly and diligently. He straightened his back. "For starters, Ziggy just centered me in a graveyard!" He shook the link in his hand, which made it squeal, and he leered at Sam, as if this were all his fault.

"A graveyard?" Sam repeated slowly. He leaned back against the sink, a luxury Al could not experience. "Why would Ziggy center you in a graveyard? She knows how much you hate stuff like that." If you really wanted to rattle Al Calavicci, you just had to mention dead bodies, ghosts, or vampires. Fighter pilot or not, when it comes to the spooky and the supernatural, Al was one part skeptic, three parts terrified.

"No," Al corrected. He stuck his thumb at his chest. "I *despise* graveyards, I don't just hate them." He pointed his thick, smoldering cigar stub at Sam. "That pea-brained, number-crunching, egomaniacal excuse for a computer— which you designed, I might add—is this far from becoming unplugged, permanently." Al demonstrated with the thumb and first finger of his right hand. The space between them was so narrow a piece of paper would have not fit in it.

"Ziggy's been known to pull some crazy stunts, but she wouldn't do that to you on purpose, Al," Sam pointed out, keeping his voice lowered. "She knows how you feel about that kind of stuff."

"Ha!" Al cried, stepping forward. His cigar hand sailed through the air. "Well, for your information, she just did. I had to hightail it out of that ghoulish place and walk all over this town looking for you."

Sam held up his hand. "Just settle down."

"I am settled down!" Al roared. "You should have seen me five minutes ago." He shifted his feet and rammed the cigar between his teeth.

"All right, all right," Sam agreed, not wanting to get into a verbal exchange. "What was happening before you had Ziggy center you here?"

Al rolled his eyes. "Gosh, Sam, I wouldn't have had a problem if she had centered me *here*." He pointed at the top of his gold shoes.

"Fine," Sam agreed. "What was going on before you stepped into the Imaging Chamber?"

Al tipped his head back toward the office area. "Can you talk?"

"Why?" Sam asked skeptically. "Is this going to take long?"

"As a matter of fact, yes it is." Al tried to pace in the confined space as he launched into his story. He was having a dickens of a time trying not to step into and through the toilet. "First of all, I've been on the phone all day with my lawyer, I have two dozen different committee reports sitting on my desk that I need to sign and file, and Verbena has been on my case about some kind of equipment she's been expecting." Al snorted to himself and snapped his gold suspenders. "Do I look like a tracking device for a phar-maceutical company?"

Sam folded his arms across his chest. "When you got into the Imaging Chamber . . ."

"Hey, don't rush me," Al warned. "Now where was I . . . oh yeah, Ziggy, that marvelous microchip maniac, can't give me two lines of complete readout regarding this Leap. Gooshie starts fiddling with the only coordinates that Ziggy can come up with and *boom!* before I know what's happening, I find myself standing in the middle of a Stephen King novel." Al batted away a fly that was buzzing around his head. As the persistent fly followed him, Al began to wave his arms in the air. Swat and move, swat and move.

"Wait a minute." Sam leaned forward. "What did you say about Ziggy and the data for this Leap?"

"Just what I said." Al paused and aimed the link at the pesky fly. The link screeched and sent the fly buzzing. "She can't pull up any data on this town during your present time frame and—"

"What do you mean she can't get any data?" Sam pushed off the sink and pressed forward toward Al. "Just what have you been doing for the past two hours?"

"Look," Al warned, "you wanted me to explain how I wound up in that cemetery, so I'm explaining. If you don't like it . . ." He made a face as he stepped back through the wall. "Man, this is a tiny bathroom."

"Forget the bathroom!" Sam winced and lowered his voice. "Please explain to me what took you so long to get here." Sam gestured wildly at the door. "I've Leaped into a sheriff in a little town. That much I know."

Al shrugged. "So you're ahead of the game. Did you know the guy you Leaped into has a wife and two kids?"

"I've got a wife and two kids?"

Al cleared his throat and hooked his free thumb into his suspender. "No. Will has a wife and two kids. Margaret O'Brien Williams is his wife and Rebecca is, of course, his daughter and Tyler is his son. And the reason Ziggy doesn't have any data for you on this Leap is because in 1965 a tornado ripped through this happy little hamlet and the big booming town up the road, . . . um,"—Al had to consult

18

the link and he yanked it up to his face—"Dunsmoore. Dunsmoore is the county seat. It's got a courthouse and library. Anyway, being the county seat, it houses all the important records for the towns in this county. You know, birth records, land purchases, that sort of thing." Al waved his hand. "When this killer tornado roared through, there was nothing left for the National Archives. Hence, nothing for Ziggy's precious memory chips to absorb. Almost all the records before 1965 were lost. About the only thing Ziggy has access to is"—Al shuddered a bit—"cemetery lists and a few death certificates. Tina is having Ziggy run a cross-check through what's left. We're looking for newspaper articles, almanacs, anything that will give us a written account about the town." He sighed and removed the cigar. "I gotta tell you, Sam, it's really tough trying to nail down 1955 in Brick, Oklahoma, right now."

"But," Sam asked, "without any records how did Ziggy figure out where I was?"

Al jiggled the link in his hand and it squawked. "See, Ziggy had nothing to do with that. Will told us."

"Will?" Sam gravitated toward Al. "The guy I Leaped into? The man back in the Waiting Room?"

"No, Sam," Al replied sarcastically, "Will the night janitor. Of course, Will in the Waiting Room. Do you happen to know another William Williams?" Al shook his head. "Why would anyone give a person a first and last name that sound so similar? It's stupid if you ask me."

"Al."

"I mean it's so confusing. William Williams. That's like Tom Thomas or ...." Al became lost in thought. "I knew this captain in the Navy that had a name like that. What was it? Bob Bobson or ... it's right on the tip of my tongue."

"Al."

"What?"

"I don't want to hear about your lieutenant," Sam wearily pleaded.

"Captain, Sam," Al corrected. "I said Captain."

19

"Whatever. Tell me what Will said."

Al pulled his shoulders back. "He told us he was from Brick, Oklahoma, and that his name was Will Williams."

"So he's awake and he can talk?"

Al laughed. "Well, they can all talk, Sam. Except for that chimp you Leaped into. Most of the time our guests prefer to scream or faint instead of engaging me in conversation. Kind of a nice change."

Sam leaned back against the sink. "Is Will okay?"

"He's fine. Once he came around and figured he hadn't been captured by the Russians or space aliens, he was more than willing to fill us in on his life. That is, what he can remember."

"And that brings us back to you. And your arrival in the cemetery." Sam rubbed his chin. "Explain to me again what was happening just prior to Ziggy sending you . . . there."

"Like I said, things were their usual hectic pace. I had been tied up all day long and we were getting zip with Ziggy when Dr. Beeks finally convinced Will he wasn't going crazy; he calmed down and began to talk about his family and this town. He remembered that he was the sheriff and was married, but that was about it. Ziggy, in the meanwhile, was scanning newspapers and archive files from another town about fifty miles east of here. The town is called Ashcroft, I think. The only thing Ziggy could pull up regarding this date is something about a murder. The town's records in Ashcroft are real sketchy in regard to the shining metropolis of Brick."

"A murder?" Sam sat up and took notice. He burrowed his brow and shook his head. "Ziggy's got her semantics wrong again. When I Leaped in, I was in the process of stopping a suicide, not a murder."

"Murder, suicide. It depends how you look at it," Al commented as he fiddled with the link. He shook his head back and forth, "No, Ziggy's still insisting it's a murder." Al continued to jab at the buttons and wave the link through the air. "That's two for two today, you bucket of bolts."

20

Al gave up and dropped the link to his side. "Only Will Williams could give us any kind of clue where you would be. So when Ziggy came up with nothing"—the link shrieked in protest—"Verbena had Will fill me in on all the details he could recall. Gooshie pieced together a target for Ziggy to aim for and I figured the next person I'd see would be you."

"And the next thing you know," Sam continued, "you're standing in a cemetery." The only sound in the room was the fly buzzing. "Where were you standing exactly?" Sam asked out loud as he thought.

"Aw, Sam," Al complained. "We've been over this already. Just face it, your computer blew it. Big time." He snapped his suspender with his fingers.

"Where were you standing? I want to know the exact spot."

Al squirmed. "I didn't hang around and soak in all the details. It was creepy." Al studied his shoes and Sam patiently waited. "I might have been standing on a grave—but I don't know for sure," Al added quickly.

"What did the headstone say?"

"Come on, Sam. You know I hate stuff like that. I certainly didn't take the time to see whose grave I was standing on. Boy, this is giving me the creeps all over again." He shuddered and drew his arms around him.

"You mean to tell me, Ziggy sends you into a graveyard and you don't even take the time to read the headstone? Surely you read the marker?" Sam tipped his head and waited for Al to reply.

Al looked down at his feet. "I kind of took a fleeting peek at it."

Sam held his breath and counted to ten. He finally asked, "And what did the headstone say, Al?"

"What has this got to do with the price of tea in China?" Al snapped his head up. "It was a headstone. I think it was . . ." Al turned his head and mumbled something inaudible.

"What was that? I didn't catch it?" Sam leaned over toward the hologram.

Al shot Sam a searing look. "I don't know. It was . . . William something." Al waved his hand over his head. "It might have been William Williams, but I'm not sure."

"Did you notice the date of death on the tombstone?" A smile was creeping up on the corners of Sam's mouth.

"It might have been June 5, 1950, but I could've been mistaken." Al started to rock on the balls of his feet again.

Sam smiled broadly. "Ziggy didn't screw up. She did what you asked her to do, with the limited data she had to work with."

Al stopped rocking and shook his head back and forth. "Nope. No way. Nohow. What do you mean, 'Ziggy didn't screw up'? I think sticking me in the middle of a cemetery is a pretty big mistake. I thought you were dead."

"I'm touched." Sam held his hand over his heart. "Al, who did Ziggy center you on?"

Al rolled his eyes, moaned, and pointed at Sam. "You! I told Gooshie to have Ziggy fixed so I would be centered on you." Al folded his arms across his chest. Now he was growing exasperated. "What'sa matter, Beckett," he scoffed, "am I going too fast for you?"

"No." Sam started to laugh. "Not at all."

"What?" Al demanded. "You're laughing? I wind up thinking you've cashed in on this Leap and you're sitting there laughing?"

"Listen," Sam pleaded. "Gooshie centered you on the only William Williams Ziggy had a record of. You said yourself most of the town's records were destroyed in the tornado." He held up his finger. "Except for cemetery and death records. The only William Williams Ziggy has a record of must be Will's father. William Williams the first. Go back and ask Will if he was named after his father. But Al, if I were you, I'd leave out that part about how stupid two similar names sound. Will might take offense at that."

Al started to say something and then clamped his mouth

shut. He scowled down at the handlink and then up at Sam. "I still say Ziggy screwed up!"

"Uh-huh," Sam commented dryly. "And what were you doing on the phone with your lawyer?"

Al swallowed and scratched his head. "I, um . . . did I say my lawyer? I meant a meeting with . . . um . . . who was that guy?"

"Maybe you can lie like a dog with Tina, but you can't fool me." Sam walked in front of Al and sat down on the toilet. He stretched out his long legs. "What do you need a lawyer for?" Sam's face fell and he gasped. "Oh God, Al! You didn't get married again, did you?"

"Me?" Al exclaimed. "Married? *No!*" Al put his free hand up to his forehead and ran it through his hair. "Hardly." He chuckled at Sam. "Me! Married! No, it's just Maxine."

"Maxine?" Sam blinked and shook his head.

Al was rubbing at his neck, trying to unkink it. "Yeah, you remember Maxine. You know, ex-wife number five?"

"Oh," Sam recalled as his Swiss-cheesed memory clicked. "The last one. I can vaguely remember that you've been married five times. What does Maxine want?"

Al was working his hand down from his neck and had moved on to his shoulder. "I have no idea. She's tucked away in a luxury hotel in Santa Fe. I'm supposed to fly into town tomorrow and meet her."

"But why? You two have been divorced a long time, haven't you?"

Al began to slowly roll his shoulder up and down. "Yeah, it's been a long time. I haven't set eyes on her since I joined the Star Bright Project. Remember, I had just finished up the Eco-Environment Project and I was all set to interview with Weitzman and the Star Bright committee members when she came breezing into town looking for a divorce? I met her at a hotel near the Capitol. All we ever did was fight. She can really pack a punch."

Sam's jaw dropped. "You two physically fought? Al!"

"*Sam!*" Al recoiled at the thought. "You know I would

23

never strike a female. We had our own unique way of fighting. *She* did the throwing while I did the ducking. Seems she didn't care for some of my comments. I could always get to Maxine with my tongue and she always would get to me with whatever she could heave in my direction." A small smile spread across Al's lips. "Actually, the fighting only put us more in the mood, if you know what I mean. I'd let a zinger fly about her wardrobe or her attitude and bang, she'd start throwing dishes, books, whatever she could lay her hands on. Soon she'd get tired of throwing furniture and we'd start wrestling. Before you'd know it, we were making love before our clothes could hit the floor."

Sam shook his head in disgust. "That's the craziest behavior I've ever heard." Sam wagged a finger in Al's direction. "Is this what you're going to do tomorrow? Destroy a hotel room? Wrestle with your ex-wife?"

"No," Al answered cynically. "Sam, it's been a while since I laid eyes on the woman. I have no idea what she wants. I've just been handed an ultimatum from her lawyer to meet with her, that's all. And I know Maxine. If I don't meet with her in Santa Fe she'll come straight to Stallion's Gate and track me down." Al responded before Sam had a chance to voice his concerns. "But don't worry. I've already made plans to meet her in Santa Fe."

Sam leaned back and folded his arms. "Oh, that's great! And what am I suppose to do? Sit around here and wait till Ziggy comes up with something? Or do I wait till Will gets his memory back?"

"You're not doing so bad," Al pointed out. He started to toy with the link in his hand.

Sam narrowed his eyes. "Let me refresh your memory. So far, I have been on a ledge, three stories high, trying to talk a three-hundred-pound crazy man from splattering his body on top of the mayor's new convertible. I then get chewed out by the very same mayor for lobbing an overripe tomato into his new car."

Al blinked. "A tomato?" Ziggy sounded off in his hand

and he read the link. "You threw a tomato in the mayor's car?"

"You're missing the point, Al." Sam stood up and stretched. "You said yourself that I'm here to stop a murder, right?"

"Solve, stop. Murder, suicide," Al shrugged. "It's all the same thing to Ziggy."

"Okay, I did that. I prevented Tom Madison's death. I changed history"—Sam consulted his watch—"over two and a half hours ago."

Al leaned forward and smoothed out his shirt. "And?"

"And why haven't I Leaped?"

There was a loud knock on the door. "Will?" Gene's concerned voice called out. "Are you okay? You've been in there a long time."

"Yes, I'm fine, Gene." Sam walked over to the sink and turned on the faucet. He rinsed off his sticky hands. "I'll be out in a minute."

Al exhaled from his cigar. The smoke curled up around his head. He tilted the link in his hand and shook it. "I don't know why you haven't Leaped. I'll go back and see what Ziggy has dug up so far." He pressed a button and the Imaging Chamber door opened behind him.

"Good," Sam said as he splashed cold water on his face. "Just don't take all day to come up with something." Al disappeared with a jab at the link. Sam shut off the water and picked up a towel. He dabbed his face off and opened the bathroom door.

Gene had returned to his desk. He tucked away the file he had been reading as Sam came back to his desk.

"I just needed to wash my hands and face," Sam explained.

"Yeah, it sure is hot, isn't it? Hottest summer on record for August, and September is supposed to be just as hot, from what I've heard. Breaking all the records across Oklahoma. We've never had a summer end this hot in Brick before." Gene got up from his desk and made his way to

25

the old-fashioned Coca-Cola machine sitting in the corner by the bathroom. He fished some money out of his pocket and dropped the coins into the slot. He pulled back the door and took out a bottle. Gene popped the cap on the side of the machine and took a long drink. He wiped his mouth with the back of his hand and gave Sam a long look. "You sure you're okay, Will? You aren't suffering from heat stroke or anything, are you?" He offered the bottle to Sam. "You seem sort of forgetful today. You might feel better if you had something to drink. You want one?"

"Yes." Before Sam could find some extra change in his pocket, Gene had produced an ice-cold bottle out of the machine. He handed it over to Sam.

"Thank you," Sam said as he tipped the bottle back. He swallowed and began to choke. He pulled the bottle away from his mouth and grimaced. "I forgot how much sugar they put in a regular soda. I usually only drink diet." He set the bottle down on the desk and smacked his mouth, trying to get rid of the sugary taste.

Gene eyed his bottle and his eyes drifted back to Sam. "Diet, Will? I never heard of a diet soda."

"Never mind," Sam said as he picked up the bottle and swallowed another mouthful. The second mouthful wasn't so bad. "So Gene, how big would you say Brick is?"

Gene took his drink back to his desk. "I guess we're still around 750. When I worked on the census in '50 it was about that. I think when Mrs. Watt's baby is born that will bring it to"—he paused and closed his eyes—"753, I think. Why?"

The clock on the wall chimed. Gene looked up at the clock. "Look at the time," he said. He picked up a pencil and tapped his desk. He glanced back at the clock on the wall and then over at Sam. Sam was too busy sorting through the desk to pay much attention to Gene. "Suppose you know what time it is, don't you, Will?"

Sam studied the clock. "I guess, if that clock is correct, it's quarter to six. Why?" Sam asked. "Am I supposed to be somewhere now?"

Gene stopped tapping his pencil. "You know me, Will. I always try to mind my own business and all, but I know how Meg feels when you're late."

Sam cocked his head. "Meg?"

Gene nodded. "Yep." He pointed at the clock. "I know we had a hectic day and all but. . . ." He whistled. "You should have been home almost an hour ago for dinner. And I know you didn't call her. She's going to have a fit when you do get home. You should run along now. I can handle this end. Doc Adams will be over later. I'll be fine," Gene as he kicked his feet up on the desk. "Just let Tom sleep it off, just like always, right?"

"Okay," Sam answered. He noticed a slight drawl to his speech. "Remember to let Doc examine his eye. You know where to reach me if you have any problems?"

"Sure do, but I can tell that it's gonna be a quiet evening. Too hot for anything else." Gene opened his drawer and pulled out a magazine. "I bought the latest comics at the drugstore in Ashcroft. It's perfect for a night like this. Yes, it's going to a long, hot, quiet night." Gene flipped open the latest issue of *Superman* and settled down to read it.

Sam nodded and walked toward the door. He looked back over his shoulder and bid Gene good night.

CHAPTER TWO

Fortunately for Sam, the town of Brick, Oklahoma, was small and he didn't have too much trouble locating Maple Street, where Will Williams lived. Sam parked the black and white squad car in the gravel driveway and shut off the engine. He sat in the car and studied the house through the windshield.

The house was two stories tall, painted white with dark green trim. It had a large front porch, complete with a porch swing. A large maple tree stood tall in the front yard. No breeze stirred the leaves on the tree.

Sam gulped, climbed out of the car, and headed toward the porch. He had taken his first step leading up to the porch when the screen door flew open. It banged against the side of the house and out ran a small girl. She nearly plowed Sam down as she came flying down the stairs. She wrapped her arms around Sam's waist and squeezed. She pulled back, her eyes twinkling with delight. "You're late, Daddy. And boy, are you in big trouble."

Sam gazed down at the little girl. She looked like she was twelve years old, maybe thirteen. She wore a red-and-white striped T-shirt (slightly soiled) underneath a pair of faded blue overalls. Her feet were adorned with white socks and a pair of red tennis shoes, the laces knotted in double knots. Her chestnut hair was parted in the middle and braided into two plaits that almost touched the middle of her back. She had knocked off a plain red baseball cap on her way out of the house and it landed on the porch steps. Sam figured by the generous sprinkling of freckles across her cheeks, nose, and forehead, she didn't wear the cap much of the time.

"What's wrong, Daddy? Did you forget what I looked like since this morning?" She cocked her head and gave Sam a delightful, funny smirk.

"No," Sam said, somewhat taken aback. He reached down and retrieved her red cap. "I did not forget what you look like. You startled me the way you came flying out of the house."

The girl motioned for Sam to lean down. Sam obliged and she spoke to him in a low voice, "Momma's really mad. She *hates* it when you're late and don't call." She scrunched up her nose and rolled her eyes.

Sam held out his hands. "I couldn't help it," he answered, matching her own soft tone of voice. "Police business."

"Oh," the girl said, smiling widely. "Well, you've got to tell it to her. Mom thinks you should be here for dinner at five sharp no matter what." She twisted her head in the direction of the door, causing her braids to swing out away from her head. When she looked back she beamed, seeing that she had made Sam smile.

"Rebecca Sue Ellen Williams!" A loud piercing voice penetrated through the screen door and out into the front yard.

"Oh no," the girl whispered under her breath. She turned around and folded her arms across her chest, her feet

29

spread apart. She stood in front of Sam in a stance as if to protect him.

The screen door creaked open and Sam found himself staring up at a woman. The woman came out on the porch and folded her arms across her chest, matching Rebecca's stance. She was very tall and she cut a good figure in her pale blue cotton dress. Her blond hair was curly and it fell in soft waves around her face. Her blue eyes blazed out as she looked at Rebecca and then at Sam. She pursed her red lips into a thin frown and tapped her fingers against her folded arm. "Will Williams!" she scolded. "Where have you been? Supper's been getting cold and I've been worried. You didn't call." Her pumps tapped in time with her drumming fingers.

Sam opened his mouth to respond, but Rebecca beat him to it. "He just got here, Momma. He was on police business." Rebecca held her head high as she announced this.

"Your father had a tongue when he left the house this morning and I'm sure he still has it. He can answer for himself, young lady. As you for, I thought I told you to watch your little brother. Honestly, Rebecca! When are you going to start minding me?"

Rebecca stuck out her chin and scowled at her mother. "Maybe when you stop calling me Rebecca. I hate that name. It's a baby-sounding name. You know I want to be called Becca."

Rebecca's mother's eyes flared from up on the porch and her toe tapping stopped. She took a deep breath and pointed her index finger toward her daughter. "Don't you start getting sassy with me, missy," she warned. "I don't have the patience to put up with you this week. Mind your manners or you'll find yourself grounded."

Becca started to reply but Sam reached down and squeezed her shoulder. "Did I hear you say dinner was getting cold?" he asked.

Becca's mother sighed. She glared at Becca and then slowly turned her attention to Sam. "Yes, stone cold. As

30

we speak. Come in and get washed up. I'll see if we can't salvage some of the dinner.''

"Here, Becca," Sam said as he gave her a push toward the house, "go inside and find your brother." Becca smiled as she waltzed up the front steps, past the watchful eye of her mother. Sam noticed the piercing stares exchanged by mother and daughter as they passed on the porch.

Inside the house Sam found himself in a formal living room with the furniture polished and arranged neatly. A closet was off to Sam's right and a big oversized sofa sat in front of the fireplace. Fresh flowers were arranged in several vases set around the room.

"Go find Tyler and you both get washed up for supper. And, Becca, don't take forever, either." Meg strode into the kitchen past Becca and Sam.

Sam started to follow Meg into the kitchen but Becca grabbed his arm. "Daddy," she warned Sam, "aren't you forgetting something?" Becca shook her head and pulled the gun out of his holster.

"Hey, wait just a . . ." Before Sam could snatch the gun out of Becca's grasp, she had opened it, emptied the chamber, closed the barrel, and handed the empty gun back to Sam.

"Who taught you how to do that?" Sam whispered in surprise. Becca had opened a closet door behind Sam and was pointing to a wooden box on the top shelf. Sam retrieved the box and handed it to Becca. She swiftly opened it and put away the gun and ammunition as Sam unbuckled the holster around his waist. "You and Grandpa did," Becca whispered back. She handed Sam the box, which he replaced on the top shelf, and shut the closet door.

"There's no lock on this door," Sam said as he fiddled with the door knob.

"You're always threatening to put a lock on that old door but you haven't yet." Becca smiled and bounced into the kitchen, with Sam following close behind.

At the stove stirring a large pot was an older, black woman. She wore a crisp, white apron and she didn't turn

31

around as Sam and Becca came through the doorway. She was watching the pan on the stove, her head bobbing up and down to Becca's mother's constant stream of commentary. A scattering of gray hair dotted her tight head of curls and only her thin, wrinkled arms gave away her age. Becca's mother stood at the sink and she was filling up large glasses of dark iced tea.

Becca maneuvered through the hubbub of the kitchen and opened the back door. *"Tyler!"* she screamed. *"Supper's ready!"*

The older woman at the stove shook her head and continued to stir. Becca's mother set the pitcher of iced tea down loudly on the countertop and made an exasperated noise.

Sam couldn't help but chuckle. He could vaguely remember calling his brother and sister in a similarly loud fashion. Of course, he had grown up on a dairy farm. If you had to call someone for dinner and they happened to be in the barn, then you needed a good pair of lungs.

"What are you laughing at?" Becca's mother snapped at Sam. She had begun to set the glasses at the table. "Do you think it's funny that the whole neighborhood can hear your daughter scream like a banshee?"

"I haven't heard that phrase since my mother..." Sam's voice trailed off as he looked into Meg's face. She wasn't smiling.

The woman at the stove clucked her tongue and set the spoon down. "Becca, you go out there and collect your brother for dinner. You haven't been brought up in the woods so don't act like it. Go on now."

Becca didn't argue with the older woman. She nodded and mumbled, "Yes, ma'am," as she went outside.

"Miss Meg, do you want me to set out those biscuits now or are you all going to eat them for breakfast?" The woman reached for an oven mitt and turned around to look at Sam for the first time. Her dark eyes danced as she looked Sam over from head to toe.

"Yes, please set them out, Miss Beulah. I swear, Will,

if this house gets off schedule for one minute, everything's ruined.''

Becca came back inside the kitchen dragging her struggling little brother with her. "Come on, Tyler. Get inside for dinner.''

Tyler laughed and dragged his feet into the kitchen. The little blond boy was dressed in a red jumper and white shoes. He came wobbling into the kitchen and looked up at Sam. He giggled and waved his small chubby fingers in the air. "Who dat?''

"It's Daddy, you lug-nut,'' proclaimed Becca. She walked over to the kitchen sink and held her hands under the water. "You're a pain, Tyler.''

"Rebecca! Don't talk to your little brother that way,'' Meg said from the table. She reached down and gathered Tyler up in her arms. "Let's wash our hands now.''

Becca threw an annoyed look at her parents as she walked around the other side of the table. "I will never understand why you and Momma decided to have another child.'' She pulled out a chair and sat down. "All I ever do anymore is watch him. He's always getting into trouble and he's disgusting when he eats. He's the worst two year old in the world.''

Meg was drying Tyler's hands at the sink. "And he probably thinks you are the best big sister in the world,'' Meg chided as she sat Tyler down in his high chair. "You could try and be nicer, Rebecca.''

Becca shrugged. "Eleven years seems like a long time to wait for a second child is all I'm saying.''

"Becca, you know better than to speak like that at the table in front of your parents.'' Miss Beulah set a bowl of mashed potatoes on the table. "I know you were raised with better manners than that. And don't give me that little innocent look either. It don't fool me at all.''

Becca started to retort but a stern look from Sam stopped her short. "Yes, ma'am,'' she mumbled as she picked up her fork and began to pick at her food.

The meal was great. Sam helped himself to seconds of

33

chicken-fried steak, mashed potatoes with gravy, biscuits, and fresh green beans. Meg said the prayer and did most of the talking, while Tyler's antics kept everyone entertained. As the family was finishing up, Miss Beulah began to clear away the dinner dishes.

"Rebecca, why don't you help Miss Beulah with the dishes?" Meg asked.

"Momma, that's not fair. Why do I always have to help with the dishes?" Becca pouted and didn't move from her seat.

"That's a silly question. I don't expect your father to do the dishes. He's been at work all day, unlike some people I know. Now, I have to give your brother a bath, young lady, and I don't have time to sit here and go over all the reasons why you have to help out with the chores." Meg held her ground firmly as she lifted Tyler out of the high chair.

"Don't argue with your mother, Becca," Sam said as he wiped his fingers with his napkin. He saw a look of defeat cross over Becca's face. She seemed to silently accuse Sam of joining sides with the enemy.

"But I can't help tonight," she protested loudly. "I was going to meet Patty and go frog hunting." Becca turned her pleading, deep brown eyes on Sam.

Sam wasn't buying into those deep brown eyes. "First, you help with the dishes. Then we'll see about the frogs." When Becca realized she wasn't going to change his mind, she reluctantly began to gather up the dishes on the table, muttering under her breath. "I always have chores to do. Tyler never has any chores."

Miss Beulah clucked her tongue. "He's only two years old, Becca. You didn't start doing any chores till you were six or seven. Seems like you had a lot of time to do as you pleased." She raised her eyebrows and handed a plate to Becca. "Besides, I like it when you help me."

"Thank you, Becca," Sam said as he gave Becca a pat on her shoulder as she went by. She made a face and clanked the dishes down on the counter.

34

"Those dishes better not be chipped," Meg warned as she cradled Tyler on her hip and headed upstairs. Tyler giggled and waved as Meg carried him away.

Miss Beulah poured a tall glass of iced tea and set it down on the table. "There's your iced tea. You go on and sit a spell on the front porch, Will. Becca and I will have this kitchen cleaned up in no time at all."

Sam thanked Miss Beulah and took the glass. "Now don't cause Miss Beulah any grief, Becca."

"Hrmph!" Becca grunted as she clanked the pots into the sink and turned the faucet on.

Sam walked back through the living room and out onto the front porch. He headed for the porch swing and eased his body into it. The sun was setting and twilight had arrived in Brick. The air was still hot and sticky. He sipped the tea and gently rocked back and forth in the swing. The iced tea had just the right amount of lemon and sugar added. Sam swallowed another refreshing mouthful. He closed his eyes and listened to the noise coming from the kitchen. Muffled voices and the sound of water running in the sink. The crickets sang off in the bushes and if you listened closely, you could hear the frogs calling out to one another. The first star of the evening appeared in the quickly darkening sky. The only breeze Sam felt was the one he made as he rocked back and forth in the swing. He sank lower in the swing and watched as the first lightning bugs began to emerge and blink on and off, on and off.

The screen door slammed open behind him and Becca ran up to Sam and declared, "The dishes are done. Can I go?"

"Hold on there. Where are you going?"

Becca's face fell. "I'm going frog hunting, Daddy. Boy, are you getting forgetful in your old age. I told you that after dinner," Becca replied as she skipped down the stairs two at a time.

"Wait a minute," Sam called out. He came down the steps and grabbed Becca's shoulder. "It's getting dark now. Why don't you skip the frog hunting tonight?"

35

Becca looked up at Sam and crinkled up her nose and forehead. "Daddy, you can only catch frogs in the dark; that's when they come out. Besides, I've done it lots of times before. I'm just going down by the creek. I'll be with Patty. I'm going to catch the best leaper for the frog-jumping contest," Becca turned away from Sam and stepped out.

"Rebecca Williams."

Becca halted in her tracks. She spun around, her braids flying out. "But Daddy!" she began to protest.

"I think you should stay home tonight."

Becca kicked at the ground with her feet. "Why can't I go?"

"Because . . . I said so." Sam winced. He'd always hated it when his parents used that kind of reasoning with him.

"That's a lousy reason." Becca dug her toes into the ground as if she were getting ready to do battle.

In the back of his mind, Sam recalled that Al insisted he was here to prevent a murder. Since he didn't have any more information to go on, Sam knew he would feel safer if everyone in this family stayed home tonight. Of course, he needed to come with a real good excuse to appease Becca. "How about if I make it up to you? I'll take you to the movies instead?"

Becca stopped kicking and thought this proposal over. "I guess so," she said tentatively.

Sam let out a sigh of relief. "Good."

"But on one condition," Becca announced, looking Sam dead in the eyes. "Just you and me, like we always used to go. I don't want Tyler tagging along. We'd have to see a baby movie if he comes and I'm too old for baby movies. And it would have to be after the Labor Day picnic, too. Momma would kill us if we tried to drive into Dunsmoore on Saturday. We're going to have to wait till after this stupid picnic this weekend."

"Well, those are a lot of conditions, but I think it sounds fair," Sam replied slowly. He flipped the end of Becca's nose with his finger and that made Becca smile.

"Okay," Becca mumbled as she climbed back up the stairs to the house. "A movie. Just the two of us," she said over her shoulder.

"Just the two of us," Sam repeated as he watched her go.

"And no Tyler and no Momma. And we get lots of buttered popcorn."

"Lots of buttered popcorn." Sam nodded and smiled. "Sounds like a date, Becca."

Becca blushed deeply and opened the screen door. "Oh, Daddy. You know girls don't go on dates with their dads. That's silly." Sam watched her enter the house, breezing past Meg as she came to the doorway.

"Will, I'm getting ready to put Tyler down for the night. You want to come up and tuck him in?"

"Sure." Sam took the porch steps in one easy hop.

Tyler was laughing and giggling as he toddled around the living room. Miss Beulah had her sweater draped over one arm and her purse in the other. She wagged a finger in Tyler's direction.

"He is a happy child, indeed." She slipped the purse onto her arm. "Reminds me of you, William. I used to change your diaper and you'd just twitter and chirp like a songbird." Meg laughed and Sam felt his ears burning. "I'll be going now, Miss Meg. It would be no trouble at all for me to come in tomorrow on my day off and help you get ready for the picnic. No trouble at all."

Meg had gathered up Tyler in her arms and was going up the stairs. "Nonsense, Miss Beulah. We can manage around here for one day. I can do the shopping myself. Maybe I can get Becca to help me. Besides, you stayed late tonight. David will be missing you. We'll see you on Thursday."

Miss Beulah laughed softly. "As long as David knows where the food is he'll be fine." She tucked the sweater around her shoulders. "He's gonna finish up his requirements at the church's school this year. Once he passes, then

37

we can see about applying for that college in Boston next fall.''

Meg sighed. ''I don't see how you could let David go so far away. All the way up to Boston.''

''He's got to go where he will be accepted.'' Miss Beulah stopped and turned her brown eyes on Sam. She smiled and paused by the door. ''I'm so proud of him. Wish your father was still alive, William. He'd just be busting to know that David's going to college, just like your father said he would.'' She reached out and patted Sam's arm. ''You better get some rest, William. You're looking mighty tired around your eyes. Can't have the sheriff looking tired at the biggest picnic of the year, now can we?''

''Yes, ma'am,'' Sam said cautiously. He cast his eyes down as Miss Beulah headed out the door. He closed the door and headed upstairs after Meg.

Sam passed what he guessed had to be Becca's room, merely by the volume of the record player. He pressed his ear to the door and heard an Elvis Presley tune playing on the turntable. He pulled back from her door and smiled. Sam thought he could hear Becca faintly singing along with the record. Sam heard the giggles and cooing of Tyler and Meg and he moved on.

Meg was just tucking Tyler under the sheets when Sam entered the room. Meg smoothed his hair back and tickled his ribs gently. She noticed Sam standing in the doorway and she got up from the bed. ''You sleep tight, little boy. Momma loves you.'' She planted a kiss on his cheek and stepped back from the bed.

Sam slipped into the bedroom and knelt awkwardly down by Tyler's bed. Tyler looked up into Sam's eyes and reached out to touch Sam's nose.

''You would go for the nose.'' Sam laughed and took the small hand and held it in his big one. ''You sleep tight, Tyler, okay?''

Tyler smiled and laughed. ''Who you?'' He blinked his eyes and watched Sam's face.

''Tyler Williams!'' Meg's voice chided over Sam's

shoulder. "That's your daddy, you silly boy. I don't know what game you're playing tonight, mister, but I don't like it. Stop fooling around and kiss your daddy good night."

Tyler did as he was told. "Nite-nite."

Sam reached over the bed and turned off the light. "You lie still and go to sleep, Tyler."

"Green." Tyler pointed at his own eye, yawned, and turned over. He pulled a yellow bunny up close to his face and snuggled down under the sheets.

Sam pushed up off the floor and found himself looking into Meg's eyes. She tipped his chin up and examined his face very closely. "What's he mean, 'green'? You don't have green eyes."

Sam smiled and batted his eyes at Meg. "Beats me. Do you have a clue?"

"No," Meg sighed as she looked at Sam closely. "I don't. I think this whole family has gone a little crazy lately."

"Well, I wouldn't worry about it." Sam gently pushed Meg out of the bedroom.

Sam listened as Meg talked all the way down the hallway about the preparations that needed to get done in time for the Labor Day picnic on Saturday. She swung open a door and Sam followed her inside.

"I'll never get all those party favors done by Saturday. I should never have said I'd be the game committee chairman and volunteer to cook all those pies for the bake sale. But what was I to do when Lucy and Herb backed out at the last minute? Can you imagine them planning a trip to Houston at this time of year? Anyway, I could really use Rebecca's help tomorrow. Do you think you could speak to her? She is becoming so difficult lately. Not that she was ever an easy child, for me at least. She'd do anything you'd say." Meg undid her earrings and dropped them in a glass dish on the dresser. She then began to struggle to undo her zipper on her dress, reaching over her shoulders and tugging at the material.

Sam stood in the doorway, surveying the room. He

39

paused and then went over to Meg. He caught her zipper in his fingers and undid it. As soon as he had unzipped her dress, he backpedaled until he ran into the side of the four-poster bed, where he sat down promptly. He cast his eyes on the floor, avoiding Meg as he spoke. "She's your typical teenager, that's all. I hate to tell you this, Meg, but it's going to get worse before it gets better."

"Lord, that's all I need to hear." Meg lowered her voice as she got out of her dress. "Here we are talking about Rebecca and the picnic and I completely forgot to ask how your day was. Since you were late I suspect you were tied up getting that fool white trash off the roof again?"

Sam began to undo his shoes and looked up. "You mean Tom Madison?" He caught Meg standing in her slip and he dropped his head back down.

"Well naturally, Will. Who else has managed to make a complete fool out of you and this town these past three months? In some ways I just wish he'd go ahead and jump. He'd save you a lot of headaches. God knows he wouldn't be missed much."

"That's a terrible thing to say, Meg." Sam stopped un-lacing his shoes. "I don't want to see him dead."

"That's not what you said after the last time you climbed up on that roof and hauled him off. After that big produc-tion of throwing a watermelon—and I must say, William, I am a little ashamed to have you, as my husband and the sheriff, tossing fruit off the city hall balcony like some high school prankster. I mean, the last time it took you all af-ternoon to get him to come in. All Tom was waiting for was for Carla to show up." Meg sighed and reached for her hair brush. "Besides, you know as soon as he's sober again he'll go right back to that Carla Sue. They'll be fight-ing and, mark my words, up on that balcony he'll go, all over again. Then you'll be expected to go up and fetch him. And the whole town will be out in the street watching this whole affair. It's downright silly. And all this trouble over a two-bit, low-life, white trash, good-for-nothing *s-l-u-t* like Carla Sue."

Sam dropped his shoe. "Margaret!"

Meg stopped brushing her hair. "Well, it's the God-honest truth, Will. Carla Sue is a waitress and God only knows what else down at that filthy drinking hole. I've heard stories about that girl that would curl your hair. Tom doesn't know any better. She sure wouldn't miss him one bit if he were to jump. Probably that's just what she wants him to do," she muttered as she pulled her brush through her hair.

"It's not a great idea to be spreading gossip about those two," Sam reminded her as he kicked off his other shoe.

"Will, it's not gossip and you know it." Meg turned toward the mirror and began to fuss with her face. "Those two have caused you more grief and trouble in just the past three months than in all the time you've been sheriff. If it's not Tom on the ledge, then it's a rowdy fight at the Hole involving Carla Sue. Do you remember that last incident? With that sailor, no less." Meg shook her head. "Reminds me of that time that traveling circus came through town . . ."

A flicker of shadow against the hallway wall caught Sam's eye. Sam got up and crept over to the door. He leaned out the doorway and came face to face with Becca, who had been eavesdropping at her parents' open door. Becca's mouth dropped open and she looked as surprised as Sam. She gathered up her nightgown in one quick motion and took off in the direction of her room, her bare feet carrying her quickly and silently down the hall. She ran to her room and shut the door.

"What are you doing?" Meg had paused and found Sam at the door. "Did you hear Tyler?"

"No, I don't think it's Tyler."

Meg walked over to the doorway and stood next to Sam. She looked very pretty, with her hair combed, standing there in her slip. "I'll go check on him on my way back from the bathroom. He's such a light sleeper," she said as she slipped out the door.

Sam thought about Becca's botched eavesdropping at-

41

tempt as he began to undo his shirt. He crossed back over by the bed and sat down. He finished undressing, folding his uniform over the back of a chair not far from the bed. He pulled back the sheets and climbed in on the far side. He listened to the sounds outside the window. He could hear the booming of thunder far off in the distance. Sam thought about Tom Madison and why he had been Leaped into this little town. Meg still hadn't returned to the bedroom. Sam dozed off about twenty minutes later and drifted into a dreamless sleep.

Wednesday, August 31, 1955

Sam awoke the next morning with the bright, warm sun shining in his face. He brought a hand up to his chin and felt a day's growth of whiskers. He opened his eyes and gazed up into the innocent face of Tyler, who was standing next to the bed. Sam sat up with a jolt and looked around the room. His memory of the Leap began to drift back and Sam brought his wristwatch up to his face. It was ten minutes after six and the sun felt like it was midday as it streamed through the bedroom windows. Sam lowered his arm and looked at Tyler. Tyler's blue eyes sparkled and danced as he watched Sam slowly wake up.

"Morning, Tyler. You're up early." Tyler giggled and handed Sam his yellow bunny. Sam held the raggedy bunny up in the air. "What's its name?" Tyler only smiled and stuck his thumb in his mouth. "Does it have a name?" Sam tried again.

Tyler nodded and pulled his wet thumb out of his mouth. "Bunny."

"Bunny," Sam repeated as he eased his body up on his elbow and got a good look around the room. Meg's side of the bed was empty, the sheets and quilt pulled up to her pillow.

"Pee," Tyler announced suddenly, watching Sam more

intently. Tyler then began to pick up his feet as if he were marching. "Tyler, pee. Pee now."

Sam flung back the covers and juggled the yellow bunny under his arm. "Wait, Tyler. Just a second." Tyler shook his head and grabbed at his pajama bottoms.

"Okay, okay, we're going." Sam groaned as he pulled himself up out of bed, offering his free hand to the little boy. Tyler grabbed his hand and pulled Sam in the direction of the nearest bathroom.

When Sam came down for breakfast, dressed and shaved, he was carrying Tyler on his shoulders. Tyler giggled and laughed, clutching his bunny as they bounced down the stairs.

Sam entered the kitchen as the aroma of bacon, biscuits, and eggs wafted through the air. Meg was dressed smartly in a yellow dress, fussing over a spitting skillet on the stove. She smiled at Sam and Tyler and nodded toward a cup of coffee on the table. She wiped her hands on her apron and took Tyler from Sam's shoulders. She tucked Tyler into his high chair and began to set the eggs and biscuits out on the table. Sam gave her a hand and she sighed a heartfelt thanks. "I have so many things to do between now and Saturday," Meg lamented as she set out a stick of butter and some homemade preserves. She stood back and smiled down at Tyler. "I've made a list up for shopping later this afternoon." She pulled out a chair next to Tyler and reached for a banana. She peeled it and gave a piece to Tyler. "Go ahead and get started on your eggs before they get cold," she scolded Sam. She looked up at the clock and pursed her lips. "Rebecca!" Meg hollered up to the kitchen ceiling. "Get down here before your breakfast gets cold."

Becca's feet thundered down the stairs and dashed past the kitchen doorway. "I don't want any breakfast, Momma," Becca hollered back to her mother as she made a beeline straight to the front door.

Sam cleared his throat and set down his fork. "Becca.

43

Come in here, please." The screen door slowly squeaked shut on its hinges and Becca came trudging back to the kitchen. She stood in the kitchen's doorway avoiding Sam's gaze.

"What do you mean you're not going to eat breakfast? Are you getting sick or something?" Meg sounded more annoyed than concerned.

"No. I just don't want to eat anything," Becca replied tartly as she studied the floor.

"Rebecca, look people in the eye when you talk to them," her mother reminded her. "And when are you going to do something about your hair?"

"What about my hair?" Becca challenged. She picked up one of her braids and inspected it closely.

"You haven't washed your hair in three days, by my estimate," Meg scolded her daughter. "You could at least comb out those braids of yours. You are going to wash your hair for the picnic, aren't you?"

"Why?" Becca snapped. "I'm just going to a stupid old picnic. It's not like I'm going to church or something." Becca tossed the braid over her shoulder and peeked quickly at Sam.

"If you're not coming down with something, then you can sit down and eat breakfast with us," Meg pointed out. "Dirty hair and all."

Becca started to retort when a warning reproach from Sam stopped her cold. She instead thumped over to the table and reached for a slice of bacon. "I'm eating now. Happy?" she announced between mouthfuls.

"Eat now," Tyler mimicked in a shrill voice and rammed a piece of banana in his mouth.

Meg sighed and tapped Tyler on the shoulder, "Close your mouth when you chew." She looked across the table at Rebecca. She was tired of arguing over the table with her oldest child. She reached into her apron and produced some cards. "I'm delighted, Rebecca. Here, I want you to run these recipes over to Mrs. King's house this morning. She needs them for the picnic on Saturday."

44

"That's clear across town," Becca whined. "I wasn't going to that part of town today. And call me Becca—please, Momma?" she added hastily. Meg simply held out the cards. Becca reached for the cards, wiping her hand on her jeans, and stuffed the cards in her pocket.

Sam took a sip of his coffee and set the cup down. "Don't fret, Becca. I'll drop you off on my way into work."

Becca had been avoiding Sam's gaze all morning long. She quickly shook her head and began to backpedal out of the kitchen. "I'm finished eating now and I can run over to Mrs. King's house faster than you could drive me," she insisted.

"Nonsense." Sam picked up a fork of scrambled eggs. "Just sit down here at the table. I'll be ready to go in a minute." Meg threw a strange look in Sam's direction. Sam just smiled at Meg and took a bite out of a biscuit he had smeared with preserves.

Becca knew when she was defeated. She ignored Sam as best as she could, and yanked out her chair. She flopped down and picked up her fork and began to stab at her eggs. In a moment she realized she was hungry after all and began to eat. She ate until Sam announced he was ready to go. Becca dropped her fork, downed her glass of milk, and bolted up out of the chair.

"Don't forget those recipes," her mother called after her. She was trying to wrestle a cup out of Tyler's grasp. "She's in a peculiar mood today."

"I'll see about having Becca give you a hand with your shopping this afternoon, Meg. I'll even try and get home early to watch Tyler." Sam leaned over and ran his fingers through Tyler's blond curls.

Meg shook her head. "I don't think Rebecca will ever want to willingly help me with anything. Especially with my shopping for the picnic. You heard how snippy she was this morning."

Sam smiled. "I think after I speak to her she'll have a

45

different frame of mind. I think she'll be glad to help you out this afternoon.''

Tyler smashed the remainder of his banana onto the top of his high chair, smearing it around with his hands.

''Tyler Williams!'' Meg admonished the boy. Sam wagged his finger at the smiling boy, slipped past Meg, and edged his way out of the kitchen.

Becca was standing next to the police cruiser, kicking the heel of her red tennis shoe into the dirt. ''You don't have to drive me, Daddy. I can walk, you know,'' Becca insisted as Sam approached.

''Well, I need to talk to you about last night,'' Sam said as he opened the door for Becca.

Becca blinked pure innocence up at Sam as he held the door open for her. ''What about last night?''

''You know very well what I mean.'' Becca climbed in the front seat, her body drooping. Sam walked around to the driver's side. He slid in and adjusted the rearview mirror. Sam turned around to back out and Al's pale face stared back at him, a black fedora pulled low over his eyes. Sam jumped. Becca was kicking the floorboard with her heel and didn't see Sam jump in surprise.

''Hi, Sam.'' Al twisted in the back seat trying to get comfortable. He looked absolutely wretched. His dark, black eyes peered out from under the rim of the black hat. His face was washed out and very pale (even for Al). He seemed distracted as he looked out the window.

''Don't kick at the floor,'' Sam said to Becca as he turned around. He readjusted the rearview mirror and backed the car out of the driveway.

Becca decided not to beat around the bush and started off the conversation. ''I already know what you're going to say and I just want you to know it won't happen ever again.''

''Good,'' Sam said as he made a left turn and headed toward Main Street. ''And I'll tell you why it's never going to happen again.'' He glanced over his shoulder at Al. Al wasn't paying much attention to the conversation taking place in front of him. He was sitting hunched over, watching the town of Brick go by. He pulled at his tie and yanked the black fedora lower on his head.

"I learned my lesson last night. I never spied on you or Momma before and that's the honest truth. I just wanted to see if you were gonna talk about Tom Madison." Becca glanced up at Sam with her eyes. It was a look that Sam was sure would melt her father's heart.

"Why would you be interested in Tom Madison anyway?"

Becca shrugged. " 'Cause he's the guy who climbs out on the balcony, right? Always saying he's going to jump. That's a lot of excitement for this little town. Everyone is talking about it. I figured who would know more about it than my daddy, the sheriff."

"Whether your mother or I talk about Tom Madison or Thomas Jefferson, you're not to start eavesdropping on another person's conversation. Besides being impolite, it's very wrong. I'm disappointed in you, Becca."

"I know, Daddy, and I'm really sorry. I won't do it ever again. I promise." She paused a moment and fingered the cards in her pocket. "You didn't tell Momma, did you?"

Sam looked down at Becca. "What do you think?"

"You didn't tell her." She looked out the window as Main Street rolled by. "Otherwise, I'd be grounded for life."

Sam kept a straight face as the trio stopped at a flashing red light. "Just because I didn't tell your mother, doesn't mean I'm not going to punish you."

Becca's mouth dropped open and she sat up in the seat. "Punishment?"

"Yes. Becca, eavesdropping on a private conversation is a terrible thing to do."

"Only if you get caught," Al mumbled from the back seat.

Sam bit his lower lip and continued. "So you won't forget the next time—"

"There won't be a next time," Becca protested.

47

"I know, Becca." Sam pulled through the intersection. "Because after you spend the afternoon helping your mother shop for the Labor Day picnic, I'm sure you'll think twice before eavesdropping again."

"No!" shrieked Becca. She balled her hands into two small fists and punched the seat. "That's not fair. I didn't even hear what you two were talking about. I should have at least heard part of the conversation to receive that kind of a sentence."

Sam put his hand on Becca's shoulder. Becca's bottom lip formed a perfect pout. "I could still make you go shopping with your mother, ground you to your room for a week, *and* tell her everything." Becca's body slumped down in the seat under Sam's hand.

"I hate shopping with Momma," she muttered as she folded her arms across her chest.

Sam pulled the car into a stall in front of the jail. He shut off the engine and jangled the keys in his hand. "It's only for the afternoon, Becca, and your mother could use some help. She is very busy putting together this picnic. I think I'm letting you off easy, to be truthful. You're only going to have to spend an afternoon with her."

Becca rolled her eyes up in her head. "But it could kill me, Daddy. Mark my words. I'll die right there in Parcin's store. All you'll get is a phone call saying that your only daughter is dead. Do you want my death on your conscience the rest of your life?" Becca seemed to shudder in the midday heat.

Sam bit his lower lip to keep from laughing, but Al chuckled good-naturedly from the back seat. "She's gonna be one to watch out for later, Sam."

Sam shook his head, "I don't think it will kill you, Becca."

"Momma hates me, anyway," Becca pointed out. "She'd lock me down in the basement and throw away the key if it wasn't for you."

Sam leaned over in the seat. "Becca, now, you know that's not true. Your mother loves you just as much as she loves Tyler. You two are just going through a phase right now. My sister and my mother went through the same thing and they managed to live through it.''

"She loves Tyler best, then you. I don't think she likes me at all sometimes." Becca began to tick off the items on her fingers. "She's always nagging me about my clothes or my hair or the music I listen to." Becca cranked her head to one side and imitated her mother's voice. " 'Why don't you act like a lady instead of a tomboy?' 'Why are you always covered in mud?' Blah, blah, blah." Becca looked out the window and resumed talking in her normal voice. "I'm telling you she *hates* me."

Sam rubbed Becca's shoulder and tried not to laugh. "You know and I know she doesn't hate you. You two just seem to be in each other's hair right now. It will pass, Becca."

Becca shot a quizzical look up at Sam. "Maybe by the time I'm twenty and too old to care." She turned around in the seat. "How come she spends so much time with Tyler?"

"Because he's your little brother and he's only two, Becca. When he gets older he won't need so much of your mother's time and attention. I bet she gave you that much time and attention when you were that age. Probably more, by the look of things. Somebody sure spoiled you rotten."

Becca just shrugged, but let Sam keep his hand on her shoulder. "I'm not spoiled. Are you sure I only have to shop with her this one afternoon? And you won't tell her about last night?"

"That's the deal."

"Okay," Becca sighed. She looked up at Sam and then reached over and put her hand on top of his. "Daddy?" she asked in her sweetest voice.

"Yes?" Sam answered.

Becca cocked her head. "Did Aunt Karen and Grand-mother Williams really fight like Momma and me?"

Sam nodded, a serious look on his face. "Ummm . . . yes, they did."

49

Becca reached for the door handle. "I still don't think the punishment fits the crime." She climbed out, and before shutting the car door, asked, "What time?"

"Be back at the house at four. And don't be late."

Becca sighed dejectedly and muttered, "Okay, four o'clock." She began to walk toward Main Street.

"And don't forget those recipes," Sam called after her. Becca turned and waved and picked up her pace down the street.

Al zapped himself out of the back seat and waited for Sam. Even though Al could not feel the oppressive humidity pressing down on the town, that still didn't stop the beads of sweat from forming on his upper lip. Al kept swiping at his mouth and pulling at his hat. He was dressed in a black silk suit, with black shoes and a plain white shirt. Even his tie was black. As Al adjusted his hat for the tenth time this morning, Sam noticed his friend's uneasiness. The link twittered in his breast pocket, but Al paid little heed to the noise. His eyes were darting around the surroundings, not focusing on anyone or anything in particular. Dark purple circles were prominently displayed underneath Al's brown eyes.

Sam stretched his shoulders and fidgeted with the gun belt he had tied around his waist that morning. "Quaint little town, isn't it? Does Ziggy have a clue as to why I'm still here?"

Al snapped his attention to Sam and blinked. "Huh? Did you say something, Sam?" He absently wiped his lips with the back of his hand.

"You're really nervous about your meeting with Maxine," Sam pointed out. He looked around, making sure no one was watching him talk and gesture to Al. "You're dressed for a funeral, not a reunion."

"Yeah, and with any luck the funeral will be mine," Al observed dryly, jabbing his thumb into his chest. "I didn't get a wink of sleep last night worrying about this upcoming meeting today. I keep thinking, What could she possibly

50

want? I started thinking maybe I did something, you know?''

"Like what?''

"I don't know, like maybe I've got a kid I don't know about or something.''

"Al, that's ridiculous. I mean, Maxine would have told you about that sort of thing . . . wouldn't she?''

"I don't know anymore, Sam. I tossed and turned all night long. I'm a wreck, Tina's a wreck.'' Al sighed and looked around at the town again. "You know, I traveled through a lot of small towns just like this when I was with the Navy. Crisscrossed the whole country every which way. You know, these little towns never change, from county to county, from state to state. Same dusty, dinky little Main Streets with a bank on one end and a Dairy Queen at the other.'' He checked his watch.

"Al, lighten up. You haven't seen Maxine for . . . what, over ten years? She probably just wants to see you again for old times' sake.''

"Oh yeah, right!'' Al snorted and adjusted his tie. "I make it a habit to call up all my ex-wives if more than a decade passes and I haven't spoken to them.'' Al held out his hand and groaned as it quivered slightly. "You realize,'' he said, focusing on Sam, "I'm going to be gone for a few hours.''

Sam nodded and began to make his way toward the jail house. "Who's the lucky hologram who'll be taking your place today?''

Al fell in step with Sam, hovering a few inches above the ground. His patent leather shoes were shined to a mirror image. "I guess Gooshie.'' Al watched Sam roll his eyes and mutter to himself. He ignored Sam and continued. "It's just temporary. I know how much you love these substitutes. I don't anticipate being gone that long, so don't get your shorts in a knot. Just stay out of trouble for a couple of hours, lay low, and everything should be fine.''

Sam laughed to himself. He had heard that line before. "What about Ziggy?''

51

Al shook his head and rubbed at his temples. He pulled the link from his breast pocket. "Nothing yet. She's still digging back through all the records of these neighboring little towns. Without the original town records even simple background checks are next to impossible to run. Ziggy's cross-referencing everything, though, so if she does pull up anything, I'll let you know."

"Like why I'm still here?" Sam added quietly as an afterthought. He had come to the entrance of the jail. He turned and looked at Al, who seemed to be dreading his upcoming meeting more with each minute that passed. Al had removed the fedora and was wiping off his forehead with the hand that held the link. Al took a look around at the town and rotated his shoulders. He replaced the hat on his head and pulled it down. "I'm sure you'll be fine while I'm gone."

"Do I have any other choice?" Now it was Sam's turn to wipe his forehead off with the back of his arm. Dark patches of sweat were appearing under Sam's arms and in the middle of his back.

"Not really," Al told him. He noted how much Sam was sweating. "Um, Ziggy did inform us that this part of the Midwest was in a heat wave during '55. Set records all over the Southwest."

"Now there's a very useful piece of information. Tell Ziggy I said thanks for that. I can tell just by standing here it's close to a hundred degrees and the humidity is . . ." Sam watched as Al zeroed in on the button on Ziggy's handlink.

"Ninety-two percent. Gotta go, Sam."

"Say hello to Maxine for me."

Al smiled thinly and his finger trembled slightly as it hovered above the blinking light. He pressed the button and vanished. Sam turned and headed into the jail house.

Gene Dupree was sitting as close to the fan as he could get, his shirt soaked under his arms and around the collar. His feet were propped up on the table and the chair he was sitting in was tipped back on the rear two legs. Gene was reading a comic book with one hand and chewing on a doughnut with the other. The minute Sam came through the door, Gene quickly pulled his feet off the table and brushed the crumbs off his shirt. He wadded the comic book up into a thin tube and stuffed it into his top desk drawer. "Morning, Will," he mumbled as he tried to swallow the remaining bites of the jelly-filled doughnut.

"Morning, Gene. Did you have a quiet night?" Sam asked as he walked over to Gene's desk. "And how's our prisoner this morning?"

Gene was reaching for a cup of coffee to wash down the doughnut. He nodded and took a big gulp of coffee. "He's loud, hung over, and very upset," Gene said, and swallowed the rest of the doughnut. "Same as always."

Sam clucked his tongue and started to head back toward Tom's cell. "Did the doctor come by and look at the cut above his eye?"

"Yes, sir, he sure did." Gene reached for the ring of keys to the cells and got up to follow Sam. "Doc Adams stitched and cleaned the cut up."

Sam arrived at the cell and took a quick inventory of the prisoner. Tom Madison was lying on the metal bed frame; his weight was causing the frame to sag in the middle. He was sound asleep on his back, his mouth open and snoring as loud as a buzz saw. His chest rose and fell with each loud breath. A fly buzzed lazily around his head and Tom would twitch his nose as the fly tried to land on it. The odor rising from the room was a mixture of sweat, urine, and whiskey. Sam still couldn't believe that someone as huge as Tom had crawled out on that ledge above the sidewalk. Gene rattled the keys next to Sam and started to unlock the cell.

Sam held up his hand. "Wait, Gene. I don't want to let him go just yet." Sam still didn't know why he was here. If Ziggy did have her facts wrong then maybe Sam was here to prevent Tom from trying to kill himself again. The thought of having to climb back out on that balcony after

Tom gave Sam a headache. Maybe Tom might feel differently about attempting to plunge off the balcony if he spent a few hours in a hot, humid jail cell thinking things over.

A look of sheer puzzlement crossed Gene's face. He clutched the keys and jingled them a little. "But Will, we always let him sleep it off and then let him go home. You said that he's pretty harmless once the whiskey wears off. He's just going to get angrier if we keep him in here. We always released him before. You know, he never causes any trouble once he's sober."

Sam shook his head. "I want him to stay put today. Let him think about what landed him in this jail cell in the first place."

Gene looked even more confused. "He could stay in here till Christmas and I don't think it would change a thing. He's not a very quiet prisoner, Will. He's gonna give us a lot of trouble unless we let him go." Gene jangled the keys again.

"He stays for now. I want to question him again. I also want the doctor to look him over." Sam started to head back down the hallway and was startled as Gene reached out and grabbed his arm.

"What's going on here, Will? Question him about what?" Gene realized he was gripping Sam's arm and released it. He took a step back. "I'm sorry, Will. I'm just confused. We've never held Tom over before and if the game plan has changed I'd appreciate knowing it." Gene stopped and looked down at his hands.

Sam leaned back against the brick wall and studied his deputy for a minute. "I want him to think about what he did, Gene. A few hours in this cell won't hurt. And after he's had some time to really sober up, then I'll ask him some more questions. This may be different from how we usually treat Tom, but I don't want to go climbing back on that balcony."

"Oh, sure, now I understand," Gene said with a disappointed look on his face. He looked at Tom sleeping in the cell. "Whatever you say, Will. You're the sheriff. You

54

know best," Gene said as he swept past Sam.

Sam left Tom Madison snoring and returned to the office. Gene was sitting at his desk, sipping his cup of coffee. Sam walked over and checked the log book.

"At least things were quiet last night," Sam noted. The log was empty. The only entry was made early yesterday afternoon.

"Uh-huh," Gene grunted as he set down his coffee. He shifted in his seat and, without looking at Sam, said, "I think it's the heat. Makes people too tired to do anything at all."

Sam cleared his throat, "Look, Gene, so there aren't any hard feelings . . ." At that moment Tom Madison moaned loudly. The moan was followed by a loud, grating metal sound.

Gene rose out of his seat. "Tom's waking up."

Tom moaned again. He then began bellowing at the top of his lungs, "Gene! Gene Dupree! Goddamn it, you come back here and let me out. Gene, are you listening to me? I know you can hear me. Don't you sit out there at your little desk and ignore me. Gene! *Gene!*"

"I'll handle this," Sam said as he headed back down the hallway.

"You're gonna need help," Gene muttered under his breath as he followed Sam.

Tom Madison was sitting up on the metal bed. A white bandage above his eye was the only clean spot on him. Dried blood had run down his face and mixed in with the short stubble on his chin. The hands that rubbed his head were dirty and greasy. Two bloodshot eyes peered out at Sam beneath a mass of dirty, brown hair. Tom flipped the hair back out of his eyes with his dirt-smeared hand. He wasn't wearing any socks and his badly worn shoes hardly covered his feet. Tom scratched his large stomach and squinted at Sam. He tried to get up but couldn't pull himself off the bed. "Sheriff Williams, 'bout time you got here!" Tom bellowed inside the small cell. "You need to get yourself a new deputy, Sheriff Williams. This one won't let me go home. And I want to go home." Tom belched loudly and held his head.

"My deputy is doing just what I've told him to do. Tom Madison, I have placed you under arrest for attempted suicide. You will remain in custody until you answer some questions. I'm also going to ask for a psychiatric exam from our doctor. Maybe after all that is over, I can let you go home. Do you understand all this?"

Tom blinked and shook his head. He lifted his soiled left hand up to the bandage. "No, I don't, Sheriff Williams. Doc Adams already came and fixed me up. Got stitches and everything. I just want to go home and sleep this off, Sheriff. You tell Gene to open that cell door. I don't need to see the doctor again."

Sam folded his arms across his chest and shook his head. "I need to ask you some questions, Tom," he began.

Tom lowered his hand. "I don't want to answer any questions. Doc Adams stitched me up and . . ." He winced. "Look, I got me a powerful headache. I'm hot and tired and I just want to go home." Tom turned his anger on Gene. "Gene Dupree, don't you stand there like a bump on a log. Open this damn door. I'm too hung over to play games with the sheriff. You tell him I don't want to waste my time sitting in his stinking jail cell. I've got to go home and check on Carla Sue. She'll be worried about me."

Gene stood next to Sam and fingered the keys nervously on his belt buckle. "Sheriff Williams says you've got to stay put," Gene answered woodenly.

Sam looked at Gene. "Go give Doc Adams a call. Have him report over here as soon as he can." Seeing Gene do a double take at that, Sam added, "Is something wrong, Gene?"

Gene cleared his throat. "You want me to call Doc and have him drive all the way over here?" Gene started to fidget in the hallway. "Doc's gonna be mad if he comes all the way back here for nothing, Will."

"Tell him I want him to examine Tom."

56

"That's right, Gene," Tom Madison teased the deputy. "You just keep kissing up to the sheriff. Just liked you kissed up to his daddy. You're still gonna be a worthless, scrawny nobody, no matter who you kiss up to." Tom demonstrated by making loud kissing noises.

Gene whirled and clutched the bars with his hands. "You watch your mouth while you're in this jail. You're a sorry sap to be bad-mouthing Sheriff Williams. You can't even keep track of Carla Sue. Bet she had a good afternoon off while you were up on that balcony."

Tom struggled off the bent bed frame and rose to his full height. He staggered toward Gene, colliding with the metal bars. He started to reach through the bars with his thick hands. When he couldn't reach Gene through the bars, Tom cut loose with a string of obscenities aimed at the deputy.

Sam pulled Gene away from the cell and gave him a push down the hallway. "Go call the doctor, Gene. And Tom Madison," Sam informed his prisoner, "you'd better make yourself comfortable. It's going to be a hot day in here."

Tom stood still, his upper lip curling into a snarl as he stared Sam down. He then began to inform Sam all about his parentage, in big colorful terms. Sam turned and headed back down the hallway. Tom's voice continued to boom all the way back to the office.

Gene was on the phone and very agitated. "I don't know why he wants you to come back. I'm not a mind reader. All he said is, you need to examine Tom again." Gene rubbed his sweaty neck. " 'Course I know you've got your appointments to keep. Yes, yes . . ." Gene rolled his eyes and watched as Sam sat down behind his desk. "Look, Doc," Gene interrupted, "Sheriff Williams wants you to come down here and—What? Yes. Fine. Yes, I'll be sure and tell him. Bye." Gene slammed down the phone. "Well, he's coming over, Will." Gene pulled out his chair and fell into it. "And Doc's about as thrilled as Tom Madison."

The arrival of Clarence Adams was marked as he barged into the jail house. Doc Adams (as everyone in Brick called him) came charging in, black bag in hand and a stethoscope dangling around his neck. He stood in the middle of the office, fanning himself with a large straw hat, his eyes blazing back and forth between Sam and Gene. His white, short-sleeved shirt clung to his hefty body. The wire-rimmed glasses perched on his large nose kept sliding down and the doctor kept pushing them up with his stout fingers. He was at least sixty years old if he was a day. His hair was silvery white and thinning. A loose strand fell down on his forehead and stirred in the breeze he was creating with his hat. The doctor set his bag down on Gene's desk with a loud thump. "What's going on here, Will? I've got my appointments in the morning. You know better than to pull me away from my patients unless it's an emergency— and I don't see an emergency here! I had to reschedule Widow Turnbull's physical examination in order to troop down here. She was mighty put off that I had to scoot her out of my office." He paused and caught his breath. The straw hat whipped through the air, back and forth, back and forth. Doc glared at Sam, waiting for an answer. "Well, Sheriff? What's the emergency?"

"It's not an emergency," Sam began to explain.

Doc Adams took three steps toward Sam. "What do you mean, there's no emergency! If I got pulled out of my practice, then by God, there'd better be an emergency here."

Sam shook his head. "I had Gene call you about Tom Madison."

The doctor blinked and fanned his face, "Oh? Why? Did his stitches come undone? Couldn't you have stopped the bleeding with a rag or something and waited until the afternoon to call me?" He chuckled and turned toward Gene. "Or was that the problem? Tom was leaking blood all over the place and poor Gene was fainting dead away?"

Gene swore under his breath and got up. "Wasn't any such problem with Tom. I can't help it when I see blood. It's bad enough to have the criminals ride me about it; I don't need you goading me too." He threw his arms in the air. "Will wanted me to call you back here to give Tom an exam and see if he's crazy."

The doctor's hand stopped fanning his face. "What did you say? Did I hear you correctly? I was yanked out of my practice—where, I might add, the temperature is *not* ninety-five degrees—and summoned here to administer an exam for mental illness?"

Sam spoke up. "I wanted you to check Tom out. Mentally and physically."

Doc Adams laughed and pulled a yellowed handkerchief from his pocket. He dabbed at his forehead and shook his head. "An exam?" He replaced the handkerchief and shifted the hat in his hands. "What is Tom doing, Will? Is he swinging from the eaves in his cell? Is he quoting Shakespeare and calling himself Donald Duck?"

"You're not taking this very seriously," Sam said. He got up from his desk and made the doctor retreat a step backwards.

"Of course I'm not taking this seriously, William. I can't believe you're asking me to do this. I think you need the exam, not Tom."

Now it was Sam's turn to get mad. "I had to crawl up on the city hall balcony yesterday and drag Tom in. I think he deserves to be examined simply for that."

"And you think that he's crazy 'cause he lounges on the balcony after a fight with his better half? Needle nuts!" Doc removed his glasses and wiped at his cheeks. "Tom Madison isn't crazy, Will. No more so than you or I. We all know he gets a little carried away from time to time. Especially when he fights with Carla Sue. Now, I admit, Will, Tom has been up to more mischief lately, but I can assure you he's not crazy. He's a little touched in the head, always has been, and that brings out the worst in him when he drinks. He's been up on that same balcony three, maybe four times and never has jumped. He won't either."

"How do you know?" Sam protested. "Are you willing to bet his life on it?"

Doctor Adams just shook his head. "Yes, I would, Will.

59

Tom Madison's not crazy. But I'm beginning to think you are for dragging me down here.'' Doc put his hat back on his head and reached into his pants pocket for a nickel. He flipped it at Gene. "Get me a soda, Gene. I'm about to expire in this office arguing with your boss." He turned and wagged a finger in Sam's direction. "Don't tell me you really dragged me down here to look at Tom Madison and decide if he's nuts." The only sound in the room was the clicking and whirling of the fan as it turned back and forth. Even Tom had grown quiet.

Sam's mind was whirling just as fast as that fan. He was trying to decide whether to say anything in Will's defense. This hayseed of a doctor was convinced that Tom Madison was as sane as everyone else in this small town.

Taking Sam's silence as an answer, Doc drawled, "Well, if I'm not needed." He turned and took the bottle of soda Gene offered him. He shook his head and began to make his way back out the door. He had a slight hitch to his walk. The phone rang as Doc was picking up his black bag. "That will no doubt be the Smiths. I'm supposed to treat a heat rash on the missus. See all the trouble you caused me, Will?"

Gene picked up the phone and listened for a second. He stopped and asked the caller to repeat something. He then pulled the phone away from his ear and handed it to Sam. "Caller said something about a murder, Will."

Sam's heart began to race as he picked up the heavy black receiver. "Sheriff's office, Sheriff Williams speaking." Gene and Doc stood by the phone, watching Sam.

The high-pitched voice on the line gasped for breath, as though the person had been running. After a few deep gasps a voice answered. "Sheriff? Sheriff Williams? You've got to come out here. Real quick."

"Whoa, whoa, whoa. Slow down there." As Sam talked into the phone he pulled the notepad from his pocket and sat down to jot the information down. His fingers froze with the pencil poised above the pad. "You're calling to report . . . a murder?"

Doc Adams forgot about having to leave in such a hurry and moved closer to the desk. He leaned over Sam's shoulder and watched what Sam was writing. "What is your name?" Sam asked the caller.

"It's Clyde. Clyde Snyder. I work at the Hole. Oh, Sheriff, it's awful. I never saw a dead person before." The voice on the other end of the phone began to rise in pitch and intensity.

"Okay, Clyde. Where are you calling from?"

"The old Gulf station just past town."

"And, Clyde, do you know who's been murdered?" Sam sat with his pencil poised frozen in midair.

Clyde had begun to sob at the other end of the line. "Oh, it's Carla Sue, Sheriff. She's dead. All cut up and blood all over the place. It's awful."

"Carla Sue," Sam muttered as he scribbled the name down. Doc leaned over the desk and whistled. "Stay put, I'll be right there." Sam hung up the phone and picked up the notepad. "There's been a murder," he announced quietly. "Carla Sue is what the caller said."

"Dear God," muttered Doc Adams as he threw a sideways glance down toward the cell block. "Well," he said as he pulled at his suspenders, "guess I didn't waste a trip down here after all. You wanna take my car, Sheriff? I just happened to bring the wagon with all the stuff from the morgue. Haven't had a chance to unpack it since that bus accident on 95 last week."

"Fine," Sam murmured.

"I can't go," Gene half whispered as he pulled at his damp shirt. "I do faint at the sight of blood." He dropped his eyes to the floor. "I'll head out there later if I'm needed, but I better stay here for now. I'm sorry, Will."

"Stay then. And, Gene, whatever you do, don't say a word to Tom until I get back."

"Yes, sir," Gene added with a curt nod of his head.

Sam picked up his notepad and started to follow the doctor out the jail's door and into the bright sun.

CHAPTER
THREE

The doctor's wagon was a beat-up old station wagon that had seen better times. It labored down the road in a cloud of smoke, jostling its occupants as the worn-out suspension hit pothole after pothole. Doc drove in silence and Sam was glad. He wasn't in the mood for small talk. Every so often a strong whiff of formaldehyde would drift forward from the back of the station wagon. Finally a deserted gas station came into view.

It was just before eleven o'clock when the station wagon pulled into what was once a Gulf gas station. The wagon chugged up to a pay phone and clanked to a stop. Parked two feet away from the phone sat an old, dusty, red pickup truck. Leaning against the passenger door was a young boy. Even though it was almost a hundred degrees, the young boy had his arms wrapped tightly around his body, his head bowed.

Sam and Doc Adams got out of the car and approached. "Clyde? Clyde Snyder?" Sam called out. A pale face with two dark, wide eyes looked up and met Sam's eyes. Clyde shook slightly and his eyes kept darting back and forth between the two men. "Are you the one who made the phone call?" Sam prompted.

"Yes, I did," he whispered through his teeth. Sam leaned closer to the boy to hear him. "I'm sorry," Clyde explained as he pulled his arms around his waist, "but I never saw a dead person before."

"I understand, Clyde. Why don't you sit down on the running board and we'll start from the beginning," Sam offered. He pulled out the pencil and flipped the notepad open.

"I just saw her yesterday," Clyde mumbled in a monotone.

Doc Adams pulled out his handkerchief and took off his glasses and began to polish the glass. "Do what the sheriff says, Clyde. Just take a deep breath and tell us what you saw."

Clyde melted down to the truck's running board, his knees giving way. He took a deep breath and tried to control his quavering voice. "Patch sent me to get Carla this morning. She was late coming to work and he figured she just overslept or something." Clyde kept staring at his shoes as he spoke, pausing to remember the details. "She'd overslept before and since she and Tom ain't got no phone I've had to go out and get her before."

"So you went to Carla Sue's house?" Sam repeated as he scribbled in the notepad.

Clyde just nodded his head. "To her trailer, Sheriff. Yes, sir."

Doc Adams replaced his glasses and pocketed the handkerchief. He reached down and patted the shivering boy's shoulder. "I'm going to get my medical bag, son. I'll be right back. You just keep talking to the sheriff."

Sam waited until Doc had left before he continued. "How old are you, Clyde?"

"Just turned sixteen, sir. I've been working at the Hole for over a year."

63

"Don't rush yourself, Clyde. Just take your time and tell me what you did and what you saw."

"I drove out there just like always. Tom's truck was gone. I figured since Carla Sue and him had that fight in the bar yesterday, he must have gone off somewhere to get drunk. He always gets drunk after they fight."

Sam looked up from his notes. "Tom and Carla had a fight, did they?"

"Yes. Yesterday afternoon at the bar."

"Go on."

"I didn't know anything was wrong, so I just walked up to the door and called out Carla's name."

"You didn't knock?"

"No, sir," Clyde said, dipping his head even further. "She wasn't always alone, if you know what I mean, Sheriff. She hated to be surprised, so I'd always let her know if I was outside." Clyde brushed his cheek and continued to talk. "I didn't get any answer so I went up to the door. See, I figured she just overslept. She does that every now and then."

"Was the door unlocked?" Sam asked. He flipped over another page in the notepad.

Clyde squinted as he looked up at the sky. "Yes. I don't know if they ever locked it. I don't think anyone would want to steal anything of Tom and Carla Sue's. I mean, I don't think anyone would."

"Hmm," Sam said. "So you got to the door . . . ?"

"You know, Sheriff Williams, it's a trailer door that opens out." Clyde demonstrated with his hand as he swung open an imaginary door. "Like I said, it was unlocked, but not opened. I pulled on the knob to open it." Clyde grew very still. "I just thought she had overslept. I was just going to yell, you know. I never thought about going inside and . . ." Clyde put his head in his hands. He shook as a spasm passed through his body. "The smell was the first thing I noticed. It came in a wave. Rotten, like a dead animal. And the air was hot that came out of that trailer. I stepped inside. . . ." His voice trailed off and his shoulders

64

began to shake. "I can't talk about it, Sheriff. I think I'm gonna be sick if I do."

Doc Adams came back to the red pickup carrying his black bag. He plopped the bag on the hood of the truck, opened it, and produced a shiny flask. "You'll be all right, Clyde. You just need a little bit of my special medicine, son." He offered the flask to Clyde. "This should help take the edge off."

Clyde tipped the flask to his lips and took a long drink. He took another long gulp before Doc could reclaim his flask. "Easy, son, you've still got to answer Sheriff Williams's questions."

Clyde wiped his lips off and nodded. "I feel a little better. Thanks."

Sam sat down on the running board next to Clyde. "What did you see inside the trailer?" he asked in a quiet voice. Clyde studied his feet and just shook his head. A bird squawked in the woods behind the abandoned station. "It's important, Clyde," Sam prompted.

"She was dead," Clyde whispered. "She was on the floor. You had to go inside to see her. The smell was everywhere; it made me sick. And the blood. God, she was covered in blood, her blood." Clyde closed his eyes and drew his knees up to his chin.

Doc Adams motioned with his head. Sam nodded, stood up, and followed the doctor until the pair were out of earshot from Clyde.

"He's pretty shaken up, Will. I don't know how much more questioning he's going to stand."

"I know," Sam agreed.

"Poor kid." Doc Adams shook his head. "He's just stumbled across his first murder victim. You remember your first murder victim, Will?"

Sam closed his eyes and lowered his head. A fleeting memory flashed across his eyes. "Yes, I do. She was a beautiful, young, blond, nineteen-year-old German girl. Murderer tried to cover it up to make it look like a drowning."

Doc Adams frowned and scratched at his neck. "I thought it was the Ferguson boy." He studied Sam closely for a moment. "Crazy drunk plowed him down on the way home from school."

Sam quickly tried to cover his tracks. He had been thinking of another Leap. "Oh, you're right, Doc. It was the Ferguson boy," Sam quickly responded before Doc could say anything else. "I feel Clyde stumbled upon the body by accident. I'm going to let him go while we head over to the trailer and have a look around. If he's already been at the scene, there's no telling who else has been there."

"Yeah," Doc Adams agreed. "I'll go fire up the wagon while you send Clyde on his way home."

Sam nodded and made his way back to the pickup truck. He realized with mixed dread that Carla Sue's body would be riding with them on the trip back to town.

The wagon bumped and pitched more ferociously as it turned off the main road onto a dirt road. A big, dusty cloud rose up behind the bumper and mixed with the noxious smoke pouring from the tailpipe as the wagon clanked along the country road. The wagon jarred over a bump, causing the equipment to rattle around in the back.

Doc Adams watched and chuckled to himself as Sam braced for each jolt. "Thought about getting the shocks replaced, but then I thought, I only haul the deceased around in this old heap. I doubt that they pay much attention to the ride."

Sam grunted as another kidney-jarring thump set his teeth on edge. "Seat belts would help, Doc."

Doc laughed. "In a hearse?"

Sam started to argue the point when the wagon veered off to the left and the pair were bumping down a new road. The wagon rumbled past a decrepit-looking house, barely visible through the tall weeds. A broken porch swing hung crookedly on its rusted chains. The porch steps were rotted through and the siding on the house was chipped and warped. A window with a crack that looked like a large

66

spider web glinted in the sun. The yard was nothing but overgrown weeds and dirt, with some junk scattered helter-skelter. The rusted mailbox read BLYTHE, Sam saw as the station wagon bounced past. The tall weeds swallowed up the view and the house disappeared.

The road became a narrow path. Old tires and rusted car parts lay in and around the path. Doc maneuvered through the debris and came to a stop just before colliding with the corner of the trailer. Sam braced himself for the stop as Doc hit the brakes. Something came loose from the back of the wagon and rolled toward the front seat. The car was engulfed in a cloud of dirt and exhaust that slowly settled around Doc and Sam.

Sam stared at a weather-worn trailer not more than three feet away. It sat dejectedly among the corpses of cars and the flat tires scattered all round. The sun beat down on the rusted tin siding. Nothing moved in the still summer afternoon. Not a bird sang or a bug buzzed. It was all too deadly quiet for Sam.

Doc began to rummage around in the seat behind him. He rattled and banged his equipment together as he gathered it up. Doc talked to himself as he sorted through his things. "Reckon some hankies will come in handy. I always carry a few around with me, just for cases like this. Damn." Doc tried to turn his body around in the front seat. "Will, could you grab that box behind your seat? The trip out here must have jarred it around."

Sam gingerly reached over his seat and felt around till he located a square box. He hauled it up over the seat and set it between Doc and himself.

"Thank you kindly." Doc opened the lid and began removing various items. Sam watched as Doc extracted two pairs of rubber gloves. He offered a pair to Sam.

Doc Adams wasted no time in snapping the gloves on over his hands. "Glad Gene didn't find her," Doc said as he worked the gloves over his fingers, "or else we'd be picking him up and hauling him back too." Doc picked up a handkerchief and offered one to Sam. Doc pushed his glasses up on his nose and shut the box's lid. "That's enough stuff for the first trip. You ready?" he asked, not looking at Sam, but studying the trailer in front of him.

"Not really," Sam replied truthfully. He was unfolding the handkerchief Doc had just given him.

"I know what you mean. This part of my job I never cared for either." Doc hauled himself out of the car with his arms loaded and began to walk toward the trailer.

Sam found his own feet shuffling toward the trailer, even though his mind and body desperately wanted to be somewhere else. He searched for Al, wishing he was here, for moral support at the very least. Al was worse than it sounded like Gene Dupree was when it came to murders, but Sam would still like to have him nearby. Sam nervously adjusted his gun belt and put the handkerchief up to his nose. He thought he could smell something in the air already, even though he figured it was just his mind playing tricks.

Two rickety, sun-bleached steps led up to the rusted and weathered trailer door. The door was closed, but not shut. Sam figured he could open the door with his shoe. Sam took his first step on the staircase. The wood groaned and creaked underneath his foot. Every hair on Sam's body stood on end and his heart began to race. Just stay calm, he kept telling himself as he stood poised on the steps. Don't panic, it's just a dead body. You've seen lots of them before in medical school. *But never a murdered one,* a small voice in his head answered back.

"You going to stand there all day, Will? Carla Sue ain't going to send us a written invitation to come in, you know."

Sam nodded. He counted silently to three and pried his toe under the door. He swung the door open and waited.

The door banged open against the trailer's side. It hit the side and threatened to swing closed again. The hinges squealed. Slowly the door swung back against the trailer and stopped moving.

The trailer was dark. Slowly the stench that Clyde had

mentioned came rolling out. It poured out the open doorway and jolted the men on the stairs. The smell stung Sam's nose through the cloth. His eyes began to water and he started to cough. Sam turned his head away from the trailer. Doc was coughing too and had taken a few steps away from the trailer's doorway.

The smell was a mixture of musty, damp air and decay. The smell began to sicken Sam and he stepped down from the steps. He rubbed shoulders with Doc and was relieved to see the smell was affecting Doc too.

"It's gonna be bad," Doc wheezed through the wadded up handkerchief in his hand.

Sam coughed and wiped at the tears in his eyes. A new wave rolled out, causing Sam's stomach to pitch. Smashing the handkerchief tightly against his face, Sam was determined not to lose his breakfast in front of Doc.

"The worst of it should be over soon," Doc said through the cloth.

"I hope so," Sam said. He blinked away the last of the tears in his eyes and walked over to the stairs. He stepped up the short staircase and stood in the trailer's doorway.

The trailer was dark and eerie. The shades were pulled down and no lights were visible from the inside. A few insects buzzed loudly just inside the doorway. Sam's right hand automatically became positioned above the butt of his gun as he took the first step into the trailer.

The inside of the trailer wasn't in much better shape than the outside. Most of the furniture was deteriorated and soiled. The carpet was threadbare in a few spots. The shades that were pulled down over the windows were ragged and ripped. A fine layer of dust covered the cluttered coffee table, which sat to the right of the entryway. As Sam's eyes adjusted to the darkness, he could make out two large brown water spots on the yellowed ceiling. A counter top sported a few glass knickknacks, a cloth, and a soda bottle. Water dripped from the faucet in a slow, annoying rhythm.

The air inside the trailer was overwhelming. It was

warm, stale, and rotten. Sweat trickled down Sam's face and neck and ran down his back. The air scarcely moved through the cloth Sam was holding to his face, but he would suffocate before he would pull the handkerchief away. Sam shuffled farther inside, making room for Doc.

Doc Adams was coughing and mumbling behind Sam's back as he pushed his way inside the trailer. He was wheezing up a storm and Sam wondered if the doctor was going to be able to stay in the trailer for any length of time. "It's got to be over a hundred degrees in here," Doc said through the handkerchief. "Gawd, what a mess."

"Are you okay?" Sam asked, turning back toward Doc.

Doc nodded and wheezed, "Let's find the body and get out of here." He pointed toward the couch. "Check over that way. My old eyes haven't adjusted to the dark yet. Yell if you find something."

Sam inched his way toward the couch, being careful not to upset anything in the trailer. He took two steps and just missed stepping on Carla Sue's foot. Sam jumped back and hit the edge of the coffee table with his leg. An empty beer bottle toppled over and clanked on the tabletop. It rolled off the table and fell on the floor.

Carla Sue was tucked away in a corner of the trailer, by one end of the couch. She was lying on her back, fully clothed except for her feet, which were bare. She was wearing a simple, short black skirt and a cotton shirt that was tied at her midriff. Beneath the coffee table were a pair of tattered, dirty brown shoes.

Huge slashes cut through Carla's clothes and had torn into her chest and neck. There were cuts on both her arms. Her right arm lay across her body, her other arm was at her side. Her long blond hair was damp and the ends were covered in her dried blood. Her blue eyes were cloudy and her face was swollen. A large black-and-blue bruise was prominently displayed on her left cheek. Her mouth was open and dried blood had caked over her lips and chin.

"Oh, God," Sam whispered and turned away from the sight.

Doc Adams stood next to Sam, examining the body. He reached out and squeezed Sam's arm. "I know it's bad, Will. If you need to go outside, I'll understand."

"I'll be all right." Sam wiped his forehead with his sleeve. "I just need a minute to get over the shock."

"It's too hot in here!" Doc set down his assortment of tools and boxes. "It feels like we're in an oven. Gonna be tough to get an autopsy with any good results." He pointed toward the back of the trailer. "Why don't you check out the rest of this place? Take your time, William."

"Sure," Sam agreed as he walked away from the body and began to make his way back through the trailer. He walked down the narrow hallway. The heat grew even more unbearable in this narrow space. Then he inspected the bathroom and bedroom at the back of the trailer. Seeing nothing that looked unusual, Sam rejoined Doc.

Doc Adams had spread out a sheet and opened the metal box. He was carefully examining the body, prodding the wounds. Doc was perspiring heavily now and wheezing like an old calliope on its last leg. "This heat is going to play hell with my autopsy. Body's in an advanced state of decay as we speak. See how bloated she is? And look how the blood has pooled underneath her and dried." Doc shook his head in disgust. "Probably pull half of her skin off prying her up off the floor. What a mess. I need some air. How about you, Will?"

Sam nodded and led them back to the front door. Sam clambered down the wooden steps and out into the hot afternoon air. He pulled the handkerchief away from his face and gulped in as much air as his lungs could hold. The hot air felt refreshing, humidity and all, after being inside the trailer. Sam trudged back to the wagon and sagged against the fender. Doc threw his handkerchief on the hood and removed his glasses.

"Well, she's dead, no doubt about that. Murdered with a capital *M*." He scrutinized Sam with care. "You sure you're doing okay, Will? You're about the color of my late wife's white cotton sheets right now."

Sam was gulping in large amounts of air and trying to shake the memory of Carla Sue's body out of his mind. "I'll be okay in a minute. I just have to get my bearings."

Doc just grunted and opened the door of the wagon. He pulled out his black bag and produced the shiny flask. He pried off the lid and offered it to Sam. "Here, Will. This should help you get your bearings." Sam hesitated and Doc offered it to him again. "Oh go on, just the two of us out here and you look like you could really use a shot. We do have to go back inside."

Sam accepted the flask and swallowed a mouthful of the liquor. It seared his throat and jarred his nose. He handed the flask back to Doc and licked his lips.

"There you go," Doc said as he took a drink himself. "You should feel better now." He replaced the top on the flask. "First thing I gotta do is gather up a few samples, then I can bag her and put her in the wagon. Looks like it is just going to be us. We should canvas the inside of the trailer next. The heat and smell will linger, I'm afraid. You can get a few shots while I dust for prints. It might take us most of the day, but I think we can handle it."

Sam nodded. "Yes. No need to call Gene."

"I didn't run across the murder weapon, did you?"

"No, I didn't, Doc. And from the wounds on the body, I'd say we're looking for a knife."

"Yes, a large one, like a butcher's knife." Doc Adams cocked his head and looked at the sun overhead. "We'd better get a move on. If we work together we should have this place done in a couple of hours."

"I should have been here to prevent this," Sam whispered to his shoes.

Doc put the flask away in the black bag. "Don't be so hard on yourself, Will. You can't expect to stop all the crime, even here in this rickety little old town."

Sam looked up at the doctor with a look of resignation on his face. "I just should have known about this, that's all."

"No way you could have, son. You know the kind of

couple Tom and Carla Sue are . . . um, were. She could run with a pretty tough crowd.'' Doc Adams pushed himself away from the wagon. ''I've got some more gloves, and the fingerprint kit is stuffed in the back somewhere. Let's get started on this mess.''

Three hours later the trailer was locked up and the remains of Carla Sue's body were gathered in a body bag and tucked in the back of the station wagon. Sam and Doc Adams were riding silently back toward Brick. The sun was setting as Doc's abused wagon pulled into a front parking space at the jail. ''I'll know more after I autopsy her tomorrow. Why don't you drop by in the afternoon.'' Sam just nodded and began to climb out of the car. ''What are you going to do about Tom Madison, Will?'' Doc asked as Sam shut the door.

Sam leaned into the open window and ran a hand through his damp hair. ''I'll question him and keep him locked up for the time being. Right now he's our primary suspect.''

Doc grunted and dropped the car into gear. ''Take care, and I'll speak with you tomorrow.'' As the wagon chugged away, Sam climbed up the steps to the jail.

Gene was still at his desk, reading his comic book. He snapped to attention when Sam appeared. ''What's happening?'' he asked in a hushed voice as Sam sat down wearily at the desk across from him.

''Carla Sue was murdered,'' Sam said as he rubbed his eyes with his hand. He was tired and sticky.

''She really was? How? Where?'' Gene asked eagerly. He caught a pained look from Sam.

''I don't have much information yet. We found her in her trailer. She was stabbed several times. I'll have to fill you in on the details later, Gene. Doc's going to do an autopsy. Have you said anything to Tom?''

Gene had melted back in his chair. ''No, I didn't say anything to him. Wow, I can't believe someone murdered Carla Sue. Tom's a suspect, isn't he?''

Sam wearily rose out of the chair. He touched his pocket

with the notepad and headed back toward Tom Madison's cell.

Tom Madison was sitting up on his bed, gently fingering the bandage over his eye. He watched Sam walk to the door of his cell. Tom eased his body off the bed as gracefully as he could and shuffled over to where Sam was standing. "Sheriff Williams," he began in his most apologetic voice, "I know I acted crazy yesterday. What with climbing up on that balcony and all, but acting crazy and *being* crazy are two different things. I just wanna go home now. I'll sign a paper or whatever you want me to do. I'll promise on my mother's grave not to climb on the city hall balcony again. I'll do whatever you want me to do; just let me go home to Carla. I have to apologize to her about . . . everything." Tom reached out and took hold of the bars of his cell.

Sam examined his hands. They were big hands, with thick fingers. Sam scanned down Tom's clothes and stopped when he came across the dried blood on his shirt. "How did you cut your eye?" Sam asked.

"I already told you that."

Sam leaned back against the brick wall. "I can't let you go just yet, Tom. I have to ask you some more questions."

Tom released his hand away from the bars and scowled at Sam. "Sheriff Williams, I've answered all your questions. I've been sitting in this cell all day long. What do you want of me? You've always let me go home before."

Sam paused a moment before he spoke. He looked down at his shoes and then up at Tom's face. He braced himself for the worst. "I just came back from Carla Sue's trailer. Your trailer."

Tom smiled, "How's Carla? Did she ask about me?"

"Tom," Sam began quietly, "I'm sorry to tell you this, but . . . Carla Sue has been murdered."

Tom Madison's smiled faded. "What kind of a game is this?" He backed away from the bars and began to shake his head. "You're lying to me, now, Sheriff Williams. Carla's not dead. Why are you lying to me?" Tom continued to back away from Sam. "She can't be dead."

"I'm sorry, Tom, but I'm not lying to you. I need to know what happened yesterday before you climbed out on the balcony. I need to know what happened to Carla Sue."

"Why are you doing this to me, Sheriff? Why are you telling me these lies?" Tom covered his ears with his hands. He was breathing hard and sweating. "Tell me you're lying, please," Tom murmured, "I don't understand. . . ."

"I'm not lying to you," Sam repeated. "Carla Sue was murdered."

Tom began to weep. He wobbled over to the metal bed and sat down, holding his head in his hands. "No, no, no," he began to moan quietly.

Sam looked down the hall and caught Gene standing in the hallway. Sam motioned to Gene with his hand that he could join them.

Sam removed his notepad and pencil from his pocket. "Tom, I want you to tell me what happened yesterday. What made you climb up on that roof? Why did you kill Carla Sue?"

Tom stopped his moaning and slowly raised his head. "No!" Tom shouted, his eyes blazing at Sam. "I did not kill Carla Sue. How dare you say that to me! I loved her!"

There was a lengthy silence as Tom studied Sam, Sam studied his notepad, and Gene looked nervously back and forth between the two.

Finally Tom began to mumble in a monotone, "I was at the Hole yesterday. I had finished up some chores and I went down to get something to eat and drink. Carla was working. She was trying to ignore me, but I sat at her table and she had to serve me." Tom shifted his weight on the bed. "I tried to get Carla Sue to talk to me. She was still in a snit about a fight we had the night before. She wasn't paying me no mind at all."

"What was it that you two were fighting about?" Sam asked quietly.

Tom rubbed his head. "She wanted to move out. I didn't

75

want her to. She said she was going to leave me. I said I'd marry her, but she wasn't interested in that. I told her she couldn't leave, I didn't want her to leave, and she threw a fit. Told me she'd be gone by the middle of September and that was that. Told me I could stay in the trailer if I wanted to. I followed her to the Hole to try and talk some sense into her.''

"Did you and Carla Sue fight yesterday morning at the Hole?" Sam asked.

Tom nodded. "Sort of." He tapped two fingers to his head. "That's where I got this. She still didn't want to talk to me. Told me to leave. I was getting angrier by the minute. She wasn't even listening to me. I asked her, Where did she think she was going to go? Who would take her in? I said some pretty mean things to her. I didn't mean what I said. She just made me so mad. Anyway, she picked up a beer bottle off her tray and smashed it over my head. Wham! That's how my eye got cut." Tom swallowed. "Can I have some water?"

Gene scrambled down the hallway and came back with a paper cup. He held it tentatively through the bars as Tom shakily rose and took the cup. He drained the cup and set it down on the floor.

"What happened next, Tom?" Sam asked.

Tom shrugged. "My head hurt and I was bleeding pretty bad. Carla just kept ranting and raving. She was very upset and was causing a scene. She kept saying how she wanted a better life. I don't think she was even sorry she had hurt me.''

"Did you slap her when she hit you?" Sam asked as he scribbled.

Tom eyed Sam coolly. "No, I never hit her. Ever. Up until this time, she never hit me either. We shouted a lot, but we always made up later. I noticed she was real jumpy and short with me lately. I thought things were okay between us." Tom paused and studied his fingers. "Patch started yelling at Carla. Said I was bleeding all over his bar and it was going to put off his customers from eating. Patch was real upset. Carla and Patch started a loud argument. Carla acted like she didn't care how Patch felt. I felt pretty stupid, having Carla treat me like she did. Her yelling at me, my head bleeding, and all those people looking at me like I was stupid. I got up and walked out of the bar."

Sam finished writing in his notebook and looked up at Tom Madison. "What happened next?"

"I was mad. I got into my truck and left. I just wanted to get out of there. I drove till I came to a shaded turnoff. I had a bottle in the truck so I sat there and got pretty drunk. Figured I'd cause a commotion and make Carla a little jealous. So I drove into town, climbed out on the balcony, and . . . well, you know the rest, Sheriff Williams."

"So the last time you saw her alive," Sam asked as he scanned over his notes, "was when you left the Hole?"

"Yes. As I was driving away, Patch had pulled her outside. They were still fighting when I drove away." Tom sighed heavily. "I didn't kill Carla Sue. I might have gotten mad at her now and then, but I would never, ever kill her. I loved her, Sheriff. And I always thought she loved me. I thought we'd always be together."

Gene cleared his throat and asked very timidly, "Do you remember seeing anybody else around at the Hole?"

Tom threw Gene a funny look and shook his head. "The Hole was pretty quiet—it was early yet. Seems like there were a couple of the regulars around. Clyde and Miller Parkinson."

"What about outside?" Gene asked. "Anyone hanging around outside?"

"No . . . wait, yes. Yes, I do remember there was a colored boy standing outside, by the soda machine. I didn't pay much attention though. Patch or Carla . . ." Tom's voice trailed off. He inhaled slowly and repeated, "Patch might have seen somebody."

Gene nodded and fell silent. Sam closed his notepad. "I'm going to have to keep you here, Tom, until I can investigate this murder further. I'll have to check out your

77

story. If you can think of anything else you remember or want to say, then tell it to Deputy Dupree.''

Tom shrugged. ''Where is Carla now?'' he asked quietly.

''Doc Adams's place. Doc's got to do an autopsy. I'm sorry, Tom. Is there anyone we can notify?''

''No.''

''What about you, Tom? Anybody I can call for you?''

''No. Just find her murderer. I didn't do it.'' Tom closed his eyes and hung his head down. ''Oh, Carla Sue.''

Sam returned to his desk and took a quick look at the clock. Almost four o'clock. He picked up the phone and dialed zero. A pleasant sounding female answered. ''Operator assistance.''

''This is Sheriff Williams. I need to phone my wife, Meg. Could you ring the number for me?''

''Certainly,'' the pleasant, but surprised voice answered. ''Are you having trouble with your phone, Sheriff?''

''Yes,'' Sam answered, lowering his voice.

''Oh?'' the now befuddled voice responded. ''One moment, Sheriff, and I'll connect you.''

Sam waited until the phone connection clicked and the line began to ring. Meg answered on the third ring. Sam explained that he was going to be late. He spared Meg the details, but did say he was working on a murder and not to expect him home by dinnertime. He mentioned that Becca should be coming home at four o'clock to help Meg with her shopping. Meg was surprisingly cooperative. She asked if there was anything she could do, and Sam answered no. He'd be home when he could. He replaced the phone and turned around to see Gene gazing in his direction.

''Let's get cracking, Gene. We've got a murder to solve.''

''Okay,'' Gene responded. He tucked the comic book in the top drawer of his desk and pulled out a white notepad.

''I'm going to check out the Hole Tom talked about,'' Sam began.

"The Watering Hole," Gene said aloud as he wrote. "The bar on the way to Ashcroft."

Sam flipped open his own notepad. "Do you know anything about that bar, Gene?"

"No," Gene said. "I don't hang out there. Not my type of crowd."

"I'm heading out there now. Why don't you call around and see if Carla was seen around the time that Tom was up on the balcony yesterday? Check with her friends, places she would go after work. If Tom says anything else or if Doc Adams calls, I want you to radio me."

"Yes, sir, I'll call around." Gene laid down the pencil. "You ought to find old Patch, the bartender, in one hell of a mood. Sure you don't want some company? It's early and the regulars shouldn't have arrived in mass yet."

"No, I can take care of it." Sam began to gather up a few items off his desk. "I want you to stay with Tom. You should go back later and talk to him. See if he remembers anything else."

"Sure," Gene acknowledged as Sam headed out the door.

CHAPTER
FOUR

By four fifteen Sam had maneuvered the big black and
white patrol car into the dirt parking lot of the Watering
Hole. The small bar was set back off the main road. There
were only a couple of cars parked outside and it looked
like the regular crowd hadn't arrived yet. Sam parked the
cruiser in plain sight and got out. He strolled under a sagging awning, past a rusted soda pop machine humming
loudly, and had to duck under a large Confederate flag that
was draped on the outside. He opened a sagging wooden
door and entered the bar.

The sun shone through dirt-caked windows and cast long
shadows across the scuff-marked wooden floor. Thick blue
smoke hung in the air like fog. A few scuffed-up wooden
tables were scattered here and there. Some men were seated
at one of the wooden tables, next to a jukebox. A country
and western tune spilled out of the box.

A dark, smoke-filled bar area was tucked away in the
back. It was just a small space, with hardly enough room

to sit at the bar. The top of the bar was sticky and a film covered the rough wood surface. The cushions of the stools were torn and the padding was spilling out of one barstool. Behind the bar stood a short, thin man with a stained apron and a black patch over one eye. His hair was cropped in a buzz cut. He rubbed his unshaven chin and stopped wiping the bar. He laughed gruffly as Sam approached the bar.

"And just what brings you down here, Sheriff?" the bartender asked with a grin. He was missing a few teeth and his voice sounded raw. The jukebox changed tunes. A Patsy Cline ballad warbled from the tattered speakers.

"I've come by to ask you a few questions." Sam walked over to the bar area but did not sit down.

"You can ask, but I don't know nothing," the bartender rasped. He laughed and pointed to his patch. "You know I don't see too good since I had my eye poked out in that fight back in '40."

"Regardless, I want you to tell me what happened here yesterday."

"Nothing happened yesterday. Or the day before that." Patch began to wipe the bar again. "Reckon you wasted your time coming here, Sheriff. Unless you want a beer?" A few chuckles drifted out of the shadows from the area next to the jukebox.

"I'll just ask you a few questions, which you'll answer, and then I'll be on my way." Sam ignored the two men laughing at the table.

Patch shrugged and turned his back on Sam. "Ask all you want, Sheriff. Talk yourself hoarse. I don't know nothing."

Sam gritted his teeth and watched the bartender's back. "Little short on help tonight, aren't you?"

Patch turned around and raised his eyebrows. "Maybe, maybe not. Heard some strange rumors flying around. Seems we got ourselves a murderer in Brick. Hey, boys," Patch hollered over Sam's head, "you hear we might have a murderer running loose?" He turned his one good eye back at Sam. "What have you heard, Sheriff?" He laughed and picked up a glass and began to wipe it with the same rag he used on the bar.

"I'll ask the questions, Patch. Let's start with Clyde Snyder. Where is he?"

Patch chortled. "Home puking his guts out, last I heard. Seems I sent Clyde off on an errand and the boy stumbled across something mighty grisly. Didn't even make it back to work. Don't worry, I'm docking his pay."

Sam was getting frustrated. He felt the gun weighing heavy on his hip. "Did you see Tom Madison and Carla Sue in here yesterday?"

Patch scratched his chin. "Maybe. Gee you know, come to think of it, I do sorta recall something going on yesterday between those two. A lot of things happen in here, Sheriff, and most of it ain't pretty. I only worry about one thing, my business. Seems to me that things turned out for the better." He leaned closer toward Sam. Sam could smell the alcohol and sweat that hung around him. "That two-bit whore is better off dead, I say. Fighting with Tom Madison all the time. Couldn't wait on tables, messed up all her orders. Hell, she was too busy drumming up business for herself. She flirted with all the men who came within ten feet of her." Patch flung the towel over his shoulder and started to walk away.

"I have more questions—" Sam started.

Patch cranked a hand to his ear. "Whaddya say? Can't hear you over the box. Look, Sheriff, why don't you come back tomorrow? I've got to get ready to tend bar tonight." Patch gave Sam the send-off with a wave of his hand.

The jukebox changed records again and a loud honky-tonk tune began. Something inside of Sam clicked and Sam didn't know if what he did next was a conscious act on his part or on Will's. In one quick, fluid motion he undid the snap on his holster and whipped the pistol out of its harness. He leveled off his arm, drew back the hammer, and aimed dead center at the jukebox. He fired off two shots, silencing the jukebox instantly and sending the Hank Williams record skidding off the turntable.

82

The gun was loud and startled everyone, including Sam. The jukebox sparked once, twice and then went dark. The men sitting at the table nearby had scrambled for cover. The bar was filled with silence as Sam turned back to face the stunned bartender. He didn't reholster his gun; he left it out in plain sight. "That song was getting on my nerves and so are you, Patch." He said the bartender's name with as much distaste as he could muster.

Patch was recovering from his shock. He snarled at Sam, his one good eye twitching uncontrollably. "That's going to cost you, Williams. You can't come in here and—"

"What do you say, Patch? Let's cut the b.s. and talk about yesterday. You get me angry again and I may just start shooting up more of this hellhole." A chair raked across the bare floor and one of the men fled outside.

Patch looked at Sam's unwavering hand that held the gun. "You're lucky you didn't try this an hour later, or they'd be carrying you out of here in a bag." Patch looked at his ruined jukebox and laid his hands on the counter. He eyed the gun uneasily. "What I've got to say I'm only saying once. Tom and Carla Sue were fighting. And don't ask me what about, 'cause I don't know. She was mad about something when she got to work and then when Tom came in that set her off again. It was lunchtime, I had customers, and she and Tom started yelling. Then she whacks him over the head with a bottle of beer. Damn fools were carrying on like no one else was around. Tom starts bellowing like a moose, bleeding all over the place. I figured if they were aiming on killing each other I wanted them out of my bar.

"Tom stormed out first, bleeding like a stuck pig. That stupid Carla Sue kept running her mouth. I chased her outside and gave her hell about wasting that bottle of beer and messing up my bar. I told her I was going to fire her and she informed me that she was quitting. She began to tell me what a lowlife, filthy person I was. I don't have nobody talking to me that way, especially a woman. I slapped her and I ain't sorry about that either. Kicked her off the lot.

She sulked off down the road with that colored boy. I figured once she cooled off she'd be back. Too many business opportunities for her to just pass up.

"See, nobody talks trash to Patch. You're lucky I can't get to my gun, Sheriff. I figure we'd have a real Old West showdown then." Patch smiled deviously and picked up a glass off the counter and began to wipe it down again. "That boy she left with could have been just another one of her customers. Carla wasn't picky when it came to color or morals. I'm through talking. Get out."

"What was his name, Patch?" Sam asked through clenched teeth.

Patch smiled widely, exposing the gaps in his mouth, and shook his head. "I don't know his name. I ain't on a first-name basis with the nig—"

Sam lifted the gun up, causing Patch to flinch. "Don't use that word in my presence. Ever again," Sam warned.

Patch eyed the gun and swallowed. "You sure got a bee up your bonnet today, Williams. I've never seen you so fired up. Anyway, like I was saying, I ain't on a first-name basis with the . . . coloreds." Patch watched and was relieved to see the gun lowered. "See, if that colored boy did murder Carla Sue, then you're going to have quite a little mess on your hands. I don't care what kind of a person Carla was. If she's been murder by a . . . colored person, then this town's going to treat her like she was a saint. And you're going to have more trouble on your hands than just her murder.

"Rumors are flying, Sheriff. At least half a dozen people saw her leave yesterday with him. Go ask that boy what he did yesterday afternoon. You're on a first-name basis with his mother. Nobody wants to see justice hindered, if you know what I mean. Now get the hell out of my place and don't you ever step foot in it again or I'll blast your head clean off your shoulders. I'm still a good shot, bad eye and all."

Sam lofted the gun. "Don't threaten me, Patch."

Patch thundered at him from behind the dingy bar, "I

84

haven't even begun to threaten you, Williams. First I'm going to report all this damage and your unruly conduct to Mayor Tilden. He's a regular customer and he'll be upset to discover you've shot up his favorite juke. He'll have a little talk with you."

Sam eased away from the bar, holding the gun out for all to see. He counted one man standing in the shadows. He backed his way out of the bar and into the parking lot. He got to the squad car as fast as he could and gunned the engine. His hands shook as he dropped the car in gear and pulled out of the parking lot. He passed two pickup trucks coming into the parking lot as he made his way out. He floored the pedal and headed back to Brick.

Al limped down the deserted project's corridor to his office. He might have made better time if he wasn't juggling a large moving box in his arms. He arrived at his door and leaned the box against the wall, balancing it with one arm and his body, as his other hand searched through his pants pocket for his security pass. He found the pass at last and inserted it into the slot on his door. The green light on the panel above the doorknob blinked and he turned the knob. The door opened easily and Al wrestled the box back into his arms and entered his office. He shoved the door closed with his elbow and worked the light switch with the same elbow. All the while the box had begun to grow very heavy and awkward in Al's arms. On the third try he got the lights on and limped over to a chair next to his desk. He deposited the box in the chair, where it balanced precariously. Al messed with the box, shifting it this way, turning it that way, until it looked like it wasn't going to topple out of the chair.

On his desk were a few pink telephone messages. Senator Weitzman's office had left two messages for Al, and Dr. Beeks was requesting a meeting with Al in the Waiting Room upon his arrival back at the project. He turned on the computer monitor and checked in with Ziggy. According to Ziggy, Sam was still a sheriff in Oklahoma in 1955.

Her records indicated that she was still searching for more data. Al noted that Ziggy was currently searching through court case files in Mississippi.

Al pulled out his leather chair and sat down. He pulled his wadded, wrinkled silk tie out of his coat pocket and threw it on the desk. He took off his coat with the torn right pocket and laid it across his desk. His shirt sleeves were both unbuttoned and he was missing a button on his right cuff. Bright red lipstick was smeared on his left sleeve. Al reached down and untied the laces on his right shoe. He eased the shoe off his foot and gently pulled off his black sock. Al's big toe was turning a nasty blackish blue. He didn't even dare try to wiggle it. "Great," he muttered.

"Your toe appears to be broken, Admiral Calavicci. Have you had someone confirm my diagnosis yet?" Ziggy's voice gave Al quite a start.

"Ziggy, don't do that! Can't you whistle or beep or . . . something, first?" Al began to replace his sock and then, very carefully, his shoe.

"Of course I can, Admiral. But I thought you were speaking directly to me, since there is no one else in your office."

"Well, I wasn't."

"I can see that not only have you acquired a broken toe from your eight-hour visit with your fifth ex-wife, but you also have lipstick smeared on your right cheek. I hope the meeting went"—Ziggy paused and drew out the next word slowly—"w-e-e-e-l-l-l-l-l."

Al laced up his shoe and hobbled over to the small mirror on the wall. He scowled at his reflection. His clothes were rumpled and askew and he did have lipstick on his cheek. He rubbed his cheek clean with the heel of his hand and began to undo his shirt. The first three buttons were already undone for him. "It's none of your business how my meeting went. What's going on with Sam?"

"Some very interesting developments have taken place in the last eight hours concerning Dr. Beckett's Leap."

Ziggy's inflection seemed to place more emphasis on the words "eight hours" than the rest of the sentence.

Al stopped unbuttoning his shirt. "What do you mean there's been developments? What's happening?"

"Which development do you want me to elaborate on, Admiral? The murder Dr. Beckett is currently investigating or the incident with the jukebox? I find them both very interesting. Each one says something different in regard to human behavior."

"*Murder!*" Al hobbled over to his desk and sat down, his shirttails flying behind him. He began to jab at the keys. "Nobody said anything about Sam being involved in a murder!"

"Yes. Dr. Beckett was also involved in a shooting."

Al stopped typing and looked up at the ceiling. He addressed Ziggy in this way when he wasn't arguing with the link. "A shooting! Sam was involved in a shooting?"

"Yes, Admiral Calavicci. Dr. Beckett shot a jukebox."

Al punched a key on the keyboard and looked at his screen. "I don't have anything on here about a murder or a shooting." Al grew annoyed and hit the keys with a renewed vengeance. "Ziggy, why can't I find Gooshie's report?"

"Because Gooshie didn't file a report." Ziggy could be absolutely maddening with her truncated responses at times.

"Why didn't Gooshie file a report? It's standard procedure. I have to file reports when I observe." Al was starting to lose his temper.

"Gooshie was never in the Imaging Chamber to observe. That is why there is no report filed."

Al sat back in his chair and looked like the wind was just knocked out of him. "But Gooshie was supposed to take my place today. Didn't I make that clear at the staff meeting yesterday?"

"Perfectly clear, Admiral. It was Dr. Beeks who made the decision this morning not to submit Gooshie to the side effects of the Imaging Chamber and thus, not to have Gooshie observe." Ziggy was almost singing her way through the explanation, which infuriated Al all the more.

Al pushed his chair away from the desk and began to hurriedly button up his shirt. He barked up at the ceiling, "Where's Verbena now?"

"In the Waiting Room, awaiting your return from Santa Fe."

Al clicked off the monitor on his desk and stuffed his shirttails into his trousers. "I swear, I leave this place for a couple hours and the bottom falls out."

"You were gone for eight point two five hours today, not two," Ziggy corrected the admiral. "Taking into account the current situation of the Leap, I think Dr. Beeks did an admirable job in overseeing the project while you were gone. I have a few suggestions I'd like to offer her so the next time will go even smoother."

Al glanced up at the ceiling with disgust. "Can it, Ziggy. Do something useful and get me a readout on everything that's happened with Sam since my last contact with him. I'll be in the Waiting Room." Al flicked off the lights, slammed his door, and limped down the hallway, just as fast as he could go.

Since Verbena Beeks had wanted to know when Al arrived back at the project, Ziggy had taken it upon herself to inform Verbena at the exact moment Al checked in with the guards at the main entrance. That had been twenty minutes ago. It had taken Al a little longer than usual to park his car and make it up to his office with his broken toe and the moving box. So it came as no surprise (to Ziggy) that Verbena and Al were about to meet, face to face, in the hallway.

Dr. Verbena Beeks had graduated at the top of her class in Psychiatry when Sam had begun to woo her to join his project. At first she had begged off, citing her own research she wanted to pursue. But Sam could be a very persistent and determined fellow when it came to his project.

Verbena was rumored to be in her late thirties. Her personal files were kept under the tightest wraps and were well guarded by Ziggy. Her black skin was smooth and wrinkle free, except for some tiny laugh lines around her eyes. She was trim and fit and always dressed immaculately. Today she was wearing a beautiful gold silk blouse, with a light tan skirt. She came clicking down the hallway, walking gracefully in her brown, two-inch, suede shoes. She paused and watched Al approaching. The usually dapper admiral was a wrinkled mess and he was favoring his right foot. Verbena stopped and acknowledged Al, "Good afternoon, Admiral Calavicci. I'm glad you made it back . . . in one piece." She paused and tried not to smile.

Al frowned at Verbena. He shifted his weight off his foot and leaned against the wall. He was all business. "Gooshie never observed Sam while I was gone. I want to know why!" Al was upset and it was taking all of his self-control to keep his temper in check.

"I see. . . ." Verbena said, nonplussed at his response. She never blinked as she answered, "Yes, Admiral. Gooshie did not observe while you were away."

"Why not?" Al interjected.

Verbena calmly smoothed out her skirt. "Shall we discuss this in the hallway or in my office?" She raised her eyebrows and looked at Al.

Al folded his arms across his chest. "Right here will be just fine. Dr. Beeks, as the project's head administrator, I demand complete cooperation from my staff. I don't understand why you changed a procedure which we agreed upon yesterday."

"I'm not going to argue the point with you, Admiral. I changed the procedure because I felt it wasn't necessary to subject Gooshie to the diverse side effects of the Imaging Chamber. The current events of Dr. Beckett's Leap didn't call for an observer. I took into consideration all the facts and that was my conclusion." She smiled at Al.

Al's jaw dropped. "But what about—"

Verbena held up her hand and silenced Al with a quick look. "Dr. Beckett's life was never in jeopardy. Surely, Admiral Calavicci, you know and trust me better than that. If I felt Dr. Beckett's life was in jeopardy, I myself would step into the Imaging Chamber.'' She leaned back against the wall.

"But the murder! Ziggy said there was a murder."

"Yes, that's right, Admiral. The murder Ziggy mentioned occurred sometime yesterday afternoon. If you hadn't returned soon I was considering sending Gooshie into the Chamber. But now you're here." Verbena smiled and shrugged her shoulders.

"Exactly, and—" Al began.

Verbena cleared her throat and interrupted again. "This issue has more to do with your refusal to appoint a permanent replacement observer than me not following your suggestions for Gooshie, if I may say so, Admiral." Verbena peeked down at her watch and clucked her tongue in disapproval. "I have a meeting scheduled back in the Waiting Room. You're welcome to join me. We are finished here, aren't we?"

"Finished!" Al's mouth dropped open with surprise.

"Good." Verbena nodded her head and stood up straight. "I'm glad that we discussed this." She turned and started back down the hallway.

"Hey, wait a minute," Al called out after her. He didn't like the turn the conversation had just taken. He hopped to catch up with her. "Slow down, Verbena. Please, *I'm* not finished discussing this yet."

Verbena stopped and turned around. Without any warning she asked, "Why are you limping?"

Al shifted his weight to his good foot and reached out with his hand to balance himself against the wall. "I broke my toe," he mumbled. He patted his shirt pocket for a cigar. "What did you mean when you said that stuff about me not finding a permanent replacement?"

"Gooshie is not a suitable replacement as an observer for this project."

Al chortled. "Gooshie is not a suitable replacement for a lot of things."

Verbena did not share Al's humorous point of view. "Admiral, we've come to the conclusion that each time

90

we've used Gooshie, the results have been rather disastrous.''

"Gooshie did . . . well, okay." Al shrugged his shoulders and began to motion in the air with his hands. "I mean he gets sick and disoriented, but that's to be expected. Hell, he is in the Imaging Chamber, for crying out loud."

Verbena folded her arms and shook her head. "He becomes deathly ill in the Chamber, so much so he is unable to function. And Ziggy has never been able to project his image very well for Dr. Beckett's benefit. Ziggy doesn't have a neuron match for Gooshie like she does for you." Al pursed his lips and ran his thumb over a small scar on his finger. "Furthermore," Verbena continued, "I think you like to watch Gooshie suffer. You can't tell me you don't get some kind of satisfaction watching poor Gooshie in the Imaging Chamber."

"Now wait a minute. . . ." Al protested.

"Besides," Verbena continued, "you promised the committee in Washington you'd have a suitable replacement by now. If something were to happen to you, Admiral . . ."

Al pushed away from the wall and put his weight on both feet. He winced a little, but quickly recovered. "Hey, first of all, nothing is going to happen to me. Second, I've been meaning to select a replacement, but I haven't had time. And third, about Gooshie . . ." Al dropped his head and studied the floor.

Verbena drummed her fingers on her arm and looked up at the ceiling tiles. "The files for a substitute observer have been sitting on your desk for six months," she pointed out in a softer voice. "We've narrowed the choices down to three top candidates and have been waiting for you to act upon those choices."

"Hey, what is it with everybody today? I'm gone for a couple hours and now I'm considered obsolete," Al complained.

"Keep that ego of yours in check, Admiral. No one wants to replace you permanently. And this has nothing to do with how long you were gone today. I, for one, think you should take more time off. Just keep in mind, at some point you're going to have to step down, be it ten years from now or ten days. Wouldn't it be fair to Dr. Beckett if he had a little experience with another observer? It's safer to iron out problems now rather than later.''

Al nodded and leaned into the wall. ''Yes, you're right, Verbena. I was gone too long today and nobody is more aware of that fact than me. And you're right also about Gooshie. We should have a permanent replacement . . . just in case. I don't like to think about somebody else looking out for Sam, other than me, but it is in the project's best interest. I'll get started on those files. I'll have a substitute observer to recommend to Washington by the end of next week.'' He glanced up at Verbena. ''Okay?''

Verbena smiled. ''There. I feel better now that we've had this discussion. Don't you, Admiral?'' She turned and let Al walk with her.

''No,'' Al growled as he limped. ''And don't ever disobey a direct order from me again.''

''Are you pulling rank on me, Admiral Calavicci?''

''Absolutely.''

''Fine. It won't happen again.''

Al nodded curtly. ''Now, what's going on with Sam?''

''Very interesting things are happening. Ziggy discovered some hard facts about this Leap just recently. Other than a jukebox, Dr. Beckett seems to be holding his own with this investigation. Oh, and Will Williams has been asking for you.'' They came to the Waiting Room and paused.

Al looked down at his clothes and shook his head. ''I need to change.'' He hooked his thumb in the direction of the door. ''You said Will wants to see me?''

Verbena nodded and punched in the code on the keypad. As the door unsealed, she gave it a push with her hand. ''It will only take a second to talk to Will. Sam's back at the Maple Street address in Brick. He's doing fine.'' She stepped back and invited Al inside. ''As far as your appearance goes, I don't think Will Williams will mind.''

Al held the door for Verbena and followed her inside. "Well, I mind. I look like something the cat dragged—" Al stopped. Sitting up on the main table, dressed in a white robe, was Sam. Actually it only looked like Sam for a brief instant as the aura around the visitor changed.

Verbena touched the admiral's shoulder and lowered her voice. "Very interesting things are going on with this Leap concerning Will's memory. Why don't you go have a talk with Will?" The door resealed behind them.

Sam Beckett sat on the porch swing, drained from the day's events. He didn't push the swing, he just sat and thought. Meg pushed the screen door open and leaned out. "You want anything besides that iced tea? Could I fix you a sandwich?"

Sam looked up at Meg and shook his head. "I'm not very hungry, Meg."

Meg let the screen door swing shut. "Okay. I'm going to put Tyler down for the night. I'll come out and sit a spell with you later, if you'd like?"

Sam smiled. "That's sounds nice."

As soon as Meg was gone Sam sunk lower in the swing, staring at the porch. He swirled the ice in the glass and took a sip. A flicker of light caught his eye and he heard the distinct sound of the Imaging Chamber door opening.

Al was wearing a wrinkled white shirt with the sleeves rolled up. His trousers were crumpled and crimped. He was leaning heavily to his left as he stepped out of the Imagining Chamber door. He raised his hand, his fingers entwined around a thick cigar, and gave Sam a small wave.

Sam just looked up at his friend. He took another long sip of his iced tea and swirled the glass again. The ice clinking in the glass was the only sound. "Hello, Al," he muttered without much feeling. He sat up in the porch swing.

"Hi, Sam." Another silence fell between them. The link twittered loudly in the admiral's pocket. "Tough day?"

"Yep." Sam stirred the ice again and took a drink. He

caught an ice chip in his teeth and crunched it.

Al tried to walk into Sam's line of vision without limping. No matter how hard he tried, he still favored his foot. Al wasn't very good with small talk and Sam was in no mood for it anyhow. So Al just began. "Ziggy tells me we've got a murder investigation going on." Al retrieved the link from his pocket and began to press the buttons with his thumb.

Sam laughed quietly and shook his head. "We?" He looked up at Al and raised his eyebrows. "Since when did *we* become involved?"

Al stopped playing with the link. He rammed the cigar in his mouth. "Okay, I deserved that. I wasn't around much today. Sorry."

Sam sat on the edge of the swing, getting closer to Al. "Hey, *nobody* was here for me today. Not you. Not Gooshie. No one. I had the distinct pleasure of investigating a murder scene all by myself. I then get to break the news to the deceased's family. Unfortunately, the only family the deceased has is behind bars. That's because I arrested and put him there. 'Course, I don't have a clue who did commit the murder. Oh, and I'm forgetting the lovely time I spent in this bar. I managed to plug a jukebox with a couple of slugs. Very sheriffy thing to do, don't you think, Al?"

"I don't know," Al replied around the cigar. "Depends what was playing on the jukebox." He smiled.

Sam didn't smile. Instead he got out of the swing and pointed his finger at the hologram. "See, none of this is even remotely funny, Al. I don't want to joke about this. I don't want to kid around." He pointed at Ziggy's link in Al's hand. "If you don't have any facts yet, why don't you just limp back over to the Imaging Chamber door and leave." Sam turned his back on his friend and walked to the end of the porch.

Al narrowed his eyes at Sam's back. He tucked the link in his pants pocket and blew a perfect smoke ring into the air. He shrugged and folded his arms across his chest. "I said I was sorry, Sam. I'm sorry I wasn't around today. I'm sorry you had to go through this mess all by yourself. I'm sorry if I'm joking about it now and it's pissing you off."

"Sorry isn't good enough, Al!" Sam turned back and faced off with Al. "It's just not good enough this time. I've got a murdered girl on my hands."

Al raised his hands into the air. "Well, that's all I can say, Sam." He brushed at some dirt on his sleeve. "You know, you're not the only one who hasn't had a perfect day."

Sam set his drink down on the porch. "Oh, please. Don't tell me you've had a worse day than me. Don't." He held his hand up to silence Al as he collapsed back into the swing. "I don't even know her last name." He lowered his head and sighed.

Al twisted the cigar around in his mouth. "It's Tritten. Carla Sue Tritten. Born April 5, 1931 to George and Marion Tritten in Millbrook, Texas." Al was glad to see Sam's head snap up with that information. "When Carla Sue was eleven years old she moved here with her older sister Joyce. Carla lived in that same trailer with her sister until Joyce married. Carla was fifteen years old at the time. The older sister split and not very long after that, Tom Madison moved in." Al had begun to pace slowly, painfully in front of Sam. "If you're depressed about stopping her murder, don't be. Ziggy's calculated that she was murdered before you Leaped in. Ziggy has found a transcript of the court proceedings in a student's law journal in Mississippi. That's where we're getting most of this information.

"According to the original history, David Bo Jefferson was arrested for Carla's murder. David is the only child of your housekeeper, Beulah Jefferson. The trial was held right after Labor Day and he was convicted and sentenced to life in prison. The evidence presented in the trial was all circumstantial and David was in the process of an appeal when he was killed in a prison riot in 1956. Ziggy says there is a 92.45 percent chance that you Leaped here to prevent David's murder, not Carla Sue's. In order to do that, you're going to have to find Carla Sue's killer before this weekend is over.'' Al plucked the thick cigar out of his mouth.

Sam sat back in the swing, amazed. "Wait, Al." He held up his hands. "How did you get Ziggy to—"

"Ziggy finally located a journal about the trial. Seems this trial was a big to-do all around this area. People from as far away as New York came down to cover it. Plus, Will helped me fill in a few of the pieces." He began to dig around in his pocket for the link.

Sam sat back in the swing. "That's a start." Sam pondered the possibilities. He looked at Al and nodded his head. "Thanks."

Al nodded curtly. "You're welcome, Sam." He pulled the link out of his pocket and started to jab the neon buttons.

Sam ran his fingers over his bottom lip and studied his friend's clothing. "Umm, tell me, Al . . . how was your day? How's Maxine? Do you have any little Calaviccis running around?"

Al pivoted and stuck his head up in the air. "Oh, that. No. But you're not really interested," he said around the cigar.

"No," Sam insisted, "I am." He pointed at Al's foot. "Looks like she got the better of you, if you ask me."

Al turned and nearly lost his balance. He waved his arms in the air in defiance. "Hey, she didn't get the better of me. Remember who you're talking to here."

"You're limping pretty badly. And I don't think I've ever seen you look so . . ." Sam bit his lower lip and cocked his head. "Rumpled?" He snapped his fingers. "Maybe that time on the Star Bright project when you were drunk, but . . ."

Al hobbled over to where Sam was sitting. He yanked the cigar out of his mouth and pointed it at Sam. "Hey, I didn't have time to change. You think I like walking around looking like this?"

"*Limping* around looking like that," Sam corrected. "Guess you and Maxine didn't hit it off very well."

Now Al was more than perturbed. His sexual prowess was on the line. "For your information, Mr. Know-It-All, Maxine and I hit it off very well. Better than well." Al smiled wickedly. "Seems like I haven't lost my touch after all these years." His eyebrows bounced up and down.

Sam's smile disappeared. He blinked at Al. "You slept with her?" He sat forward in the swing. "You actually slept with your ex-wife!" he almost shouted.

"Sam," Al scolded, drawing his finger to his lips, "keep your voice down."

Sam was on his feet again. "How could you sleep with your ex-wife?"

Al took a long drag on his cigar. "Easier than you think. Maxine and I didn't hate each other when we split up. It was my fifth marriage and it was never what you'd call stable. We lived in New York, but I spent a lot of time working in Washington. First came the Eco-Environmental Project. Then Star Bright. When I signed on for Star Bright, Maxine filed for divorce. That's one of the reasons I was drinking so much when you met me. My marriage was over and my career seemed to be headed for the dumper.

"Seems Maxine's going through this rebirth/reborn–type experience thing and wanted to come to terms with everything in her past. That's why we had the meeting in Santa Fe."

"And that's why she wanted to see you again?" Sam asked in disbelief. "So she could sleep with you?"

"No!" Al snapped. He tried again to explain. "She wanted to return all my stuff she had boxed up. I was in Texas on Star Bright when I received the final divorce papers. Maxine had all my things shipped to storage in New York."

Sam's curiosity was getting the better of him. "Stuff? What kind of stuff?"

"Stuff. You know," Al said, waving the link through the air, "photo albums, school records, moon rocks, old pictures, medals, military records, boxing gloves, that kind of stuff. She and I had a great time talking over the memories. We had a lovely lunch served in her hotel suite. She was very grateful that I took the time to come and see her. We began to reminiscence about the good old days in New York and . . . well . . . one thing started to lead to another.'' Al paused and smiled impishly at Sam.

Sam shook his head. "But that doesn't explain the limp," Sam pointed out.

"Oh, this," Al walked toward the steps. "It's nothing. I just broke my big toe."

"Please, Al." Sam held up his hands. "I don't even want to know how that happened."

"Well, it's not what you're thinking. Maxine and I fell asleep afterwards. Remember, I hadn't slept the last few nights and, well, things caught up with me. She woke up, got dressed, and slipped out before I woke up. On her way out, she placed a wake-up call for me at the front desk. That damn phone rang and startled me out of the best sleep I'd had in days." Al took the cigar out of his mouth and rolled it between his fingers. "I thought the wake-up call was Ziggy. I had forgotten where I was. I got up and headed straight for where Ziggy's monitor would have been in my quarters. Only I wasn't in my quarters. I was in this hotel suite. I ran smack into the coffee table with my big toe." Al jabbed at his foot with his cigar. "And that, Sam, is how I broke my toe." He limped over to Sam and tipped the cigar in the air.

The screen door banged open and Meg joined Sam on the porch. She sat down in the swing and began to rub his shoulders. "Boy, you must have had a bad day. Your shoulders are so tense." She began to knead Sam's shoulders.

"This is where I came in," Al announced. "I'll see you tomorrow, Sam." He brought the link up, winked, hit a button, and vanished.

"That feels so good," Sam sighed. "Tell me, Meg . . . what do you know about David?"

Meg continued to massage Sam's neck and shoulders. "You mean Beulah's boy?" She laughed as she worked.

"Miss Beulah raised him all by herself and she did a fine job. He's going off to college just like your daddy said he would."

"What are your impressions of him?"

"Impressions? Of David?" Meg muttered. Sam was pleased to let Meg launch into a long discussion about David. She didn't need any other prompting. Sam sat back and listened as Meg rubbed his back.

CHAPTER
FIVE

Al stepped out of the Imaging Chamber and rammed the link into his pants. He poked his head around the corner and caught a glimpse of Gooshie sitting idly behind the humming control panel. Gooshie was sitting on a stool, his hands running over the control panel in front of him. "Is it clear?" Al hissed, his head turning this way and that, scanning the room.

"All clear, Admiral," Gooshie called out.

Al stepped away from the Chamber and Gooshie shut the door behind him. Al limped up to the panel, chewing on the end of his cigar. "Where is she, Gooshie?"

"Tina is currently tending to General, I believe, Admiral Calavicci," Gooshie replied slowly, his eyes avoiding the admiral's. "At least, that's what she told me approximately eleven minutes ago."

Al made a face. "Good. It usually takes Tina over half an hour to feed that damn pet alligator of hers." He rubbed his chin as he thought. "If Tina comes looking for me, you haven't seen me, got it? You have no idea where I am or what I'm doing. I don't want Tina to see me like this.''

"Yes, Admiral." Gooshie pushed at his wire-rimmed glasses, which were always slipping down on his nose. "Do you happen to know where General resides these days?" he asked, his eyes darting this way and that across the floor. It was as if Gooshie expected General to appear in the control room.

"Are you kidding?" Al exclaimed. He dusted off his shirt front as he spoke. "I don't want to come within ten feet of that overgrown reptile handbag. I hope wherever she keeps that gator it's as far away from me as possible." He turned away from the humming control panel and headed toward the ramp that would lead him out into the hallway. "And remember, Gooshie," Al warned, "you haven't seen me."

"Deception and mistrust are the first signs that a relationship is in trouble, Admiral Calavicci," Ziggy's smooth, alto voice chided Al as he made his way to the door. "You should try being open and honest with Dr. Martinez-O'Farrell, Admiral. You might be surprised at the results."

"And who asked you?" Al growled up at the silver ball on the ceiling. "You're supposed to be cross-referencing files concerning Sam's Leap, not spewing out marriage counseling mumbo-jumbo," he reminded the computer.

Ziggy loved a verbal match, especially with Al. "Oh, yes, Admiral," Ziggy cooed back. "But from the way you've been limping since your return from Santa Fe, I'd say you could use some form of counseling. And I shouldn't have to remind you, of all people, that I can easily do two functions at one time without the—"

"Listen, Ziggy," Al began to reason. He caught himself and glanced over at the control panel. Gooshie dipped his head down, trying to avoid eye contact with the admiral. Al snapped his head up in the direction of Ziggy's glowing silver ball on the ceiling. "Why am I standing here trying to reason with an overblown circuit breaker?" He shook his head as he limped through the door. "I'm certainly not going to inform you about my love life."

"Tina fills me in on that subject quite nicely," Ziggy responded in her same neutral tone. "And reverting to name calling is so beneath you, Admiral Calavicci."

Al gave Ziggy a distracted wave of his hand as he hobbled out of the control room.

A few hours later, Al was in the process of balancing two cups of steaming coffee as he waited for the Waiting Room door to open. He had changed into a silk shirt with a red, white, and green paisley design. A thin, metallic green tie hung loosely around his neck and his silver loafers matched his pewter-colored slacks and coat.

The door opened and a cool breeze blew past Al into the corridor. It was past midnight at the project and only a small skeleton crew remained on duty. Al entered the Waiting Room and waited for the door to shut silently behind him. He walked past the nurses' table, which was unmanned, and proceeded to the main table in the center of the room. He shot a quick glance up at the main observatory windows and was relieved to see the observation deck dark, the shades drawn. He had almost lost his limp completely, thanks to his well-broken-in silver loafers. He carefully approached the padded table.

Will Williams was sitting on the table, his legs pulled up underneath him, leaning on an elbow, and jotting something down on a yellow notepad.

Al gently set the cups down on the table, near Will's hand. "Careful, it's hot," Al cautioned.

Will Williams smiled and wrapped his hand around a steaming cup. Two dark brown eyes blinked back at Al. Will took a swallow of the black liquid and tipped back his head, letting the coffee flow down his throat. "Thank God for small miracles."

Al listened to the voice. It was familiar and yet strange at the same time. "Strong, black, and lethal is the only kind of coffee the cafeteria serves," Al pointed out. He picked up his cup and also took a swallow. He grimaced and set the cup down on the table. Al took a shoe box he had carried under his arm and set it down on the table.

Will took another soundless drink. "This is great. The cranberry juice was getting old."

"I see you've been keeping busy." Al tapped at the yellow notepad on the table.

Will laughed. "I've got to tell you, I'm beginning to feel like a hamster in a science experiment gone awry." He nudged the yellow legal pad. "At least this keeps me sane." He turned the corner of the pad with his finger and surveyed its contents. "Dr. Beeks has been taking my notes and analyzing them, I think. I told her I like to scribble and doodle when I'm not writing and she seemed to get more excited about my scribbling than my note taking."

"Well, Dr. Beeks is thorough." Al pushed the shoe box toward Will. "This should help." Will cocked his head and picked up the box. "I don't know what rules I'm bending by getting these for you, but try not to draw a lot of attention to them, um, if you can."

Will opened the box and took out a white running shoe. "Mighty fancy-looking footwear." He turned the shoe over in his hand.

Al tapped the box with his index finger. "They're running shoes. You were complaining about your feet."

Will pulled the protective tissue booty off his foot. He eased the shoe over his bare foot. "Wow, that feels so much better. Not a bad fit either. 'Course, I'm not planning on doing any running." He began to lace up the shoe. "Thanks, Admiral."

"It's Al. Call me Al."

Will dug out the other shoe from the box. "I appreciate this, Al. I really do." Will noticed the lag in the conversation so he shifted gears. "My wife and kids—are they all right?"

Al seemed relieved that the subject had changed. He looked up and put his arms behind his back. "Yes, your wife and kids are fine."

Will stopped wiggling his feet and grew silent. "You

mean they can't tell that Sam is there and I'm here?'' Will seemed more than a little disappointed.

Al began to rock on the balls of his feet. "No, but it's nothing to be worried about. We'd have a real mess on our hands if everyone noticed Sam every time he Leaped. Your memories of this place will fade once you return."

Will shook his head in disbelief. "It's amazing when you come to think about it. Except . . ." Will folded one of his legs underneath him and pointed at the yellow pad. "That Sam's a physicist, not a sheriff, and he's got a murder to solve."

"That's where you come in," Al moved around to the head of the table. "You've been a tremendous help in filling the gaps. Ziggy, Dr. Beeks, everyone is astonished at how much you remember." Al pointed at the pad. "Just keep writing the details down that you remember."

"But I can't remember that much," Will protested. "A flash here, a detail there. It's maddening. It comes and goes."

"Don't let it get you down," Al reassured him. "Whatever you remember, write it down. No matter what detail or how small, it could be important."

Will picked up his pencil and pulled the pad closer toward him. "I've been a good sport. I've been answering your questions, writing down what I can remember. I've answered a long list of questions from Dr. Beeks and Lord knows I've let them take enough samples to start their own blood bank." Will's deep brown eyes looked into Al's eyes. "Would you answer a few questions of mine?"

The men stared at each other. A machine beeped softly in the background. Will shifted on the table and the rustling of his robe was loud in the room.

Al stopped rocking. "Depends on the questions."

Will nodded. He thought a moment. "How come, with all this future high-tech stuff, you need the help of little old me?"

Al ran his index finger over his bottom lip and studied the table. "Ziggy would have a conniption fit if I told you too much. I'd also be breaking more rules than I care to

104

admit. Let's just keep this simple. Yes or no answers."

Will tapped the pencil on the pad. "Okay. Ziggy's the supercomputer, right?" Will asked.

Al nodded. "Yes. She keeps track of everything." Al glanced nervously at the door.

"Except she doesn't have records for Brick?" Al hesitated in answering. "Come on, Al," Will coached. "I've been getting all kinds of questions about 1955 and Brick. I can put two and two together."

"Normally, Ziggy should have the data we're discussing. But she doesn't." Al looked very uncomfortable.

"So something happened to the records of Brick for 1955?"

"Yes."

"Something that wipes out a whole year of records." Will paused and watched Al flinch. "Official records for Brick are kept in Dunsmoore, I remember that much. What happens, Al?"

Al stood very still and closed his eyes. "I can't tell you that."

Will picked up the notepad and hugged it to his chest. "Then I can't help you anymore either. Fair is fair."

Al opened his eyes and saw Will clutching the pad. "Will," Al began to reason, "you've got to understand. Sam needs this information to help solve the murder and catch the killer. Without your help, history won't be changed."

"And you've got to understand my position. I'm the sheriff in a small town. Something so terrible happens to that town that vital records are destroyed. I know records don't simply disappear unless something drastic happens. You know what happens and when. I want that information. We'll swap details."

"Will, don't you understand? I can't tell you that." Al stepped forward and spread his hands out. "It's highly classified. It's against the rules."

"I'm sure we can work something out. An exchange of information seems fair, in my opinion. I'm willing to tell

105

you everything I can remember, but I want the people who make up my little town out of harm's way. I've been co-operative enough. Bend a little, Al. Please?'' He extended his hand.

Al looked like he was being torn in two. He kept biting his lower lip and studying the floor. He finally exhaled and reached for Will's hand. He gave it a firm shake. ''I can get in big trouble here,'' he grumbled as he reached for Ziggy's link. He turned on the link and the lights blinked to life. Will picked up the pencil on the table. ''Wait. You can't write this down,'' Al cautioned.

''Then how will I remember it?'' Will asked.

Al shook his head. ''I don't know. But for now listen, don't write.'' He consulted Ziggy's link and began in a soft voice. ''In May of 1965 a tornado touches down in the middle of the night in the towns of Brick and Dunsmoore. There was no forewarning. Dunsmoore suffers the worst damage. The city hall, courthouse, and library are destroyed along with a couple homes and most of the businesses. All of the records for the towns of Dunsmoore, Brick, and Miller are destroyed. Very few vital records remain from prior to 1965. The town of Brick fares better, with only a couple buildings destroyed.'' Al stopped talking. He continued to read the information on the tiny data line.

Will was shocked. ''No warning?'' he repeated. ''Any casualties?'' Will clutched the robe around his chest. ''There had to be some.''

Al continued to read. ''The storm caught everyone by surprise. Five persons were killed in Dunsmoore.'' Al lowered the blinking link. ''Seven killed in Brick.''

''Who are they?'' Will demanded.

Al struck the link with his palm. ''It doesn't say.'' The link stopped blinking. ''I'm sorry, Will, that's all it says.''

Will dropped the pad on the table. ''I appreciate that, Al.'' He seemed to be having trouble digesting the information about his town.

''I shouldn't have said anything. I should have kept my mouth shut,'' Al lamented.

106

Will blinked and pushed the pad of information toward Al. "You wanted as much information on David as I could remember." Al picked up the pad and scanned it as Will continued. "David Bo Jefferson is the only child of Beulah and Lucas Jefferson. He's almost eighteen, I think. He works doing chores for folks around the area, white and colored. He's been attending a school set up at the Baptist church. Miss Beulah calls him her miracle child. Miss Beulah and Lucas were married a long time before David came along. Miss Beulah was hired to take care of me and my father after my mother passed away. I was five years old when she came to cook, clean, and care for us. She stayed with my family even after David came along. Her husband died in some kind of accident, I can't remember what exactly. Seems to me that David was about ten years old. David is a good kid and a hard worker, just like his father. He had a couple of scrapes with the law when he was a teenager. He got mixed up with the wrong crowd. Miss Beulah steered him on the right path. She's hoping he can get accepted at a Negro college next year."

"Do you think he would murder Carla Sue?"

"No," Will answered strongly. "I don't. He doesn't mix with those kind of people. I can't imagine why he'd be tried for her murder. Does he know her?"

"The first time around he did," Al replied. "Or it was implied pretty heavily at the trial."

"Doesn't make sense, Al." Will had picked up his coffee cup. "I mean, you've got a murder, you need a motive. What would David's motive be? I mean, if he didn't know her. David doesn't strike me as a person who could murder another person."

Al wasn't about to get into the complications or allegations brought up at the trial. He again shifted gears. "What do you remember about Carla Sue?"

Will tapped his head with his finger. "Hardly anything. She lived in a trailer on some land owned by . . . um . . . B-somebody. Crazy as a coon dog that guy was, I do remember that. He rents the land to Carla and Tom dirt cheap.

Carla worked at the Hole as a waitress. She did other things on the side, so I've heard. I don't recall ever arresting her for anything. I think she had a nice smile and a polite manner about her. Didn't come across as a hard person, if you know what I mean. But there were those rumors around the town and it sure didn't cast her in a very good light.''

Al nodded. ''Anything about Tom?''

Will lowered his head and a small smile crossed his lips. ''Slow, well-meaning oaf. Lived with Carla Sue for as long as I can remember. Does odd jobs. Fixes cars mostly. Seemed devoted to Carla Sue. Caused me a few headaches over the years but nothing serious. He doesn't seem a likely candidate for murder either. Never seen him get really angry. Their fighting consisted mainly of yelling matches. Tom might get drunk afterwards, but nobody complained. But something different was happening with Tom. It seems to me he was getting in some kind of trouble lately, I just can't recall what it was about.''

Al spied over his shoulder. ''I just got a few more things to ask you, then we'll call it a night. If Beeks finds out what we've been up to, I'll be toast for sure.''

Will snapped up his head and smiled. ''I like Dr. Beeks.'' He shook his head back and forth in amazement. ''I never thought I'd meet someone like her, doing what she does. And her being a doctor and all.'' He caught Al smiling slightly at him and Will leaned back on the table. ''I keep forgetting I'm not in Oklahoma in 1955 anymore.'' He cocked his head, ''This isn't Oklahoma, is it?''

Al folded his arms and smiled broadly at the amused look on his face. ''It's New Mexico and the year isn't important. I'm glad you like Verbena. Dr. Beeks is a top-notch doctor. You are in perfect hands with her, none better.''

''I'm not questioning her ability, by any means, Al. She's been very nice and professional and everything. . . . It's just such a shock to—''

''To see an African-American woman who happens to be a doctor?''

Al watched as the color in Will's cheeks rose and turned

a bright red. "Don't be embarrassed, Will. You're on the edge of a lot of change for the South in 1955. Civil rights, the freedom marches, the bus boycotts, all this will take place in your lifetime. The old stereotypes and roles will start to crumble, but it will be at a price. A lot of innocent blood will be spilled before . . ." Al let his voice trail off.

"Al, if this really is a time experiment in the future, why can't you change all that suffering and pain?"

"Good question," Al sighed. "I find myself asking that same thing on every Leap. Believe me, if I was running this experiment, I know the first thing I'd change, but it's not up to me."

"Well, who decides on what needs to be changed?"

Al stepped back from the table and checked his watch. "We still haven't figured the 'who' part out yet."

Will made a face. "Seems like you got a lot of bugs to work out of this so-called experiment," he observed. "What about the names? Can you get me the names of those casualties from Brick?"

Al drummed his fingers on Ziggy's link. "I'll see what I can do, but I can't promise you anything at this point." He picked up his coffee cup and dumped it in the trash by the wall. "Oh, I almost forgot." Al snapped his fingers. "Gene Dupree, your deputy."

"He hasn't fainted on Sam, has he?" Will ran his hand over the notepad. "Gene's a good person. My father took to him when he was thirteen years old. He was headed for trouble. Mother abandoned him right after he was born. Gene was being raised by an alcoholic father, who beat him at every drop of the hat." Will shuddered. "What a mess. My father arrested Gene on a petty crime. His father wouldn't bail him out. Left him in jail. My father was appalled. He spent the next two days and nights talking to Gene. Finding out what made him tick. My dad was good at talking to people and figuring out what made them do the things they did. He discovered that Gene was an impressionable kid with good intentions. My father put up the bail money, went to court with him, and, when he was released, brought Gene home.

"Gene adored my father. It was strange having him around at first. Gene was a funny kid. Shy, quiet. He wasn't dumb or stupid. Pretty smart, in fact. My father convinced Gene to stay in school. He got Gene interested in law enforcement. I made him my deputy when I took over the sheriff's position from my father. He's been a good deputy."

Al had more information than he had planned on asking. "What about as a sheriff? Isn't he going to follow in your footsteps?"

"I don't think so." Will saw the look of surprise on Al's face. "He's just not what I would consider sheriff material. He gets ribbed a lot about his appearance. He's as skinny as a stray dog. He faints at the sight of blood, so he stays away from the messy traffic accidents and mishaps. Kind of hard to have a deputy that won't investigate a murder or accident scene. Won't have a thing to do with autopsy reports. But he is a good deputy despite all his flaws. Trustworthy, loyal, dependable, honest."

"Sounds like a regular Boy Scout." Al picked up the pad from the table.

"Gene is a Boy Scout, in some ways. Nobody in four counties can handle a gun like Gene. Best damn sharpshooter I've ever seen. Now that's one thing I wish I could do. Handle a gun like Gene." Will whistled and the sound bounced around the empty room. "I've never had a problem with him backing me up."

Al checked his watch again and stood drumming his fingers on the pad. "I should be going now. Try and get some sleep, Will."

Will laughed. "I'll try. Sleep isn't coming very easy though."

Al shook his head. He held the pad up. "Thanks for the notes."

"Can you get me the exact date and time I need for 1965?"

110

Al took another quick look around the room. "I don't know. I'll try. Good night, Will,"

"You can do better than try, Admiral." Will raised his hand. "Good night."

Thursday, September 1, 1955

Sam pounded on Doc Adams's door again. It was seven fifteen in the morning. The heat was already rising up from the warm pavement, promising to be another hot, miserable day. Sam had spent a sleepless night tossing and turning, going over the details of the case in his head. His time was running out.

Sam tipped his ear next to the door. Silence. He assaulted the door with his fist. "Doc! You awake?" Sam shouted through the thick oak door. He picked up the brass knocker and rapped as hard as he could. "It's Will Williams."

Through the door Sam thought he heard a muffled cough. A drowsy, deep voice called out, "I'm coming, I'm coming. Hold your damn pants on." It took forever before the lock on the door slid back and the front door opened a crack. A bloodshot eye peered out at Sam. Doc recognized the sheriff and pulled the door open wider. "What'sa matter, Will?" He smoothed down his hair, which was standing out in all directions. His face had the start of a scruffy beard. "Has there been an accident?"

"No. I need to talk to you about Carla Sue's autopsy. I need to see your report."

Doc stopped smoothing out his hair and looked at Sam. His eyes narrowed and a red flush from anger spread to his cheeks. "You mean to tell me you've gotten me up at this hour in the morning for an autopsy report? Hell, I haven't even finished it yet." Doc started to shut the door in Sam's face. "Come back at a decent hour. I distinctly recall telling you to come *this afternoon*."

"I've got to talk to you now," Sam insisted as he pushed

111

at the door. "I don't have much time and I need your help."

Doc was surprised at the tone of Sam's voice. He let the door swing back. He pulled a frayed bathrobe around his middle. "I don't even have any coffee made yet," Doc complained. His eyes squinted in the early morning light.

"I'll make the coffee," Sam offered. "I'll even make breakfast if you want. Please let me in."

"You don't have to cook breakfast, Will Williams. But I do expect you to get that coffeepot going. I'll let you see what I've done so far. But mind you, the report won't be finished."

"That's okay, Doc. We'll talk about what you've found so far. Where's the kitchen?"

Doc snorted and pointed. "In that direction. Don't make a mess either. I don't want Esther giving me hell about messing up her kitchen." He shuffled in his slippers in the opposite direction. "I've got to get dressed and find my glasses. Won't be able to find the right drawer in the morgue unless I've got my glasses." He began to trudge upstairs muttering to himself, "Damn sheriff is off his rocker, waking me up at this time in the morning. I'm getting too old for this. Let that fancy doctor from Ashcroft handle this stuff. I'm getting too old."

By seven thirty Doc had gotten dressed and had Sam join him in the back of the house. This part of the house was reserved for the pathology lab and the morgue. The room was a large one, built onto the back of the house. It might have been a garage at one time, but now it was a makeshift morgue for the small town of Brick. The stainless freezer with four unmarked doors hummed loudly. Doc ambled into the room and switched on a bright overhead lamp. He pulled a file from the top of a filing cabinet.

"I'll go over what I've found so far. Remember the report is not complete yet. I had to reschedule the rest of my patients around yesterday. After I see my few morning patients, I'll work on completing the report. " He straighten his glasses and scanned the report. "Victim: white, female, age twenty-four. Cause of death: multiple stab wounds to the upper torso. Stabbed at least thirty times with a sharp pointed instrument. Swelling on her left cheek is due to a blow she suffered before the time of death. Some contusions and bruising on her back and shoulders, no broken bones. The bruises on her back occurred when she fell or was pushed down. The exact time of death hard to pinpoint because of the heat in the trailer. I haven't done a full autopsy on the body yet. I was going to get started this afternoon,'' Doc grumbled.

"She was at the Hole around twelve or twelve thirty,'' Sam noted.

Doc nodded and thought a moment. "If she was last seen alive at noon, I would hazard to say time of death anywhere from two to six P.M. More likely occurred between three and four, but I can't say for sure." Doc ruffled through his notes. "What time did you go after Tom?''

"I think it was after three o' clock. Could have been closer to four." Sam watched Doc pour over his notes. "Tell me, Doc, would you consider Tom a suspect?''

"I wouldn't, no. I don't think Tom did it.''

Sam reached for the notepad in his pocket. "Why not?''

Doc pulled a stool away from the table and eased his large frame onto the small stool top. "Don't make sense to me. Why would Tom kill Carla? They've been together all this time. What would cause him to do this to her, now? Just don't feel right.''

Sam leaned against a counter. "What if Tom found out that she was seeing other people. It makes him angry. Pushes him over the edge.''

Doc shook his head back and forth. "Tom's feeble-minded. Even if he knew about her seeing other men, I doubt if he'd believe it. He's been around and heard the rumors. Tom never believed them before. Why should he start now?''

"But the suicide attempt—''

"That was no suicide attempt!'' Doc interrupted. "I keep telling you that was an attempt to get Carla worried about

113

him. That's all. He'd never jump. Might fall by accident, but never jump." Doc pointed to his report. "Let's see here, she was thrown or forced back down on the floor. Okay, Tom's big enough to do that all right. He must weigh close to three hundred pounds. There are those bruises on her back and shoulders. Someone forced her down and she was stabbed repeatedly. Not once or twice, but over thirty times. Overkill. What does that tell you, Will?"

Sam thought a moment. "The murderer was angry, enraged. Out of control."

"Yes," Doc agreed. "And so out of control he didn't stop. I've determined the third or fourth blow cut clear through her aorta. She would have bled to death in minutes and stopped struggling. Yet the killer kept stabbing her, even after she gave up the fight. Deep penetrating wounds. I found that the stab wounds on her stomach and hips weren't driven nearly as deep as the ones on her neck and shoulders. It's as if our killer was getting tired as he worked his way down the body."

Sam stopped writing and shook his head. "All this created a bloody mess. When her aorta was cut it would have sprayed the killer with blood. He would have been covered in blood."

"Yes. This was a gory murder. To find the killer all we have to do is find someone who was covered in blood day before yesterday." Doc laughed and took off his glasses. "I don't recall anyone in Brick walking around like that Tuesday, do you, Will?"

"No." Sam pointed at Doc's notes. "Do you mind?"

Doc shrugged and handed over his report. "Remember it's not complete."

"Was the murderer right-handed or left-handed?" Sam asked as he scanned Doc's notes.

"Very difficult to say. I'm going to guess our boy is right-handed, judging from the angle of the stab wounds on the body, but don't hold me to that." Doc shifted his weight around on the stool. "It's just a guess." Doc turned and pointed at the report in Sam's hands. "Got any suspects, Sheriff Williams?"

"No," Sam said as he shuffled through the paperwork, "just Tom."

"I still think Tom didn't do it," Doc quickly interjected. "I know he and Carla had been living together. They were known to fight. Tom had fought with her prior to going out on that balcony. But he's still not your man, Will."

"He's right-handed, isn't he? He's big and strong," Sam argued.

"He's right-handed all right. I'm way ahead of you, Will. I picked through his medical records last night." Doc pointed to a thick folder sitting on the countertop. "Tom was raised in a large family. Ten brothers and sisters in all. His family lived down the road toward Ashcroft. Dirt poor. The kids would go work on farms for money instead of going to school. When Tom was about ten years old he was involved in a farming accident. Nearly lost his right arm above the elbow. He can still use his arm, but he favors it. He doesn't have much strength in that arm and I know for sure he can't raise it above his shoulder. Tom had a bad case of the mumps too. He had just turned sixteen. Whole family came down with them. Tom had to be hospitalized, along with his older brother. Was in the hospital for two weeks. He was very sick. Guess that's why he and Carla never had any little ones running around."

"You think he was sterile due to the mumps?" Sam asked with little interest.

"That's my guess. They lived together for almost ten years." Doc pointed at the notes. "Back at the murder scene, some evidence turned up that bothered me. Flip through that report. I think I mention something on page five." Sam began to flip pages. "See, we're back to motive, Will. I don't think Tom paid much attention to the rumors surrounding Carla Sue. He'd always shrug off the slightest bit of information about Carla's infidelity. He'd always said nobody knew her like he did. She sure had the wool pulled over his eyes, but then Tom was easy to fool. He was never very bright. I found that appointment card in the trailer. It's for a doctor in Ashcroft. I've always treated Tom for all his ailments. He'd come to me with the slightest problem. However, I never treated Carla Sue. She and her sister always went into Ashcroft. I called the doctor listed on that card, but he's out of town till Tuesday."

Sam had found the card and was studying it carefully. It listed a general practitioner who resided in Ashcroft.

"How long would you say she'd been having affairs?" Sam asked.

"Don't know for sure. Couldn't really call them affairs. Tom and Carla were never legally married. They were common-law husband and wife. Happens quite often with the poorer folks. If I had to hazard a guess about her sideline, I'd probably say since she started working down at the Hole. She was fourteen or fifteen then. It's a shame, she was quite a beautiful girl." Doc stood up from the stool and consulted his watch. "Esther should be arriving at any time now. I've got my first patient at nine this morning. She's going to have a fit if she finds me back here." He motioned at the reports. "Help me gather all these things up." Doc began to shuffle papers back into files.

Sam handed back the files to Doc. "Some witnesses saw David Jefferson walking away from the bar with Carla Sue."

Doc stopped shuffling the papers. "Have you questioned David yet?"

"No," Sam admitted. "I was going to do that after I talked to you. I have to either charge Tom or let him go. Looks like I'm going to be letting him go for now."

"Will, . . ." Doc began. He paused and wrung his hands. "Were Carla and David . . . um, involved together?"

"I don't know. I don't think so." Sam picked up his untouched coffee. "He just walked her home."

Doc tossed the files down on the countertop and shook his head. "Don't you find that kind of strange? A colored boy walking home a white girl who he doesn't even know?"

116

Sam thought for a moment. "It does seem kind of odd, but I'm sure David had a reason."

"Could it be the same reason other men followed Carla Sue home?"

Sam shook his head as he handed Doc the file. "I don't know, Doc."

"Look at the facts, Will. David walks Carla home. Why did he do that? Did they know each other? He's probably the last person to see her alive. Why was he at the Hole in the first place? That's a notorious hangout for the Klan after dark. You know how Patch treats Negroes. If he and Carla were involved—"

"Don't jump to conclusions," Sam interrupted.

"But let's just say they were, for argument's sake. What if they were more than just acquaintances and what if someone finds out about them? What does Carla do? If she cries rape, she might have a case. No matter that most folks wouldn't give her the time of day if they passed her on the street, she cries rape by a Negro, those same folks would submit her name for sainthood."

"I don't believe this and I won't believe anything until I hear David's side of the story." Sam poured his coffee down the sink.

"You know, Will, I like David and Miss Beulah. I don't have anything against them. But if what I'm saying is true, you're gonna have real messy investigation on your hands."

"What are you talking about?"

"Let's just say it was David who murdered Carla." Doc held up his hands to ward off Sam's protests. "Just listen. Let's say it's true. If this gets out, this town will come apart at the seams. There are people in this town who aren't afraid to don a sheet and take justice into their own hands over a case like this." Doc patted Sam's shoulder. "Tread lightly, Will, and watch your back. I hope I'm wrong about David, I really do. Don't let your loyalties cloud your judgment. Someone wanted her more than just dead." Doc looked at his watch and led the way back into the main

117

part of the house. An older woman was just letting herself in through the front door when Sam and Doc emerged from the back. "I'll call when I finish up the rest of my report."

Sam thanked the doctor and nodded at Esther who was giving Sam a good once-over. "Your first patient will be here in twenty minutes," she reminded Doc as she slipped past the men. "And you better not have messed up my kitchen."

Sam opened the door and stepped out into the hot sun. "Watch yourself on this case, Will," Doc warned again as he shut his door.

When Sam entered the jail he was more troubled than ever. Gene was filling out a duty roster behind his desk and was eating a doughnut. A paper cup of coffee sat not far from his right hand. Sam doubted if the doughnut ever touched Gene's system before it was gobbled up by his metabolism. Sam checked the log by the door.

"You're up bright and early," Gene noted.

Sam didn't look up. Instead he made a mark in the log. "I'm not going to charge Tom with Carla's murder. I'm releasing him today."

"What!" Gene turned suddenly and tipped his coffee over on his desk. The coffee soaked through the blotter and splashed over the top of the desk onto Gene's leg. Gene jumped up and began wiping at his leg with a napkin.

"Are you okay?" Sam reached for some tissues from his desk and began to blot up the coffee spill on the desk.

"Damn. Oh yeah, I'm just too clumsy. I'd thought I'd outgrown it, but . . ." Gene rubbed his pants leg. The duty roster was soaked. Gene picked up the roster, coffee dripping off its corners, and threw it in the trash.

Sam tossed the wet tissues in the trash. "Do you have an extra pair of pants to change into?"

"Yeah, I'll just go and—Oh, wait a minute. My extra uniform isn't here. I forgot I . . . left it at the cleaners in Dunsmoore." Gene sucked his breath in and looked up at

118

the ceiling in frustration. "I do have a spare pair of pants at home though."

"I'll let you run home in a minute. Wait till I get Tom released and then you can go," Sam offered.

"Okay," Gene said with a sigh of relief. "I won't be more than a few minutes."

Sam held out his hand. "I need your keys."

Gene pulled the ring loose from his belt buckle and handed it to Sam. "Holler if he gives you any trouble."

Sam took the keys and headed down the hallway. "I don't suspect that Tom will."

Tom Madison rose off the bed when Sam came down the hall. He walked over to the door of his cell and gripped the bars. He didn't say a word as Sam approached and found the correct key.

"I'm releasing you on your own accord, Tom. You'll have to stay around town if we need to ask you more questions."

Tom grunted and peered through the bars at Sam. "Are you charging me with Carla's murder?"

"Not at this time. Her murder is still under investigation." Sam inserted the key in the lock. The lock opened and the door swung open. Tom stepped out into the hallway.

"I'm going to find who murdered Carla and then I'm going to do to them what they did to her." Tom stood in the hallway, watching Sam very carefully.

"That would be a mistake on your part, Tom. Let us handle this case," Sam said as he shut the cell door.

"We'll see whose mistake it is." Tom's eyes flared with anger as he started down the hallway. The men entered the office and Tom headed straight for the door. He grabbed for the knob. "Does Doc Adams still have Carla?" he asked without turning around.

Sam had opened his desk and pulled out a folder. He emptied the contents of the folder on his desk. "Yes."

Tom swung the door open and was momentarily blinded by the sunlight.

"These things are yours, Tom. You're gonna have to sign for them before you go."

Tom squinted as he turned around. He marched over to Sam's desk, picked up his wallet, and shoved it in his overalls. He then picked up the pen and scrawled *T-O-M* across the envelope. He turned and strode across the room toward the door.

"You're forgetting these." Sam held up a set of keys and jangled them. Tom turned around. Sam palmed the keys and tossed them to Tom. Tom started to catch the keys with his right hand. When his hand was level with his elbow he winced. The keys sailed through the air and dropped at Tom's feet. He bent down, picked them up, and left the office. He didn't close the door on his way out.

Gene stood in the doorway and watched him walk away. "I got a bad feeling about him. Did you have to let him go?"

Sam swept the envelope off his desk top and into the trash. "I can't charge him, Gene. You know I don't have any proof."

Gene pulled at his damp pants leg. "Do you think he left the Hole and went back to their trailer to wait for Carla Sue? Could it have happened like that?"

"I don't think Tom could have been up on the balcony if he had murdered her. He wasn't covered in blood for one thing." Sam pulled the notebook from his pocket. "Go home and change your uniform."

"Okay. I'll take the car out front." He picked up some keys from his desk and started out the door, where he almost collided with Mayor Tilden.

"Dear God, Gene Dupree, where's the fire?" the mayor bellowed. Gene stepped aside and let the mayor pass. "What happened to you?" The mayor asked, pointing at Gene's damp leg. "You look like you wet yourself."

Gene squared his shoulders. He gave the mayor a nasty look and pushed past him out the door. The mayor whistled and watched Gene storm off. "He's a might bit touchy, wouldn't you say, Will?"

Sam watched with dread as Mayor Tilden pulled off his wide-brimmed hat and sat down on the corner of Sam's desk.

"You might say we're all a might bit touchy this morning. Did you come by for a reason, Mayor Tilden?"

"Yes. Yes I did." The mayor pulled a piece of paper out of his coat pocket and set it down on Sam's desk. "That's a cleaning bill for the upholstery in my car." He smiled at Sam.

Sam took the bill, wadded it up, and deposited it in Will's top drawer. He smiled back at the mayor. "Anything else, Mayor?"

The smile disappeared from Mayor Tilden's face. "Are we alone?"

"Yes." Sam was growing annoyed with the mayor.

"You released Tom Madison?"

"Just now, Mayor."

"Fine." The mayor replaced his hat.

"Mayor Tilden, I don't have time to play games with—"

"That's about the only thing I like about you, Will. Straight to the point. As you know, we've got our big Labor Day picnic coming up this weekend. Three days of fun and festivities. I'll be looking forward to your wife's home-baked pies again this year." He smiled and reached for a red bandanna in his back pocket. "As the mayor of Brick I'm concerned about this murder investigation. I don't want anything to dampen the atmosphere surrounding the picnic."

"The picnic?" Sam asked incredulously. "You're worried about the picnic?"

"In a way. Frankly, I'm more concerned about this town and its citizens. Seems we may have a problem on our hands."

"What are you talking about, Mayor?"

"Let me spell it out for you, Will. There's that little

121

matter concerning David Jefferson and Carla Sue,'' Mayor Tilden said suggestively as he eased himself off the desk. ''Seems my wife's cousin, Clark, heard a rumor down at the Hole. He heard that boy was walking Carla Sue home on the day she was murdered. Seems to me, he heard a rumor that they were more than just friends. Now Sheriff, I know you'll do your utmost to protect this town and its citizens and to uphold the law. You're like your father, a man of your word. When you became sheriff, you promised to uphold a high level of integrity.''

''Save your speeches for the campaign.'' Sam pushed back his chair. ''I'm busy, Mayor Tilden. Now if you'll excuse me.''

The mayor stuffed the bandanna in his pocket and stuck a fat finger in Sam's direction. ''Be warned, Will. If that boy killed Carla there'll be hell to pay. And I don't want my town being turned upside down by the Klan. Handle this fast and swiftly and see that justice is taken care of. I want that boy questioned and if he is responsible for her murder I want him arraigned the day after Labor Day. Anything less and we'll have a war erupting on our hands. Do your job as you see fit, Williams. But I want someone in custody by Tuesday. I'm just warning you.''

Sam licked his lips and looked at Mayor Tilden closely. ''I bet you know more about the things that go on down at the Hole than you're letting on.''

Mayor Tilden laughed. ''Maybe I do, and then, maybe I don't. We're very different men, Will. You didn't want me to become mayor and I sure wasn't thrilled to see you be elected sheriff. But that's water under the bridge, as they say. Just understand that this town won't back up a yellow-bellied coward who keeps a felon loose and endangers this town and its citizens. Especially the citizens who vote.''

''You can leave my office the same way you came in.'' Sam pointed to the door. ''I don't like to be threatened, Mayor.''

''No one is threatening you, son. Believe me, you'll know when you're being threatened. Just don't mess up this

122

investigation. Keep your well-meaning, liberal intentions out of this investigation and we'll just see if you understand what I'm trying to tell you or not. We'll just see." Tilden started to leave. "Oh, by the way, Will. It's a shame about that jukebox down at the Hole. Are you going to plead self-defense?" Tilden brayed loudly.

"Get out, Tilden."

The mayor laughed as he left. Sam got up and slammed the front door behind the mayor. He was surprised a few minutes later when Gene eased the door open and poked his head in.

"What happened with Tilden, Will?" Gene had changed his coffee-splattered pants for a crisp, clean pair. "You look ticked."

"I'm fine. Just had to deal with Tilden. You sure did get back here fast." Gene just nodded. "I'll be leaving for a while." Sam retrieved his notebook from his desk. "I'll be back later. Call me if anything happens."

"Sure," Gene answered as Sam banged the door closed.

CHAPTER SIX

The Williamses' kitchen was full of laughter and the aroma of fresh baked pies. Miss Beulah and Meg were standing over two rolling boards. Miss Beulah had just set down her rolling pin and was dusting off her hands on her apron. Tyler held a blue ball in his arms and walked underfoot, dropping the ball here and there.

Meg was laughing and the latest gossip was being swapped back and forth between the two women about the picnic committee. Miss Beulah smiled and listened as she stepped around Tyler on her way to the oven. She pulled on the oven mitts and pulled two more pies from the oven. Meg made some room on the counter. "Five pies baked, five more to go."

Miss Beulah set the pies down and wiped her forehead with her hand. "Thank goodness we got a start on them early. It's going to be another hot day."

"I'll die if it stays this hot for the picnic." Meg had picked up a handful of flour and was sprinkling it over the rolled-out dough on her board. "Worst hot weather in years."

The screen door banged shut and Miss Beulah looked at the kitchen clock. "That's probably Becca coming in from outside."

"Rebecca," Meg called out from the kitchen, "is that you?"

Tyler threw the ball at the doorway. "Play wit' me."

Meg looked up and stopped rolling out the dough.

Miss Beulah took off the gloves and set them down by the stove. "Oh my."

Sam nodded at the surprised women. He reached down and tousled Tyler's blond curls. He squatted down and rolled Tyler's ball into the living room. Tyler screamed in delight and waddled after the ball.

Meg wiped her hands on her apron. "Will, what's going on? You've still got your gun on."

Sam put his hand on the belt and looked at Meg. "I know. I need to speak with Miss Beulah. I'm not staying."

Meg turned and looked at her housekeeper. Miss Beulah was walking across the room, her eyes wide with concern. "Has there been an accident?"

"No accident," Sam reassured her. "I need to speak to David. Do you know where he is now?"

Miss Beulah narrowed her eyes at Sam. "Yes. Today he should be home from school by now. He does a few things around the house before going to do his chores."

"Will, what's going on?" Meg asked.

"I need to ask David a few questions. Miss Beulah, why don't you take a ride with me out to your home? I'm sure Meg can manage by herself for the rest of the day." Sam gave Meg a look that told her not to protest.

"Is David in trouble? Did he do something wrong?" Miss Beulah looked from Sam to Meg, and began to pull at her apron strings.

Meg put her arm around Miss Beulah's shoulders. "You go ahead with Will. We're almost finished here anyway."

"Let me get my things, William. I'll be with you in a

125

moment," Miss Beulah said as she walked out of the kitchen.

"Will," Meg hissed, "what is going on?"

"I can't talk about it now," he answered in a hushed tone of voice. "It's got to do with that murder investigation we talked about last night. If I'm going to be late, I'll call you."

Meg caught his hand. "David's not in trouble, is he? I can't believe that David would do anything wrong."

Sam squeezed Meg's hand and released it. "I hope not."

Miss Beulah reappeared with her purse and hat. Sam let Miss Beulah lead the way out of the house. Tyler came giggling back to the adults, his ball captured again. Meg picked him up as Sam and Miss Beulah left.

David and Beulah Jefferson lived across the railroad tracks, on the east side of Brick. All of the black families in Brick lived there. Sam pulled the police car in front of a house with a dirt yard. The Jeffersons' home was kept in better shape than most of the homes on the street. Some bright geraniums bloomed in a window box and the storm windows were freshly painted. The yard, although without grass, was neatly lined with red bricks. Sam got out and opened the door for Miss Beulah. She didn't say a word as she climbed the stairs and took a key from her purse. She opened the door and invited Sam into her home.

The house was dark and the air inside felt stifling. There was a small parlor with a sofa and a chair. Miss Beulah pointed to a verandah. "Make yourself at home, William. I'll go see where David is. Would you like some iced tea?"

Sam smiled but politely declined. He sat down on the couch and patted his shirt pocket for the notepad. He watched Miss Beulah enter the kitchen, open the back door, and call for David.

Sam heard a voice answer back. The screen door opened and David appeared. He looked surprised to see the sheriff of Brick sitting in the living room. Miss Beulah whispered anxiously to him.

126

David was seventeen years old. He wore a white T-shirt that was soaking wet with perspiration. He reached for a towel with his well-toned arms. He wiped his forehead and nodded in Sam's direction. David walked into the parlor and stood awkwardly before Sam.

Sam smiled and pointed to the opposite side of the sofa. "Why don't you sit down, David? I'd like to ask you a few questions." Sam smiled at Miss Beulah, who was standing in the kitchen. "You're welcome to join us, Miss Beulah."

"I think I will join you." She sat down in the only other available chair, facing David and Sam. Her back was straight, her chin held high, and her hands folded tightly in her lap. She nodded her head in David's direction as he sat down nervously on the edge of the sofa.

Sam flipped open the pad with his pen. "You look like you've worked up quite a sweat, David."

"Yes, sir, Sheriff Williams." David cleared his throat. He spoke in a deep, strong voice. "I was out back chopping wood for my mother's stove. It's going to be another hot day."

"We don't get electricity or gas out this way," Miss Beulah explained. "We're lucky just to have a phone. It's a party line, but I don't mind. David chops the wood for my stove and keeps this house from falling down around our heads." Miss Beulah smiled at her son.

Sam smiled and checked his notes. "David, I need to ask you a few questions about your whereabouts Tuesday afternoon."

"Why?" David asked.

Sam looked up at David. "There's been a murder," Sam told him in a quiet tone of voice.

"A murder?" David repeated. "But I don't know anything about a murder. Who's been murdered?"

"Let's not get ahead of ourselves," Sam cautioned. "Now David, what did you do Tuesday?"

David shrugged and looked down at his hands. "I usually attend the school the Reverend Niles runs out of his

127

church. I attend from seven in the morning till eleven or so. It varies on how I'm doing with the schoolwork."

"David's a smart boy. He's going to finish up his basic requirements this year. Then with the reverend's help and the Lord's blessing, he's going to apply to college come next fall." Miss Beulah reached over and patted her son's leg. "He's been working around the community to raise some money. Books and tuition are going to be expensive."

David seemed embarrassed by his mother's boasting. "Now, Momma," he complained, "no need to go on about me in front of Sheriff Williams. I practically grew up in the sheriff's house." He bowed his head and continued his story. "Tuesday I didn't go to school because I was caught up with my lessons and I had promised a farmer I'd help out on his farm. He's getting ready for the fall planting."

"What was the farmer's name?"

"Mr. Nicholas. It's the old place out on the highway. I started working for him last year. I do chores for him. The pay is good and I can work the hours around my schooling."

"What kind of chores do you do on the farm, David?" Sam asked as he jotted down his notes. He glimpsed up and watched the boy's hands twist in his lap.

"Cutting up wood, baling hay, cleaning out the barn, tilling the fields. Farm work."

Sam turned over a new page in the notebook. "Hard work?"

"Yes, sir," David replied. "I don't know any kind of work that ain't hard."

Sam smiled briefly and nodded. He knew how hard working on a farm could be. "When did you finish at the farm?"

"About noon."

"How did you know it was noon, David?"

David laughed a little. "White folks went in for their supper. They always take supper at noon. I finished up and left for another job back in Brick that afternoon."

Sam paused and studied his notes. "You went right from the Nicholas farm to this other job?"

David sat very still on the couch. He looked down to his shoes. "Not exactly, Sheriff Williams."

Miss Beulah leaned forward in her chair and studied her son. "You always go from one job to the next." She turned to Sam. "He's got lots of folks wanting him to work for them. He's a good worker and strong too."

Sam smiled at Miss Beulah. "I bet he is, Miss Beulah." Sam addressed David again. "What do you mean, 'not exactly'? Did you stop in between the two jobs?"

David had grown very still. He couldn't look up at Sam or his mother.

Miss Beulah grew concerned. "David, Sheriff Williams has asked you a question."

David remained silent, studying his shoelaces.

Sam coughed and leaned back into the sofa. "David, I've got witnesses that can place you at the Watering Hole Tuesday between twelve and twelve thirty." He paused and tapped his pencil against the notepad. "I need the truth, David, and I need to hear it from you. You did stop by the Hole Tuesday, didn't you?"

David moved his head to the left and right. "I haven't done anything, Sheriff," he muttered.

"But you were at the Hole? These eyewitnesses that claim they saw you there, are they telling the truth or aren't they?"

Miss Beulah sat riveted on the chair, looking at her son. "Tell the truth, David."

David swallowed and slowly looked up into his mother's face. His lips trembled. He turned and frowned at Sam. "So what if I did stop by the Hole? It's not a crime to get a soda, is it?" A small, audible sigh escaped from Miss Beulah.

"No, it's not, David. Do you remember anyone at the Hole that day when you stopped?" Sam asked.

"I don't know. I didn't go inside. I got a soda from the machine outside and then I left. I know better than to hang

129

around that place even in the broad daylight. I just got my drink and left. I didn't see anybody.'' David's tone was very defensive.

"Why would you stop at that place anyhow?'' Miss Beulah snapped. "I warned you to stay away from that place. It's an evil place. Bad things happen there.''

"I know what you've told me, Momma,'' David insisted. He lowered his voice. "I don't usually stop there on my way home. Except yesterday I did. You know how hot it's been. I'd been tilling fields all morning under the sun. I was hot and tired and I wanted a cold drink.'' David turned to Sam. "That soda machine sits out front for anybody to use. Patch don't care as long as you don't disturb his customers. I got a bottle of soda.''

"So you paid for a soda outside and never went in, is this right?'' Sam asked quietly.

"That's right,'' David agreed. "Going inside would have been stupid on my part. I was only looking for a drink, not to cause a scene.''

"And you didn't talk to anybody outside the Hole?'' Sam coyly asked.

David hesitated slightly as he answered the question. "No. . . . I didn't want anyone to know I was there.''

"You're lying,'' Miss Beulah whispered. She trained her eyes on her son. "I can tell when you're lying.''

David turned toward his mother and he shook his head. "Momma, please. . . .''

"You can't even look me in the eye,'' Miss Beulah declared.

"David,'' Sam began, "I've got witnesses that place you at the bar Tuesday and have you speaking to Carla Sue. This is a very serious matter. I'm trying to get to the bottom of this.''

"I keep telling you I didn't do anything!'' David's voice began to rise. He shot a quick glance at his mother and fell silent. His hands twisted into two tight fists. "I got my drink and . . . I left. That's all that happened.''

Miss Beulah leaned over to her son. "David, you have

130

got to tell the truth. Sheriff Williams is trying to help you."

"But I don't need his help. I didn't do anything," David protested. A clock ticked in the kitchen. A dog barked down the street.

Sam jotted a few more notes down on his paper. "So these eyewitnesses that say you spoke to and later left with Carla Sue are lying?"

"You were seen leaving with Carla Sue?" Miss Beulah shrieked, her voice shattering the quiet afternoon. She slapped at her son's leg. "You left with that girl in plain sight? David Bo Jefferson! What were you thinking?" She brought both hands up to her face. "You know better than to walk down the road with that girl."

"That's why I'm here, David. Carla Sue was murdered Tuesday." Sam saw the look of utter surprise on David's face.

"What!" David looked from Sam to his mother. "I didn't know she was murdered."

Miss Beulah pulled her hands away from her face and tried to calm herself. "I've heard rumors all over town. People are saying a black man killed her." Miss Beulah fought back tears. "I didn't know they were talking about my son. That girl was nothing but trouble." She turned to Sam. "Please, Will, don't let them take my son from me. He didn't kill her. I know they're going to blame him. They're going to put him in jail or . . . worse." She stifled a cry of anguish.

David sank back in the sofa. An expression of shock crossed his face. "I was just hot and thirsty," David began in a soft voice. "I had worked the whole morning away on the Nicholases' farm. I was headed back to town. I didn't even think about a soda till I'd almost passed the place. I've walked past the Hole every day now for over a year. Tuesday afternoon I was so hot. The place was deserted and all I wanted was a soda.

"I just had gotten my drink and started to leave when the front door flew open. First Tom Madison came stumbling out. He was holding his hand over his eye. He was

131

bleeding. He tottered down the stairs toward his truck, moaning all the way. I didn't think he saw me at all. He scared me and I guess I just froze where I was. I watched as he got in his truck and drove off. I got my feet moving and had just hit the parking lot when I heard a women scream. I looked back and that bartender, Patch, was pulling someone out of the bar. He had ahold of Carla's hair and was yanking her out of the place."

Sam was writing like a madman. "What did you see next, David?"

"I was trying to get to the main road without trouble." David shook his head. "Patch and Carla were fighting, real nasty. Carla had gotten Patch to turn loose of her hair and she was screaming at him, threatening him. She swung at him and missed. That made her even angrier. She warned him not to touch her or he'd be sorry, or something like that. Patch backhanded her across the face. He hit her hard, Sheriff Williams. Knocked her flat down the stairs. He started to kick her. Poor Carla was scrambling away in the dirt. Her nose was bleeding and she was crying. Patch grew weary of chasing her and started to go back inside. He yelled at her, calling her nothing but a cheap whore." David dipped his eyes and nodded at his mother. "Sorry about that, Momma, but it's what he called her."

David resumed his story. "Carla's nose was bleeding and her face was swelling up where Patch hit her. She was just sitting in the dirt, holding her nose. She ripped up her shirt and with the torn piece, she tried to stop her nosebleed." David stopped talking.

"Did you talk to Carla, David?" his mother asked quietly.

David murmured quietly, "Yes, I did. I knew I shouldn't. I knew I should just keep on walking but . . . she was hurt. I went over and made sure she was all right. She was pretty upset. I helped her up. She was pretty woozy on her feet and her nose was still bleeding. She thanked me for the help. She was limping as she walked away. She turned around and asked me which way I was headed. I told her and she asked me if I would mind walking her home.''

Miss Beulah closed her eyes and sighed heavily, ''Oh, Lord have mercy. Don't tell me you did?''

David didn't have to answer; his posture and eyes gave his answer away. His mother stifled another cry and shook her head angrily at her son.

Sam turned another page in his notebook. ''David, did Carla Sue know you?''

David started to shake his head. ''No. But . . .'' David looked over at his mother. ''You all don't want to know the real truth. I didn't have to walk her home, but . . . I owed her a favor.''

Miss Beulah stared at her son, her mouth agape. ''What do you mean you owed her a favor?''

David could not look at his mother. He lowered his head. ''I never wanted you to know about this, Momma. I know how much you worry.'' He wrung his hands. ''About a year ago I started working on the Nicholases' farm. Pay was good, but the hours, at first, were long. One day I got tied up with the livestock. It was almost dark when I started for home. I had just passed the Hole when a pickup truck went by. Instead of turning into the bar's parking lot it turned around and started coming my way. There were three white boys in the cab. I didn't recognize any of them. I got off the road and started to cut across a field. I figured if I was off the road they'd pass me up and go back to the Hole. They started following me, across the field.

''I started running as fast as I could. That truck just kept on coming. I was scared, Sheriff Williams. I kept running toward a light. I thought it was that crazy's house, Blythe's place. But it turned out to be Carla Sue and Tom's trailer. That truck was almost on top of me. I pounded on the door and yelled for help. When nobody answered I took off again. The pickup cut me off before I could get five feet away. Those boys got out and they had a baseball bat. They were taunting me, calling me names. I was caught in the truck's lights like a deer. I tried to get away and wound up backing up into a tree.

"Those boys were circling me and swinging that bat. They kept telling me what they were gonna do with my body. I thought for sure I was dead. Then that trailer door bangs open and somebody runs down the stairs and back through the field. Whoever it was ran away fast, off behind the trailer. That person must have seen what was happening, but they just kept on running. The boys got jumpy after that happened."

David took a breath. "The next thing I know there's this gunshot. Bang! The shot took the bat out of the boy's hand. Then there's another shot just inches in the dirt from where one boy is standing. We all just froze.

"Carla Sue comes out of the shadows and moves into the light thrown by the truck's headlights. She's holding a big pistol and pointing it at those boys. She was wearing hardly anything at all and she was barefoot.

"One of the boys starts to take a step forward. Carla Sue just plants a bullet in the dirt right at his feet and makes that boy dance like he was sidestepping with a rattlesnake. Carla ain't afraid. Never takes her eyes off those boys for a second. Carla waves the gun and accuses us of scaring off her best customer. Those boys warn her to mind her own business. Carla said something like, 'You're on my property, making this my business.'

"They started taunting her. She fired a shot and took out one of those headlights. She points that gun at the other headlight. 'I might hit something or somebody in the dark,' she warned us. Those boys aren't interested in me anymore. They just head back to their truck, cussing her and calling her all kinds of names. She just stands there, smiling with that gun in her hand. They warned her they'd be back. They got in the truck and went back through the field."

David rubbed his hands on his pants. "Now I'm afraid she's gonna turn that gun on me. She aims the gun at me and asks me my name. I tell her. She then wanted to know what I was doing running across her place. I told her how I was chased. She lowered the gun. She told me how to cut across Blythe's place. She even warned me to stay off the main highway in case those boys came back looking for me. She then turned around and went back in the trailer.'' David looked over to his mother. "I never told you this 'cause I know you'd worry yourself sick, Momma. You wouldn't let me work on that farm again and the pay was too good to pass up. From then on I just told the foreman at the farm I'd have to leave before sunset. And I've never had a problem since. Carla Sue remembered my name and face yesterday at the Hole. She even asked me if I ever had any more trouble. I didn't want to leave her by herself. She said she was afraid that Patch would send his buddies out after her. That's why I walked her home, Sheriff Williams. And that's all I did. I walked her to her trailer steps and then came back into town.''

Sam looked up at David. The young boy bit his lower lip and met Sam's gaze. Sam knew that David was telling the truth. "Did she say anything to you on the way home?''

"Nothing special. I didn't have to do much talking, she just kind of rambled on. Said she was never going to work at the Hole again, that she was going to have a better life for herself soon. People who put her down and talked behind her back would be sorry.'' David looked down at the floor. "She wanted the money back on my soda bottle, so I gave it to her and left.'' David watched as Sam and Miss Beulah exchanged looks of dread. "Now what's wrong? I told you the truth. That's what happened.''

"Besides the witnesses, you left your fingerprints at the scene of a crime when you gave Carla that bottle,'' Sam explained. "Doc Adams was able to lift some good prints off it.''

David sat in silence as the implications sank in. "But I didn't do anything except walk her home. She was alive when I left her, I swear.''

Sam closed his pad and tucked it away in his pocket. "I'm going to be honest with you, David. This is not good. I was hoping you might have seen someone at the trailer or that maybe Carla told you about someone who was threatening her. See, your prints were left at the murder scene and there are witnesses that saw you leave the Hole with Carla Sue.'' Sam looked up at Miss Beulah and shook his head. ''I'm sorry, David, but I think it would be best if I take you back to the jailhouse with me.''

''Jail!'' David jumped up off the sofa. ''But I didn't do anything. You can't take me to jail.''

''Oh, Will, please don't take my son to jail,'' Miss Beulah whispered desperately. She reached out and grasped Sam's arm. ''He can't go to jail. You can't take him away.''

''David, I had to come out here and question you about this murder. Other people know you were with Carla before she was murdered. If I don't take you to the jail, there is no way I'll be able to guarantee your safety. Right now the jail in Brick is the only place where I can keep you safe.'' Sam reached over and closed his hand over Miss Beulah's. ''I'm sorry, Miss Beulah, but I've got to do this.''

''But I didn't kill her,'' David protested loudly. ''I didn't kill her. I'm telling you the truth.''

''David, I believe you. Now we've got to prove your innocence. Until I can do that I have to take measures to keep you safe and alive.'' Sam rubbed his neck. ''Miss Beulah, I don't think you should stay here by yourself either. You come and stay with Meg and the family.''

Miss Beulah raised her head and removed her hand from Sam's arm. ''I will not burden you and Miss Meg with our troubles.'' She squared her jaw and smoothed out her dress. ''It won't look right to folks if I stayed with your family.'' Miss Beulah sadly shook her head. ''I won't stay at your home. I'll just wait until David is cleared, then no one can say you favored anyone in this case.''

''But you can't stay alone,'' Sam insisted.

Miss Beulah looked at her modest house. ''I won't stay alone and I won't stay here. I'll ask the Reverend Niles to put me up. He'll have room for me and if he doesn't, then someone in the congregation will.'' Miss Beulah nodded and turned to her son. ''David, please get my Bible out of

136

my bedroom. Go change into some nice clothes and wash your face.''

David rose silently from the couch and faced his mother. He embraced her and whispered fiercely, ''I didn't do anything wrong. I didn't do nothing to shame you. Momma, I'm so sorry for all this.''

Miss Beulah patted her son's back as she fought back tears. ''I know you didn't and the Lord knows you didn't. And Sheriff Williams knows you didn't do it either. We've got to place our trust in him for now and let him find the person who did commit this terrible crime.'' She motioned with her head. ''Go on now and fetch my Bible.''

When David left, Miss Beulah looked up into Sam's face. Tears rolled down her cheeks. ''Please, Will, promise me you'll see that no harm comes to David. You've got to make things right. You've got to see that David is cleared. My son did not murder anyone. He was foolish to walk that girl home, but he did not murder her.''

''Yes, ma'am,'' Sam said quietly. ''I'm going to do the best I can.''

''You've got to do better than that,'' Miss Beulah warned. She grasped Sam's hand. ''You've got to clear David. He's my only child, Will. He's all I have.'' Miss Beulah released Sam's hand. ''I cannot stand by and watch him go to prison for something he didn't do. He's innocent, so help him God.''

Sam embraced Miss Beulah. ''I know. Now I've got to prove it.''

The jailhouse was a swarm of activity when Sam, David, and Miss Beulah arrived. Several men were sitting on the steps, fanning themselves against the day's heat. As Sam pulled up, the men scampered down the steps and swarmed over the squad car.

''I'm from the *Dunsmoore Bulletin,* Sheriff Williams. Is this the murderer of Carla Sue Tritten?'' a reported demanded as a photographer next to him snapped away.

''No comment,'' Sam replied tersely as he helped Miss

137

Beulah out of the car. She held up her hands to fend off the questions and flashes. When Sam opened the back door for David the reporters descended on the young man. Sam wedged his body in between Miss Beulah's and David's and herded them up the stairs.

"Why isn't that boy handcuffed, Sheriff?" one of the reporters shouted.

"You can't get away with murdering a white woman," another one taunted.

Sam pushed and shoved his way through the men, leading Miss Beulah and David up the stairs and into the jail, where he heartily slammed the door on the reporters.

Gene was involved in a heated discussion with someone on the phone. Gene warned the caller about making threats and slammed the phone down. The phone began to ring again.

"Where'd all those reporters come from?" Sam growled as he herded Miss Beulah over to his desk. He pulled out his chair and let her sit down.

"Hell if I know." Gene nodded at Miss Beulah, "Sorry, ma'am. They pounced on this place about ten minutes after you left. It took me forever to get them out of the office. Then the phone started ringing about half an hour later and it hasn't stopped. There's a reporter that claims to be from a newspaper in Tulsa, if you can believe that." Gene picked up the ringing phone. "Sheriff's office." He grew disgusted and hung up on the caller. "We're starting to get an occasional death threat too, Will."

"Dammit," Sam kicked his desk out of frustration. "Someone leaked this murder investigation to the press. That's all we need, the press here to stir up the animosity."

Gene ignored the ringing phone and walked over to David. David and Gene took a long look at each other. "Hi, David." David stared silently back at the deputy.

"Take David, fingerprint him, and put him in a cell near the front," Sam said as he picked up the phone. "Sheriff's office." He listened for a second and then snapped,

"Where did you get that information?" He shook his head and replaced the phone on the hook.

Gene led David down the hallway. Someone began pounding on the outside door, demanding to speak to Sheriff Williams.

Miss Beulah sat behind Sam's desk dazed. Her heart ached as David was led down the hallway and out of sight. "You be strong, David. You keep your head held high. You didn't do anything wrong," she called after her son.

"Sam."

Sam whirled around. He looked down at Miss Beulah.

"Over here."

In the back of the room, standing in the corner, was Al. He stood out against the pale yellow walls in a white silk shirt with baby blue polka dots. A trail of blue smoke wound up around his head and over the top of the filing cabinet he was leaning on/into. "We need to talk." He motioned with his head toward the bathroom and pocketed his lighter in his crisp white pants.

Sam looked down at Miss Beulah. "I need to freshen up. I'll be right back. Gene is just down the hall if you need anything."

"I'll be all right. You, however, look like you've just seen a ghost."

Sam gave her shoulder a squeeze and followed Al into the bathroom. Sam turned on the light and bent down to the sink. He turned on the faucet and let the cold water run. He dipped his hands underneath the stream of water and splashed his face. After two or three handfuls he reached for a towel. He straightened up and looked at the reflection in the mirror. Will's reflection stared back at him. Sam wiped his face and turned to Al.

"You're looking a little worse for the wear," Al pointed out with his cigar. "When is the last time you got a good night's sleep?"

"Not during this Leap, that's for sure. This is all starting to come apart at the seams," Sam complained as he dabbed his face. "Those reporters, for instance. Do you know who

139

called them?'' Sam buried his face in the damp towel.

"Could have been the mayor. Or Tom Madison. I don't know.'' Al stuck his cigar back between his lips. "That's not the reason I'm here, Sam. You've got an even bigger problem on your hands now.''

Sam pulled the towel away from his face. "How so?''

Al pulled the link out of his other pants pocket. "Ziggy is now predicting there is a ninety-five percent chance that David will be killed if he stays here in Brick.''

"*Killed?*''

Al winced and shushed Sam. "Lower your voice. Yes, killed as in dead.''

"How could he get killed?'' Sam insisted at a lower volume.

Al removed his cigar and rolled it between his fingers. "You've changed history, Sam. When David was arrested in the previous time line, Will took him to Dunsmoore. I've been running some figures by Ziggy and she concluded that Dunsmoore is going to be a lot safer for David than keeping him here. Ziggy ran across an article from a paper in Tulsa that reported an alleged jailbreak that takes place late tonight. The jailhouse is going to be stormed by some Klan members. David was killed in the melee that followed. The paper reports he was shot when he tried to escape. Gene Dupree was also wounded in the attack.'' Al juggled the link in his hands. "I've run this by Ziggy and conferred with Will. They both concur that you should move David to Dunsmoore. The sheriff in Dunsmoore is Billy Joe Cooper. He's an old friend of your—er, I mean Will's family. He and his four deputies can keep an eye on David until the trial.''

"Trial?''

Al nodded solemnly. "David still stands trial for Carla's murder, even if he is moved to Dunsmoore.''

Sam tossed the towel into the sink. "You've been running this by Will?''

"Sure. He's retained some of his memory and he's been helpful.'' Al shrugged his shoulders and held out his hands.

"Hey, don't look at me like that. I'm just using all my available resources."

Sam rubbed his eyes and considered Al's suggestion. "If I move David to Dunsmoore, will he be safe?"

"Yes." Al gestured with the link. "Ziggy says if you move David, then the raid on the jail will never take place. Thus, David will be safe."

Sam clicked the light off with the chain. "But he still stands trial?"

Al stuck the cigar back in his mouth. "You've still got to prove that he didn't murder Carla, Sam."

Sam grunted and leaned back against the sink. "Just what else have you been running by Will?"

Al made a noise. "Oh, don't worry. I'm not giving away any big secrets." Al waved the link at the bathroom door. "You'd better go back out there. I'll be back. We're still digging up more information." Al pushed a button on the link and disappeared.

Sam returned to the office and was confronted with the persistent ringing from the phone. He ignored the phone and knelt down by Miss Beulah. "I'm sorry, Miss Beulah, but I've decided to move David to the jail in Dunsmoore. In light of all that's happened, I hope you can understand why."

Miss Beulah looked crestfallen. "Dunsmoore! But that's so far away. Are you worried about those pesky reporters out there?"

"No. I'm worried about David's safety." Sam paused. "I don't believe David will be safe if we keep him here. This move will be the best thing for David."

Gene came back down the hallway. He pointed at the phone. "Do you want me to get that, Will?"

Sam stood up. "No. Clear the line and get Sheriff Cooper on the phone. Tell him I'm bringing over a murder suspect who's going to need some protection."

Gene blinked and didn't move. "Dunsmoore? Sheriff Cooper? But—"

"Don't argue, Gene. Just do it."

141

Gene shut his mouth and moved over to the phone. He lifted the receiver. He cleared the line and waited for a dial tone.

As Gene dialed the sheriff's office in Dunsmoore, Sam tried to reassure Miss Beulah. "David's going to be all right, Miss Beulah. After Gene gets through, why don't you call the Reverend Niles and have him meet us at Dunsmoore." Miss Beulah simply nodded, overwhelmed by everything.

Gene pulled the phone away from his ear and motioned with the receiver toward Sam. "It's Sheriff Cooper. He wants to talk to you, Will." Gene lofted the receiver in Sam's general direction. He scowled and made his way to his desk.

Sam caught the phone and watched his deputy sulk off. He held the phone to his ear and began to make arrangements for David.

Al strolled out of the control room on his way back to his office. He was just passing the Waiting Room (with his smoking cigar in hand) when a nurse rushed past him. She was in such a hurry she hadn't even tried to salute as she pushed her way inside the door. The missed salute didn't bother Al, but the urgency of her trip into the Waiting Room did.

Al started to move on to his office but hesitated. He walked over to the Waiting Room door and punched the keypad. He didn't feel anyone would mind if he just stuck his head in for a second. The door opened. From behind the door Al could make out the pings and beeps of machines sounding off. Voices were raised and there was a buzz of activity in the normally quiet room. Al pushed the door open and stepped into the Waiting Room.

From the looks of the room, all hell had broken loose.

The room was filled with many doctors and nurses all scurrying around and snapping at each other. They talked loudly over the main table in the center of the room. Verbena and three other doctors stood with their backs to Al, huddled over the body on the table. Dr. Beeks talked rapidly to the other doctors, her head bobbing up and down, back and forth. The body on the table was out of sight, hidden by the medical staff, a row of machines, and a white blanket.

Al walked into the room, his mouth ajar. The machines were beeping endlessly and an IV bottle was being placed at the head of the table. Verbena was still deep in a discussion with the other doctors.

"Admiral? Pardon me? Admiral Calavicci?"

Al was startled by the voice to his left. A nurse was giving him a sharp salute. Al returned the salute and started to walk away.

"I'm sorry, Admiral, but you're not allowed to smoke in here." She pointed at the cigar in Al's hand. "It's a no-smoking area."

Al searched and found an empty wastebasket, which he tossed his cigar into. "What's going on in here?"

The nurse rose from her desk, her arms loaded down with charts. "The patient had an incident. Excuse me, Admiral." The nurse walked around Al and headed toward the table.

"What's an incident?" Al asked loudly as the nurse walked away. A few heads turned in his direction. One of them belonged to Dr. Beeks. She said something to a doctor on her right and walked briskly toward Al.

Dr. Beeks's mouth was drawn in a tight line as she hurried away from the table. A loose strand of hair had worked its way out of her bun and she tucked it behind her ear as she advanced. Underneath her open white lab coat flowed a bright red sweater and matching red and black skirt. She reached Al and touched his arm. "I tried to reach you as soon as this happened, but you were already in the Imaging Chamber."

Al looked past Verbena to the table. "When what happened?"

"Approximately ten minutes ago, Will . . . fainted, for lack of a better term."

Al motioned around the room with his hand. "All this

143

over a fainting spell?'' He looked at Verbena. ''I don't think so.''

Dr. Beeks shook her head. ''It was more like a blackout. He just dropped the pad he had been working on, went as white as a sheet, and passed out.'' She pulled at her coat. ''I've got Dr. Larson, the neurologist, checking him out now.''

Al blinked in disbelief. ''Is he all right? Has Will come around yet?''

Verbena nodded. ''He's given us quite a scare, Admiral. He was out for almost three minutes. He's very groggy and disoriented. I've ordered a sedative and I'm restricting his visitors to just his immediate medical team. His vitals are stable and that's a good sign.''

''Is he going to be okay?'' Al listened as the beeps and clicks of machinery began to soften.

''I think so. There doesn't seem to be any neurological damage. However, his recall seems to be affected.''

Al raised his eyebrows, ''His recall? You're talking about his memory, aren't you?''

Verbena nodded. ''Will had retained more of his memory than other patients I've observed. It was uncanny how he was able to help fill us in on the details that Ziggy couldn't. I guess it's all catching up with him now. He's lost most of what he could remember. It could be temporary; I don't know yet. He's back to where all our other patients seem to be when they first arrive. Disoriented and with large memory gaps. I want him to rest for the remainder of this Leap. No more sessions with you discussing possible murder suspects. I'm sorry, Admiral. I know he was helping you and Dr. Beckett.''

Al was straining to peek around Verbena. ''Can I see him? Just for a second?''

Verbena turned the admiral's request over in her mind. ''Yes, but just for a minute. He's very tired and that sedative should be starting to take effect now.''

''Thank you.'' Al walked cautiously toward the table.

144

The men in the white coats parted and let Al come to the edge of the table.

A variety of different machines were gathered at the head of the table. A white blanket was pulled over the body and it came up to Will's neck. Al gazed upon the face at the head of the table.

Will was very pale. His eyes slowly opened and focused. "Al?"

Al leaned down and smiled at Will. "Hey, Will, how are you doing?"

Will licked his dry lips and struggled to remain awake. "I passed out, I think. Can't remember. Dr. Beeks gave me a shot. I'm really sleepy but . . . I wanted to tell you something." Will's eyes began to close.

Al leaned closer. "Will?"

Will's eyes flew open with a start. "What we talked about—you have to write the information down in 1955. I can't remember the details. Sam's got to help me."

Verbena had joined Al at the table. She touched Al's arm, letting him know his time was up.

"Get some rest, Will. Don't worry, I'll handle everything."

"The details . . ." Will sighed and drifted off to sleep. Al put his hand on Will's shoulder. He withdrew his hand and turned away from the table. Al thanked Verbena again and headed out the door.

By the time Gene and Sam returned to Brick it was dark. It had taken all day to get David transferred into the Dunsmoore jail and make arrangements for Miss Beulah to visit each day. Some of the press had tagged along with them to Dunsmoore and that had meant more pushing and shoving when they arrived. Miss Beulah had made arrangements with the Reverend Niles to stay with his family. Sheriff Billy Joe Cooper promised Sam that David would be well protected and chided Sam for not dropping by more often. The press had disappeared by the time Sam and Gene arrived back in Brick.

Sam was glad to see that the reporters were gone. He opened up the roasting office, tossed his keys on his desk, and sat down wearily. Gene, who was in a foul mood, went to the soda machine and got a bottle out. He drained most of the drink in one swallow. He turned the fan on and it began to blow warm air around the room. Gene sat down in his chair and studied his partner.

Sam was trying to figure out where this Leap had gone so wrong. He was depressed over the fact he hadn't been able to keep David from being arrested. If he couldn't come up with the killer before Tuesday, then David would go on to stand trial and eventually be convicted of Carla Sue's murder. Sam was lost in thought when Gene coughed.

"Um, Will? Excuse me for interrupting your thoughts, but I need to discuss the work schedule for the next few days." Sam turned and looked at Gene with a puzzled expression on his face. Gene set down the bottle and wiped his hands on his pants. "I know it's not the best time right now, but I don't know when the right time would be. These past few days have been so crazy and strange. The duty schedule has changed now that David's at Dunsmoore. I'd figured he'd be staying here and I'd be taking the night shift. Now with David housed up in Dunsmoore, that makes this place empty at night. Do you think it would be safe if we left this place unoccupied at night?"

Sam realized that Gene had been staying at the jail each night since Tom's arrest. He nodded his head in agreement. "With David in Dunsmoore I don't think anyone will try and storm this place. We should be able to lock it up without any trouble."

"Good. I don't mind sleeping on the cot, but I was sure hankering for my own bed." Gene reached for his keys in his pocket. "What about tomorrow, Will? Can I still take my usual day off on Friday?"

Before Sam could reply the front door flew open. It caught Gene and Sam both by surprise. Gene was on his feet, his pistol in his hand, before Sam could get out of the chair.

146

Mayor Tilden, his chest all puffed out, came bounding into the office. His sleeves were rolled and his shirt untucked. His cheeks were flushed with color and he held onto the doorknob to steady himself. He looked around at the office and wagged his finger at Gene. Gene muttered under his breath and replaced the gun in his holster. The mayor swayed over to Sam and stuck out his hand. "I wanted to congratulate you both on a job well done." His words were slightly slurred and he rocked like a boat on rough seas.

Sam looked at the mayor with disgust and didn't make an effort to shake his hand. "What job well done?"

Mayor Tilden slowly withdrew his hand. He cleared his throat. "Why, the fine job you both did in rounding up Carla Sue's murderer. This is the way I like to see crime handled, fast and quick." He turned to Gene and nodded. "Gonna be a big write-up in the *Dunsmoore Bulletin* tomorrow. I was very generous to give credit where credit was deserved."

Gene just shook his head and pulled out his chair. He sat down and propped his legs up on the corner of the desk.

"This murder investigation is just beginning." Sam's tone made the mayor take notice. "It's just getting started, in fact. And I don't appreciate leaks to the press."

The mayor eyed Sam closely. "Huh? I don't know what you're talking about, Will."

"He's talking about the idiot who sicced the press on us this afternoon," Gene commented from across the room. "Hell, Mayor, we could have had a riot on our hands. Or didn't you stop to think about that when you were mouthing off to those news hounds from Dunsmoore?"

"You watch who you're talking to . . . boy." Mayor Tilden put his hands on his hips and turned around to face Gene. "I didn't call anyone regarding this arrest. They contacted me. I must say that I felt pretty foolish not knowing what was happening in my own town. I'm the mayor, by God, not some two-bit little deputy."

Gene slammed his feet down on the floor hard and pushed himself up out of his chair. "I'm getting tired of

147

everybody riding me tonight,'' Gene warned.

Sam's brow furrowed and he cautioned his deputy, "Easy, Gene. Don't get too—"

"Don't tell me to relax, Will. I suppose a drunk mayor waltzing into your office and spewing out insults doesn't bother the great and wonderful sheriff of Brick?''

"Gene!'' Sam glared at his deputy.

"I am not drunk,'' Mayor Tilden informed the men with loud indignation. "I've just been celebrating the arrest of that colored boy.''

"We've placed David Jefferson under arrest, but we're just investigating. I'm not convinced he did anything,'' Sam pointed out to the mayor.

Mayor Tilden turned and laughed. "It looks like an open and shut case to me, Williams. You've arrested the right boy. He was last seen walking Carla Sue home. There are witnesses at the Hole that saw them together. Everyone knew she'd take anyone into her bed for cash, black or white. Something went wrong, that's all. He panicked and killed her.''

"You don't know the first thing about this murder case, Tilden,'' Gene responded angrily. "You don't know the facts.''

"I've got all the facts I need, Gene Dupree. And I plan on making an announcement at the picnic.''

"What do you plan to announce?'' Sam pushed his chair out of the way and stood up. "That the murder investigation is continuing? That we're still talking to possible suspects?'' Sam took a step toward the mayor.

Mayor Tilden's face darkened and he raised his index finger in the air. "Now, you just wait a minute here. You got your murderer at Dunsmoore, plain as I and this town can see. Carla Sue was murdered by that boy. He couldn't afford to let anybody know about the way they were carrying on, so he killed her. And your job, Williams, is to see that he stands trial and is convicted. That's exactly the way I see it.''

"You can't see past the racist nose on your face!'' Sam

148

stepped closer to the mayor's face. He began to raise his voice. "You don't have any hard evidence that will stand up in a court of law. All you're worried about is your job and your standing with some very questionable men in this town. You could care less about David Jefferson."

"How dare you call me a racist!" The mayor came nose to nose with Sam. "You care too much about that boy. I think it's clouding your judgment. I think I might need to replace you with someone who can deal with this case with an open mind."

"You mean someone who thinks like you do," Sam challenged. He pushed the mayor with his shoulder and the mayor wobbled. "Someone who thinks like a bigot and reacts like one. Someone who listens to men beneath white cloaks, cowards who refuse to show their faces."

Mayor Tilden recovered his balance and stuck his finger inches from Sam's face. "By God, Will Williams," the mayor shouted, "I'll have your badge by morning if you call me a bigot again and slander my good name." He started to jab at Sam's chest, but Sam shoved his hand away, which infuriated the mayor all the more. "I don't care if your daddy was a sheriff, Williams. I will not have you speak to me in that tone or manner. I'm the may—"

"You're drunk, Tilden." Gene elbowed Sam out of the way and pushed Tilden. "You've been down at the Hole and got all liquored up, drinking with those idiots who inhabit that place after dark. You have no right to show up in this condition and order us around like a couple of stooges."

"Now wait a minute, Gene," Sam said, moving forward.

Gene's eyes blazed at Sam. "Shut up, Will, and butt out of this." He turned back to Tilden. "You need to sober up and keep that mouth of yours shut until this investigation is over. That mouth just might get you into trouble." Gene eyed the mayor coldly.

"Is that so?" The mayor watched Gene with contempt in his eyes.

Gene nodded. "As you know, Will and I have both been

149

busy trying to crack this case. I don't know who called the press today, but it only made matters worse. This case is only a couple days old and already we're ready to try and convict. A full-blown race war isn't going to sit well with the citizens of Brick. You may just wind up getting blamed for causing it to happen in the first place.''

Mayor Tilden puffed out his chest. ''You think you've got this handled, Gene Dupree?''

''Just watch your mouth. We'll try and keep you up to date as soon as we can,'' Gene finished.

Mayor Tilden pushed away from Gene and walked toward the door. He turned around and pointed a finger in Sam's direction. ''I still might have your badge, Williams. There are a lot of people watching your moves very carefully on this case. Watch where your sympathy lies—it could put you out of a job. The time is ripe for change around here.'' He reached for the doorknob, missed, and found it the second time. ''I'll be waiting for a full report on my desk by Monday morning.'' He threw Sam an angry glance over his shoulder and slammed the door.

Sam melted down in his chair. He pulled the notebook out of his pocket and laid it on the desk top. Sam's hands were still shaking from his encounter with Tilden.

Gene had taken his seat at his desk. ''Your daddy always said he was just a windbag that somebody needs to deflate every now and then. Got his name in the paper and with David's arrest, he's probably got a lot of pats on the back from the guys at the bar.'' Gene dropped his head down and studied his hands in his lap. ''He's right about this murder case though. We misstep and we're liable to have more than just reporters camped out at our doorstep.''

Sam tapped his fingers on the top of the notepad. ''Does Mayor Tilden spend a lot of time at the Hole?''

Gene shrugged. ''I wouldn't know. Just hear things. He seems to know a lot of what goes on in this town behind the scenes, if you know what I mean. He got a lot of his votes from the guys who hang out at old Patch's place.

Why, that's one of the reasons you opposed him running for mayor. Everyone says he has an inside source to the Klan, but nobody can prove it. Let's just say he would fit in real good with some of those men at the bar.''

Sam glanced at his notes. "Would he have known Carla Sue?"

Gene laughed. "Well, sure. Anyone who goes into that place would know Carla Sue. She's been known to flirt with everyone. Wouldn't surprise me one bit if she and the mayor took a roll in the hay.'' Sam jerked his head up. "Don't look so surprised, Will. Mayor Tilden has been seen with some pretty young things now and then. His wife doesn't seem to know or care.'' Gene pulled at his damp shirt. "What about tomorrow, Will? Do you want me to stay here in Brick?''

Sam looked back down at his notes. "Do you have plans?''

Gene picked his key ring up off the desk. "Nothing important. Just headed into Ashcroft for the day. I've got some errands to run.''

Sam shook his head. "Go ahead and take tomorrow off. In fact, why don't we call it a night? We both could use some time to relax.''

"Fine,'' Gene agreed, "I'll stop by the office here on Saturday morning. The picnic starts on Saturday and we agreed that I'd stay here while you attend the picnic with Meg. I'll be here or at the lake on Sunday and, of course, everyone will be at the lake on Monday.'' Gene got up from his desk and headed out the door. "I'll come in bright and early on Saturday morning so you won't have to worry and miss a thing at the picnic. Oh, sorry about the elbow in your ribs. Tilden just makes me so mad sometimes.''

Sam rubbed his fingers over the spot where Gene had nailed him. "I should have stepped in and ordered him out of the office.''

Gene scoffed at Sam's remark. "Oh sure. I'd like to have

seen that.'' He caught the knob in his hand and shut the door.

Sam sat in the quiet office and wondered what Gene meant by that last comment. He pocketed the notepad and reached for the phone to call Meg.

CHAPTER
SEVEN

When Al located Sam, he was bent over his desk in the jail's office, working on his notes. He had transferred the notes to a bigger pad and was scribbling away when Al popped in.

Al was a sight for Sam's weary eyes in his black fedora; black, white, and pink striped silk shirt; black trousers; red socks; and gold shoes. Sam looked up from the notepad and rubbed his eyes. He leaned back in his chair and stretched out his legs.

Al's right hand cupped the link and he rubbed his brow with the back of his hand. "Been doing that long?" he asked as he pointed to the pad.

"Since four this morning. I couldn't sleep so I came down here to work. It's"—Sam glanced at his watch—"almost eight o'clock now."

"Any progress?"

153

Sam's smile disappeared. "No. I keep going over David's testimony, looking for something, anything that will clear him. What about you?"

Al waved his arm through the air, making Ziggy's link, held in that hand, wail. "I can't talk to Will. Beeks has got him under strict supervision. No visitors."

Sam drummed the pencil on the desk top. "Why? Did something happen?"

"Yeah, the Leap is catching up with him. Looks like we're on our own for a while."

Sam pointed at the link. "What about Ziggy?"

Al snorted. "She still can't piece together enough data to help us. Although she is rather proud that she suggested the move for David." The phone rang on Sam's desk. It rang. And rang. Al pointed at the phone. "Aren't you going to pick that up?"

Sam turned back to the pad. "Why bother? It's just another reporter calling."

Al began to tap his foot impatiently. "You can't just let it ring!"

"Why not?" asked Sam. "I've been doing it for most of the morning."

The phone kept ringing. "Sam!" Al cried, putting his hand to his head. "It's starting to drive me nuts. Pick it up."

Sam picked up the phone on the tenth ring. "Sheriff's office, Sheri—" Sam winced and pulled the phone away from his ear.

"What? What?" Al asked quickly.

Sam put the phone back to his ear and whistled into the receiver. "Hey, hold on. Try that again without yelling."

"Where have you been?" Doc Adams demanded. He began to pace back and forth in his kitchen. "I've been trying to call you for the last hour. I thought you liked to get up with the chickens."

"You and a hundred reporters have been trying to reach me," Sam informed the doctor.

"That's what I'm calling about," Doc snapped. He rattled his morning paper by the phone. "Have you seen the Dunsmoore *Bulletin* this morning?"

Al was trying to listen in on the conversation. Sam moved away from the hologram. "No, Doc. I haven't been reading the paper. Any newspaper, for that matter."

"Judas H. Priest, Williams! You've got yourself a snitch on your hands," Doc began to protest.

"What are you talking about, Doc?" Sam flipped to a clean page on his notepad.

"My damn autopsy report, that's what I'm talking about. Who leaked it to the press?"

"Your autopsy report? You mean Carla Sue's?"

"What's going on?" Al hissed. "I hate being left out." Sam motioned with his fingers to be quiet.

"Of course Carla's. I'm reading from the front page. . . . 'And other evidence to support the arrest of David Jefferson of Brick was a bottle with his fingerprints left at the murder scene. The murder weapon is suspected to be a sharp knife, which has not been found." Doc rattled the paper. "That's what I'm talking about. I thought you wanted this to be kept quiet. The whole front page paints David as the murderer. Some unnamed source is quoted as seeing David and Carla leave the Hole together. Tom Madison is running his mouth too. Looks like Tom is getting involved with those fellows down at the Hole. That can't be good, Will."

"Doc, I haven't even seen the report." Sam moved the phone to the other ear.

"How could you not have seen the report? I dropped it off at the jail yesterday afternoon while you were out. I gave it to Gene," Doc grumbled. "Gene said that he would make sure you got it."

Sam nearly dropped the phone. He covered the mouthpiece with his hand and motioned to Al. "Go look over on that desk."

Al drifted across the floor to the other desk. "Well, what am I looking for?"

"An autopsy report."

155

Al jumped back from the desk. "That's disgusting, Sam. I don't want to look. . . ."

Sam got up and carried the phone over to Gene's desk. He cut in front of Al and began to rifle through the desk's contents.

"Will, are you still there?" Doc asked gruffly.

"I'm still here," Sam answered. "I'm looking but I can't find the report. Are you sure you dropped it off? Did Gene say where it would be?"

Doc laughed. "Now who's getting senile? Of course I remember what I did with that report yesterday. You had your shorts all in a knot when I didn't have it finished yesterday morning. So I brought it by the jail just as soon as I finished. Don't tell me Gene has already misplaced it. I told him specifically not to let anyone but you see it. I told him it was Carla's autopsy. He looked like he was going to pass out just by handling it."

"Don't just stand there. Help me look for the report," Sam hissed at Al and indicated the desk.

Al held up his hands. "I don't know where to look. Besides, I can't pick anything up."

"Who are you talking to now?" Doc asked.

"Nobody," Sam answered in frustration. He shut the bottom drawers of the desk with his foot. "I've got to track down that report."

"You'd better," warned Doc, "or else the whole county will be reading about this murder case before it goes to trial. And Will, be sure to read the part about Carla's—"

"I'll call you back." Sam hung up on Doc and carried his phone back to his desk. "Come on," he said, gesturing to Al as he headed out the door, "I'm going to need your help."

"Where are we going?" Al asked as he started to slip through the wall.

"To find that autopsy report."

"So where is it?"

Sam paused by the door and kept his temper in check. "I don't know where it is. Obviously it's not here. Maybe

156

Gene accidentally took it home yesterday.'' The phone began to ring again.

"How do you accidentally take—'' Al began.

"Al!'' Sam opened the door. *"Let's go.''*

The pair drove out of Brick on Route 21. The business section quickly fell away to long, open farm fields. Al gave Sam directions to Gene's house via Ziggy. They had just driven past a field of cotton when a lone house came into view.

"Is that it?'' Al asked from the back seat. He peered through the car's window, looking for a street number.

"It's not the right address, unless Ziggy's wrong.'' Sam slowed the car. "Gene's place can't be much farther. He made pretty good time the other day when he had to hurry home and change clothes.''

Al swatted at the link. "This house belongs to a family named King.'' Al leaned closer to the window. "This is a really big place. They've got their own garden on the side.'' Al suddenly sat up in the back seat. "Sam! Look! Do you see that?''

Sam hit the brakes and brought the car to an abrupt stop. He looked out the driver's side window. "What! What do you see?''

"That's air pollution,'' Al announced proudly. He pointed at the thin trail of smoke snaking up behind the house. "See that black smoke coming from behind the house?''

Sam turned so he could get a better look at Al. "You gave me whiplash because of some smoke?'' Sam turned around. "It's probably just the trash pile burning. We used to burn trash on the farm.''

"But it's not just a trash pile burning. It could be the start of the breakdown of the ozone layer.'' Al leaned forward over the seat. When it came to environmental issues, no one was more determined than Al to drive a point home.

"I'm not interested in burning trash piles, Al. Besides, what am I supposed to do about it?''

"You're the sheriff," Al pointed out. "Arrest them."

"I can't just arrest people who burn trash, Al. It's not illegal." Sam hit the gas and the car moved on down the road.

"Not yet, but it will be." Al sighed wistfully and watched the house grow smaller.

Another mile down the road from the Kings' house was a small, one-story house set back from the main highway. Sam pulled into the deserted driveway and shut off the engine. A detached garage sat at the back of the driveway. The house looked well cared for.

"Ziggy says this is the address she got off the court records for Gene. Looks kind of lonely, doesn't it?" Al scrunched forward in the back seat.

Gene Dupree's house was nestled behind two big weeping willow trees. Al leaned over, his elbows disappearing into the seat. "Now what?"

"If Gene's got the report it's got to be here. Why don't you and I go do some investigating?"

Al moaned. "Fine. If you want to waste your time digging around in an empty house . . ." He hit a button and appeared on the front porch.

Sam joined Al on the porch. Sam tried the door and found, to his dismay, that it was locked. He knocked on the door and called out Gene's name. "Why would you keep your door locked in a small town like this?" Sam asked as Al paced the length of the small porch.

"Well I would," Al chimed in. "Especially if I was a deputy and happened to be involved in a murder case that's going to make headlines fifty miles away." Al waved his hands in the air and the link chirped. "Nobody's home, let's go."

Sam stepped back away from the door and looked at the windows. "All the blinds are drawn too."

"So he likes privacy. Big deal. We're wasting our time."

Sam stepped back. "I've got to get my hands on that report. Gene's supposed to be spending the day in Ashcroft." Sam put his hands on his hips. "I'm going around to the back. Why don't you go in through the front door and take a look around?''

"This is breaking and entering, *Sheriff*,'' Al started to point out. But Sam was down the steps and around the corner of the house before Al could finish.

Mumbling to himself, Al slid through the door and into the living room. The room was dark and it took Al's eyes a moment or two before they adjusted to the dimness. The drapes were closed and heavy curtains hung in front of the windows, blocking out the sunlight. Al walked around blinking until he could make out a stream of sunshine coming from the kitchen. He walked into the kitchen and waited for Sam.

Al inspected the countertop with the glasses neatly lined up and the plates all stacked. The table was bare. A small 1955 calendar hung on the back of a door that Al guessed led down to a cellar. The calendar was opened to Miss September and showed a very bosomy girl in hot pants and a midriff top.

Sam jangled the doorknob and the kitchen door gave way. He cracked open the door and peered into the kitchen. He eased his body through and gently shut the door. "I'm in,'' he whispered. "Did you see anything?''

"Yes,'' Al whispered back. He rocked on the balls of his feet and pointed at the door. "Check out this calendar.''

Sam took one look and turned away. "That's not what I meant, Al. Let's just find that report and go. I don't want to get caught breaking into my deputy's house.'' Sam headed out of the kitchen and into a narrow hallway. "What's down this way?'' Sam whispered.

"Why are we whispering?'' Al answered in his normal speaking voice, causing Sam to jump a bit.

"Because,'' Sam said, spinning around. "Just . . . because,'' he answered in his normal voice. "Did you see anything in the living room?''

"No. Too dark. Let's head this way. This is not a huge house by any means.''

Sam walked down to the end of the hallway and opened

a door. It was a bathroom. He walked back and checked out the room to his right. It was a small bedroom. There was a bed and a dresser, and another small bathroom.

"The kid lives kind of Spartan style, don't you think?" Al noted as he drifted from the bedroom to the bathroom behind Sam.

Sam nodded in agreement. "Let's check the last room and get out of here. This is starting to give me the creeps." Sam walked down the hallway to a doorway. He tried the knob and the door swung open. The men entered a small room that appeared to be a study. Sam and Al separated, looking in different areas. Al paused by a wooden desk and let out a low whistle. "Hey, Sam, come here."

"What?" Sam strode across the room. "Did you find the report?"

"Um, I don't think so," Al responded truthfully. He pointed at the desk top, which was covered with loose papers and magazines. "Pick up that magazine near the top there and flip it open." Sam pulled out the magazine from under two other magazines and flipped it open. It was difficult to make out what Sam had picked up from the desk. Like the living room, the windows were shut and the drapes drawn. Sam reached over and turned on the lamp sitting on the desk. A smiling, naked woman striking a provocative pose emerged from the pages of the magazine.

"Bingo!" Al smiled and leaned over the desk. "I was right."

"Of course," Sam sighed with disgust. He flipped the magazine shut. "Concentrate on finding the autopsy report, Al."

"Hey, that's a 1955 *Playboy*." Al patted his chest and produced a cellophane-wrapped cigar. He undid the wrapping and tossed it into a trash can. As soon as the wrapping left Al's fingertips, it vanished. "That's a collector's item and I haven't seen the centerfold yet." Al found his lighter and lit his cigar.

"And you're not going to see it either. Why couldn't you have been this helpful earlier?" Sam asked as he set the magazine down on the pile where he found it. He hit another stack of magazines with his forearm and sent them scattering onto the desk top and the floor. Sam caught the pile and steadied it before more magazines tumbled off. "These are all the same type of magazines, Al."

"Over against the wall too. Look, two more stacks." Al sighed. "Boy, I wish I could turn pages. Seems like Gene Dupree knows how to take care of his spare time." Al began to walk around the desk. He whistled again. "These run the gambit of taste, I see. Chains, bondage, S & M." Al shuddered. "This is some bizarre stuff, even for me. I would have never guessed by looking at the kid either. Wow." Al stepped around a small stack. "There are some weights tucked over here in the corner."

Sam was searching the cluttered desk top, trying not to disturb anything. He picked up a photo by the corner and moved it to another pile.

Al walked over to the desk and studied the photo in Sam's fingertips. "How does she do that?"

"Hey Al, look." Sam was moving some more magazines and pictures away from one corner of the desk. He had discovered some handwritten notes. He picked up a few more items off the desk and discovered Doc's autopsy. The report was opened to the description of the murder scene.

"What did you find?"

"The autopsy report. Gene's been taking notes, it looks like. Damn. I can't remove it without Gene knowing we've been here. It's half buried." Sam moved a few more pictures on the desk top, uncovering more of the report.

Al tipped his head and read a line of the report. He made a noise and looked away. "Boy, that's pretty descriptive." He paused and looked down at his cigar. "You know, something's not right about this."

"How can I get the report out of here without Gene knowing I've moved it?"

Al shook his head. "You can't."

Sam popped his head up and listened. "Did you hear something, Al?"

161

Al cocked his head toward the door. "Naw, I didn't hear anything. We got zilch here. Unless you want to lift that report. Gene's gonna know you broke into his house, and worse"—Al motioned around the room with his cigar—"he's gonna know you've found his Den of Love."

"I know, I know. But I don't want to leave the report here. Why didn't he tell me yesterday?"

"Because he forgot?" Al shrugged and sucked on his stogie. "Remember the joint was really jumping yesterday," Al chuckled to himself.

Sam ran his fingers over Gene's handwritten notes. The phrase "locate murder weapon" was circled and underlined.

"Look," Al reasoned, "just get the report tomorrow morning. I'll try and have Ziggy run a check on it until then."

Sam stepped away from the desk and brushed off his hands. "What if Ziggy can't come up with the report? I hate to wait till tomorrow. In the meantime we'll explore a hunch I have."

"Now where are we going?" Al asked as he drifted through the door. Sam swung the door shut and continued down the hallway and back into the kitchen.

Sam was listening and looking all around as he paused in the kitchen. "I checked the garage in back. The windows are boarded up."

Al rolled the cigar in his mouth and juggled the link in one hand. "What hunch are you talking about? You found the report. I don't think I like the sound of this."

Sam opened the kitchen door. "I've got to find the murder weapon. Time is running out for David."

Al rolled his eyes. "I *know* I don't like the sound of this. Just where are you off to, Sherlock Holmes?"

"*We're* off to Carla Sue's trailer."

"That's where I draw the line, Sam. I'm not going to the murder scene." Al waved the link in the air. "I don't like murder scenes. Count me out!"

"Al, I'm running out of time. You won't have to go

162

inside the trailer. Just walk around outside and look for clues."

Al pondered this a moment. "You promise I won't have to go inside?"

Sam nodded. "I promise." He let himself out the door.

Al heard Sam going down the steps. He mumbled to himself as he pocketed the link and blew a thin blue trail of smoke into the air. The house was still. "Sam's getting me spooked," Al mumbled as he started to walk through the back door after Sam. Al stopped to admire the calendar once more. He looked at the calendar and froze. The calendar was swinging ever so slightly back and forth on its nail. Unless you looked closely you could hardly detect the movement. Al looked closer at the door. It was open just a crack. He racked his brain, trying to remember if that door had been open before. The hair on Al's neck stood up and the cigar trembled in his fingertips. The calendar's momentum had stopped. Miss September smiled back at Al. Al swallowed and took a step closer toward the door. "Gene?" he called out in a shaky voice, even though Al knew no one could hear him. He stared at the door, waiting for it to open further.

The window banged loudly behind Al's back. Al yelled and flew backwards, away from the door. He dropped his cigar and it disappeared through the floor. Al staggered away from the door and window, managing to step through the table. Someone was standing at the window.

Sam smashed his face up to the dirty window and spotted Al. "Come on, Al," Sam's muffled voice shouted through the glass. "Let's go."

Al put a trembling hand over his heart. His knees were turning to water and he had nothing to hold himself upright. "You just scared me to death, Sam Beckett," Al yelled at the window. "And I've lost my cigar too." Al scanned the floor looking in vain for his cigar.

"Quit messing around." Sam was motioning with his head and body.

Al stomped over to the window and shouted back at Sam,

"I'm coming." Al stepped away from the window and swore under his breath. He pulled the link from his pocket and it almost slipped through his shaking hands. He hit a button that put him outside.

Inside the deserted kitchen the sound of the car starting up drifted in from the outside. The cellar door slid soundlessly shut, causing Miss September to swing back and forth, ever so slightly on the nail.

Al was trying to light another cigar. He was having a difficult time getting his fingers to work the lighter. After the fifth try the lighter glowed to life and Al lit the end of his cigar. He pocketed the lighter and took a long drag on his cigar, hoping to calm his jagged nerves.

Sam was emerging from the trailer. He came down the steps and wiped his face off with the back of his shirt sleeve. "How are you doing?"

Al sneered and exhaled a trail of smoke. "I'll live. What about you? Find anything?"

"No, nothing." Sam dusted off his hands on his pants leg. "The inside of the trailer has been gone over with a fine-tooth comb. Let's take a walk." Sam headed away from the trailer, keeping his head down as he walked.

Al walked a few paces back. "What exactly are we looking for? And how are we going to find it in all these overgrown weeds?"

"I don't 'exactly' know," Sam confessed.

"You don't really think the murderer is going to just drop the weapon out here, do ya?" Al asked as he stepped around an old, rotting tire.

"Could have happened," Sam muttered. "No one would ever find it. Why don't you stop jabbering and start looking? Get Ziggy to help us."

The weeds were growing thicker as Sam and Al wandered away from the trailer. Al shook the link up and down in his hand. "I can't rewire this thing on such short notice. I'm no Einstein, you know. You should have warned me ahead of time." As Al walked, his legs from the knees down began to disappear into the weeds.

"You've gotten Ziggy to work through that link before. Now is a fine time to feign incompetence."

Al halted. "Incompetence?" He snapped his head up. "Who are you claiming is incompetent?"

Sam turned around and wiped his sweating brow. "I don't want to argue, Al."

"I'll show you who the incompetent one is." Al straightened his shoulders. "Just watch this." Al thumbed his nose at Sam and disappeared into a large patch of tall weeds.

Sam began to pick through the weeds ahead of him. He heard a click up ahead in the grass. Sam paused and listened. "Don't fool around here, Al," Sam called out, "we're supposed to be looking for evidence." A formidable silence met Sam's rebuke. "Al?"

Al suddenly came charging back out of the tall weeds, his arms held high in the air. His eyes were wide and he began to wave his arms frantically. "Run, Sam, run!"

The weeds parted where Al had just charged out and Sam found himself looking down the barrel of a shotgun.

Sam whipped his hands up into the air and shouted, "Don't shoot. It's Sheriff Williams." The barrel of the gun remained pointed at Sam and time stood still.

Slowly the barrel was lowered and a dirty hand parted the weeds. Two dark eyes peered out.

Al jogged over to Sam's side, one hand smashing the fedora down on his head, the other hand holding the handlink pressed tightly to his chest. Al had lost his second cigar of the day. He breathed through his mouth in short, raspy breaths. "It's . . . him . . . the . . . killer, Sam."

"Who's out there?" Sam called out, his hands still in the air. "Show yourself."

The weathered hand, twisted with arthritis, separated the weeds. "You're trespassing on my land," a scratchy, deep voice shot back. An old, wrinkled man stepped through the weeds and squinted in Sam's direction. He lowered the shotgun a bit and took a step forward. "Is that you, Gene Dupree?"

"No," Sam answered back, keeping his hands in plain sight. "It's Sheriff Will Williams."

The old man put a hand up to his ear. "Who?"

"He's deaf, Sam." Al tugged at his brim. "And he's gonna shoot us."

Sam took a step closer and bellowed, "I'm Sheriff Williams. From Brick?"

The gun dropped down to the man's side. He turned his head to one side and spit a long, brown stream of tobacco out on the ground. Tobacco juice dribbled into the man's beard.

"On top of everything else," Al announced as he watched the old man, "I think I'm going to be sick."

"You're on my property, Sheriff." The old man held his hand up to his brow. "You're lucky you aren't dead."

Sam looked at the old codger. "Can I put my hands down?" Sam asked.

The old man laughed and set the butt of the shotgun on the ground. "Suit yourself."

"I didn't know I was on your property." Sam lowered his hands until they were resting near his gun belt. "You must be Mr. Blythe. You gave me quite a scare."

The old man spit again and Al moaned quietly behind Sam. "I should have killed you, running around on my land. This is private property, Sheriff. Been in my family for three generations."

"And what prime real estate too," Al snipped.

Blythe shrugged his shoulders and turned back into the weeds. "You know the way off my land," he called over his shoulder.

"Wait, Mr. Blythe," Sam called out. He surged forward after the man.

"Sam," Al cried, "that guy's a nut. Come back here."

Sam ignored Al and continued in his pursuit of Blythe. Al muttered, readjusted his hat on his head, and glumly followed Sam.

The old man made good time striding through the weeds. He reached the deteriorating house before Sam could catch him. He carried the shotgun as he climbed the rickety stairs.

Sam broke through the weeds and came into the yard.

The old man turned around and stopped. He watched Sam approach. Blythe was dressed in a torn and tattered shirt and a pair of dirt-caked pants. He spit another stream of tobacco shot, which splattered down on the porch. Most of his teeth were gone and he ran his blackened tongue over his gums as he spoke. ''You're still here?''

''Sam!'' Al stepped through the weeds and into the yard next to Sam. ''Come on. This guy isn't going to tell you anything.''

''Mind if I ask you a few questions?'' Sam shouted.

The old man shrugged and came back down the stairs. He cradled the shotgun in his arms. ''Go ahead and ask.''

''Sam,'' Al warned. ''He's going to tell you about the little green men from Mars.''

Sam walked into the yard and stood about a foot away from Blythe. The odor from the man nearly knocked Sam down. Sam didn't even want to hazard a guess as to when the man had bathed last. ''I just want to ask you a few questions and then I'll be on my way.''

Blythe looked up at the sky. ''Yeah?''

''The trailer in back?'' Sam pointed in the direction of Carla Sue's trailer.

Blythe followed Sam's finger. ''You want to know about the girl?'' Blythe acted like Sam was boring him. ''I let that girl live there with her man as long as they kept to themselves and didn't cause me no trouble.''

''She was murdered. Did you know that, Mr. Blythe?'' Sam had reached for Will's notebook again.

The old man shrugged. ''Figured that's what brought out all those people. What's done is done.''

''Sam,'' Al called across the yard, ''Ziggy's got nothing on this guy.'' He stuck his finger next to his head and twirled it.

The old man spit and pointed to the tall weeds next to

his house. "They messed the grass up. Those demons who roam this land at night. Can't kill them with guns or knives. I should know, 'cause I tried."

Sam saw the crazed look in the old man's dancing eyes. He started to put the notepad away. "I'm sorry if we troubled you, Mr. Blythe."

The old man roared with a wicked laughter that sent chills up Sam's spine. "All those damn visitors coming and going. Making tracks back to that trailer. Going to see the tooth fairy for a treat." He chuckled loudly and spit. "They come and make the demons go away. Do you know what I mean, Sheriff?" Blythe scratched at his arm with his dirty hand. "I know there were a lot of men going back to her trailer when Tom wasn't around. 'Course Tom is so dense and thick you'd have to hit him over the head to get him to see things the way they were. I may be crazy, but I saw what went on." He pointed at the tree not far from where Al was standing. "She was shooting at that tree one day. Her and that boy. He was teaching her how to hold a gun. He was teaching her to shoot and she was teaching him things by night. They stood on my property shooting at my tree. I guess he was better than that lying windbag who came around. Brazen hussy, Carla was." Blythe stopped talking and looked up at the sky again. "She attracted all kinds, Sheriff. Good, bad. Black, white. Mostly white. Mayors, city councilmen, deputies, pastors, young and old. Mostly good on the outside, but some were bad and dark on the inside."

Sam turned and studied the tree. Al shrugged his shoulders and consulted with Ziggy's link. "Who was teaching Carla Sue to shoot a gun?" Sam asked.

Blythe snorted. "One of her regulars. Used to come and park his car back behind my house. Thought I didn't know. I watched him. He was just a demon in disguise. He'd been courting her for more than a year. He was here the day she died. Tore out of here like a bat from Hell. Half dressed, running through the weeds, like the true demon that he was.

168

Splattered with demon's blood." Blythe wheezed and coughed in the sun.

Sam felt his heart and his temples pounding. "The man that you saw running away that day—was he a colored man?"

Blythe shook his head. "I hadn't seen a black one in a while. Like I said, mostly white." Blythe turned around. "I'm done talking. You've got two minutes to clear off my property. You go back to Brick and deliver a message for me. Tell that upstart deputy of yours to stay off my property. And you tell the mayor I want my electricity turned back on or I'll tell the town what kinds of underwear he really likes to wear by the light of the moon." Blythe turned and pointed at Sam. "You got that, Sheriff?"

Sam's pencil became still. "My deputy? Gene Dupree was here? On your property?"

Blythe laughed as he climbed the stairs. " 'Course he was. He was here this very morning." He pulled open the rotting screen door and before disappearing inside said, "Those demons come at night and steal parts of my house. Those demons will be back, I'm telling you. They always come back."

Sam turned and briskly headed back toward Al.

Al tipped his fedora back on his head. "What a wacko." He saw the look on Sam's face as he approached. "Now what?"

Sam didn't stop as he pushed back through the weeds. "Meet me back at the car."

"Sam? What'sa matter?"

Sam pushed through the weeds and disappeared.

Al was standing next to the patrol car when Sam joined him. Sam was sweating profusely and had to wipe his face off with the back of his arm. He leaned against the car and looked down at the ground. "It's Gene. It's my deputy."

"What are you talking about, Sam?" Al had both his hands in his pockets. "You can't believe the things that crazy old man said. His testimony would never stand up in court. Heck, you'd be laughed out of the state if you tried

169

to bring that old geezer in." Al pulled his hands out of his pockets and gestured with them. "Look what he said about the mayor. You can't take what he says seriously."

Sam opened the car door and sat down. "He said a lot of things. He claimed he saw Gene teaching Carla Sue to use a gun."

Al dug the link out of his pocket. "He's crazy, Sam. Besides," Al pointed out, "Gene's a good guy. I mean, forget about his den and the magazines. We all have our little faults."

Sam dug his heel into the dirt and weeds. "That's just it. I can't forget about those magazines or the pictures. And why was he at the murder scene this morning?"

"I dunno, maybe he was investigating?"

"Then why did he lie to me about going into Ashcroft today?"

Al squinted up into the sunshine. "I don't know. But you've got to prove it to me that Gene Dupree could commit murder, Sam. From what I've seen of him he looks like a young Barney Fife. Besides, I know *I* wouldn't be investigating a murder scene no matter what. Not even in broad daylight." Al stopped talking and a puzzled look crossed his features.

Sam rested both his arms on the car door. "I know I'm jumping to conclusions. It could have been Tilden too. But why would Tilden murder Carla Sue? He's had lots of affairs according to Gene. Why would this affair be any different?" Sam shook his head. "I'm really confused now." He tapped the seat and closed his eyes. He opened them a few moments later. "Al, have Ziggy run a perimeter on this area."

Al stopped thinking about Gene and began to punch at the link. "Okay. How wide?"

Sam looked around. "Say two to five miles. I'm looking specifically for residences."

Al was quiet as he entered the data into the link. "Less than a mile due west is Gene Dupree's house." Al tapped the link with his fingers. "And the only other house after

170

Gene's is the King residence. It's about two and a half miles down the road.''

"Let's take a ride. I'm working on a theory.'' Sam shut the car door and started the engine.

Al walked around and leaned down at the window. "Where are we going now?''

Sam dropped the car into gear. "To the Kings' house.''

CHAPTER EIGHT

Al and Sam were subdued when they arrived at the King residence. The house was surrounded by woods on one side. A large garden was spread out to the other side and back of the house.

Sam opened a tall wooden gate that led them into the yard. A woman with a large sun hat was bent down and working a row of flowers not far from the house. Sam called out and waved. The woman waved back.

Mrs. Sally King was kneeling beside a row of flowers. She put down her shovel and dusted the dirt out of her work gloves. "Afternoon, Sheriff." She tipped her wide brimmed hat back on her head. "What brings you out here? Have you got another jumper?"

Sam shook his head. "No, nothing that serious. I understand we borrowed a tomato from your garden. I wanted to thank you."

"Oh, Will Williams, no need to do that," the woman told him, laughing. Her laugh was deep and hearty. "I had tomatoes rotting all over the ground from this year's bumper crop. Besides," she added, her blue eyes sparkling beneath her hat, "I heard it landed in the mayor's car. Good shot, William."

Sam knelt down and admired the flower bed. "Marigolds. My mother used to grow marigolds."

"Gardening keeps me occupied now that the children are all grown up and on their own. I love working out here."

"Mrs. King . . ."

Sally swatted playfully at Sam's knee. "You've known me too long to call me anything other than Sally."

"Sally," Sam began again, "did you see Gene Dupree, my deputy, when he came by the other day?"

"I saw him from a distance." She pointed back toward the house. "I was in the kitchen doing some canning. Saw him wave from over by the fence. He said he needed a tomato. I told him where the tomatoes were and he let himself in. Why? Is there something wrong?"

"Um . . ." Sam began to hedge.

Al stepped up to Sam's back. "Tell her Gene lost your favorite pocketknife and you've come by hoping to find it."

"It seems," Sam continued after a moment's pause, "Gene's lost my favorite pocketknife."

Sally King frowned. "Oh no. Not that nice one your daddy gave you when you became sheriff? With the engraving on the handle? I remember the day when he gave it to you. Oh, what a shame."

Sam cast a worried glance up at Al. "Yes. That's the one, all right. Do you mind if I go and hunt around for it?"

" 'Course not," Sally insisted with a wave of her hand. "Go ahead. I don't get many visitors out this way. The tomato patch is back by the trash pile. I could fix you some iced tea while you look."

"No, don't get up," Sam said as he rose, "I'll only be a minute and I don't want to trouble you."

"I'll be right here if you change your mind." She turned back to her flower bed. "Take your time."

173

Sam and Al followed the trail of smoke from the smoldering trash pile. It brought them through the garden, out by the tomato vines.

"Look at this," Al complained as he circled the trash heap. "This is a major source of pollution. Look at all the stuff that's burning here. It's going to give off enough toxic fumes to get to even me." He waved his hand in front of his face.

"You're one to talk," Sam pointed out. "You're lucky I can't smell those cigars you keep smoking or I'd be the one complaining about toxic fumes." Sam paused and walked over to the trash heap. Al was pacing around the perimeter of the pile, grimacing at what was smoldering at his feet. "We used to burn trash on the farm," Sam said as he eyed the heap. "By the looks of this heap, I'd say this trash has been smoldering for a day or two, wouldn't you?"

Al shrugged, clearly disgusted. "I wouldn't know. It just looks like a bunch of burnt trash to me." Al held his stomach with his hand. "Man, this has *not* been a good day for me."

Sam looked around and headed in the opposite direction from the pile. When he came back he had a rake in his hands. He began to rake apart the trash pile.

"Where did you get that rake?"

Sam kept raking. "Over by the compost pile. Seems Mrs. King does recycle."

"Good," Al decided. "But what are you looking for?"

"The murder weapon."

Al sighed. "So who do you think committed the crime? Loyal, trustworthy Gene the Boy Scout? or Tilden the adulterous mayor? My money is on the mayor."

Sam paused. "You're calling Gene a Boy Scout?"

"No, I didn't but Will did." Al wrestled with the handlink. "He said some good things about Gene." Al began to read the data silently to himself. His face fell and he studied the link closely. "Wait a minute. . . ."

174

Sam was busy raking through the trash and didn't bother looking up. "You found something?"

Al looked up from the link. "I remembered what was troubling me back at Gene's house when we were in his den." Al's tone had gotten Sam's attention. "You know, Will told me Gene faints at the sight of blood."

Sam was a damp mess. His shirt was soaked with perspiration and it clung to his back and chest. He stopped and wiped his face with his shirt sleeve. "Yeah. Doc mentioned it too. It's a real sore point with Gene."

Al began tapping his fingers to his chin. "Will also mentioned something about Gene not being able to read autopsy reports." Al looked at Sam with concern. "Gene was not only *reading* that report but he was making detailed notes regarding the murder scene." Al grunted and he began to stab at the link with his finger.

"Maybe Gene is just trying to solve the murder. I think there's more to Gene Dupree than meets the eye. I mean, those sure weren't comic books in that study."

Al was frantically punching keys on the link. "Something's not right." The link blinked and chirped and twittered at the admiral. "Aha!" Al cried out a few moments later. "Wow, Sam, listen. I don't know why I didn't think of this before. I had Ziggy run through the town records of Brick from 1965." Al tapped the display with his fingertips. "Gene Dupree isn't listed as your deputy in any newspaper accounts. In fact, Ziggy can't find Gene Dupree anywhere in her data banks for 1965." Al punched a few more buttons. "It seems he just disappeared. He got a driver's license in Nebraska in 1957 but after that, it's like he dropped off the earth."

Sam stopped raking. "Nebraska? What about Tilden?"

"Ziggy's got more on him. He resided in Brick until his death in 1974. You're gonna love this. He was recalled as mayor in 1956 and never held a higher office. Tried to run for the House of Representatives in 1958 but got tangled up in an investigation with the IRS. He withdrew and never was elected to anything again."

Sam went back to raking the trash pile and started thinking out loud. "Carla Sue was murdered in the early afternoon, very close to the time Tom was on the balcony. If Gene was at the trailer and if he killed her, he'd be covered in blood. Blythe said he saw a white person running from Carla's trailer with blood on his clothes."

Al stepped around the trash Sam was raking. "Yes, but he didn't say it was for sure Gene. Remember Carla had quite a little sideline of activity and it could have been anyone. You can't go on what Blythe saw anyway. He's nuts. You're going to need solid proof to clear David."

Sam nodded in agreement. "Okay, but let's say it was Gene. He must have changed clothes, since the duty roster shows him as being on duty that afternoon. On the way home to change he hears Will's call over the radio about Tom. He goes home, changes his clothes, but he doesn't have time to get rid of the murder weapon or his bloodied clothes. He stops here on the way into town to get a tomato, sees the fire, and gets rid of both the knife and his blood-stained clothes."

Al grimaced and shook his head. "Talk about a long shot. You don't have a lot of evidence to back that theory up."

"That's why I'm looking for the murder weapon. This would be a good place to ditch the weapon and clothing."

Al wagged his fingers in the air. "You don't know that *David* didn't stop here on his way into town. Granted it's a little out of his way but if you're going to get rid of a murder weapon . . . ?"

Sam bit his lower lip and wiped off his forehead. "Maybe. But remember David was on foot. I'll have to see what time he arrived back in town that afternoon. Sally King seems to keep a close eye on her property. She didn't mention seeing David back here. I still think Gene or even Tilden could have come from Carla's place and gotten rid of the knife. They were both in the area at the same time. And whoever it was might have gotten rid of the murder weapon in those woods out back."

176

Al turned and looked out toward the back of the yard. "Gee, Sam, you don't have a week to search through those woods. The way things are going, David's going to be arraigned on Tuesday. Even with a dozen deputies you'll never get those woods searched."

Sam picked up the rake and began vigorously spreading out more of the pile. "Does Ziggy have any information regarding the weapon in the court papers?"

"Let me find it. . . . Here it is. In the original history no murder weapon was ever found." Al backed away from the pile as Sam raked trash over the top of his shoes. "Sam, you're making a mess. Won't the clothing and knife be burned up anyway?"

Sam knelt down at the edge of the pile. "The clothes, yes, and most of the knife. I'm looking for the blade." He combed the debris with the rake. The trash was spread out over a large area of the yard now. Sam fished his pencil out of his pocket. "Ever get the feeling, Al, that you're on the right track? I've got that feeling. I think the murder weapon is here and Gene planted it."

Al searched the ground. "I don't know, Sam. You are making a big mess."

Sam pulled and separated and cleared the debris away at his feet. "I know David is innocent and it's going to be up to me to . . ." He surged forward and stepped over the smoldering pile. He knelt down and picked through the trash until he had uncovered a blackened, burnt piece of metal. He reached for a half-burned newspaper and scooped up the charred remains of a knife blade in his hand. Sam carefully wrapped the blade in the paper. "I'm going to take this to Doc Adams and see if he can get any prints off of it." Sam held up the paper and carefully retreated from the trash pile.

Al was unconvinced. "It's 1955, Sam. You know Doc Adams isn't going to get much from that knife—if that is a knife. It's hard to tell if this is even the knife we're looking for. You wanna know what Ziggy says the odds are that's the genuine article?"

"No, I don't. But it is a knife blade, that much I know. And I didn't see any other cutlery out here. I doubt Sally King would just throw a knife into the trash pile. It's the only hard evidence I can produce right now, even if it's not much." Sam set the paper-wrapped knife down in the grass and began to rake up the mess he had made.

Ziggy's link shrieked and Al read the display. "Ziggy's located a paper in Tulsa that did a follow-up story on the murder a year later. Nothing much has changed, according to the report, except that Will Williams has a new deputy. Seems Gene Dupree left Brick about two months after David's trial ended." Al looked up at Sam. "Tilden could be involved in some way too. You still think Gene acted alone?"

"I don't know. Tilden is still here a year after the murder and Gene isn't. Can't figure why Gene would up and leave Brick. Seems he wants to hang around and follow Will's father's footsteps. If Gene did commit the murder then he could flee once David is convicted. I would guess that Will would be looking for some way to get David's sentence overturned once he's convicted instead of looking for the real killer." Sam had raked up the trash pile and returned the rake where he had found it. "I don't really have a motive for Gene and that troubles me. Looks like I'll have to question Gene tomorrow morning. I'm not going to stake out his house tonight. He might get suspicious and flee. Maybe he didn't do it, but he might know who did. Especially if Blythe is right and Gene was involved with Carla Sue." Sam tucked the wrapped blade in his arm and led Al back through the yard.

Sally King spotted Sam and called out, "Did you find the knife, Will?" she asked hopefully.

Sam gripped the paper wrapped blade in his hand. "I sure did. Thank you for letting us have a look around. By the way, Sally," Sam added as he tucked his blackened hands around his back, "could someone get inside the gate without you knowing it?"

Sally King scoffed. "Not hardly. I lock the gate at night

and if I'm not going to be at home. Otherwise I'm out here ninety percent of the time. The other ten percent I'm in the kitchen or house. Almost all the windows face this yard. I'd know if someone was in the yard. Why do you ask, Will?''

''Just wanted to make sure you're taking precautions. Part of my job of keeping the town safe.''

Sally laughed. ''This murder is the most interesting thing this town has to talk about since Tom Madison started climbing out the city hall window. I sure hope you find out who did it. I've read in the papers that your housekeeper's boy may be involved. I hope he didn't do it. He seems like such a nice boy.''

Sam bowed his head. ''Thank you again. I'll let myself out.''

''What if it's not Gene?'' Al asked quietly as Sam shut the gate and headed back toward the patrol car.

''Then I've run out of time and suspects,'' Sam said as he climbed into the car.

''I'm going to run a few more things by Ziggy,'' Al said as the Imaging Chamber door opened up behind him. ''I'll go with you tomorrow morning when you talk to Gene.''

''Good idea,'' Sam agreed as he started up the car. ''I'll get Meg and the kids headed off to the picnic tomorrow before I swing by the jail and question Gene. First I'm going to run this by Doc's place and see what he thinks.''

Al watched Sam drive off. He had a bad feeling about this Leap all of a sudden. He stepped into the Chamber and closed the door.

As twilight descended upon Brick, a car pulled along beside Sally King's garden. It coasted up to the gate and stopped. The figure in the car watched the house. Bright lights in the kitchen and the upstairs signaled someone was at home.

A few minutes later a lone figure crept up to the gate and opened the latch. The gate opened easily and without a sound. The person blended into the long shadows the setting sun was casting. Along the row of cornstalks this person walked, being careful not to rustle the dry stalks. The person was heading toward the back of the garden, toward the trash pile. Just a few more feet to go, around by the fruit trees and then into the tall protective vines of Sally King's prize winning tomatoes.

Sally King tossed the last of the weeds on the pile and listened. She looked at the tomato vines and spotted the intruder, hiding in the shadows.

The intruder felt the gun tucked under his belt, next to his skin. The fingertips of the intruder brushed down across the small bulge it made in his shirt.

Sally King walked boldly over to the vines. "Who's there! Come out." She had a shovel in her hands, which she held up protectively in front of her. She was still quick on her feet for sixty.

The intruder looked around. Nowhere to escape, nowhere to run. The gun tucked away seemed heavy and so accessible.

Sally King raised the shovel in the air. "Come out of those vines now. Don't think I can't see you."

Gene Dupree felt beads of sweat forming on his neck. He stepped out of the vines into the fading light. "It's just me, Mrs. King. Gene Dupree." He held his hands up as he walked. "Don't hurt me with that shovel, Mrs. King."

Sally King slowly lowered the shovel as Gene approached. "Gene Dupree, you scared the living daylights out of me."

Gene lowered his hands and smiled. "I didn't intend to scare you, Mrs. King. I thought you were in the house. All the lights were on."

Sally King studied Gene carefully. She didn't put down the shovel. Something about his manner made her uneasy. "You just can't go walking into people's backyards. Didn't Will's father teach you better than that? Why, I didn't even recognize you without your uniform."

Gene stopped smiling. "I have manners." His tone was bitter. He saw the surprise on Sally King's face. Gene made himself grin again. "I just forget to use them sometimes. I

180

am sorry, Mrs. King. I'll just let myself out." Gene stepped back into the vines.

"Did you come looking for the knife?" Sally King asked as Gene retreated.

Gene stopped. He slowly turned around and looked at Sally King with a neutral face. "Pardon me?"

"Will's pocketknife? He came by earlier today and was looking for it too. Said you misplaced it when you came by the other afternoon. You don't have to worry about it, Gene—Will found it."

Torrents of sweat began trickling down Gene's face and chest. He could feel his heart hammering. "Oh. Will's knife." Gene needed time to collect himself. Could she see his anxiety? Could she hear it in his voice? She would be easy enough to kill, he reasoned. What to do with her body would be the tough part. He ran his hand over the gun under his shirt. "I'm glad he found it," Gene lied.

"I've got a lot of work to do before the picnic tomorrow, Gene, so if you don't mind?" Sally pointed at the gate.

Gene heard the disgust in her voice. She wanted him to leave. Gene pulled his hand away from his shirt. "Of course you do, Mrs. King. Why, it wouldn't be a Labor Day picnic without you winning all those blue ribbons for your canned goods." *And you'd be sorely missed at the picnic tomorrow if you didn't make an appearance,* Gene thought to himself.

Sally King stood where she was. The last traces of light were fading rapidly from the horizon. "How could you look for a pocketknife in the dark, Gene Dupree?"

"Good night, Mrs. King. I'll see you at the picnic." Gene turned and began to make his way back through the yard. He walked rapidly and didn't bother looking back.

Sally King watched Gene leave. She carried the shovel with her as she followed behind him. She watched as he swung open the gate and jogged to his car. She sighed and shook her head as she closed the wooden gate. She listened as his car pulled away into the night.

Sally King thought about calling Sheriff Williams and

181

telling him Gene had come looking for his knife. She also thought about all the preparations she had to do before tomorrow and decided in the long run she was just over-reacting. Will was too busy to be concerned about his deputy's whereabouts. She locked her gate and went inside.

Saturday, September 3, 1955

Sam spent yet another sleepless night tossing and turning. He rose before dawn and tiptoed out of the bedroom. He quickly dressed, made some coffee, and waited for the sun to rise. A small breeze had begun to pick up and blow through the open windows, bringing with it the first relief from the heat in three days. Sam stood at the window and let the cool breeze blow into his face. He watched as the eastern sky began to turn pink.

Meg came down the stairs, fully dressed and with Tyler in her arms. Tyler looked priceless in his blue jumper, all scrubbed and shampooed. Meg was dressed in a beautiful sleeveless pink dress with a white satin ribbon for a sash. A matching white ribbon was tied around her blond curls. She set Tyler down and wandered over to the window by Sam. She inhaled deeply. "Lord, thank you for that breeze. Do you think it's the end of the heat wave?"

"I hope so." Tyler toddled into the kitchen and Meg dutifully retrieved him. "You're up early," Sam noted as he headed into the kitchen after Meg.

"I've got to get to the lake as soon as possible," Meg answered as she began to pull box after box off the kitchen table. "Becca stayed at Patty's house overnight. I sure hope Wilma can get them ready. I'll need everyone helping this morning."

Sam walked over and began to help Meg box the pies. "I need to do something this morning before I head over to the lake."

Meg stopped boxing the pies and looked at Sam.

182

"What!" Meg grew slightly irritated. "What could be so important so early this morning?"

"I can't explain," Sam began as he handed another box to Meg. "I shouldn't be gone very long. It has to do with the murder investigation."

Meg looked down at the kitchen table loaded with food and items for the picnic. "Can't it wait, Will?" she demanded. "How am I supposed to cart all this food and supplies over to the lake by myself? You said you would help me."

"Becca will help you. I said I shouldn't be gone very long." Sam watched Meg out of the corner of his eye.

"I can't possibly carry all these things," Meg complained. "Maybe if I had Miss Beulah here to help, but she'll be in Dunsmoore," Meg finished in a lowered voice.

"Meg . . ."

"No," Meg nearly shouted. "Not today, William Tyler Williams. Of all the days to go wandering around on police business, why today? Let Gene handle whatever comes up. I thought we agreed you'd come to the picnic with me today and we'd spend it together as a family. You can't go back on your promise. You promised me nothing was going to spoil this day. It's Saturday, for goodness' sake. Surely this investigation can wait. . . ."

The screen rattled and a friendly voice called out, "Hello? Anyone awake this morning?"

Meg pointed her index finger at Sam. "Don't leave. We're not finished talking yet," she snapped, and walked out to the living room. Meg smoothed out her dress and opened the door for Miss Beulah and the Reverend Niles.

Sam wandered out to the living room, trying to calm himself and hoping to get a moment alone with Meg.

Miss Beulah was dressed in her Sunday best, with matching shoes and purse. "I'm off to visit David this morning," she said, looking at Meg and Sam. "The reverend and I need to keep his spirits up. I understand they may arraign him as soon as Tuesday. Is that so, William?"

Sam nodded curtly, "Yes, ma'am."

"So soon." Miss Beulah shook her head. "How can they be so sure they've got the right person?"

Meg took Miss Beulah by the arm. "I know it isn't much, but I've got a basket made up for David. I know how much he looked forward to this picnic. It's in the kitchen."

"You didn't have to go to all that trouble, Miss Meg. I'm sure you've got your hands full today. Thank goodness you've got Will to help."

Meg and Sam exchanged blistering looks across Miss Beulah's head as Meg led the party into the kitchen.

"Look at all this food and all those preparations," declared the Reverend Niles in a loud voice. "My, but you ladies have been working hard."

"Yes." Meg smiled. "I'm so glad Will's going to help me. I'd be lost without his help today."

"Meg, I need to talk to you." Sam pulled at Meg's arm.

Meg just ignored Sam. "Wish you were coming today, Miss Beulah. Wish things were different."

Miss Beulah turned and glanced up at Sam. "I wish they were too, Miss Meg."

The screen door opened and shut in the living room. Tyler, who had been playing in the kitchen, bounded out into the living room calling, "Bec, Bec, Bec."

"Rebecca? Patty?" Meg called. "Is that you?"

"Yes," Becca called from the living room. "Momma, call Tyler, he's bothering us."

"Becca and Patty come in here and show the Reverend Niles and Miss Beulah your outfits." Meg turned to the reverend. "Patty's mother made them matching dresses. They're gonna look like twins today." Miss Beulah smiled and waited for Becca to make her entrance. Sam glanced at his wristwatch. It was ten minutes after six.

"Becca, don't keep these people waiting," Meg chided.

Patty appeared in the kitchen doorway at once and smiled. Her hair was in two braids and she was wearing white tennis shoes and her brand new, freshly ironed yellow cotton dress. Becca slowly walked up behind Patty. One of her braids was coming undone and her shoes were missing. She stood behind Patty in her stocking feet. Meg leaned forward, reaching for Patty. Patty jumped out of the way, exposing Becca. Becca's dress was wet, torn, and covered with dirt. Both her legs were splattered with mud and her socks were soaking wet.

Meg was stunned. Sam was shocked. Miss Beulah was amused and the Reverend Niles cast a watchful eye on Meg.

"My Lord, child," Miss Beulah clucked at Becca, "you look like you rolled in the mud."

Becca raised a sorrowful face; her eyes were filling with tears. "I'm sorry, Momma and Daddy. I slipped in the creek."

"Slipped!" exclaimed Meg as her face turned red. "What were you doing down by the creek? The creek is not between here and Patty's house."

"It was an accident, Mrs. Williams," Patty bravely spoke up. "She didn't mean to fall in."

Meg shot Patty a look that silenced her. "An accident!" Meg's voice began to rise. "This is no accident, Rebecca Sue Ellen Williams. This is a disaster." Meg towered over her daughter. "What were you thinking?"

"We should be going," the Reverend Niles said as he guided Miss Beulah away from the kitchen. "You all have a wonderful time at the picnic." Miss Beulah smiled sympathetically and gave Becca's arm a squeeze on the way out.

Sam eased himself between Meg and Becca. "Calm down, Meg. You're going to have a stroke."

"Calm down! How can I calm down when we're supposed to leave for the lake in five minutes? Rebecca looks like she just crawled out of a pigsty and I've got fifty boxes to haul to the picnic by myself 'cause you need to go off on some mysterious, last-minute investigation! How dare you tell me to calm down!"

Sam kept his tongue clamped firmly between his lips and looked down at Becca. Tears were spilling down her cheeks. "Becca, I must say I'm very disappointed in you."

"I'm know, Daddy. I'm sorry. I didn't mean to slip."

"Are you all right, Becca?" Sam looked over the wet and scratched girl who stood in front of him. "Are you hurt?" Becca shook her head. Sam sighed. "All right now, you're too old for tears. You go upstairs, wash up, and change out of those clothes." Becca turned and fled up the stairs, relieved not to be the center of attention anymore. "And don't leave a mess. And don't dawdle," he called after her. Sam then turned to Meg, who was looking absolutely exasperated. "Meg, I'll help you load the rest of the picnic supplies into the car. Then you take Tyler and Patty and go on to the picnic. I'll bring the rest of the food and Becca as soon as she's ready. I'll drop the food and Becca off, but then I'm going to leave." Sam held his hand up in the air, "And I don't want to hear any arguments. I'll return to the picnic as soon as I can. It lasts for three days, Meg. I doubt if I'll miss much."

"But, Will," Meg began to complain, "all those boxes of pies? You promised. . . ."

"Please, Meg, let's not argue now. I'll drop the pies and Becca off later. I'll join you as soon as I can and I'll give you a full explanation. Right now, let's get you, Tyler, and Patty loaded into the car." Defeated, Meg turned and gathered up an armload from the table and headed toward the screen door.

As Sam was loading the last box in the trunk the phone rang.

"It's probably the game committee wondering where I am," Meg groaned and rolled her eyes skyward.

Sam dumped his load of gunny sacks into the back of the car. "I'll catch the phone. You head on over to the picnic."

"Oh great." Meg dug around in her purse for her set of keys. "I could just kill Rebecca. And I wish you'd tell me what's so important."

"Later." Sam waved at Tyler as he watched Meg climb behind the wheel and start the engine.

The phone was still ringing as Sam came back in the house. He walked through the living room and heard the water running upstairs. Sam came into the kitchen and picked up the phone. "Hello?"

The line was silent. Sam hung up the phone and began to box up the pies. It was six fifty-five on Saturday morning.

CHAPTER
NINE

Rear Admiral Al Calavicci sat at his desk early this morning poking and pecking away at the computer. His smoldering cigar was sitting in a LAS VEGAS SANDS ashtray, just an arm's reach away. A cup of Verbena's fresh-brewed mocha almond coffee was steaming in his favorite mug. Al had been up most of the night going over Ziggy's data for the Leap. That pile of paperwork was almost as tall as the paperwork he needed to complete for the project's monthly reports. After working on Ziggy's pile of readouts Al had opted for a break. He had gotten in four hours of much deserved sleep, showered, and shaved. Now he was ready to work on the project's pile of paperwork for a while, until Ziggy came up with something else for the Leap.

Al had dropped by the Waiting Room to check in on Will, only to have Verbena veto the suggestion. Will Williams's condition was still unchanged and Verbena was worried he was getting worse. She was in the middle of running more tests when Al dropped by. So instead Al had settled for a mug of Verbena's fresh coffee and her take on Will's condition.

Al had hoped to be spending part of the day in a romantic liaison with Tina, but Tina was still miffed about Al's visit to Santa Fe. He hoped the red roses and baby doll lingerie he was having delivered to her would change her mind.

So Al found himself sitting behind his desk, with a ton of paperwork and no Tina in a slinky teddy. Since he planned to work behind his desk for a few hours and since he wouldn't be meeting with Tina, Al resorted to something he rarely ever did in the presence of the project's personnel. He chose to dress down this morning. Way down, by Al Calavicci's clothing standards.

After his shower Al had pulled on a pair of well-worn, faded blue jeans, his favorite pair of high-top tennis shoes, and a horizontal-striped, purple and gold polo shirt. Al vowed if he was going to be alone with all those Sat-Com reports due for Washington, at least he was going to be comfortable.

He ran his hand through his still-damp hair and reached for his coffee mug. He had closed and locked his door before extracting a pair of tortoise-colored reading glasses from his locked top drawer. Vain though he was, Al knew his eyesight was going, slowly but surely. He could still pass the mustard when it came to flying. It wasn't as though he was flying bombing missions anyway. He just needed the glasses for occasions like this, when he was alone and had a ton of reading. Fortunately, those conditions didn't occur very often. No one else knew he wore glasses. Not Verbena or Gooshie or Tina. Not even Sam. So far Al had managed to get by reading the tiny print on Ziggy's hand-link. Al pledged he would get a bigger handlink rather than wear his glasses.

Al sipped the coffee and slipped on his glasses. He pulled a heavy manila folder off the top of the pile and opened it with dread. Most of these reports were overdue to the committees in Washington. He had missed a few deadlines; other deadlines he had bargained for extensions and won. Al turned to the computer screen and hunted down the file he needed. As he waited for the report to pop on the screen, his eyes drifted to the moving box from Maxine. It was still sitting where he had dumped it upon his arrival from Santa Fe. He looked at the deteriorating corners of the box and the sagging bottom. The computer beeped and Al turned his attention back to the screen. He updated the report in front of him with a few jabs at the keyboard. When he finished the update he sent the copy back to D.C. with another jab. As the computer confirmed D.C. had received the report, Al's attention drifted back to the box.

The box was an ugly sight sitting in his neat and pristine office. It was covered in dirt and grime. The tape holding the box together had long ago lost its tenacity. The lid of the box bulged, as did the sides. Al looked around his office. He selected a corner where he could put the box for now. He'd have to wait until later to go through its contents. He should have hauled it to his quarters instead of his office. Sitting here it was creating an eyesore. The computer beeped and waited for its next command.

Al slipped from behind his desk and walked around to the chair that held the box. The moving box was almost as wide as it was tall. Al remembered how much trouble he'd had when he carried the box up to his office. He calculated the distance from the corner to the chair. Five short feet, easy. The box could sit back in the corner for the next millennium and at least he wouldn't have to stare at it. Al jiggled the box. Things rattled and clicked together inside. Probably wasn't filled with anything of value anyhow. Maxine would have scrounged through it before she packed it away.

Al wrapped his arms around the side of the box. It seemed wider now than he remembered it being when he carried it up to his office. He tried to lift it. It seemed heavier too. Al pulled his arms away and noticed his polo shirt was covered with dust and grease. That did it. Al grabbed the box and lifted it away from the chair. The contents inside shifted wildly. It sounded like something broke. The box began to slip through the admiral's arms. "Oh no, you don't," he grunted. He brought his knee under the box's bottom and nudged it up. He was balancing on one leg, his knee pushing the bottom of the box and his arms squeezing the middle. Al's face was getting red and he was beginning to sweat. He carefully lowered his knee. The box stayed intact. "Just five feet," he wheezed. He eased the box between his desk and the chair and took his first step. He took another step. The box slipped an eighth of an inch through his arms. Al's back began to hurt. On his third step the bottom gave way and a lifetime of memories and mementos exploded out of the box. The box collapsed and emptied. The box was now very easy to hold.

Al's tennis shoes were buried under broken glass, yearbooks, awards, trophies, and a silk negligee just for starters. A large textbook from MIT landed on the admiral's broken toe. A rosary hit the floor and its string broke, sending glass beads everywhere. A pair of boxing gloves hit the pile and rolled under the desk.

Al flung the tattered, empty box against the wall at the far corner of the office. He was buried up to his ankles in junk. A broken bottle of wine began to seep its contents from one spot of the pile. The air was soon pungent with the aroma of sweet grapes. Al could just picture Maxine laughing at him, wherever she was. "Aw . . ." Al angrily kicked his wine-stained shoes free of the pile. The toe that had been on the receiving end of the MIT textbook had begun to throb.

Al sat down in the vacant chair and stared at the pile on the floor. He moved the silk teddy with his shoe and discovered an old black-and-white photo. It's frame's glass was intact, just dirty. Al reached down and picked up the photo. He wiped the glass off on his jeans. Al, his father, and Al's little sister, Trudy, waved and smiled into the camera. Al caught his breath. He rubbed the picture with his hand and tilted it in the office light to get a better look.

His glasses slid down his nose and Al pushed them back into place. Suddenly, Al felt very old. He took off his glasses and set them on the desk.

A drama award Al won while he was in the orphanage caught his eye. More photos, black and white, their frames broken and bent were catching his attention. He set the family photo on his desk next to his glasses.

Ziggy's monitor behind Al's desk gave off a shrill whistle and at the same time, the handlink next to his cigar began to blink.

Al couldn't take his eyes off the pile. He was finding all kinds of treasures he had forgotten about. "What is it, Ziggy?" Al said as he bent down to retrieve a crumpled, pink paper umbrella. "What did I save this for?" he exclaimed, turning the umbrella around and around with his fingers.

"Admiral, I would like to update you on the current time lines which are now forming."

"So update." Ziggy had been updating this Leap for the last twelve hours or so. Another tidbit of useless information had probably found its way into her data banks. Al continued to pick through his lost belongings.

Ziggy didn't like to be ignored. Al's voice patterns indicated to her that he was preoccupied. She ran a quick check on several of the project's female personnel and determined that none seemed to be missing from their current posts. "There has been a major change in the time line," Ziggy began in a deliberate and slow monotone voice. Al was rummaging around and had retrieved a book of matches. "Dr. Beckett has once again altered history as we know it." Ziggy waited patiently for a response. Instead her audio circuits picked up broken glass and heavy grunting. She increased her voice playback a decibel. "Admiral Calavicci?"

Al had just picked up a heavy trophy and he shoved it over to one side. "What?" he growled.

"Are you listening to my report? Are you paying attention? I would not have troubled you if I didn't think it wasn't of the utmost importance."

"Yeah, yeah, yeah, and yeah," Al said as he dusted off his hands on his shirt. He sat up in the chair and addressed Ziggy. "You've got my undivided attention, Ziggy. Shoot."

"Precisely," Ziggy seemed to sigh.

"Precisely what, for crying out loud," Al demanded.

"Shoot, Admiral Calavicci. That is precisely what is going to happen to Dr. Sam Beckett in exactly three minutes and twenty-four seconds."

Al leaned forward in the chair and forgot about the mess on the floor. "What did you say?"

"The current time line indicates—" Ziggy began again tediously.

"Forget the current time line," Al said, getting to his feet and stepping around the junk. He reached over and snatched Ziggy's handlink. "Cut to the chase."

"But there is no chase, Admiral. Just a shooting. In two minutes and fifty seconds. An intruder will enter the Williamses' home and shoot and kill Dr. Beckett, who the intruder thinks is Will Williams."

Al forgot all about feeling old. He spun around and headed for the door. He unlocked it and threw it open. He stepped out into the hallway and pulled the door shut as he began to run. "Details, Ziggy. I need more details," Al called out as he ran toward the Imaging Chamber.

Ziggy's voice boomed throughout the corridor. "Will Williams's body was discovered by Deputy Gene Dupree, who pronounced Will dead at 07:06 A.M. on Saturday, September . . ."

Al bumped into a guard who was in the middle of saluting the admiral. Al didn't bother returning the salute as he planted the Marine into the wall. "Where, damn it? Where is Sam shot?" Al was running at full tilt toward the main control door. He punched the handlink. The door eased up as Al bent down and scooted through.

"The autopsy report states that Dr. Beckett will be shot

193

in the upper chest at close range in less than . . ."

Al scrambled upright and began to run for the Imaging Chamber door. Gooshie and Tina were startled by Al's sudden appearance and Gooshie dropped his clipboard on the panel. Tina gasped and pulled away from Gooshie. She had never seen Al dressed in jeans before.

Al flew in the Imaging Chamber (which Ziggy had opened only seconds before) and jogged to the middle of the room. No sooner had Al entered the Chamber than the door shut behind him and the floor began to disappear beneath his feet.

"You have one minute exactly," Ziggy reminded the admiral.

"Gooshie!" Al barked as the walls and ceiling inside the Chamber dissolved. "Get your grubby hands off Tina and center me on Sam! *Right . . . now!*" Al caught his breath and brought the link up to his face. "Where is Sam shot, Ziggy? Where?"

"Why, in Brick, Oklahoma, Admiral Calavicci."

Sam had just two more pies to finish boxing. He was carrying the last two pies from the table to the counter when without any warning, Al came flying through the kitchen wall, his face beet red, his hands waving in the air. He startled Sam, who leaped back out of the admiral's way and in the process dumped two berry pies on the kitchen floor.

"Get out of the kitchen, get out of the kitchen," Al yelled, the link going crazy in his hand. He was hopping across the kitchen, going through the kitchen table and chairs, and pointing at the back door.

Sam watched Al dance across the floor. "You startled me," he barked at the dancing hologram. Sam was still sore from his encounter with Meg. He reached for a dish towel, only to have it slip through his fingers and land on the floor. Disgusted, Sam bent down and began to peel the pie tins away from the floor.

Al had almost disappeared through the back door. He

halted, charged over in front of Sam, and stood jumping from one foot to the other. "Get up. Leave the mess. You've got to get out of the kitchen." Al was frantic.

Sam pointed at Al's feet. "I've never seen you in sneakers before," he exclaimed, his eyes drifting up from Al's feet. "Or blue jeans for that matter. I didn't know you owned a pair."

"Sam," Al pleaded, "forget my shoes, forget my clothes. Just get out of the kitchen."

Sam had pried one pie pan off the floor. "I can't go anywhere now. I have to wait for—"

Al checked his watch and stomped his foot. "Forget the pies, Sam! Come on, move your ass." Al sprinted toward the back door. "It's the only way out."

Sam stood up and set the pie pan in the sink. "Al, what's going on?"

The screen door opened and banged shut in the living room.

Al moved quickly and stood in the doorway of the kitchen. "Sam, please. I don't have time to explain. . . ." Al glanced down and noticed a gun protruding out from his purple and gold polo shirt. The figure holding the gun walked through Al, blocking his view.

Sam Beckett watched the intruder pass through Al and emerge into the kitchen. Sam swallowed and took a cautious step back. "My wife has a strict policy about guns in the house." Sam's back made contact with the kitchen counter.

Gene Dupree stopped and cocked his head. "Does she now?" His dark, small eyes never left Sam. Gene was dressed in his deputy's uniform. The uniform was neatly pressed and clean except for the dark, wet patches around the collar and under his arms. His hair was slicked back away from his forehead. Slowly Gene proceeded forward and closed the gap between Sam and himself.

Al had stepped around Gene and hurried over by Sam's side. His eyes darted back and forth between Sam and Gene as his fingers slapped at the handlink furiously.

"Gene, what's going on here?" Sam began to creep along the counter.

"You know perfectly well what's going on here, Will," Gene answered in a calm and steady voice. "Don't move." The sound of Gene's voice made the hair on Al's neck stand up. "I thought I'd pay you a visit. Save you a trip."

Sam looked at the gun pointed at his chest. "What trip? And why are you here, in my home, pointing a gun at me?"

Gene pushed farther into the kitchen. "Don't play dumb with me, Will. You and I both know that you're about to crack this murder case wide open. We both know who murdered Carla Sue."

"Sam," Al warned, "this guy could go off at any moment. Don't aggravate him." Al swatted at the link and read the display desperately. "The time line is all jumbled up. Ziggy can't give me a prediction of how things turn out." Al looked up from the link. "Just take it easy with this guy. Keep talking to him."

"Why did you kill her, Gene?"

"Careful, Sam," Al urged.

A thin line of sweat began to bead up on Gene's forehead. "That's what I always liked about you, Will. Straight to the point. No useless questions." Sam leaned back against the counter and Gene snapped the gun up and aimed it at Sam's head. "Don't you move or try anything funny, Will. Or I guarantee you Doc will be scraping your brains off the ceiling."

Sam eased his hands away from his sides and into the air. "Okay, okay. Take it easy."

Gene looked at the pies boxed on the table and chuckled. He motioned with the gun at the box. "Look at those pies, all ready to go. I bet Meg baked herself silly getting ready for this affair. You always had it easy, Will. You came from a good family and your father was a very respectable man. I always looked up to him. I loved him like he was my own father. My real father didn't amount to much, you know? He didn't care about me like your father did." Gene wiped his forehead with his free hand. "I always wanted to please your father. No one else would have taken me in like he did. He made sure I stayed in school. He died before I could show him how grateful I was. Before I could do him proud.

"You never had things rough. Life's always been good to you, Will. Married your high school sweetheart. Settled down and had two kids. You became sheriff after your father died. You've never had to prove yourself. You never had people whispering behind your back, second-guessing you. You never were a loner. You were always well liked. Never had people laughing at you. You always had the respect. I wanted the respect, but I never got it. Until two days ago."

"You killed Carla Sue for respect?"

"No!" Gene shouted and waved the gun in the air. "No, no, no. Don't you get it? You're usually so smart, Will." Gene giggled. "I killed her because she thought I was a fool. She thought old Gene was going to be her ticket to good fortune and high community standing. She thought if she got knocked up, I would do the right thing." Gene sniffed and stared off in the distance, looking past Sam. "Well, I tried to do the right thing, the way your father would have handled the situation. I gave her the money to take care of the problem. But she wanted to keep the baby. The baby probably wasn't even mine. She thought if she had the baby I'd have to marry her. She thought she had outfoxed old Gene Dupree. But instead she made me very mad."

Sam lowered his hands and steadied himself against the sink. "She was pregnant!"

Al lowered the link and blinked back his shock. "You rotten son of a . . ."

Gene snapped out of his daze. He looked at Sam and shrugged. "Carla Sue was nothing but a whore. A whore who got herself knocked up and wanted me to do right by her. All the time I kept thinking what would your father think of me? I'd be the laughingstock all over again. I couldn't marry her. It was Tilden's, no doubt. He was seeing her behind my back.''

"Killing doesn't solve anything," Sam shot back. "My father never would have made you a deputy if he knew you were—"

Gene grew angry. "Shut up, Will. I know what your father wanted. You didn't know. You didn't have a clue. I knew! Just me!"

"Sam!" Al waved his arms and shook his head back and forth. "Don't provoke him."

Gene began pounding on his chest with his free hand. The hand with the gun remained trained and steady on Sam. "I had everything planned out. I knew I was going to become sheriff. You'd be headed to the bench soon, just like your father wanted. It might take a year or two, but eventually I'd become sheriff. Then Carla announces she's pregnant. Hell, it could have been anybody's kid, white or black. I'd look pretty stupid marrying Carla and then having a half-and-half kid, don't you think? Anyway, Carla threatens me that either I marry her or she lets everyone know I'm the father. Either way I lose. If I marry her, then the whole town has another excuse to gossip and ridicule me. If I don't . . . well, you can see my problem.

"If you had released Tom right away in the first place none of this would be happening. Either Tom would be charged with the murder or he'd have gone out and killed whoever he thought murdered Carla. Either way, it would have been taken care of. But no, you didn't release Tom. You kept him locked up." Gene was sweating profusely now. "You destroyed my plans."

"Did you really think you would become sheriff?" Sam asked angrily, stepping away from the counter. "Did you really think you could commit murder and get away with it?"

Gene began to step back, his eyes darting all around. His shoulder blade collided with the doorway and he stopped. "Don't move. I warned you. I know exactly what I'm doing. You put me in this predicament, Will."

"Put the gun down, Gene." Sam took another step forward. "You know it's the right thing to do. Turn yourself in."

Gene blinked as sweat began to run down into his eyes. "Don't come any closer."

Sam stopped with his hands held out. "Put the gun down. You can still make my father proud of you. He'd be so disappointed in you right now."

At the mention of Will's father, Gene's expression changed. Gene gritted his teeth and steadied the gun. "My plan will still work. I've got it all figured out. Your father always said you had to have a plan, a direction in life." Gene took a deep breath and smiled. "See, Will, you're gonna be Carla Sue's killer. You were having the affair with her. Doc's already discovered her secret. It's in his autopsy report. I guess you didn't get a chance to read that part of the report, did you, Will?" Gene sneered and laughed mischievously. "Did you like any of those magazines?" Gene laughed and shrugged. "Don't matter what you know about me now. You won't be alive long enough to tell it to anyone. I'm going to tell everyone how I found out about you and Carla Sue. How I discovered in Doc's report that she was pregnant. See, that gives you a motive, Will. You killed her and then you tried to frame David for it. You even went back to Mrs. King's house yesterday and retrieved the murder weapon, fearing you'd be found out. I'm also going to produce an eyewitness at the Hole who will swear in court that you used to come down to the bar and sneak off with Carla Sue in the afternoon. Heck, even Tilden will testify against you if I threaten him just right. He never liked you much. I'll say I was coming to arrest you this morning when we struggled and you grabbed for my gun. I shot you in self-defense. Then I'll be appointed sheriff. Tilden will appoint me."

Sam calmed his outrage and narrowed his eyes. "It won't work. No one will ever believe you, Gene."

"My plan will work," Gene insisted. "Who do you

think called the newspapers?'' Gene smiled wickedly and tapped his hand to his chest.

"Gene, your story will never hold up in court."

"Shut up, Will. Just shut up. I'm through listening to you." Gene blinked back the sweat running in his eyes. "My plan will work," he said in a small voice. "I know it will. I thought it all out." The hand holding the gun lowered. "I know it will work . . ." Gene muttered.

Sam was close enough to kick the gun out of Gene's hand. All he had to do was drop his weight back to his left leg, pivot, and bring his right foot up and around. Sam shifted his weight off his right leg.

It was a quick movement but Gene still caught it and raised the gun up in a flash. He aimed.

Al watched Gene pull the trigger. Al leaped into the bullet's path and lunged for the gun.

Sam tried to move out of the line of fire. He dove for the floor.

The gun made a loud pop when it fired. Sam heard the sound of the gun. That was followed by the crack his bone made as the bullet passed through Sam's upper left arm. A white, hot flash of pain spread from above Sam's elbow up to his shoulder. The bullet traveled out of Sam's arm and smashed into the tile countertop.

The impact sent Sam falling backwards. His legs buckled and he slid to the floor. Sam's vision blurred, causing the linoleum pattern and berry pies on the floor to smear and run together. Sam's nose tingled with the smell of gunpowder. His ears were ringing and his mouth was dry. Blood was flowing down his left arm and dripping off his fingertips onto his pants and the kitchen floor.

Al saw the gun pass through his hand as he reached for it. He also saw Sam spin and fall away. At first, Al thought Sam was okay and that Gene had missed. But then Al saw the blood.

Sam landed on his butt and began tilting to the right. His face was drained of color and his eyes were dazed. Al scrambled over and squatted next to Sam. Sam was leaning so far over that his nose was almost touching the floor. He reached out with his right hand and tried to steady himself. Sam's hand slipped and he almost tumbled into Al's lap. Al reached out as a reflex to steady Sam. The handlink tumbled out of Al's grasp and for a split second Al disappeared as the link left his fingers. With lightning reflexes, Al snatched the link out of midair. He rammed the link into the waist of his jeans, where he wouldn't have to worry about it.

Sam blinked and shook his head. His vision cleared and he found himself looking at Al's high-top tennis shoes.

"Sam, can you hear me?" Al leaned over. "Hang on, Sam. Don't faint on me, buddy." Sam was just staring at Al's shoes. Al began snapping his fingers and talking in his gruffest admiral's voice. "Come on, Sam. Answer me."

Gene lowered the gun. His shirt was soaked with sweat. Gene looked sad and confused, standing there in the kitchen doorway as Sam struggled on the floor. "I'm sorry, Will." He started to raise the gun again and then stopped. "I didn't want it to be this way." He ran his left hand through his slick hair. "I wanted it to end in one quick, painless shot."

Sam licked his lips and tried to sit up against the cabinets. He shook his head and looked at Al. Al's image floated and shifted like a kaleidoscope.

The link was shrieking in Al's waist. "Sam, can you hear me? We've got to do something, Sam. He's going to shoot you again."

Sam tried to heave his body up and was floored by the pain in his left arm. He inhaled and cradled his bleeding arm. He looked up and made eye contact with Al. "My arm," Sam said with a thick tongue. "Al, my arm hurts. I think the humerus is shattered."

Gene's steely eyes flipped around the kitchen, looking for the person Sam was addressing.

Al balled his hand into a fist and pulled it down through the air. *"Yes!"* he roared with relief.

"My arm," Sam said thickly, "is broken."

"I know, Sam," Al said, talking slowly. He looked over

his shoulder at Gene standing in the doorway. "There's a dish towel on the floor. Pick it up and wrap it around your arm. You need to stop the bleeding."

Sam reached for the towel with his right hand. He closed his fingers around the towel and draped it into his lap. Sam picked up the towel and gingerly pressed it against the wound. He muffled a cry of pain.

"That's it," Al encouraged, wiping his perspiring face with his hands. "Just hold it there."

Sam groaned loudly. "It hurts."

"I know, I know, Sam. But you've got to stop the bleeding. Do you understand?"

Gene pushed away from the door. "Who are you talking to, Will? There's nobody here but me."

"Al, I'm so dizzy." Sam had begun to lean to his right again.

"Don't faint on me, Sam. It's just the shock. Take some deep breaths." Al frantically looked around the kitchen. There was only one way out and that was through the back door. Al doubted if Sam could stand, let alone try and make a run for it.

Gene looked down at the spreading pool of blood beneath Sam. He scratched his nose. "You know, she bled a lot too, Will. I didn't know there would be so much blood." Gene's voice was quiet and calm and he looked like he was daydreaming as he spoke. "Guess the sight of blood doesn't bother me anymore."

Sam looked up, too spent to respond. He just leaned against the cupboards for support, his wounded arm dangling down at his side.

Al leaned closely into Sam's face. "You have to try to get up and out of here, Sam."

"I can't." Sam's head sank back wearily against the cupboards. "I can't."

Gene wiped his forehead off with his shirt sleeve and began to whistle a tune. As Gene whistled he traced his toe along the patterns in the linoleum. Gene stopped whistling without warning and snapped his head up. "I didn't like it when she struggled. I didn't want her to suffer either. Even though she tried to trick me into marrying her, I still liked her."

Al stood up and walked over to Gene. He scowled into the deputy's face. "You're nothing but a coward. A scum-sucking, psychopath coward." Al was so angry he began to tremble. "Don't you touch him," Al warned, his voice just barely above a whisper. "Or I'll kill you myself. I don't care how long it takes, I'll track you down. I'll find you in the future, do you hear me? I'll find you!"

Gene looked at Sam on the floor. His eyes focused. "Don't be afraid when you die, Will. I'll be sure and look after Meg and the kids when it's over." Gene took aim. His eyes became two dark pits.

Al's face was contorted as he uselessly slapped at Gene's hands. "No!" Al shouted. "Stop!"

Sam tried to move. He tried to pull himself along the floor, but his feet couldn't get any traction on the slippery surface. His arm burned and ached as he moved.

Suddenly the room was filled with another bang, causing Al to flinch.

The window in the back door exploded, sending a shower of glass everywhere. Al watched as the glass rained down all around and through him. It tinkled on the floor and skidded across the linoleum.

Al turned and looked down at Sam. "Sam?" he whispered.

Sam was lying on the floor, his right hand covering his eyes. Glass was sprinkled in his hair and on his clothes.

Al turned around to look at Gene Dupree.

Gene Dupree blinked and smashed his hand into his chest. A crimson spot began to grow and spread beneath Gene's fingers. The gun slipped from Gene's grasp and landed on the floor. Gene gasped for breath and dropped to his knees. He pulled his hand away from his chest and looked at the dark blood.

Al recoiled as Gene slid to the floor, coughed once, and

became still. Al whirled. "Sam! Are you all right?" Al's voice broke with emotion as he knelt down.

Sam stirred and moaned. Sam slowly raised his head. Broken shards of glass fell onto his shoulders and into his lap. His pallid face looked up into the hologram's. "Al?" Sam whispered through dry lips. Sam slowly eased his body up off the floor. He rested his head against the cupboards and looked over at Gene sprawled on the floor. "What happened?"

"I don't know," Al whispered back. "Gene shot himself somehow."

"What?"

"I don't know," Al said, his emotions almost getting the better of him. "He was going to shoot you. I saw him aim the gun. Then he was shot. I guess he shot—"

"Oh no. No." Sam was trying to sit up. He reached up to the counter above his head and grabbed at the tile countertop. He winced and cried out in pain.

"Sam, where are you going?"

Sam continued to pull himself up off the floor, ignoring Al and his throbbing arm. He wrapped his right hand around the countertop and pulled.

"Sam! *Sam!*"

The room rolled violently and Sam stopped to regain his balance. "Al, go help Becca."

"Becca?" Al shook his head. "You're going into shock, Sam." He pulled the link out of his pants. "I'll have Ziggy figure out how—"

"Al, please." Sam shook his head to clear it. "Becca. Out there."

Al leaned toward Sam. "You mean Becca was in the house?"

From the living room came the faintest, softest voice. "Daddy?"

Al's jaw dropped. He stepped around Gene Dupree's body and charged into the living room. There stood Becca, shaking, her teeth rattling, her father's gun in her hand. Al bent down and tried to calm the distraught child. He wrapped his arms protectively around her, his shimmering hands passing through Becca's shoulders. Becca started to sob. *"Sam!"* Al bellowed. "Get in here. Quick. I need your help."

CHAPTER
TEN

Sam pushed away from the counter and headed toward the living room. He didn't look down as he stepped over Gene Dupree's still body. Sam lunged for the kitchen doorway and leaned against it as large, black spots swam before his eyes. Sam tucked the damp dish towel carefully around his left arm and concentrated on the figures in the living room. A thin dripping trail of blood marked his path out of the kitchen.

Becca stood shivering in the living room. Tears ran down her face and she absently wiped them away. Her father's big gun dangled in her small hand, where it threatened to drop to the floor at any second. Becca gasped when she saw Sam emerge from the kitchen. ''Daddy,'' she cried, ''oh Daddy.''

Sam walked stiffly over to Becca. Becca collapsed into Sam, trembling violently against him, her teeth chattering, her chest heaving as she began to sob. Sam eased the gun out of Becca's grasp and set it down on the floor. He wrapped his right arm around Becca's shoulders and led her to the couch, where he sat down beside her. He spoke to her in his gentlest, softest voice as he cradled her with his good arm. Meanwhile, Al was ferociously pacing back and forth behind the couch, feeding data into Ziggy as fast as his fingers could hit the keys.

Sam smoothed Becca's hair away from her wet face and tried to calm her down. She was still sobbing. He felt her pulse as he kept talking quietly to her.

Al paced at a killer rate, his big brown eyes glued on the handlink. "I've got Verbena on top of this, Sam," he reported from behind the couch. "She's getting the data as fast as Ziggy can process it to her." The admiral's eyes squinted and he brought the flashing cubes closer to his face.

Becca shook uncontrollably against Sam, her small body wracked with deep soulful sobs. "I-I-I din-did-didn't want t-t-to hurt Gene," she sobbed. "But I w-wa-was afraid h-h-h-he wa-was going to hurt you. He had-d-d-d a g-g-g-un in his han-n-nd."

Sam hugged Becca the best he could. "I know you didn't want to hurt Gene, sweetheart. Everything's fine now."

"He shot you," Becca sobbed, growing more upset. "He shot you, Daddy."

"I'm okay, Becca. I'm going to be all right."

"Is . . . is Gene okay?" Becca looked up into Sam's eyes. "I just wanted him to leave you alone. I didn't hurt Gene, did I?" She began to cry all over again.

Sam rocked her on the couch. "He's fine, Becca." Sam looked around the living room and saw the opened closet door with the dining room chair pulled over in front of it. He looked back at Al. "We both need to go to the hospital. I'm worried that she might start going into shock," Sam whispered urgently, "and I may not be far behind her."

Al stopped pacing and came around to the side of the couch. He knelt down next to Becca, his gaze never wandering from her face. "I know," Al replied quietly. "Verbena confirms that she needs to be hospitalized. She also says to keep talking to her and reassuring her.''

Becca shivered against Sam, jarring his left arm. Sam bit his lip and stifled a cry of pain. The white dish towel covering his upper arm was slowly turning red.

Al stood up and ran his fingers through his hair. "Ziggy says the nearest hospital is in Dunsmoore and that's thirty minutes away. How are we going to get you both to the hospital?"

Sam was checking Becca's pulse again. "I can drive Becca to the hospital. I'll take the police car."

The data display on Ziggy's link had jammed up and Al was in the process of hammering the link with the heel of his hand when he stopped in midwhack. "You can't possibly drive her. You've got a broken arm and you've lost a lot of blood. You're in no condition to drive."

"Well," Sam whispered, "someone has got to drive. You certainly can't."

As if on cue the screen door opened and Miss Beulah stuck her head inside. "Oh, Will, I'm so glad I caught you before you left for the picnic. I forgot that basket Miss Meg . . ." her voice trailed off.

Sam was never so glad to see another human being. "Miss Beulah, please help us."

Miss Beulah entered the living room cautiously. "Why, Will, what's going on here?" Miss Beulah walked over to the couch and looked down at Becca. "Dear God, William! What's wrong with this child?" Miss Beulah reached down and wrapped her hands around Becca's hands. "She's as cold as ice and shivering so." She turned and looked at Sam. She noticed his arm. Her eyes registered concern. "Oh my God, Will. You've been shot."

Sam couldn't take the time to explain. Although Becca had stopped sobbing, she was growing too quiet for Sam. "Is the reverend waiting outside?" he asked Miss Beulah. She nodded without looking away from Becca. "Please go get him."

Miss Beulah seemed torn about leaving Becca and Sam. "But you're hurt, Will."

"Please, go get the reverend, Miss Beulah."

Miss Beulah hurriedly retraced her steps to the front porch and called for the Reverend Niles. She returned to the couch and gently eased Becca out of Sam's arms. "You're hurt bad, William. Let me hold her." Sam held onto Becca's cold hands as Miss Beulah began to rock Becca in her arms.

The Reverend Niles opened the screen door. "You called for me, Miss Beulah?" The reverend looked at Sam with bewilderment. "What's going on in here?"

Sam leaned back into the couch. "Reverend Niles, you've got to call Doc Adams. You'll have to use the phone in the kitchen. Tell Doc it's an emergency. Tell him Becca's hurt."

Reverend Niles eyes bulged at the sight before him. "Why, Sheriff Williams, you've been—"

"Yes, I know."

"Don't stand there," Miss Beulah snapped. "This child needs a doctor. Do what Will says and call Doc Adams."

The Reverend Niles bobbed his head up and down and headed for the kitchen. He halted in the doorway and brought his hand up to his chest. His mouth dropped open and he exclaimed loudly, "Great Jesus in Heaven!" Everyone in the house jumped, including Al. Becca's eyes flew open and she moaned.

The reverend staggered back into the living room and sank back against the wall. "Lord have mercy," he said in a subdued voice.

Sam started to get up to call Doc Adams himself, but Miss Beulah put her hand on his shoulder. "Regardless what is in that kitchen, Reverend, you've got to call the doctor."

The reverend pulled himself away from the wall and cleared his throat. "I'll go call the doctor." He gathered himself up and strode into the kitchen, keeping his eyes focused straight ahead.

Miss Beulah removed her hand from Sam's shoulder. "Something terrible happened in the kitchen, didn't it?"

she whispered and patted Sam's shoulder. "It's over now, William. Isn't it?"

Sam dropped his head and mumbled, "Yes, ma'am."

The Reverend Niles emerged from the kitchen and shuffled back to the couch. He tripped over Sam's gun on the floor and caught the back of a chair to steady himself. He seemed to be lost in a fog.

"Reverend Niles," Sam began. The reverend looked down at the gun on the floor. "Reverend Niles?"

The Reverend Niles closed his eyes. "Doc Adams is on his way, Sheriff Williams. Would you mind if I said a prayer? I feel a prayer is needed."

"Please do." Sam squeezed Becca's hand. "A prayer would be nice."

Doc Adams arrived less than five minutes later, pulling up in his station wagon. He pushed open the screen door and emerged with his black bag in hand. He was dressed for the picnic, wearing a short-sleeved shirt and blue walking shorts. His white legs stood out in contrast with his black socks and shoes. "Where's Becca? Will?"

"No need to shout," Miss Beulah declared. "We're all here in the living room."

Doc began to open his bag as he walked over to the couch. He looked down at Becca cradled in Miss Beulah's arms. "What happened to Becca?" he asked as he rummaged through his medical bag.

"I think she's in shock," Sam said.

Doc paused. "Shock?"

Miss Beulah continued rocking Becca. "She's as cold as ice, Doc Adams. And she's gotten so still, like she's asleep. Only I know she isn't sleeping 'cause she keeps trembling in my arms."

Doc reached down and cupped Becca's head in his hands as he examined her. "What caused this?"

"It's in the kitchen," the reverend said softly.

"She needs a sedative," Sam urged. "And we need to get to the hospital in Dunsmoore."

Doc looked at Sam for the first time. "Dear God, Will! You've been shot."

Miss Beulah nudged the doctor with her foot. "Keep your voice down. This child jumps at the slightest noise."

Al, who had been watching this scene unfold before him, leaned over the back of the couch. "We've got to get you and Becca to the hospital, pronto. We're wasting time."

Doc pulled out a needle and syringe from his bag. "I had no idea," he mumbled. "The Revered Niles said Becca was hurt, but I didn't know . . ." He looked up at Sam. "I tried to reach you after you hung up on me, William. I wanted to tell you about the part of Carla's autopsy report that didn't make it into the paper. I couldn't reach you and then I got a call from Julius Watt saying his wife had gone into labor. She was carrying twins and I had to get her to Dunsmoore. I was with her most of the afternoon and night. Esther said I missed you yesterday afternoon when you stopped by. I got back into Brick around three thirty this morning. Managed to deliver a mighty handsome set of boys."

Sam leaned over to Doc and winced as he inched forward on the couch. "Doc, Becca needs to get to the hospital right now. You can examine her thoroughly later."

"You're one to talk," Doc said as he swabbed Becca's arm with a cotton swap. "You're not in much better shape. Let me call for an ambulance from Dunsmoore. It shouldn't take too long to—"

"No," Sam insisted. "You've got to drive us."

"All right, all right. Goodness, Will, don't get yourself in a stew. Let me give you and Becca a shot, then we'll go to Dunsmoore."

Sam shook his head back and forth. "Not me, Doc. Take care of Becca, but I need to stay alert."

Doc made a face and turned to Becca. "Okay, Becca, you're going to feel a little prick now." Doc inserted the needle and gave Becca the injection. "I'm not going to argue with you, Will. You're going to be sorry though."

"Fine," Sam said, as he turned around to check with Al.

Doc Adams picked up the loose, damp ends of the dish towel wrapped around Sam's left arm. He made a knot and in one quick twist pulled the knot firmly against the wound. Sam yelped out in pain. "I should have warned you that might hurt," Doc said as he checked the towel. "The bleeding seems to have stopped for now," he told Sam.

Sam grimaced at Doc. He wasn't about to thank him for that. "Doc, take Becca and put her in the patrol car. Miss Beulah, you and the Reverend Niles can stay behind. I'll notify Sheriff Cooper in Dunsmoore by radio. And Meg. Someone needs to get Meg."

Miss Beulah released Becca into the doctor's arms. "I'm going with you, Will. The Reverend Niles can go get Meg. She'd never forgive me if I left you and Becca." Miss Beulah helped Sam get to his feet. The reverend looked shaken as he helped Miss Beulah steady Sam.

Sam was also very wobbly on his feet. Doc shot him a warning look over his shoulder as he carried Becca. Sam spoke to the reverend as Miss Beulah guided him toward the screen door. "Reverend Niles, please go to the lake and find Meg. Don't tell her about the shooting. Just say I've hurt my arm and she needs to come to the hospital."

Al opened the Imagining Chamber door. "I'll meet you at the hospital, Sam." He gave Sam a thumbs-up, stepped inside the door, and disappeared.

Sam, Miss Beulah, and Doc barged through the emergency door at Dunsmoore City Hospital and found themselves surrounded by a room full of people. Doc cradled Becca in his arms as Sam followed close behind with help from Miss Beulah. People with their heads bandaged and arms in slings paid little attention to them. Doc pushed his way to the reception desk and hunted down the first available nurse he could find.

She looked tired and overworked. She glimpsed quickly at Becca and laid a clipboard on the top of the counter. "You'll have to fill this out to admit your granddaughter," she said as she picked up a handful of folders.

"She's not my granddaughter," Doc said. "I'm her physician."

Sam leaned against the countertop. "I'm her father and she needs to see a doctor immediately."

The nurse sniffed indifferently. "She didn't arrive by ambulance, so she'll have to wait her turn."

"She didn't arrive by ambulance," Sam interjected, "because we drove her here by way of a police car. And she needs immediate attention."

The nurse spotted Sam's arm and made a face. She pulled another clipboard free and laid it down in front of Sam. "You'll have to be admitted too."

"Look," Doc said, trying to keep his voice down, "I want to see Dr. Brown right now."

The nurse just kept gathering up her files from the desk. "He's not here today."

Al opened the Imaging Chamber door and stepped into the room. He maneuvered around a candy striper rolling a wheelchair down the corridor and hurried to the counter next to Sam.

The nurse cast a contemptible glance at Doc Adams. "It's the Labor Day weekend. We've had a pileup on the interstate, a bar fight, and the usual weekend traffic. You're going to have to wait your turn."

"Horse feathers!" Doc snapped. He jerked his head toward an empty gurney sitting by the wall. Before the nurse could protest, Doc rushed Becca to the gurney. Miss Beulah picked up the clipboards and a pen. She gave Sam a smile and a nod. Sam's grateful smile said it all as he held Becca's hand and let Doc lead them through the hospital.

They pushed their way through two double doors and searched for a doctor. Al had to jog along behind the gurney just to keep up. He only took his eyes off the link momentarily to follow a pretty nurse along the corridor.

The group came to a main intersection in the hospital, with elevators at one end and a registration desk at the other. Al jogged around a man in a tan uniform, who was blocking his path to the registration desk. Al paused for just a second to get a better view of the man. Was it something about his stance? That uniform? Doc was pushing the stretcher ahead and Al had to pick up his pace just to keep up.

The gurney took a quick right past the registration desk and banged through another pair of swinging doors.

A young doctor nearly collided with the gurney in the corridor. He lowered the chart he was reading. He looked like he was fresh out of medical school. He eyed the stretcher. "What happened to her?" he asked Doc nonchalantly.

Sam pushed his way in front of the young doctor. "She's suffering from shock. You'll need to get a saline drip started and I'll need to see the head of your psychiatry staff, right away." Doc's mouth hung open as he listened to Sam give orders.

The young doctor looked at Sam. "I see," he said slowly. "Well, I'll examine her in a minute and make sure she gets taken care of. Why don't you follow one of the nurses down to X-ray and we'll get that arm attended to."

"I'm staying with Becca until her mother arrives." Sam looked at the doctor's name tag pinned to his white coat. "Dr. Stevens."

Dr. Vincent Stevens looked perplexed. "Who are you?" he asked Sam.

Doc Adams cleared his throat. "This is Becca's father, William and I'm her doctor. I would appreciate it if you could locate Dr. Joseph Brown."

Dr. Stevens laid the chart down. "I'm not getting paid to page doctors, gentlemen. Now, if you'll just follow this nurse back to the waiting room . . ."

"What an idiot!" Al exclaimed. "Sam, you've got to find another doctor. This guy's a bozo."

A tall, no-nonsense nurse appeared next to Sam. "I'm not leaving her side," Sam said loudly. "And she needs to be examined by your staff psychiatrist too."

Dr. Stevens rolled his eyes. "Suit yourself. But you've lost a lot of blood." The doctor sighed as he lifted Becca's wrist to check for a pulse. "You gentlemen are aware that it's the Labor Day weekend, aren't you? All our permanent staff have the weekend off. Dr. Logon, our psychiatrist, and Dr. Brown will return on Monday."

"If he calls me a gentleman one more time . . ." Al lamented. Becca moaned and stirred on the gurney.

"But we're not waiting till Monday," Sam informed the rookie doctor as he reached over and grabbed the startled doctor's lapel with his good hand. "You're going to reach Dr. Logon now. And while we're waiting for Dr. Logon to arrive, I want Becca taken care of." Sam released the young man's coat, pleased to see he had smeared it with blood. Sam's left arm was just a dull throb now compared to the anger he felt for this cocky doctor.

"But I don't know where he is," Dr. Stevens whined. "Besides, this girl hasn't suffered any kind of major trauma that I can see."

"That's because you're still green around the gills," Doc informed the distressed doctor. "Anyone with any good medical training can see she is suffering from posttraumatic shock."

The tall nurse smiled to herself. "Dr. Stevens," she began, "I know for a fact that Dr. Logon usually spends the weekends with his wife's family in Ashcroft. I'm sure he keeps that number around here so we can reach him in case of an emergency. I would try the reception desk at the main entrance. And I bet you'll find Dr. Brown's number there too. I think Dr. Brown is staying home this weekend."

"All right, sister," Al commented next to the nurse, "way to put Bozo in his place."

The nurse pushed the gurney toward a door. "Let's put her in here for the time being. I'll get a drip started."

Dr. Stevens scoffed at the nurse. He shook his head at them before turning on his heel and heading down the hallway.

"Thank you," Sam said as the nurse wheeled the stretcher into the room.

"You're welcome. He's such a fuddy-duddy doctor. Although we are a bit shorthanded today, I'm sure she'll be in good hands until we get Dr. Brown or Dr. Logon here. I'm going to get that IV started. Then I'm going to call X-ray and schedule an appointment for you," Nurse Watkins said to Sam.

"Do it sooner than later," Doc advised the young woman.

Al found a corner away from the action in the room and retreated to it, with the squawking handlink.

Becca cried out and Sam leaned down over the railing. Becca's shaking had been reduced now to a slight quivering. With the shot, she would drift off to sleep soon. Sam squeezed her shoulder. "It's okay, Becca. I'm here." Becca's eyes flew open for a second and looked at Sam. He smiled and stroked her cheek.

"Daddy?" Becca answered wearily and closed her eyes.

"I'm right here, honey. Everything's okay."

Al edged a little closer to the bed. "That's a good sign if she's talking."

"Yes," Sam agreed as he ran his fingers lightly over Becca's arm. "It's a very good sign."

Becca opened her eyes and struggled to keep them open. Sam leaned over, ignoring the numbing pain in his left arm. "I overheard you and Gene talking," she said, beginning to shudder again. "I didn't mean to listen. Gene was so angry. I didn't want to break our promise."

The nurse came back in the room and began setting up the IV bottle. "She's fighting the sedative. She needs to rest."

"Becca," Sam said softly, "you didn't break our promise. We can talk about this later. Don't worry, your mom is on her way here. Just lie still and go to sleep."

Doc clucked softly to himself and patted Sam on the back. "I'm going to check on Miss Beulah. I'll be right back."

Sam looked up at Doc Adams and smiled gratefully. "We'll be fine," he whispered.

Doc left the room quietly. Al shook the link and it protested noisily. "Sorry, Sam. I still can't get Ziggy to produce a current time line."

Outside in the hallway a shouting match was taking place. In a flash the door to the room burst open and banged against the wall. Meg came charging through, her arms waving madly through the air, her eyes trained, looking for her daughter. Two nurses were trying in vain to stop Meg's forward motion. Once Meg spotted Becca she was no match for the nurses who were trying to take her back outside. "Unhand me. I've just spoken to Dr. Adams and I demand to see my daughter at once. Let me go or I'll have my husband arrest you. He's a sheriff. Rebecca!"

Becca's eyes flew open and she reached up with her arms. "Mommy."

Sam thought Meg never looked more beautiful as she bent over the railing and carefully gathered up her daughter in her arms. The nurses saw what was going on and let Sam contend with Meg.

Sam lowered the rail on the bed, letting Meg get closer to Becca. She smoothed her daughter's hair and hummed to her in a soft voice, "Easy now, Becca, you're in Momma's arms now. You can cry all you want to, 'cause I'm here and your daddy's here and everything's all right." Sam watched Becca's eyes close and her breathing become heavy. He leaned over the bed and gave Becca a quick kiss. Meg reached out and caught Sam's shirt. Then she noticed the towel wrapped around his arm and she opened her mouth to scream. Sam's hand covered her mouth and he shook his head back and forth. Meg gasped and her eyes filled with questions.

Sam uncovered Meg's mouth and touched his fingers to her lips. He shook his head. "It's not as bad as it looks," he whispered.

"Oh, Will," Meg mouthed and bit down on her trembling lips.

"You stay with Becca now while I go get this arm looked at. I'll find you later," Sam reassured Meg. Sam winked, brushed his hand against Meg's cheek, and headed for the door. He pushed open the door with his shoulder and disappeared into the corridor.

Al smiled warmly at Meg and Becca as he passed the bed. He slid through the door behind Sam and emerged into the hallway. The link had finally started to quiet down and he studied the blinking cubes in his hands. "Hey, Sam, I think you did it. The time line is still all jumbled, but Ziggy's prediction of you succeeding is going up. See?" He turned to show Sam the link and found himself talking to empty space. He turned in a full circle. "Sam?"

Al noticed the double swinging doors leading back to the main corridor. He stepped through the doors and collided into Sam. Al had to step through Sam, who was leaning against the wall. His face had taken on a very ashen color.

"You okay, Sam?" Al knew it was a pretty stupid question. One look at Sam's face and you knew he was anything but okay.

Sam didn't even bother to sneer in Al's direction. He just rested his damp back into the wall and studied the floor. "No." He cleared his throat and shook his head. "I think . . ." He paused and inhaled deeply. "I've got to sit down."

Al stepped away from the wall and scanned the main corridor. "There's a bench over by the elevators. It's only a few feet away. Right past the nurses' station. Do you see it?"

Sam didn't take his eyes off the floor. "A bench?"

"Yeah," Al insisted. He thumbed to a point over his shoulder. "Just a few steps."

Sam swallowed and took a wobbly step away from the wall. "Oh boy."

"Just a few steps like that and you're there." Al was all encouragement as he walked ahead of Sam over to the bench. "See, it's right here. Walk, walk, walk, and you're here."

Sam reached out and tried to steady himself against the wall. "Al? I . . . don't . . . feel . . ."

Al darted back to Sam's side and began to wave his arms

218

around. "Sam! Don't faint. Not here. Not in the middle of the hallway!"

Sam closed his eyes and felt his knees give way. He tried to brace himself for the impact. He hoped he would land on his right side.

First he was falling, then he was jerked to the right. Two strong arms lifted him up and dragged him over to the bench. The hands eased him down on the leather seat and then pressed Sam's head forward.

Sam waited as his vision cleared. His left arm was throbbing in time with his heartbeat. Sam realized his head was bent down between his knees and was being held in place by a pair of firm hands. As he came around, he found himself staring at two pairs of feet. One pair wore spit-polished black shoes, framed by tan pants with a sharp crease. The other pair were adorned in high-top tennis shoes and were rocking nervously back and forth. Sam slowly tried to raise his head up and get a look at the owner of the black shoes. The person who saved him from taking a header.

"Hold it there, buddy. I don't want you to take another dive on me."

The person's face was still obscured from Sam. "I'm okay," Sam insisted as he slowly sat up. He leaned back against the wall and came face to face with his rescuer. "I wanted to thank y—" Sam's mouth dropped open. Sam blinked and studied the face closely, making sure his brain wasn't playing a trick on him.

"Hey, boy, are you some lifesaver, kid." Al sighed and looked at the kid who still had his hands on Sam's back. "I thought for sure Sam was—" The pair of high-tops stopped rocking.

Sam clamped his mouth shut and studied the kid in front of him. The boy was in his early twenties. Two large, brown eyes peered back at Sam from under bushy eyebrows. The kid had a pale complexion, which only made his black, wavy hair stand out around his face. The young kid broke into a smile and pulled his hand tentatively away from Sam. He wasn't very tall, but his uniform seemed to add a foot to his height. He looked down the hallway and his eyes narrowed in a very familiar way.

"Hey," he barked in a slightly raspy voice, "can we get some medical help here?" Sam knew that voice, and he knew it would have a decided edge to it in another forty years, after a few hundred cigars. The young kid turned back to Sam and thumbed over his shoulder, saying, "If my pals would stay out of the nurse's hair for five minutes, we'd get you some help." He lost the smile. "You're not gonna faint on me again, are you?"

Sam was too dumbfounded to speak. He shook his head.

"Good." The young kid seemed relieved. "Your color is still out to lunch, but at least you seem to understand what I'm saying to ya. I got to tell you, this is one hell of a way to meet. My friends call me Bingo." The kid offered Sam his outstretched hand.

Sam looked at the hand, with the round, thick fingers. Choking back his utter surprise, Sam grasped the kid's hand. "I'm Sam."

Bingo smiled and firmly shook Sam's hand. "Well, Sam, it's nice to meet you. Let me find one of those cutie-pie nurses to have a look-see at your arm. We'll have you ship-shape in no time."

Al Calavicci stood motionless by the bench, his mouth also slightly agape. He gazed back at his younger self and his face gave way to a whole slew of emotions. The link squawked and shrilled in the observer's trembling hand. Ziggy's link could have been on fire and Al wouldn't even have noticed. He never took his eyes off the kid just inches in front of him. When he finally pulled his eyes away he looked down at the link, as if it had just been handed to him out of the blue. Al ignored the data display and tipped his head up. He looked over the young kid who had helped Sam to the bench. "That's me," he whispered through lips that barely moved. "My God, that's me."

"You still hanging in there, Sam?" Bingo asked. The kid reached out and put his hand on Sam's shoulder as he studied Sam's face.

"I'm fine. Much better now," Sam muttered.

Al Calavicci snapped out of his daze. "Sam! You're not Sam. I mean, you're Will. You can't tell me—er, I mean him, which is me—" Al stopped and started all over again. "You can't tell me you're Sam." Sam was not paying attention to Al the hologram. He was riveted to Al the person in 1955. Bingo turned away and looked down the hospital's corridor. Al ran his hand through his hair and swayed on his feet. "Now I'm not feeling so good." Al stared up at his younger self. "I can't believe it—that's me?" Al shuffled closer to the bench. Never taking his eyes off the young man standing in front of him, he motioned to Sam. "Move over, Sam. I got to sit down for a minute too." Al reached out with his hand for the bench.

Sam turned and looked at Al edging over to the bench. Sam's eyes grew wide with the realization that Al (the hologram) intended to sit on a bench that didn't exist for him.

"No, Al, wait!" Sam called out a split second too late.

Bingo spun around and eyed Sam closely. "What did you call me?"

Rear Admiral Calavicci heard Sam and remembered suddenly that there was no bench to sit on. "Oh shi . . ." Al waved his arms frantically, trying to regain his balance. He clawed the air while Ziggy sounded like a cat in heat as the handlink was waved about. Al lost his balance, toppling backwards, falling through the bench, slipping through the floor, and disappearing out of sight.

Sam leaned forward and looked under the bench. "Al?" he whispered.

"And just what do we have here?" another kid, dressed in an outfit similar to Bingo's, came around the corner, a smoldering stogie planted firmly between his teeth.

Bingo snapped his head up. "For your information, Chip, this guy needs some medical attention. And if you hadn't scared all the nurses off this floor he'd be getting it by now."

Chip whistled. "I'll say he needs some attention. Look at that arm."

"Just ignore my best friend, Sam. He has a case of bad manners today."

"He sure does smile a lot for a person who's been shot," Chip observed as he stepped back and began to puff on his cigar.

Nurse Watkins came around the corner pushing a wheelchair. She spotted Sam and wheeled the chair toward the bench.

"Here comes the cavalry," Chip announced and smiled at the nurse as she went by.

"There you are. I've been looking all over for you." Chip watched the nurse as she bent over and set the handbrakes on the chair. "Dr. Adams wants you down in X-ray, STAT. I would have been here sooner but . . ." She threw a frown aimed at the airmen. "Along with everything else we've had our hands full with a squad of wayward pilots who happened to get into a nasty barroom brawl last light."

"What?" Chip said, feigning innocence. "I didn't do anything."

"Do something constructive, Chip," Bingo said as he put his hands under Sam's good arm. "And help me get him into the wheelchair."

"A piece of cake," Chip said as he rammed the stogie between his teeth and helped lift Sam off the bench and into the wheelchair. "You're in a pair of fine hands now," Chip said, giving Sam a slap on the back. "And not to mention legs and thighs and hips."

Nurse Watkins shook her head and released the brakes on the wheelchair. "Say your good-byes, boys. It's time to move this patient."

"Are you two boys through playing wet nurses?" A tall, dark man called out, sounding annoyed. He was wearing a leather jacket over a uniform like Chip's and Bingo's. The guy's hand was bandaged and he was waving it at his friends. "We better get going if we're going to get back to Ashcroft and make New Mexico by sundown."

"Hey, we wouldn't even be in here if you hadn't got

your hand all busted up in that fight last night, Stacker,''
Chip yelled back around the cigar.

"Look, why don't you all go outside and shout," Nurse
Watkins turned and admonished the men. She reached over
and snatched Chip's cigar out of his mouth. "And if you
want to smoke, do it in the smoking area." She ground the
cigar out. She gave the chair a shove and began to wheel
Sam down the hall.

"She told you!" Bingo pointed and laughed at Chip.

"Hey, wait a minute." Sam was twisting around in the
chair trying to get a good look at Bingo.

"Your first stop is X-ray and then to bed."

"But . . ." Sam began helplessly. The nurse paid no
heed; she just rolled him down the corridor away from the
pilots.

"Come on," Chip said, elbowing Bingo in the ribs,
"let's go."

Bingo jabbed Chip back and turned to look at Sam one
last time. He raised his hand. "Take it easy, Sam."

"Thanks, Al," Sam called out as he was wheeled around
the corner and out of sight.

Bingo pulled his hand back. Chip was already heading
down the hallway. "Hey," Bingo called out as he caught
up with his buddies. "Did you hear what that guy called
me?"

Chip began to hunt around his pockets for another cigar.
"What?"

"He called me Al. Did you hear him?"

Chip shook his head. "You're beginning to lose it,
buddy."

"I am not," Bingo shot back. "I know what I heard."

"Ladies," Stacker said with an edge of irritation in his
voice, "let's get the lead out. We've got to drive back to
Ashcroft and we're running late."

Bingo turned back and looked down the corridor. "How
did he know my name was Al?" he muttered. He shrugged
and joined Chip and Stacker as they walked down the corridor.

• • •

Al landed hard on his butt in the Imaging Chamber. Ziggy's link flew from his hand and skittered across the floor. The walls and floor around him slowly dissolved. He sat and watched as the hospital corridor turned into the deep blue tiles that made up the Imaging Chamber's floor, walls, and ceiling. He looked at the link, lying four feet away. He sighed and slowly laid down, gazing up at the blue ceiling.

Al hardly ever forgot he was a hologram, that he couldn't grasp items or sit down. He hardly ever got rattled as a hologram either. Al closed his eyes and braced himself, waiting for it to happen. "Just be gentle, that's all I ask." His voice echoed against the Chamber walls and floor.

The memory began as just a flicker. A memory he did not recall until a few seconds ago. The memory grew and the details began filling in. Al's own memories were being sorted and shuffled like a deck of cards. The new memory began to blend with all the other memories of Al Calavicci.

As Al lay flat on his back, feeling the cool, hard tile floor under his shoulder blades and head, he began to feel the first eerie traces of remembering. Something, he was positive, he had never experienced until a few minutes ago. Accompanying his brand-new memory was the beginning of a dull headache.

Al rubbed at his temples and began to recall his trip to San Diego in 1955. He and his buddies had graduated from Annapolis and were flying across the country to the top-gun school in California. Al knew they had covered a lot of territory on that trip. Most of it spent in bars and pursuing females. But landing in Ashcroft, Oklahoma? Stopping at a hospital in Dunsmoore for Stacker's broken fingers? Helping some guy to a bench? Al's eyes snapped open. Not only did this all take place some forty-odd years ago, making it difficult to recall all the details anyway, but this memory was already being shuffled with Al's "original" memories. That is, if Al had any original memories left. It was becoming increasing difficult for the admiral to sort out his original memories from the new ones Sam created for him.

Al seemed to recall a nasty barroom fight that took place between some local yokels and his buddies toward the end of their cross-country travels. He vaguely recalled Stacker breaking his fingers and the drive to a hospital. Al could also picture, just as fuzzily, the young nurse pushing Will down the corridor in the wheelchair, as he stood there waving with Stacker and Chip. And yet, wasn't it just less than an hour ago that Ziggy had informed him about Will dying?

"Awww . . ." Al began to squeeze his fingers against his temples. In a few hours Al would never recall the original history at all. Only Ziggy would know. Ziggy was keeping track of all the history before and after Sam Leaped. Running two parallel lines of history in her trillion-zillion zigawatt brain. Al dropped his hands away from his head. He had come through another ripple effect in time, thanks to none other than Sam Beckett. Al slowly pulled himself up into a sitting position and rubbed his neck. The admiral had a throbbing headache forming at the base of his skull and he had really crunched his tailbone when he fell.

Al got to his feet and began to brush off his jeans. The big changes always seemed to pack more of a wallop when they arrived. Al had spoken to Verbena about it once. Sam had been involved in a Leap where he saved an undercover detective's life, but could not fix Al's marriage to his first wife, Beth. Al had gone to Dr. Beeks the next morning after the Leap with his head feeling like he had been on a two-week drinking binge. Al's head continued to hurt three days after that particular Leap and he would have gladly welcomed the relief a migraine would have brought by the end of the third day. Dr. Beeks could only sympathize with Al and suggest he belt down the aspirin and keep a cold compress handy if Sam ever got tangled up in his past again.

Al limped over and retrieved the handlink, massaging his tailbone. He began to walk around the Chamber, trying to work out the kinks in his body. "Hey, Ziggy," he called out after his stride began to return to normal.

"Yes, Admiral Calavicci?"

"Ziggy, has Sam Leaped yet?"

"No, Admiral. Dr. Beckett is currently undergoing an X-ray."

Al rubbed his neck, feeling his head pound. He had a feeling this was going to be one whopper of a headache.

"Anything else, Admiral?" Ziggy purred contentedly.

"He hasn't Leaped yet?" Ziggy hated to repeat herself and Al's question was met with silence. He tried a different tack. "Getting Will's arm set isn't going to cause any problems, is it?"

"No problem, Admiral. Some rather unpleasant pain for a few days."

"And the little girl, Becca? She's okay, right?"

"According to my new current time line, yes."

Al involuntary winced at the mention of a new time line. "So . . . ?"

"So?" Ziggy repeated. "A needle pulling thread, perhaps? Or are we speaking of sow, to plant seed for growth, to set something in motion?"

Al tightened his grip on the link. "So . . . why . . . hasn't . . . Sam . . . Leaped?" Al drew each word out and ground his teeth for emphasis.

"There is obviously something he still needs to correct. Oh, by the way," Ziggy added as an afterthought, "Dr. Beeks wanted me to relay this message: Will is alert and awake. He's asking for you in the Waiting Room."

Al tucked the link in his back pocket and walked over to the door. "Ziggy, please inform Dr. Beeks that I'll be in to see Will in about an hour," Al said as he opened the door of the Imaging Chamber.

Al entered his office and was confronted with the mess he had left earlier. The admiral stepped around his memorabilia strewn all over the floor and sat down behind his desk. He opened the drawer and took out a bottle of extra-strength aspirin. He popped the top and shook out four capsules in his hand. He tossed the bottle back into his drawer and started to get up to get some water, when something in the mound caught his eye. Al reached down with his free hand and pulled a partially concealed black and white snapshot from the pile at his feet.

Al felt goosebumps appear on his arms as he studied the shot. "I'll be damned," he muttered as he laid the photo down on his desk. His head was starting to pulse big time, so Al hastily got up and went out in the hallway to locate a drinking fountain.

The black and white photo on the desk had slightly ruffled edges and was turning yellow in some spots. Three men, all young and smiling, were posing around a sign. They each wore identical uniforms and short military hairstyles. One of the two men who flanked the sign had a huge cigar clamped between his teeth. The third young man was kneeling down in front of the sign so he wouldn't obscure the words. Above the black, wavy hair of the kneeling pilot were big, black letters that read: YOU ARE ENTERING THE TOWN OF DUNSMOORE, OKLAHOMA. THE TOWN OF DUNSMOORE WELCOMES YOU.

CHAPTER
ELEVEN

The nurse at the small desk looked up as the door to the Waiting Room opened and Admiral Al Calavicci stepped inside. The nurse snapped to attention and drew his hand up in a sharp salute, which the admiral returned with an equally impressive salute of his own. Verbena Beeks waved from the observation deck above the room. Al returned the wave and strode briskly over to the table.

Will Williams was lying down, his hands folded across his chest, with a light blanket covering him. When Al entered his line of vision, Will sat up, his eyes scanning over the person standing in front of him. Will beamed and offered a curt but effective salute of his own. "Rear Admiral Calavicci."

Al seemed to glow with a blinding brilliance in his dress whites as he stood under the fluorescent lights in the Waiting Room. He snapped his hand up to the brim of his hat and saluted back.

"I guess I'm going home soon?" Will's eyes looked

tired and yet hopeful. He pulled at the blanket that covered his arms.

"That's what Ziggy says." Al put his hands behind his back and assumed a perfect at-ease. "Sam hasn't Leaped yet, but Ziggy is predicting he will at any time. I'm here to tell you how much we appreciate everything you did. You were helpful in helping us with the murder." Al pointed at Will's left arm under the blanket. "I know how bad you must feel about your arm."

Will flexed his arm as he spoke. "Dr. Beeks spent about two hours discussing what I can expect when I get back. She's prepared me for the broken arm." Will's features clouded. "But I'm not half as concerned about my arm as I am about Becca. If it's all the same to you I'd like to speed this process up so I can return to my family. I'm needed there."

"I understand," Al said.

A few moments of silence hung in the room between the two men before Will spoke up. "Admiral? Do you remember the discussion we had?"

"Oh yes." Al spied Verbena as she entered the room. "I know just how to handle it."

"My, but you're looking especially sharp today, Admiral Calavicci." Verbena Beeks smiled as she approached the table. "And how's your headache, Admiral?"

"It's still there."

Verbena glanced up at Al with raised eyebrows and then back at Will. "And how are you today, Will?"

Will smiled and tipped his head. "Just fine, ma'am. Ready to go home."

Verbena sensed something going on between Al and Will. "I'm sorry, but did I interrupt something?"

"No," Al and Will answered at the same time.

Will smiled sheepishly. "Al was just proving to me he's a real Navy guy after all. He's got the suit and scrambled eggs to prove it."

Verbena looked puzzled. "Scrambled eggs?"

Al pointed to the bright gold zig-zagging trim on the

brim of his hat. "Actually, we were saying good-bye, Dr. Beeks."

"Well, I want to say good-bye too," Verbena added. "You've been an exceptional patient, William." Will offered his hand to Verbena. "Well, a handshake won't do for me." Verbena walked over to the edge of the table and embraced Will. "Take care." She pulled back out of the embrace and smoothed out her lab coat. "I'll leave you two alone now." She threw Al one more look as she headed out of the room.

Will tipped his head to Al. "I always believed you were a real admiral. But thanks for wearing the uniform just the same."

Al snapped his shoulders back. "Before you know it, you'll be back in Brick. I've one more little piece of business to settle with Sam before he Leaps. So I'll be on my way now."

"Well, so long, Al. If you're ever in Brick, look me up. That is if you can remember me."

"Oh, I'll remember," Al answered. A wide smile broke out on his face. "I never forget a friend." Al nodded and headed for the Imaging Chamber.

"Sam."

Sam opened his eyes and peered around the darkened hospital room. His mind remained in a haze from the painkiller he had been given. Sam's left arm was encased in a cast from his hand to his shoulder. It was anchored above his head by a large metal hook. Sam closed his eyes and settled back down in the pillow, where he began to drift off to sleep.

"Hey, Sam."

Sam fought off the urge to wake up. "Mom?" he answered groggily.

Al's shoulder sagged and he rolled his eyes to the ceiling. "Hey!" Al leaned over the railing on the bed and shouted in Sam's ear. "What kind of drugs have they got you on, anyway? Do I look or sound even vaguely like your mother?''

Sam sat upright, jerking his arm and causing it to ache at a new level of pain. "Where—what—Al?" Sam turned and blinked at the sight of Al, standing by the side of his bed, in his admiral's uniform. He was smoking a cigar which rested between the first and second fingers of his left hand.

Sam narrowed his eyes and frowned. "I'm still here? I haven't Leaped yet?"

Al detected more than a little irritation in Sam's voice. "No, you haven't Leaped yet, but according to Ziggy you're about to." Al smiled. "How's your arm, by the way?"

"My arm hurts like hell," Sam retorted curtly. "How the hell's your tailbone?"

"Touché." Al stuck the cigar in his mouth. "Boy are you in a lousy mood." Al began to hunt around in his pocket for the handlink. "Didn't they give you enough pain medication?"

"Not enough to make a difference." Sam sighed as he settled back into the pillows. He looked wistfully up at the ceiling. "So when do I Leap?"

Al rammed at the link in his hands. "How should I know?"

Sam lifted his head off the pillow. "You're the one with the link," he snapped, clearly exasperated.

"Since when has that ever made a difference?" Al smacked the link with his fist. It bleeped noisily at the admiral.

Sam swore and closed his eyes. "Why did you wake me up if you haven't got anything?"

"Who says I haven't got anything?" Al tipped the link to read the display. He was startled as a metal bedpan flew by his head and crashed into the wall behind him. The bedpan smacked loudly against the wall and dropped to the floor by Al's white shoes.

Al took a step to the left away from the pan. "You're gonna be sorry you did that, Sam."

231

"Albert Calavicci." Sam was seething.

Al figured he had pushed this as far as he wanted to go. "Relax."

"Don't tell me to relax. I don't feel like playing twenty questions right now. You can't or won't tell me why I haven't Leaped. My arm feels like it's been ripped out of its socket." Sam inhaled and shook his head. "And that just for starters."

Al held up his hands. "Sam, don't have a cow."

"Speaking of cows," Sam barked, "our vet on the farm gave better injections than that incompetent rookie medical school jerk who jabbed me this afternoon."

"That's your own fault," Al pointed out. "That's what you get when you argue with a doctor. I remember on my first tour of 'Nam, there was this cocky upstart—"

Sam hung his head down. "Al, please don't start." He lay down and slung his right arm across his face. "I'm not up for one of your stories."

Al brought the link up to conceal his smile. "Well, okay. You did good, Sam. Back in Brick, David is cleared of the murder and released. He eventually becomes a lawyer. It takes him a long time, but he does it."

"So he's okay?"

"Yeah, according to Ziggy, he's fine. Got a law practice set up in Oklahoma City."

Sam exhaled. "That's good to hear. At last some good news." He moved his right arm. "What about Becca?"

"I had a long talk with Verbena about her. Becca's going to have a rough six months at first. Flashbacks, bad dreams. But her parents help pull her through. She eventually comes to realize if she hadn't fired your gun, then Gene would have killed you."

"What about her future?"

Al dipped the link. "Ziggy says she went on to graduate from Oklahoma State and follow in her father's footsteps. She becomes the first female sheriff ever appointed in Oklahoma."

"Al, that's great," Sam said with a genuine smile.

232

"That's the first time I've seen you smile in a while."

Sam's smile turned into a frown. "What about Gene Dupree?"

"D.O.A. Carla Sue was seeing him and Tilden at the same time. No one can determine for certain who the father of the baby was It could have been Gene's but it could have also been Tilden's. Seems Carla didn't want to end up in another dead-end relationship, so she chose Gene. Gene showed promise. He was young, single, and headed on his way up in the community. But then Carla never counted on Gene backing out of her marriage proposal. Gene panicked when Carla threatened to spill the beans about her and the baby. I bet Carla knew a lot of things about Gene that Gene didn't want anyone to discover. He confronted Carla that day in the trailer and when she wouldn't change her mind, he killed her.

"Tilden's going to come forward in a few days and bring Gene and Carla's affair to light. He's trying to cover his own bases and only manages to get a little mud slung on his name and reputation. But it's all for the best. Tilden's through as far as his political ambition goes. And Tom Madison, who was going to be Gene's pawn in this whole mess, packs up and moves away by the end of September. Things slowly start to return to normal, if this town ever was normal to begin with." Al chuckled to himself and jabbed at the link. With his fingers he began to rummage around in his coat pocket. "Um, now comes the tricky part. . . ."

"Tricky part?" Sam asked suspiciously.

"Yeah, where's that notepad you were carrying around with you all the time?"

"My notepad?"

Al pulled the cigar out of his mouth. "Will's notepad, actually. The one you're always writing on. Where is it?" Al smoothed out the piece of paper he'd pulled from his pocket and held it up to his face.

Sam cast his eyes around the room. "In this nightstand, I guess." He shot a quick look at Al. "Why are you holding that paper so close to your nose? Can't you read it?''

"Yes, I can read it. It just happens that the light in the Imaging Chamber is lousy for reading.'' Al waved his hands in the air. "Don't change the subject. Just find the notepad.''

Sam made a face and reached with his right hand over to the drawers by his side of the bed. "Why do you need it, anyway?'' Sam grunted and groaned as he opened up the drawer. Feeling around with his fingers, he pulled out the pad.

"And don't forget a pencil,'' Al reminded him from across the room.

Sam muttered something as he reached in and found a pencil.

"Okay,'' Al began when Sam had the notepad balanced on the bed and the pencil in his grasp. "Flip it open and write this down.''

"Wait a minute. What do you mean, 'write this down'?''

"Don't worry.'' Al rattled the paper in his hand. "Just jot down this date.''

"Date? Al, I'm not writing anything about a date in here.''

Al knew no matter in how much pain or how heavily sedated Sam was, he was bound to encounter this typical kind of behavior from his friend. "That's it,'' Al said, throwing up his hands, "you're the one bellyaching about not Leaping. If you don't want to Leap, fine. If you want to stay here, fine. I bet in another hour that arm ought to start really hurting—and itching too. I bet right now you can feel places you want to scratch, but can't reach. And not to mention . . .'' Al nudged his foot in the direction of the bedpan and rolled his eyes.

Sam looked at his arm sealed in a cast and then over at Al. He reluctantly flipped open the pad.

"Write this legibly.'' Al found himself on the receiving end of a look that could kill. "May twentieth, 1965.''

Sam dropped the pencil. "That's in the future. You know the rules, Al.''

"Rules, schmules." Al began to walk toward the bed. "I bet that arm is really starting to ache. Just a slow, dull, burning ache you can't do anything about. Just think how it's going to feel in an hour. How's your shoulder feeling with your arm all strung up like that?"

Sam picked up the pencil and scribbled in the pad. This process was beginning to burn up a lot of his reserved energy. He tried to stifle a yawn. "Okay, I wrote down the date."

"Now write down: Tornado hits Brick. Two fifty-four A.M."

"I know what you're doing," Sam mumbled as he moved the pencil over the paper. Sam no longer cared about the rules. He wanted to Leap. He wanted his arm to stop hurting and he wanted Al to leave him alone so he could get some sleep. "You're doing this for Will."

"You're right." Al folded the paper and tucked it back inside his coat. "I owe him this, Sam. Think of this as a little tiny warning. It saves lives."

"You owe him. . . ." Sam leaned back against the pillows. His eyelids were growing heavy. "What about . . . what . . . about . . ."

"That's it." Al stuck the cigar in his mouth and sucked on the end. "You're finished here."

"Good." Sam sighed wearily as he laid the notepad on the bed. "I'm ready to go home now. . . ." The arguing had drained what little energy Sam had left. He closed his eyes. The pencil rolled out of his fingers and into his lap. Sam's head rolled to one side as he drifted off to sleep.

Al tiptoed over to the bed and watched Sam sleep. He leaned over and read the notepad on the bed. In a fairly legible scrawl were the words Al had dictated. Al cast his eyes up at Sam and smiled. "You never know where you'll Leap next. It could be home." Ziggy's handlink chirped in his hand. "Bye-bye, Sam."

The whole room sparkled and twinkled as Sam Beckett Leaped.

ACKNOWLEDGMENTS

I am deeply indebted to the following people in helping me make this book a reality. To Ginjer Buchanan, who gave me the chance of a lifetime. I cannot thank you enough. To Don P. Bellisario, who created *Quantum Leap*. To Scott Bakula and Dean Stockwell, who breathed life into the characters. To Sherry Woodrum, who patiently read my early drafts and offered her words of encouragement. And to my husband, Terry, who always believed.